TALES OF MANTICA

DROWNED SECRETS

By BEN STODDARD

ZMOK
BOOKS

Cover Art provided by Mantic Games
Tales of Mantica: Drowned Secrets
By Ben Stoddard
This edition published in 2020

Published by Winged Hussar Publishing, LLC
Zmok Books
1525 Hulse Road, Unit 1
Point Pleasant, NJ 08742

ISBN 978-1-94543-099-2 Paperback
ISBN 978-1-950423-32-3 E-book
LCN 2020935582

Bibliographical References and Index
1. Fantasy. 2. Action. 3. Adventure

Winged Hussar Publishing, LLC 2020 All rights reserved
Copyright by Mantic Games

For more information on Winged Hussar Publishing, LLC, visit us at:
https://www.wingedhussarpublishing.com

Acknowledgements

Writing and publishing a novel has been a dream of mine ever since I was a child, and with that being said there are a lot of people who I must thank for making that dream a reality.

For starters, thanks to Brandon and Vince at Winged Hussar for taking a chance and giving me this opportunity. I got the email with the offer to write this book on my birthday in 2018, so that was one of the best birthday gifts ever.

The Kings of War community is far and away one of the best communities I've ever been a part of and beyond the general gratitude I feel towards everyone included in that, I need to thank a few members in particular.

Thanks to Mark Marber for taking the time to help go over my manuscript and for the exchange of ideas back and forth. It was a pleasure to work with a fellow author and to be welcomed into the field so amicably was a great boost to my confidence.

A big thanks to Rob Phaneuf and Mark Zielinski for bringing me onto Counter Charge way back at the start of 2nd edition and for helping me to network within this community. A special thanks to Mark for bringing me onto the Narrative Workshop and helping me to share my writings with a larger audience.

A thank you to Mark Cox and Kris Kapsner for bringing me onto the International Campaign Day as a story writer, that gave me some exposure and helped me grow immensely!

Saving the best for last. I must thank two of the most important women in my life. First, my mom always encouraged me to write, and without that encouragement I think I would have given up on the idea of creating stories long before the crushing realities of adulthood would have pressed me to give it up. I wish she could be here to read it in person.

Finally, thank you to my wife, Andrea, who has supported me throughout this process by giving me time, encouragement, and feedback. She read through this story multiple times helping screen for errors and mistakes in the storyline as well as descriptions and flow. She is amazing and I'm lucky to have her.

All of you have been integral in helping me accomplish this dream. It's a huge step towards accomplishing bigger dreams and goals that I have and that I hope to accomplish as I build more stories that I hope you all will enjoy.

Ca'ohm onwei nah my friends

-Ben Stoddard

Part One

RED SKY BY MORNING

Ashal!" Her name echoed through the great marble pillars that stretched up toward the impossible ceiling far above her. The young naiad often found herself staring upward in this great hall which was part of the small palace that had been graciously offered as a residency for her mother, Ai-ellain, during her tenure as an envoy to the Hegemony of Basilea. Ashal knew that she should respond to her mother, whose voice still reverberated among the pillars spread about the hall, but she didn't want to go to the courts of the Hegemon again. The Basileans had such strange customs and they were boring to listen to, as well. Why her mother had accepted the post here as the Trident Realm's envoy to the Golden Horn, as the people here referred to the massive capital city, was beyond Ashal's understanding. But because she was so young, still only in the seventh brood, ten more of her people's yearly spawnings would come to pass before she would be considered independent from her family and able to live on her own.

She scratched at her neck, bothered by the uncomfortable dress that was gifted to her by the court of the Hegemon as a sign of respect for her mother and those she represented. The reflective, fish-like scales of her skin chafed under the silken threads and caught on already frayed edges of the costly material. Her form, while similar to the humans of Basilea, was just alien enough to the other children at court, all of them sons and daughters of men, that it caused many to look away when she entered a room. Ashal was tired of the sideways glances and the open staring. Many of the children refused to even talk to her, and she spent most of her days sitting alone in the corners of the play yards. There were other naiads who had accompanied her mother, but none were of her age. Part of Ashal hated her for making her come to this awful place.

"Ashal!" Her mother's voice rang out again and Ashal ducked behind one of the cold pillars right as her mother came into view. She could hear her muttering under her breath in the strange, trilling language of her home, and a wave of sadness washed over Ashal. She stifled a sigh, but it came out in a sobbing gasp instead; and before she could stop herself, tears spilled out of her large, oval eyes and her breath came in sucking wheezes. She felt an arm on her shoulders.

"Ashal, my fountain!" Her mother cooed in their native tongue. "Why do your eyes weep? What cause have you to sadden?"

"I wish for home!" Ashal sobbed, throwing herself into her mother's embrace. Her mother wrapped her webbed fingers around Ashal's head and drew her close, laying her head down on top of her daughter's while her voice swished like the distant crashing of the waves.

"Ah, my heart, I know that you shed water for our home and would that we return to the depths where you spawned. But you know why this cannot be."

"No, I do not know!" Ashal cried. Her mother continued to make comforting noises and held her daughter close. After a few moments, they heard the sounds of boots clicking against the hard stone floor and then someone politely cleared their throat behind them. Turning, they saw a beautiful young Basilean woman dressed in the traditional robes of the Sisterhood. Blue fabric over white cascaded down a slim figure topped by a short-cropped head of blonde hair framing eyes that were the color of the sea on a dark night. The sister smiled shyly and looked down at Ashal, who responded in kind and buried her face in her mother's arms coyly.

"Is my little sea flower having a rough day?" The sister knelt down to look at the young naiad on her own level.

"Sister Laurine!" Ashal's mother smiled. "She is missing her home waters this day. I also think that she is not wanting to visit your high king's court." Her voice was heavily accented as the awkward words did not sit well with the thicker tongue of the naiad anatomy. Laurine laughed, a melodic sound, and held a hand out to Ashal. The sister had been assigned to help their household settle into their new surroundings and was a kind face in a sea of strangers. Ashal smiled shyly out from behind her mother's arms.

"I hate going to court, too, little one. How about you and I indulge in some truancy? We can always beg forgiveness from His Holiness later." She looked up at Ashal's mother. "And I would try to avoid calling him the high king, he gets upset by that. Remember that he is the Hegemon." Ashal's mother grimaced.

"You know I can not say this word." The naiad shook her head. Laurine laughed again.

"Then you can simply call him His Holiness, or Your Grace."

"You are a strange people. Divinity is not a title a mortal should wear." Ashal's mother smiled slowly down at Laurine who stood up.

"You have a different perspective, *Ishouren*," Laurine spoke using the proper title given to Ashal's mother in the naiad tongue which meant, roughly, 'Blessed One.' The older naiad blinked in surprise and then inclined her head in acknowledgment.

8

"I see your meaning, Sister. You are too much of the wisdom to be bowing in this Holiness courting." Luarine laughed at this response, her eyes dancing as she did so.

"Unfortunately, the priesthood is unwelcome to women I'm afraid," she gave a sad smile as she spoke. "But perhaps your daughter and I can avoid the whole messy situation. I have some things that I would love to show her, and it is far too nice a day to be spent listening to those high priests drone on about the activities of the Abyss and whatnot inside that dark palace." Laurine turned her eyes to Ashal. "Would you like that, little sea flower? This city holds some amazing things to behold!"

"Oh yes!" Ashal exclaimed, her accent less than that of her mother, she felt she had acclimated to the Basilean tongue easier than her parents had. "Please, *Ss'enwei?*" Ashal used her private name for her mother that translated roughly to the Basilean word 'starfish', the one she used whenever she was trying to sway her mother.

"I am unsure," her mother responded, leaning back to look down at her daughter, but Ashal could see the hidden smile in her eyes and knew that she had won.

"Please! I will take Magdolon! He will make sure that I am safe!" Ashal gripped her mother's skirts, she had been forced to wear one of the uncomfortable human dresses as well. It was the custom of the Hegemon that the envoys should not come to court improperly dressed, and so the whole family had been forced to switch from their comfortable clothes suited for the sea into these terrible folds of woolen and silken cloth that hung about them like dead weight. Ashal unconsciously again reached back to scratch at her neck where the high collar of her dress chafed against her skin.

"Very well," Ashal's mother sighed. "But only if you take Magdolon with you. He is to be in charge, ya? You do as he tells you to do."

"Oh yes! Thank you, *Ss'enwei!*"

* * * * *

The smell. That was the worst part of the surface world. Magdolon wrinkled his snout as he tried to ward off the various odors that threatened to overwhelm him as he strode through the massive bazaar trailing behind the skirts of his master's daughter. Towering over the rest of the crowds, the reptilian guard caused a few sideways glances from passers by, with the sun glittering of his emerald scales and a viciously hooked snout that gave him the appearance of a snapping turtle. Strange spices choked the air with heady perfumes that stung the back of his throat and made it hard to breathe. The odor of so many unwashed and sweaty bodies pressed together caused his stomach to churn. But the worst smell was that of the smoke generated by the smoldering fires that burned every couple of hundred feet in any food vendor's stall where various and exotic foods sat sizzling and steaming over the open flames. Magdolon sighed and found his eyes wandering out to the barely visible ocean that lay so close that, if the placoderm listened carefully, he could hear the waves lapping against the city walls over the raucous din of the marketplace.

The Golden Horn was an awe-inspiring feat of human engineering. Effectively it was a land bridge that spanned between two continents and served as the largest trading port between the Sea of Suan to the northeast and the Sea of Eriskos to the south which eventually fed into the Infant Sea further west. The Basileans had a stranglehold on trading routes that had made them one of the richest nations in the world. Even the naiads, the masters of the many waters, were forced to parley and trade with the Hegemony in order to gain passage through their mighty sea gates. It was either that or travel miles out of their way to reach the same destination and be subject to brigands and ogre raids along the way. Today was one of the many market days, and a vendor could make a month's wages in a matter of hours if he could afford to set up his shop here in the mighty bazaar and then pay someone to keep away thieves and pickpockets. Magdolon did a quick inventory of his possessions as he thought of some degenerate cutpurse sneaking up behind him.

The giant reptilian guard shifted his spear to his offhand and focused his eyes on the child with whose safety he had been tasked. Ashal giggled as the Basilean sister accompanying them handed her a strange piece of food made up of a sticky substance poured over a spongy biscuit and stabbed with a long stick so that she could eat it without getting her hands or face messy. The young naiad was unsuccessful, however, as the sticky substance, honey Magdolon thought it was called, was quickly smeared all over her hands and dress as she devoured the sweet treat. Magdolon smiled in spite of himself. Ashal was the pearl of his assignment, and although he still hated being away from the depths where he felt his real duty lay, he could stomach days like these where the sunlight was tempered with the smiles of this hatchling and her high pitched squeals of delight. Such days seemed to be coming further and further apart of late, though.

Gradually the amount of vendors began to dwindle, the trickle of shouted prices and advertisements slowed to the point where Magdolon felt a ringing in his ears at its absence. Great walls loomed in the distance dividing this sector from the others that made up the city as a whole. Outsiders and non-believers of the Basilean faith were only permitted within certain areas, and for the most part these partitions were heavily guarded to prevent someone from wandering into a place where they were not allowed. The walls before them seemed less grand, with crumbling bits of stone and a general air of neglect settling over them like a layer of paint. Sister Laurine pulled them onward toward the run-down gate that separated this section from the next. As they drew closer,

Magdolon felt a thrill of excitement as he heard the sound of surf pounding against rocks.

"This next section is one that I think you will find particularly interesting." Laurine spoke while holding Ashal's hand, pulling her onward. Magdolon frowned, a chill settling in the air and with it was a dampness that accompanied it. His gut twisted and he felt as though someone was watching them from the shadows, but every way he looked all he could see were the ramshackle buildings that made up this poorer neighborhood of the market sector. He could see that at one point there had been a lot of very fine architecture and expensive buildings that had made up this part of the city, but they had since fallen into disrepair, and now only homeless squatters dared venture here.

"Sister Laurine, I feel this is a place very bad for us," Magdolon voiced his unease. Laurine glanced over her shoulder at him.

"Yes, it is a bit of a rougher area of the city, I'll grant you that, but there are still hours before it gets dark. During the day, we are relatively safe, so long as we stick to the main streets and don't venture down any dark alleys." The Basilean sister did not slow her pace as she walked. "We are very close now, there is something that I think you will want to see that makes the journey worth it."

"Please, Magdolon?! We can go with her, yes?" Ashal beamed. The twisting in Magdolon's stomach increased.

"We are approaching the gate, see? There are men at arms guarding the passage." Laurine pointed ahead at where the path lined up to a rather poorly maintained gate. Rusted bars made up a portcullis that looked as though it hadn't been opened in years. Two soldiers stood leaning against it with wrinkled uniforms and rather shaggy plumes sticking out of the top of their helmets. As they cleared the last street of broken down buildings, Magdolon noticed that the wall that separated this district from the next ended abruptly about a hundred yards down from the rusted gate, and the sound of the pounding surf was becoming increasingly noticeable.

"Where is this that you are taking us?" Magdolon questioned.

"If I told you, then that would ruin the surprise!" Laurine laughed in response. Magdolon reached forward and took hold of her shoulder gently, but forcibly, and brought their progress to a stop.

"This is my duty, to be sure of the safety of Ashal. You will tell me, or we will be returning to the home of my master." The placoderm guard stared down at the Basilean sister, his golden eyes piercing through her forehead as he spoke. Laurine stared back for a few moments before sighing.

"It is called the Quarter of Woe, and it lies submerged beneath the waves. I thought you might like to see it and explore our city's past, as there is much of our history that lies beneath the waters that you can visit unmolested by the crowds. I thought it might be something different and unique for you. Not many are allowed in there, but I have special rights as I have been studying the ruins

11

in an attempt to catalog the history lost in those waters." Laurine chewed her lip thoughtfully. "Also, if I'm being honest, I brought you here for selfish reasons, to see if you could help me recover some things. I'm a good swimmer, for a human, but I can't reach the places that you two could, and I've hit a bit of a dead end in my research." Magdolon squinted at the sister suspiciously.

"This sounds fun!" Ashal cried out before Magdolon could respond. He looked down at the little girl who was swirling back and forth with her hands clenched before her face. Her big eyes looked up at him, filled with anticipation.

"This place. It is dangerous?" Magdolon asked, returning his gaze to the sister.

"Nothing that I have found has made me worried," Laurine responded. "If you prefer, however, we can go back. I understand how this might make you uncomfortable and I can respect that." Ashal stopped swirling and the look in her eyes seemed to fall away.

"We are not going?" Ashal's voice was small. Laurine knelt down to look her in the eyes.

"Not today, my little sea flower, Magdolon doesn't think it's safe, and he's in charge. Maybe another day when we can get some more of your mother's guards we will come back and you can explore, maybe with your mother, even! Wouldn't that be more fun?" Laurine reached up and brushed a tear off of Ashal's cheek.

"My mother, she will never come. She is too busy with your holy man. It will be many days before we come here again. Maybe never." Ashal's voice cracked as she spoke. Magdolon understood her disappointment. Her mother was a busy individual and her staff was limited. If they didn't go today, then it was likely they would never go at all.

"Sister, you say that there is no danger?" Magdolon spoke, pushing his nerves down.

"None that I have found."

"Then we will go. If I see danger, we leave." Ashal's face broke into a wide smile at Magdolon's words.

"Oh! Thank you Magdolon!" Ashal cried out, rushing forward to wrap her arms around one of his massive legs. Magdolon smiled and reached down to pat her head. Laurine nodded in approval and then continued on toward the rusty gate. The soldiers, upon seeing her approach, snapped to attention and attempted to straighten their uniforms. She quickly put them at ease with a few quick comments and a laugh. As she was speaking with them, Magdolon knelt down beside Ashal.

"Listen to me, little one," he spoke in their native tongue. "I want you by my side for all of this adventure. You do not wander off, understand?" Ashal nodded vigorously, still smiling, and hugged him again. Laurine had finished her conversation with the guards and was walking back toward them. Behind her, the rusted gate screamed in protest as one of the guards cranked on a handle, twisting it around slowly to raise the portcullis and admit them entry to the Drowned Quarter.

"Shall we go in?" Laurine smiled, motioning toward the sound of the waves crashing beyond the gate.

* * * * *

They spent hours diving amongst the ruins of a golden age long past. Seaweed and barnacles clung to ancient statues and crumbling pillars of stone. When they had first arrived, Ashal had quickly shed the uncomfortable dress she had been wearing for a much more comfortable swimming shift better fitted for her body type. She laughed wildly as she felt the cool water gliding past her while she spun through the lengths of flooded hallways and buildings that held untold wonders for any who dared venture deep enough.

The entire time she explored, Magdolon was always there. Often times he had to grab onto the exuberant child to make sure she didn't get too far ahead of him in her glee, but he was glad for it. Ashal was profoundly unhappy in the stone halls of the Hegemony, any true citizen of the Trident Realm would struggle to be happy living in these stagnant houses of rock when the sea lay so tantalizingly close that one could hear the waves at night. These moments of unbridled joy were far too few and far between for little Ashal. So much had been required of her at such a young age, all because of the duty of her parents. It wasn't fair.

Ashal suddenly pulled up short as she rounded a corner in another submerged building. Bubbles exploded from her mouth as she gasped and then froze still. Magdolon rushed forward and pulled her behind him as he looked down the passageway, trying to follow the direction of her gaze. He quickly saw what had been the cause of her alarm and felt instant relief flood through him. A skeleton, encrusted with barnacles and wrapped in a decayed and tattered piece of cloth, lay strewn across the ground. It must have been the unfortunate victim of whatever catastrophe had befallen this sector and caused the whole thing to sink below the waves. Magdolon was surprised that they had not encountered more of these eerie corpses floating about in the darkened passages of this dead city.

Magdolon quickly pulled Ashal away and they retreated back to the shore where Sister Laurine was waiting for them. As they swam, Magdolon again pushed the gnawing sensation he'd felt at the gate to the back of his mind, but it would not go quietly. A thought bubbled into the foreground of his mind: *Where is all the life?* Even with this city section being flooded as it was, there were no sea creatures here. No fish, no coral grew in the briny depths where they had explored. Nothing but the barnacles that had attached to the skeleton they had encountered even suggested that such a place as this could even maintain life. This didn't make sense to Magdolon, as the water was fresh, it filtered in from the sea and did not appear to be polluted in any way that would prevent sea life from finding a way to survive here. Yet nothing did. Magdolon had a harder time suppressing this thought.

As they surfaced next to where the Basilean sister waited for them, a cold wind blew in from the east, causing little Ashal to shudder. Laurine called out to them and motioned for them to join her around a small fire she had built using some scraps of dried timbers she'd gathered. Magdolon lifted Ashal out of the water before pulling himself free and plodding over to where the warm fire crackled. He settled down on his haunches to absorb its small comfort.

"I cannot thank you enough for your help today!" Laurine spoke, motioning toward the small pile of items that lay a way off. The sister had a small notebook where she had been cataloging their finds while the other two had been diving into places that only they could reach. "I would never have been able to retrieve these wonders without you." Ashal giggled and held out her hands to the fire to warm them. Magdolon nodded in acknowledgment.

"Why is there only you to explore this place?" Magdolon asked. He had noted that there were no other sisters or workers there to help them, and this had fed his growing sense of unease.

"I've asked for more help," Laurine sighed, "but they never say they can spare the hands needed. Even I have a hard time finding my way here on a regular basis. With all the fighting that is a constant in our day-to-day lives, and wars that must be planned, campaigns to be drawn up and discussed, logistics for surviving the winter and foodstores, there just isn't enough time in the day for us to preserve our past. Especially a past so frustratingly out of reach as this one."

"What is it that happened here?" Ashal chimed in, rubbing her hands together.

"I don't know," Laurine replied. "There are several records that claim one thing or another, but there are conflicting accounts, and the limited amount of diving I've been able to do has brought less than desirable results. Some historians say it was magic that caused this part of the city to crumble. Others that a Shining One smote it down for the sins of its inhabitants. One argued that it was a feat of sabotage from our enemies that hoped to gain entry to the city, although I find that one highly unlikely as no enemy has ever gotten closer than within cannon shot from our walls. What I think is most likely is that it was a faulty construction decision that eventually lead to the city sector breaking under the strain and falling beneath the waves." Laurine shrugged. "We may never know for certain. All that I do know is that there is a treasure trove of knowledge that is just outside my reach, taunting me."

They sat in silence for a few more minutes until Magdolon looked up to the horizon. "It is becoming the time to return home." He grunted, indicating the darkening sky as the evening sun sank behind the walls of the Golden Horn. Laurine sighed again and nodded.

"You're right, of course. I'm sad we didn't have more time, I would've liked that. But then, I've grown used to not getting what I want." She walked over to the pile of recovered items. "Do you think you could help me with one last thing? It won't take long. I have a small chamber that I discovered not too far from here, it goes down into the ground but it makes for a good private study for me to store the artifacts that I find here. It's not far and it'll be easier than carrying them all the way back to my quarters at my abbey." Magdolon shrugged and reached down to start picking up the cataloged items. Ashal jumped over and helped, too.

Laurine lead them through a portion of the ruins that had not fallen into the sea. The dilapidated buildings looked ready to crumble at a stiff breeze, but the air seemed as dead as the city under the water, and not even a whisper of wind disturbed the centuries of dust that had accumulated. Their passing only minorly disturbed the dirt and grime, throwing up small motes that drifted lazily down to settle almost exactly where they had lain moments before.

Eventually they came to a small opening in the ground. It seemed odd that a hole should appear in the midst of a series of buildings, but the gaping maw stretched wide enough for a man to fit through easily, and Magdolon could see a rope ladder attached to one side that would allow someone to climb in and out of it. Laurine walked right up to the edge.

"I think it was a well, once, but since the quarter was drowned, it has crumbled into disrepair. Surprisingly, there is the remains of what seems to have been an extensive network of tunnels that leads a good distance in all directions. Perhaps those tunnels were the cause of the collapse? Anyways, I found a small cave-like room down there that is dry and more sturdy than any of the buildings left in this district, so that's where I store my treasures until I can study them more precisely." With that, Laurine slid down through the hole and grunted as she landed a few feet below.

"Hand me down Ashal, Magdolon, I will catch her, no worries!" Laurine's voice called out of the darkness. Magdolon looked at the hole dubiously, but then he set aside the trinkets which he carried and lifted Ashal up with one of his powerful arms. The young spawnling giggled as she flew off the ground and was gently lowered into the hole. Laurine quickly lifted her hands up and grabbed Ashal when she dropped low enough for her to hold. Shortly after, Magdolon dropped down, landing with a loud crackling noise as his heavy frame caused the packed earth to shudder and loose rocks to tumble down around him. Ashal smiled and ran up to hug his leg as he straightened from his fall.

"Let us be quick, Sister. I must be seeing Ashal home soon." Magdolon seemed to growl in the stunted light of the dark tunnels. Laurine simply nodded. Reaching over to the wall, she removed an unlit torch from a makeshift sconce

15

that hung there. Quickly producing a flint and steel, she lit it with practiced ease and took Ashal's hand, walking down a tunnel that stretched out before them. The path twisted occasionally, and a few times there were other branches that twisted off in other directions. At one, Magdolon was certain that he heard the sound of dripping water coming from the inky blackness of its depths, out of sight.

After a few minutes of walking, they finally came to a small cavern that was obviously different from the dirt tunnels outside it. For starters, the ground was cobbled stone and several bookshelves lined the walls, each shelf packed with very old and musty looking books. A chair and several tables were packed on one side of the room, and on the other side there was a deep looking pool, a strange looking apparatus sitting at its edge. The apparatus consisted of a series of tubes and large gears with a long coil of what appeared to be a hose linking the machine to a crude looking mask made up of stitched together snakeskin. Laurine caught Magdolon eyeing the device.

"I use it for my own diving adventures; not all of us can breathe underwater, mighty placoderm." She walked over and indicated one of the tables on the other side of the room. "Place the items we recovered here, I'll take time to look over them at a later date." Magdolon complied, walking over and depositing his armload of relics and other items. He turned and saw Laurine staring down at the pile of trinkets.

"It's so sad that this is what our lives are reduced to." She spoke slowly, picking up what looked like a child's toy, the remnants of what must have been a soldier on a horse so long ago. "All of our hopes, desires, our aspirations, all wiped away with the turning of the tide, a fissure in the earth. In the end, our descendants will barely know who we were. Even those famous enough to be heralded in the stories that shape our world, we do not know what they wanted of their lives, what they felt. All we will be left with is their possessions and our best guesses as to what they were really like." She tossed the broken toy back into the pile and turned to smile at Magdolon.

"I'm sorry," she sniffed, as her eyes clouded over with unshed tears. Magdolon was taken aback by this sudden shift in her behavior.

"Why must you sadden?" he asked. "Of what do you have to be sorry?"

"For so many things," she gave a mirthless laugh and sniffed again. "For starters, my lack of decorum in crying in front of you. But there are so many things with which I am burdened. I have many sins for which I must atone. I only hope that the end result will be enough to absolve me." She turned and leaned against the table, her head bowed.

"It all started when I finally gained access to the Drowned Quarter. I was allowed to come here and begin searching the ruins as best I was able by myself. I was given some token servants to help at first, but after a while and no results to speak of, even they were taken away. I was left alone to continue my search for answers. I don't know why it was so important to me. I guess I wanted to be reassured that so many lives could not just be taken away like this, and not just taken away, but completely forgotten! I couldn't stand the idea that someone could just cease to be like that. My mother had always believed so stalwartly in the blessings of the Shining Ones, but that hadn't saved her when the orcs descended on our village."

Laurine's tears flowed freely now, falling down her face in streams that dripped onto the table and over the relics they had recovered. Magdolon shifted uncomfortably, unsure as to how he should react. Humans were so volatile! Their emotions raged like a storm, crashing against the rocks and leaving him to feel as though he were a small ship left adrift in the midst of the tossing waves. He preferred the company of his fellow placoderms, with their stalwart and stoic presence to bolster him up and remind him of his duty.

"I am sorry for your sadness," he ventured. Laurine turned her reddened eyes on him.

"Thank you," she smiled through her tears. "It feels good to tell someone about it." Magdolon nodded at this and then turned as if to leave. "But," the sister spoke before he could walk away, "I'm afraid I cannot repay your kindness, at least not in a way that would be worthy of you. For you see, you are one of my sins."

Laurine lifted her hand and a bolt of energy flew from her fingers to slam against Magdolon, who grunted with pain and went flying into a shelf, crushing the wooden plank and causing the books to rain down on him as he slid onto the dirt floor, dazed. Ashal screamed. Laurine lowered her hands and began to chant in a strange language. Mist-like tendrils of power seeped out of her hands and writhed into the ground beneath her, causing the earth to tremble.

"One of my earliest discoveries in my excavation here was a strange book that told the most… inconvenient truths." Laurine stopped her chanting and closed her eyes in concentration, the tendrils of power still leaching into the ground from her closed fists. "It taught me the ways of power and the lies of eternity. At first I didn't want to believe, but then I began to look at the advantages the book offered. It taught me the ways of the dead, and how to bring them back!"

Ashal screeched again as a skeletal hand punched its way free from the hard packed earthen walls in the tunnel outside the room and watched in horror as a body pulled itself free from the dirt, shaking off debris as it did so. Ashal edged back, further into the room.

"At first I thought to use the dead only as a means of excavating the lost city. They didn't need to breath and surely this was no evil purpose that I was using my power to accomplish!" Laurine leaned back and seemed to grimace as more energy rushed out of her and into the dirt. More undead creatures began to pull themselves free from the earth. Magdolon, still dazed from her earlier attack, worried indistinctly as to whether the tunnels could stand this much disruption.

"Now, however, I have come to the realization that our society is flawed, our memories are too short, and we forget where we have come from!" Laurine lowered her head as the last of the power left her clenched fists and entered the dirt beneath her. "The Hegemon does not serve the people *or* the gods. He is a foolish man who forgets the poor and the needy and leads his people on hopeless and pointless campaigns against those who he claims are our enemies when the Abyss, and the orcs, and the evil northmen rage across our lands. He does not care for his people, and he does not serve a higher purpose!"

Magdolon shook his head to clear his vision and pushed himself to his feet. He pulled his spear out of its strap holding it to his back and rushed over beside the young Ashal who stood trembling and petrified. He counted about a dozen skeletons that stood between them and the exit into the tunnels. Behind them, Laurine took a step forward and almost fell, clutching the edge of a table and pushing herself up with a grimace. The giant placoderm took up a defensive stance against the undead minions and stabbed with his spear at the closest one. The sharp point punched through the exposed eye socket of the first skeleton, and the creature stepped back under the force of the blow. But as Magdolon brought his spear back in preparation for another attack, the undead creature once again began its forward advance.

He switched his stance to a series of efficient motions, his spear stabbing in a steady rhythm of pinpoint thrusts. Magdolon grunted, the precision of these strikes that he normally used to fight within the heavier confines of underwater combat struggled to find killing blows against the already decayed bodies of his current opponents. The first skeleton finally succumbed when one of Magdolon's thrusts took its head from its shoulders, and he repeated this measure with the next one, also managing to drop this opponent. But the rest of the animated skeletons continued their shuffling attack and threatened to overwhelm him.

A quick glance behind showed that Laurine was still recovering from the effects of whatever spell she had cast. Magdolon pulled Ashal behind him and backed further into the room as more skeletons appeared from out of the darkness of the tunnels. There were far too many for him to defeat. They would soon crowd in and tear both him and Ashal to bits! Magdolon lunged forward and stabbed his spear at Laurine who twisted desperately to the side, narrowly missing the point of the weapon. Magdolon quickly followed up with a series of blows, but she turned and fled behind the advancing wall of skeleton warriors that continued to shamble into the room.

"Surrender! If you do so, I promise I will not hurt you or the child unless it becomes necessary." Her voice called from behind her undead minions who ceased their advance and now stood staring at Magdolon and Ashal, the latter of which was whimpering quietly, tears streaming down her face as she stared in abject horror at the scene before her.

"Why do you do this thing, Laurine?!" Magdolon cried out, moving once again to stand between Ashal and the skeletal corpses. "Why are you forcing Ashal to suffer as this?"

"I do not seek the child's death! Nor yours for that matter," Laurine responded. "She is simply leverage for something greater."

"You mean to be using her against her mother? To what cause?" Magdolon glanced around the room once more, his eyes focused on the pool to the side of the room. Only a couple of skeletons stood in their way. Could they make it? Did the pool lead anywhere? Or was it just a deep hole that had filled with water? It didn't look stagnant, which meant that it had to have a source to the ocean from somewhere. They had to try. Magdolon reached down and took Ashal's hand.

"Oh, Magdolon, do not have me speak of such things in front of my little sea flower." Laurine laughed, and it was a dry, humorless sound.

"You do not be calling me this anymore! I am not your sea flower!" Ashal screamed through her hot tears. "I hate you!"

"That makes me sad, Ashal," Laurine sighed, "but I understand, and I don't blame you. Life is so unfair, especially to children." She paused a moment. Magdolon took a deep breath, drawing Ashal closer to him. "This is your last chance, Magdolon, surrender and I promise you that you will live. I have enough of my soldiers to bury you in their bones despite your obvious skills. Will you yield?"

"No." The placoderm gripped Ashal to his side and sprung forward. He swung his spear in a wide, sweeping motion that felt awkward in his hand. It swept the first skeleton out of his path easily, and the next one also went down quickly. His spear caught in the ribs of the last corpse, and as it toppled over, he was forced to abandon his weapon as he ran past and dove into the pool with Ashal screaming as he went.

The icy cold of the water washed over them, and Magdolon pushed them down with his powerful tail. Darkness covered their escape as they dove deeper and deeper into the tunnel. Eventually they came to a branch, and Magdolon swam to the right, hoping that it would take them further into the city and away from Laurine's drowned quarter. He did not look back, even if Laurine sent her minions after them, there was no way they would catch him in the water, even carrying Ashal with him.

He didn't know how long he swam before stopping. His muscles sang out in synchronized pain from the effort. They were hopelessly lost, and he had no idea if there even was an exit to these tunnels besides the entrance that was controlled by Laurine. But even if that were the case, he knew that he couldn't find the way back now even if he wanted. He turned to Ashal who had slumped against one side of the tunnel, her knees were against her chest and she hugged them to her, all the while shaking. Magdolon signed to her with his hands in the language of his people.

We. Rest. Now. He said. His body ached and he could feel the cold temperatures beginning to take its toll on him. This water was colder than the waters of the ocean, and he wondered if it had ever seen the sun on its surface, or if it had been warmed by the volcanic fissures in the ocean floor. Had it always been stowed away in these dark tunnels? Magdolon could only make out vague shapes of anything that wasn't more than a few feet away from him. Even Ashal's form was obscured for the most part, only the most obvious of details were discernible in the murky gloom. It would make future navigation nearly impossible.

Magdolon took a small knife out of his belt and reached out to touch the side of the tunnel. He felt dirt, and it gave way to his knife when he tested it. He nodded; he didn't know how well the marks would last, but it might give him some semblance of order in his attempts at finding their way out of this labyrinth. They rested a few more minutes before Magdolon finally took hold of Ashal and placed her on his back, instructing her to wrap her arms around his neck so that she could hold on to him while he continued their slow advance.

Keeping his knife in contact with the wall to score it with the blade, they swam onward. At every branch, Magdolon followed a simple process of elimination and constantly chose the left branch, continuing to score the walls. He found himself redoubling back on his marks, sometimes not noticing them until they had been traveling down the same tunnel for some time. He always tried to correct their course whenever he found himself going in circles, but it was slow progress and there was no way to track how much time they had been in the darkness except for when Ashal began to complain about her hunger.

Magdolon also felt the pangs gnawing at his stomach. How long had it been since they last ate? It had to have been hours ago and so much had happened since then. Magdolon felt a sting of panic as he wondered whether they would be able to find their way out of these tunnels before starvation set in. He could already feel his limbs becoming shaky as the adrenaline rushes and lack of food took their toll on him. He was a soldier and used to light rations when the times required it of him, but how long could he go without any food at all? Worse yet, how long could Ashal survive without any food? Right now it was a minor inconvenience, but what would happen when the hours stretched into a day or two?

Being so wrapped up in these thoughts, he didn't notice as a rotting corpse shot out of the darkness and slammed into him. The placoderm reeled backward and Ashal went spinning away into the inky water. The bloated zombie took advantage of Magdolon's hesitation and bit down hard on his exposed forearm. Blood blossomed out into the water and Magdolon cried out, bubbles escaping his mouth. He quickly brought up the small knife he held in his other hand and brought it down on the base of the zombie's skull. The creature instantly went limp and floated away to the ceiling of the tunnel. Gripping his forearm, the wounded guard glanced around him to try and spy Ashal, but she was nowhere to be seen.

Taking deep breaths to try and calm himself, Magdolon began moving about slowly in the direction he thought that he'd seen Ashal go when the zombie attacked them. He cursed his poor vision for these circumstances and fought back a grimace as another wave of pain washed up his arm. After several long minutes of searching, Magdolon fought down the foolish urge to hurry forward in a vain attempt to catch her and their imaginary attacker. Where was she? Had there been other zombies around them that had snatched the little spawnling away from him? Was she even now being ripped apart somewhere nearby, her muffled screams unable to carry to his ears because of the water between them? Magdolon sniffed the water, there was no sign of blood in its currents other than his own. But what if they'd been under control of Laurine? Could she not have ordered them to carry the young naiad back to her?

Just as he began to despair, a small hand lurched out of the dark and took hold of his wrist. Magdolon reacted slowly, bringing his knife up in a defensive stance before he recognized Ashal's tiny grip and her scared eyes staring at his wound. He waved her away and had her retake her position on his back before once more restarting their wanderings.

After what felt like hours, Magdolon shook his head. His vision kept blurring and the pain in his arm was driving him to distraction. He hadn't been marking the walls, so he wasn't sure they were even following the same path or had been wandering in circles for the entire time. He shook his shoulders to signal Ashal to step off, but she clung on even after a second shake. Magdolon grew a little impatient and reached back to grab her, but she waved his hands away and then signed in front of his face with her other finned hand.

Can. You. Feel. It? She signed. Magdolon furrowed his brow but forced his body to grow still. At first, there was nothing but the surrounding darkness, but then he felt it. A slight tremor in the water that felt like something small hitting the surface, like droplets falling and making ripples that flowed out though the water. Magdolon waited for what felt like an eternity before the vibrations came again, and this time he was certain. They were underground, but that vibration proved to him that there was an end to the water somewhere nearby if they could just find it. If there was a surface, then they were making progress toward the end of these accursed tunnels and might find access to the city above that way.

As they approached the source of the vibrations, Magdolon noticed that the water had begun to lighten, although it was still murky and it seemed to be less clean than before. Bits of detritus and debris hung suspended in the water as more light began to penetrate the darkness. Finally, Magdolon spotted ripples above them and swam upward to break through into the air.

They found themselves in a dark tunnel. Blue light pierced the gloom through a grated opening several feet above them. It was small, but Magdolon could see stars through it and breathed a sigh of relief. They were close to being above ground once more and there would be an end of the darkness at long last. He noticed an outcropping of crumbling stonework that jetted out as a narrow ledge over the water and made his way over to it. He helped Ashal climb onto the ledge before wearily pulling his own weight onto the slick stone. His head swam with the effort - he hadn't realized how close to absolute collapse he had been, and now that his body rested on the cool floor, he found that he couldn't keep his eyes open. They slowly slid shut and darkness took him completely into its embrace.

* * * * *

Ashal woke to the sounds of bells tolling. Their frantic ringing cascaded into the narrow space where the slumbering form of Magdolon still lolled, one arm, the infected one, lay submerged in the filthy water from which they had emerged the previous night. Ashal was surprised to see bright sunlight streaming in from the grated opening above them to illuminate their surroundings, they must have slept through the night! Ashal saw the familiar stone patterns of human masonry that built up their cold and square houses. She took this as a good sign and one that they were close to returning back to the city.

Up above them, the sounds of the bells were mixed with the sounds of heavy boots stamping past and voices shouting in the heavy sounding accents that the humans held along with their awkward language. Ashal walked over and tried to shake Magdolon awake. His skin was hot to the touch and his chest barely rose when he breathed. It took Ashal several attempts to get a response from him and increasingly violent shaking.

"Magdolon!" she cried out. He stirred and opened one bleary eye, groaning as he did so. He pushed himself into a sitting position and smacked his lips.

"Is there anything to be drunk, spawnling?" he rasped. "I thirst so desperately."

Ashal shook her head.

"Nothing but mucky water all around us. But listen! There is music and men above us!" Magdolon tilted his head to listen to the clamor happening up above them. His eyes seemed unfocused and his speech was slurred. He groggily pushed himself to his feet, stumbled once, and then righted himself with his hand against the wall.

"We must go," he growled. "Must get you to your mother before Laurine can hurt her through you." They staggered forward for several yards before they turned a corner and came across a ladder that led upward toward another grated opening, but this one was bigger and seemed to have a hinged gate attached to it. Magdolon was leaning heavily against the wall and kept blinking and shaking his head. His breath was ragged and uneven as well.

Ashal climbed up to the grate, but when she tried to pull it open, it only came a few inches and screamed loudly in protest as ancient metal scraped on itself. The hinges gave a final groan of protest and then refused to budge any further. Ashal called down to Magdolon, who climbed unsteadily up behind her. He reached out his injured arm to try and pull on the opening but was only slightly more successful than Ashal had been, opening the grate a few more inches. The gap was now barely wide enough for Ashal to push her head through after a determined effort. She saw that they were now in a large open square with tall marble arches, and in the distance she spotted the great domes of the Golden Horn, but this was a part of the city that she didn't recognize. Several Basilean soldiers were running around and she called out to them. At first no one heard her, but her cries became increasingly more frantic until some passing uniformed officers hurried over with a few other guards in escort, a confused look on their faces.

"What is the meaning of this? How did you get down there?" A tall, blond officer yelled as two of the soldiers attempted to place the shaft of their spears in between the grate and the opening in order to try and pry it open further. Ashal fell silent before the stern gaze of the tall man who was yelling at her; he seemed unnecessarily angry, and after the stress of all that had happened to her, she could feel sobs rising up from her chest and tightening her throat.

The soldiers heaved on the spear and gradually the opening was wide enough to permit Ashal's whole body through. She wriggled and twisted until she landed on the stones of the square, her body aching from the effort.

"Please!" she gasped. "My guard, he is still in the dark. Do keep the pushing on so that he might be free, too!" The soldiers looked confused, but after some gesturing from the young naiad, they understood and continued to lever their spear shafts into the hole. With a groaning screech, the grate opened up completely and Magdolon was able to throw his arm through and pull himself into the square. He lay there gasping on the ground for a few moments, and Ashal ran up to hug his wounded arm. She didn't notice how eerily quiet the soldiers had become, not until she heard the whispers.

"He fits the description we were given," one soldier hissed.

"All these fish-folk look the exact bloody same! Of course he fits the description! But why does he have the little one with him?" another replied. Ashal felt Magdolon shift, and a low, defensive growl emanated from his throat. The soldiers' spears lowered to point at the placoderm and the small hatchling naiad.

"I hereby place you under arrest by right of the Holy Hegemon of Basilea! Please do not resist!" One of the soldiers stepped forward and pulled Ashal away from Magdolon. Ashal struggled, but the man's grip held firm. She clawed at him with her webbed hand, but a second soldier came forward and grabbed her free arm and held her fast. Magdolon groaned and tried to rise, but another human stepped forward and slammed the butt of his spear into the back of the placoderm's skull. Magdolon's eyes rolled back and he fell forward in a crumpled heap. Ashal began screaming as her captors came forward and lifted Magdolon's prone form off the ground to carry him away. The two humans holding her followed behind the struggling soldiers hauling the massive bulk of her guard between them.

* * * * *

The prison cells were dark and uncomfortable. Ashal shifted on the hard wooden bench that was bolted to the stone wall and served as the only furniture within her room. Stone stretched all around her and towered up about ten feet in each direction. There was no window, so the only light came from the flickering torches in the hall who diffused their radiance through the barred window of the thick wooden door to her cell. She shuddered as she watched the flickering shadows dance across the cold masonry. The humans loved their stone so much! To her, it was abhorrent, plain and drab in comparison to the coral palaces of her homeland. Stone was cold and dead, it was not a thing to build a home from.

She did not know how long they forced her to wait in the dark, but it felt like days. Magdolon lay slumped on the floor, he was too heavy for her to move, and there was no other place for him to lay in any case. His breathing was shallow and ragged, his arm and flesh were burning to the touch. Ashal shivered in the dark, tears streaming down her face as every so often a sob would tear itself from her throat. She wanted to go home! Now more than ever she longed for the warm tides and salty tang of the sea. She wanted to feel the golden sands of her underwater kingdom where she could fly through the water and play with the brightly colored schools of fish. When she opened her eyes and was greeted by harsh stone before her, it only brought new waves of dread with it.

After an eternity, there was the sound of footsteps in the corridor outside her cell and then that of a key turning in the lock. The door groaned as it opened outward to reveal a Basilean soldier standing there, his shadow flickering across the floor as the torch sputtered behind him. Then, as Ashal watched, the guard fell forward onto the floor, a large, red stain growing on his back. The young naiad gasped and stared at the quickly cooling corpse before her. Another flickering shadow fell across the floor and Ashal looked up in surprise.

"Calm yourself, little sea flower," Laurine cooed quietly. In her hand was a long dagger, dripping with the guard's blood. Ashal cried out in terror and huddled back against the wall. There was nowhere to run!

"Magdolon!" Ashal cried out her protector's name, but the placoderm didn't stir. Laurine advanced slowly. She knelt beside Magdolon's body and reached a hand over his wounded arm. The hot, red marks of the zombie bite there were oozing a yellow liquid that looked the consistency of honey. A blue light blinked into being beneath the sister's hand and she began to mutter some words under her breath that Ashal could not understand. Her eyes widened in fear and anger and she leapt at Laurine, a screech on her lips. She clawed the Basilean's face with her sharp little nails and Laurine yelped, falling backward to land on her back in surprise.

"Do not touch him, witch!" Ashal screeched, crouching over Magdolon's body. "You will not be turning him into a creature of death!" Laurine sat up, touching her face where three bloody lines stretched across her cheek. She sighed and held up her hands as if surrendering.

"I suppose I deserved that after everything I put you through, little one. But I was not planning on making a zombie of your guard there. That wound is heavily infected, and if I don't treat it, he will die." Laurine spoke slowly, not moving a muscle as she did so. Ashal pondered what she said for a moment.

"Why would you do this thing?" Ashal asked. Laurine laughed mirthlessly.

"Because I do not wish him to die. Quite simply. I have attained everything that I needed from both of you. I do not wish anyone to die that does not require it. I do not take life lightly, little sea flower."

"You were to kill us in the tunnels before!" Ashal accused.

"Only if I needed to, and as it turned out, I did not. Your mother was most accommodating." Laurine sighed and cast her eyes to the floor.

"What did my mother do?" Ashal asked, confused. Laurine refused to meet her questing gaze. The silence stretched out for a long time. Finally, Laurine spoke.

"I must heal Magdolon, the wound is dire and will kill him if I do not." With that, Laurine pulled herself forward and placed her hands on Magdolon's wounded arm. A dull, gray light emitted from beneath her palms as she chanted under her breath, her brows furrowed in concentration. At times she seemed to jerk her head to the side as if arguing with someone, but after a few moments she sat back, panting. Magdolon's breathing eased and he opened his eyes, which now appeared focused and clear of fever.

"I need to study up on my medicinal magics, they've been getting harder to work with over the past few months." Laurine panted as she pushed herself backward to put her back against a wall. Magdolon tried to push himself up, but his arms shook as he rose, and he tumbled back to lay on the ground. He pointed an accusing finger at the Basilean sister.

"You," he gasped, his voice scratchy and weak, "why are you here? You were to feed us to your undead things!"

"We're past all that now, and I have no intention of killing you anymore," Laurine sighed. "I already explained this to your ward, I have what I need and now I see no point in you two suffering further. You are free to go." Magdolon's eyes narrowed as he stared at her, torchlight causing the golden flecks in his bulbous fish eyes to shimmer.

"What is this thing that you have done?" Magdolon whispered. Once again, Laurine's eyes fell to the ground and she shuffled awkwardly before rising to her feet. "Laurine!" Magdolon called as the sister turned toward the door.

"You cannot stay here," Laurine paused by the door, not looking back at the two former captives behind her. "And you must leave quietly. I can distract the guards and mislead them for awhile, but you will have to be silent and quick. If you make it down to the docks, I have a boat waiting for you at pier thirty-seven. The shipmaster's name is Arden and he..." She turned, trailing off as Magdolon's webbed hand wrapped itself around her throat, lifting her off the ground.

"I will kill you now and tell my master the truth of your deceit." Magdolon's voice growled now, his scratchy whisper from before mutated into something much more threatening.

"You cannot..." Laurine choked. "She's dead! And you will be, too, if you do not release me!" Magdolon hissed. Ashal felt a lump of iron form in her lungs and her vision swam as she watched Magdolon slam Laurine against the stone wall of the cell. However, even as he did so, his legs buckled and he fell forward, releasing his grip on her and collapsing to his knees while his hands gripped his head. Ashal watched it all with a sudden detachment. The cold of her cell seemed to have infected the core of her very being. Her mother was dead. The coldness took hold of her gaze and she fixed that dead stare on Laurine, and just as suddenly, the ice in her eyes turned to a burning flame that threatened to overwhelm her. She wanted to scream, she wanted to scratch the human's eyes from her skull, but the numbness inside stopped her and so she just stared, unable to tear her gaze away.

"Your infection was rather severe," Laurine gasped at Magdolon, her voice cutting through Ashal's thoughts. "I'd recommend no sudden movements like that for the next few weeks while your body recovers." She pushed the placoderm back and he fell weakly to the floor, groaning quietly. Ashal rushed forward and attacked Laurine with her small claws, but Laurine danced to the side.

"You lie!" Ashal screeched turning to face her foe. "My mother is not dead, I will be having your tongue for this deceit!" She lunged again at Laurine, but the sister stepped into her attack, and in a blur, her hand flashed across the young naiad's face to send her sprawling onto the floor in a sobbing heap. The wretched sound filled up an empty silence that threatened to smother them all.

"I am so sorry, little sea flower..." Laurine's voice was thick, as if her throat were constricted.

"Do not call me this!" Ashal sobbed. Laurine took a sharp breath and seemed to fold in on herself, hugging her arms around her stomach.

"What is this thing that you have done?" Magdolon's weak voice finally cut through the somber sounds of Ashal's crying. Laurine looked at him, and the weak light of the torches in the hall reflected off her glistening cheeks. Magdolon started at this. Was she crying? What cause had she to weep?

"It wasn't supposed to go this way!" Laurine sniffed. "She should have only been banished. But the Hegemon, in his mercy," she spat this word with a vehemence that contrasted sharply to the choked sound of her tears, "His Holiness simply had her household executed and a warrant issued for both you and the little one."

"I do not understand." Magdolon pushed himself unsteadily to his feet, his hand gripping the wall for support. "For what would your Holy Man kill my people?"

"Because I framed them." Laurine closed her eyes and leaned back against the wall. "I blackmailed her mother into playing along, saying that I had Ashal and that if she wanted to see her again, she would need to admit to whatever crime she was accused of. All I had to do was show her the dress that Ashal left from our little outing. The one she took off in order to go swimming. She agreed unconditionally." She breathed a ragged sigh.

"Then what is it that happened?" Magdolon's voice was flat as he stared at her.

"I went to the Hegemon's guard and said that Ai-ellain was planning an assassination on His Holiness, saying that I had overheard it while I was in their quarters when I shouldn't have been. I openly accused her, and because of my blackmail, she admitted to the crime. But her political position should have granted her immunity!" Laurine's voice squeaked and she trailed off, turning to look at the flickering torches. Ashal on the floor had grown still, her small voice sobbing quietly into the stone beneath her.

"The Hegemon didn't even hesitate; he had his guard cut Ai-ellain's head from her shoulders on the spot. I found out later that he had already received a message from the Trident Realm that Ai-ellain was being investigated for... Abyssal dalliances. Evidently, they found occult artifacts at her estate and she had been seen descending into the Forbidden Trench that runs through her territory there before she requested her transfer here to the Golden Horn. Those accusations, along with her forced admission of attempted assassination, sealed the Hegemon's judgment. His guard then stormed the Neritican embassy and slaughtered everyone there under suspicion of infernal involvement. The Hegemon simply watched, and in the end, condemned their whole household as dangerous heretics that had threatened the sanctity of the Basilean crusade." She paused at this then turned to gesture toward Ashal. "She and you are scheduled to be executed tomorrow at the steps of the Hegemon's palace, a final example for her mother's supposed treachery. When this was announced, I knew I couldn't allow it."

"Why would you do this thing?" Magdolon asked. "What did my master do to earn such scorn at your hands?" Laurine flinched under his words.

"She did nothing." Her voice came out in a whisper. "I thought that if I uncovered a plot, that I would be given status at court. I cannot accomplish what I need to do if I remain a lowly cleric for the rest of my life! Too many innocents have died under the Hegemon's negligence! I have to have power if I am to help the powerless!"

"And now it is you who kills the innocent." Magdolon moved to kneel beside Ashal, and she felt his arms fold around her. The small naiad did not struggle, and the massive placoderm lifted her easily off the ground. Her quiet sobs were muffled against his cavernous chest. Ashal glanced up to look at Laurine, and saw that her eyes had grown cold and her face placid despite the rivulets of tears that still stained her face. Laurine reached up and scrubbed her eyes with her wrists before turning to walk toward the door.

"The guard will be changing soon. I have a few people who I've been able to bribe with either money or… favors. You must make haste to the docks and meet my man at pier thirty-seven. You must leave the city and never come back. You cannot return to the Trident Realm, either. Already news of Ai-ellain's attack has reached your kings there and they have sent a quick response condoning the Hegemon's actions. It seems that the Golden Horn's place in the world of commerce is too great a boon for your royalty to risk jeopardizing in order to avenge a single lost household of their nobility. They will gladly turn you back over to the Hegemon if they were to discover you in their realm."

Magdolon paused as he rose, cradling Ashal. "You mean," he whispered, "we cannot go home?"

Laurine's shoulders fell as he spoke.

"No, you must never return home. And you must not stay here, or anywhere within the shadow of our Hegemon."

"I should kill you." Magdolon's voice was empty. Laurine nodded.

"Yes, you probably should," she sighed. "But you won't, because if you do, I have left information regarding your escape in the hands of someone I trust. If I do not return, then he will take that information to the authorities, and they will find you before the sun has crested the horizon. I am your only path to escape, and you will not condemn Ashal to that."

"How do I know that you are not lying? You say that our kings have sent a message condemning my master for your crime. How is this possible? That would take days to do!"

"You don't know that I'm not lying." Laurine answered without turning. "But if you stay in this cell, you will die for certain. I can promise you that you have been here for too long as it is. I am leaving now, after that you may do as you wish, but I caution you against going back to your homeland as it will not be safe for you."

With that, Laurine swept out of the room and Ashal listened to the sounds of her footsteps receding down the hall. Silence pervaded the cell and Ashal would have thought she had gone deaf if not for the sound of her own sniffles as her tears began to dry in her chest, forming a cold lump. Then, she felt Magdolon step forward. She felt as he lifted his feet over the body of the slain guard before the door, too. Her eyes were already drooping before he walked out of their cell, and by the time he was walking down the stone corridor outside, she had succumbed to the empty darkness of a dreamless sleep.

* * * * *

The waves washed gently against the sides of the small fishing boat as it pushed out and away from the wharf. Magdolon watched as the great city of the Golden Horn slowly began to recede under the moonlit sky, the water turning more rough and turbulent as they passed out beyond the protective borders of the sea walls that hemmed in the docks and framed the shipyards surrounding the sprawling metropolis. Arriving at the docks had been surprisingly easy, as if someone had cleared a path for them. No one had even tried to stop them, although they had been forced to hide in dark alleyways whenever a patrol of soldiers came close. About the time they had arrived at the pier indicated by Laurine, there had come a ringing of bells from throughout the city, but the fisherman who waited with his boat paid the sound no heed and pushed off the docks with a long pole, allowing the water to pull them away from land.

Turning, Magdolon looked down at little Ashal, who stood staring back at the city; her eyes were narrowed and rimmed with shadows. He knelt beside her and reached out a comforting hand to rub her head. She shook it away, never breaking her gaze on the Golden Horn.

"I make an oath this night," she spoke quietly and in her native tongue. "I will kill those responsible for my mother's death. I swear it by the blood of my mother that they will pay!" Magdolon winced at her words.

"Do not make idle of these things," he said softly. "You make impossible oaths against untouchable people."

"Nothing idle is in my words," she replied. "They will feel the death at my hand, and they shall suffer before I will release them. As Kyron's dark shadow as my witness, so shall it be." She continued staring out at the disappearing city until the horizon swallowed the shadowed place and the sun began to peak its red-eyed face out from the eastern sky. Magdolon stood by her the entire time, his eyes equally fixated on her. The ship tottered back and forth against the waves as the grumbling fisherman tried to correct their course. The day promised to be a hot one, and the wind blew gently from the west, pushing them farther and farther away from their pain. Magdolon watched as Ashal's shoulders squared, her eyes narrowing to focus on the Golden Horn as it diminished, not tearing her gaze away until the city fell from the horizon. For now, the day was young, but when its light reached the peak of the sky, there would be a harsh reckoning to all who stood below its gaze.

Ashal shuddered and reached out to clutch Magdolon's hand, finally closing her eyes as she did so.

Part Two
BEWARE THE RIPTIDE

10 years later...

One

A FRAGILE FAITH

Yvette's pen scratched furiously across the parchment in the light of a single, flickering candle. All around her were cast dancing shadows by the inconstant light, but she paid them no heed as she continued to compose her missive. Words that she had practiced and crafted to perfection scrawled across the blank space before her in a neat, but intricate hand. The message had to be perfect so as to only convey its meaning to the right parties, and even then it must only be the right amount in order to entice. Should the letter fall into the wrong hands, it would reveal very little to anyone who did not understand the hidden meanings. To the side of her current writings lay a second letter, already complete and sealed with blood red wax and a black ribbon. The seal was that of her personal crafting, showing a skull with tears of blood emanating from its eyes. A bit morbid, but fitting to her current situation.

Outside her window, the wind howled forlornly as it whistled on toward the mountain peaks. The Abbey of Danos was nestled right against the beginning of the rugged peaks that made up the majority of the dwarven realm of Abercarr to the east. Only a small forest separated them from the shores of the Sea of Eriskos to the southwest, and the wind was constantly blowing through the trees as it came off the salty waters and journeyed on into the mountains beyond. The abbey was located firmly within the boundaries of the Hegemony of Basilea, and ostensibly the occupants there followed the tenants of the Shining Ones, but Yvette knew better.

The sister bit her lip as she read over the contents of her letter. Her critical eyes scanned the document for any fault. Yvette was very young, and she felt she was gorgeous by most standards. Her chestnut hair fell in lazy ringlets down to the small of her back, complimenting her almond colored skin and soft, brown eyes. Many had claimed that it was a shame that her upbringing had forced her to join the Sisterhood, as it seemed a waste of such a pretty face. This, combined with her other 'assets' that even the plain clothing of the sisterhood could not hide often lead to jealousy among the other, homelier sisters of the abbey. But that had all been before Laurine had arrived. Since then, things had changed.

Before Laurine, there had been quiet mornings filled with accompanying devotions and prayers. Choirs would sing praises to the Shining Ones throughout the day. Now the prayers were quieted, and though the pretense of holiness was maintained through the angelic voices of the choir, the psalms were sung at midnight with a heavy cloak of irony laid over the words of their cantos. The Abbey of Danos had never been a perfect place to live, but at least before, Yvette could speak with her mother. At least she had some friends with whom she could talk and laugh. Now everyone walked through the hushed hallways with an all too familiar hunger hanging behind their eyes.

No, they were not the sisters of Basilea any longer, only puppets wearing masks. If the Hegemony knew of the evil that was sleeping in the beds of this abbey, they would have descended upon them with cleansing fires and holy swords long ago.

She brushed a softly curled tuft of brown hair out of her eyes and sat back, sighing. The letter was done. She still felt unsure about some parts, but overall she was satisfied and couldn't delay sending it any longer; not if she wanted it to arrive in time for its recipient to act on the information provided within. She quickly folded the parchment up into a neat square and sealed it with the morbidly weeping skull, this time with a blue ribbon. As she pulled the stamp away from the still cooling wax, there came a knock at her door. Quickly, she pulled a dusty old tome over the two letters and hid the stamp and the wax.

"Come in," she called out. The door to her room creaked inward as a stately figure stepped into the light of the small, flickering candle. She seemed to flinch as the light touched her, as if it hurt her eyes. Straight, blonde hair was hidden beneath an abbess's veil, and a gaze that could chip glass stared out at the young woman sternly.

"Abbess Laurine!" Yvette exclaimed. "To what do I owe this honor?" The older woman came forward and sank down onto the edge of Yvette's bed.

"My child, we missed you at evening devotional." Laurine's voice was gravelly and she sounded weary.

"I apologize, Abbess, I became engrossed in my studies and lost track of the time. I will be sure to do my penance tomorrow, I assure you." Yvette kept her eyes pointed fixedly on Laurine's face, desperately trying to keep her gaze from wandering over to where the book hid her letters and the sealing wax. The words that came out of her mouth were a lie, of course; she'd missed devotionals because she'd needed to finish her letters so that they could leave first thing in the morning with their departing guests who had stayed at the abbey on their way back to the Golden Horn. That, and the fact that she hated that nightly ritual. That wasn't entirely true; she thought the devotionals a beautiful idea, but she also knew how vapid and meaningless their purpose was in her present circumstances.

"There is no need, my child." Laurine placed a hand on Yvette's shoulder. "I can see that your mind is elsewhere. Tell me, what troubles you?" Yvette flinched, wrinkling her brow as she tried to think up a suitable response.

"It," she stammered, "it's the other sisters." An honest lie, for sure, but it made it easier to keep track of when asked to elaborate or if the subject came up later on. Laurine sighed and nodded.

"Yes, there are many of them who do not see the worth of what we do, is there not?" The abbess pulled her hand back, but Yvette continued to hold her gaze, the young sister's eyes glistening with a subdued defiance that she could not suppress. She made a quick decision, diving deeper into her deception.

"Why is it so? Why do they mock you for your devotion?" Yvette saw Laurine's eyes flash in response to her question. Whether her reaction was one of surprise or anger, Yvette couldn't tell, but it was a long time before she responded.

"They are bitter, I suppose." Laurine's words fell heavily from her lips. This was not the response that Yvette had expected.

"Bitter? How?"

"They resent the change that I brought when I came to the abbey. I think almost everyone does, even you my child." Laurine's response caused a flare of panic to stab through Yvette's chest. *No she doesn't suspect you, at least not of your real purpose!* She took a deep breath to calm herself.

"I am not bitter toward you, Abbess." Yvette spoke slowly, and her words sounded hollow even to her own ears. Laurine laughed.

"You are too pure for such lies, my daughter, do not sully your pretty mouth with them." Laurine shook her head. "I am sorry for the sorrow that I have brought to you and the others that live here. I wish you could see what I do. That you could see the horrors living beyond the safe walls of our abbey. We are here to protect the faithful from those horrors, and I have done everything in my power to ensure that their faith does not go unrewarded." She hesitated at this last part for a moment before continuing. "I know what unanswered prayers feel like, and I swear that I will not allow faith to go unrewarded so long as I am capable of rewarding it."

"I..." Yvette began, but Laurine cut her off.

"You do not need to explain yourself, my child, I am well aware of what your devotion has cost you, and how much of that cost was brought on by me. I am fully willing to bear the brunt of everyone's displeasure, it is a weight I have forced myself to carry for many years now, and I will continue to do so as long as is necessary." Yvette noticed the sag in Laurine's shoulders as the older woman spoke.

"Surely this is unnecessary suffering? Is there nothing that you can do to help alleviate your own trials?" Yvette's voice was soft, she forced herself to reach out and grasp Laurine's arm. "What is the source of your troubles?" Yvette's question was well-placed, and Laurine smiled ruefully at the young sister.

"You would have me gossip of the other devoted members of our abbey?" Laurine spoke softly, and Yvette's gaze hardened.

35

"I would not gossip, Mother Abbess, but no one should be forced to endure these ungrateful goslings alone." Her voice was hard, and she felt a cold shiver travel up her spine as she thought of her own indignation at the treatment she had received from the other sisters in the abbey. Laurine gave a weary sigh in response to her outburst.

"It is alright, child, I know you meant nothing by it. You have a sweet disposition and you merely wanted to help me unload some of my cares. You would become my confidant, then? Have me share my darkest secrets with you?" The abbess's gaze bore through Yvette's skull; she did not look away though her breath quickened as she awaited whatever came next. Laurine took a deep breath and raised her eyes to the ceiling.

"If I were to be completely honest, I think my first mistake was bringing Sister Rose with me. She does not seem content with my vision and constantly hounds and undermines me at every turn." Laurine's voice was oddly husky, as if she was struggling to get the words out. Yvette watched the older woman with interest. Years seemed to accumulate on Laurine's face in the flickering shadows of the sputtering candle. The abbess did not speak for several moments as the wind howled outside Yvette's window. When she finally lowered her gaze and focused on Yvette again, the dark circles around her eyes seemed to have deepened and her brow was furrowed.

"I say this in absolute confidence with you, child, it must not be spoken of outside of this room, is that understood?" Laurine's eyes flashed dangerously.

"Of course, Abbess." Yvette maintained her gaze. Laurine stared at her a moment longer and then nodded.

"I fear that Rose is trying to remove me from authority. That she envies my position and would see me cast out. I do not know why she wishes this, but I feel that it is true." Laurine reached up and rubbed her temples, another sigh escaping her lips. Yvette did not respond right away, none of this was new information to her. Hearing Laurine confess her knowledge of it was the only surprising thing in this. Laurine never sought to defend herself and otherwise seemed oblivious to Rose's attacks.

"I also fear for you, too, Yvette." Laurine's voice cut through Yvette's thoughts and she froze.

"What do you mean, Abbess?"

"How is your faith, my daughter? You seem distracted of late. It may not seem so to many, but I am well aware of my flock and those whom I serve. That is something Rose does not understand." Laurine paused and took a deep breath. "You have had something on your mind, my child, feel free to share it."

"I..." Yvette's mind raced, what could she say? "I... find myself... questioning the path of discipleship... due to the infighting and bickering I have witnessed between the sisters. I feel that this is not what the Shining Ones would have us do." Yvette knew that this was a lie, she had abandoned her faith in the Shining Ones long ago, shortly after her mother had died. Laurine laughed mirthlessly, and it was a dry, hollow sound.

"You speak as if you had a choice my child." Laurine's mouth curled into a cruel smile. "Where else would you go? Who else would take you in? You have no family left, no friends outside of these walls. We are all that is left to you. And even should your faith falter, self-preservation must urge that you continue on." Yvette closed her eyes at Laurine's stern words and sat back, anger pulsing in her temples forced her to take long, deep breaths in order to calm herself. The abbess sighed and Yvette was grateful that she had misinterpreted her silence.

"But I understand what it is to be trapped by circumstances beyond your control," Laurine continued. "I am sorry that this has been placed on you. It is not fair that you should be shackled with such a burden at such a young age when you have so long that you must carry it still ahead of you." Laurine stood and walked over to where Yvette sat. She reached out and took hold of Yvette's hand as it rested in her lap, patting it affectionately. Yvette flinched away from the touch, her eyes flashing open and a growl escaping her throat. Laurine pulled her hand back quickly, a hurt look in her face. The younger woman closed her eyes again and took a deep breath before opening them.

"I'm sorry, Mother Abbess," she said slowly. "I know that you are right, but as Saint Lorikus tells us: 'The truth, when spoken aloud, can oft times lead to resentment in those of a proud countenance.' I feel that applies to me far too often." Yvette reached out and took Laurine's hand, squeezing it affectionately. "Please forgive me my weakness."

"There is no need to apologize, my child, I understand completely. I am glad to see that you are keeping up with your studies. Be strong, daughter, your faith shall not go unrewarded." Laurine stood and began to walk toward the door. She stopped as her hands grasped the handle and turned to look back over her shoulder.

"I would focus my studies on the lectures of the Divine Marcouth. I feel that his words would better apply to your present circumstances, dear girl."

"Yes, Mother Abbess, thank you." Yvette stood and bowed as Laurine pushed on the door and walked out, closing the door behind her. The young sister sat at her desk, counting the seconds and holding her breath. When sufficient time had passed, she quickly pulled the old book away and swept up her two letters. Throwing on a cloak, she stuffed the letters into the back of her belt and swept out the door, throwing her hood over her head to hide her face.

She stalked silently down the hallway, her footsteps echoing through the stone corridor. She quickly found herself outside in the walled courtyard as she walked from the building where the sisters slept and that which housed any visiting guests. The wind whipped her cloak about her thin frame, and she clutched the letters in her belt to keep them from flying away. The courtyard was completely empty, unsurprising for this time of night. The Great Hall dominated the center of the courtyard, its high steeple towering over the rest of the buildings with a bronze statue of the likeness of Mescator, God of Justice, at its pinnacle. The rest of the building was made up of some simple stained glass windows and a sloping metal roof that had been designed by the dwarfs in more peaceful times. Besides the Great Hall, there were four other squat and rectangular buildings. One was the barracks, where the standing contingent of soldiers meant to guard the abbey and the citizens of the town that lived below were housed. The other was the quarters for the sisterhood who made their devotions to the abbey, and the third was more of a house or manor, meant for housing visitors and guests who stopped by the out of the way abbey. The last was a small, crude chapel which was a relic of days long past, from a time before the war with Winter.

Usually the guest building stood empty, as the abbey was so far out of the way of any normal trade routes or other kinds of traffic. But at least annually there was a regular inspection sent from the Basilean capital city of the Golden Horn. This was possibly the one time that Rose and Laurine worked together in order to charm the visiting dignitaries and their attendants. Most of the time, the visitors were anxious to finish the unpleasant task of visiting this remote outpost anyways, and so getting them to abbreviate their visits was never a hard feat to accomplish.

Yvette had been lucky with this batch of attendants who had accompanied the paladin in charge of this inspection. There had been a young man, only a few years older than herself, whom she had been able to charm with a few batted eyelashes and shy glances. Strictly speaking, sisters were not allowed romantic entanglements, but there were very few things that were traditional or restricted for the sisters of this particular abbey, and Yvette was well equipped and willing to exploit the weaknesses of the flesh if it suited her purposes. She had begged of him the favor of carrying a few letters back on his return journey to the Golden Horn, and he had acquiesced with very little resistance. Yvette smiled in spite of herself, sometimes her beauty had its advantages, and sometimes being thought of as inconsequential or simple due to that same beauty could be useful as well.

She approached the door to the guest building and knocked on it, feeling slightly idiotic as she pounded out a simple rhythm that she and her messenger had agreed upon to be their sign. After several minutes, the door cracked with a loud creak that was quickly swallowed up in the howl of the wind. Yvette breathed a sigh of relief when she saw the familiar face of the young man, who beckoned her to step inside.

"Many thanks, Korman." Yvette's voice seemed to resonate loudly once she was out of the wind. The young man nodded and turned toward her, reaching out a hand to her waist to pull her in closer. Yvette playfully shoved the hand away, shaking her head.

"There's no time for that now! What if we're heard?" she whispered; Korman's face fell, but he nodded. Yvette reached out a hand and caressed the side of his face. "Perhaps another time, my pet," she cooed and then produced her two letters.

"Now, remember, the blue ribbon I want you to carry back to the Golden Horn and give it to your contact within the Free Dwarf quarter to deliver it to my friend. The black ribbon is to be left on your way out of town. Do you remember? There is a dead oak with a wild rosebush growing up around it. Deposit the letter with the black ribbon there, and do it without drawing any notice. Understand?" Korman nodded and took the letters from Yvette. She smiled and reached up to kiss him on the forehead. Then she turned and quickly ducked back outside into the windy night.

After struggling back across the courtyard, she made her way back to her room and quickly stepped in and closed the door behind her, making sure to twist the latch. She leaned against the aged wood, breathing a deep sigh and closing her eyes. Now that the letters were sent, it was only a matter of waiting for a response. Something stirred within the shadows of her room, and a lone figure rose up from behind her desk. A tall, curvaceous figure stepped into the sputtering light of the barely lit candle. Yvette opened her eyes in surprise, focusing on the person before her. Long, raven hair framed a pale face and ruby lips over which sharp, icy blue eyes stared out with intense concentration. Dreadful recognition dawned on her face.

"Sister Rose! I…"

"Don't bother with the pleasantries, little duckling," a sultry voice purred. "I know that Laurine has been here, and I wonder where it is that's kept you out so late after curfew…" Quickly, Rose closed the difference between them and was suddenly inches from Yvette's face.

"I… I…" Yvette sputtered.

"Don't worry, my little duckling." Rose traced the curve of Yvette's cheek, following on down to the side of her neck. "You will talk. We have all night to catch up."

Two
STIRLING INDIFFERENCE

T he giant burlap sack threw up a cloud of dust as Ashal dropped it onto the dirt floor of the small, roughshod building; the smell of fish wafted up from the top, and three more, similar shaped bags sat off to the left. She stood in a semi-permanent storage house constructed of rough cut timbers and tar. It was not the testament to dwarf craftsmanship that most people would associate with the hardy folk, but it served its purpose well and was solid in its construction. The dwarf that sat in front of her stood up and walked around his desk to inspect the contents, just as he had with the previous two bags that Ashal had brought in, scribbling in a small notebook he carried.

"That's thirty pounds of smoked fish, sixty pounds of dried venison, and about twelve rabbit skins and another three deerskins tanned and ready for use." Ashal rattled off the contents of the sacks for the dwarf. She stretched her back as she spoke, stifling a yawn. Her body was a mass of lithe muscle that rippled as she moved. The fins surrounding her head had expanded and grown deep red as she had risen from childhood into adolescence. The scales on her skin had deepened to a blued steel color which shimmered from patterns of light that danced around her when the sun hit just right. However, the most stunning of her features were her eyes. Gone were the googled fisheyes of youth and in their stead had come golden spheres that constantly scanned the room like a predator searching for its next meal.

"That's a little more than we asked for." The young dwarf grumbled as he sifted through the last bag. "The foreman won't want to pay any extra." Ashal forced herself not to sigh and roll her eyes as she thought of the foreman. These dwarfs were slightly more nomadic than others of their kind tended to be. They would take odd jobs to finish mining out old veins of whatever ore was left over after larger nations or companies had decided that such veins were unprofitable. Also if ore was discovered in areas that were rather remote and thus not worth the effort to reach with a regular operation, then teams like this could be hired to set up mining outposts for a much smaller cost than sending in a large team. When those situations arose, camps like these proved quite useful as they would move in to finish off what was left, and once the vein was dry they'd hire out to another location and move on to the next job. Such mining camps were not uncommon, especially among the Free Dwarfs, and they served a purpose in a world that was in constant need of metal for weapons, armor, and coin.

"No worries," Ashal shook her head, the thick tendrils of her hair whipping back and forth as she did so. "Just consider it a bonus. We're running out of buyers in the area, although I'm curious as to why you placed such a large order." The dwarf, who Ashal had taken to calling Gravel in the time that they had lived in the area due to his guttural voice and the fact that she couldn't pronounce his real name, sighed and looked up at her.

"There's no easy way of telling it, so I'll just come out and say it." Gravel didn't want to meet her eyes as he spoke. "We'll be moving out shortly. The copper vein we were mining in this area is running low, we're having to work twice as hard for half as much pay. The foreman's been looking for a new site for us to dig for some time. He sent out a bunch of feelers through the various unions and even out to some neighboring kingdoms for work, and it just so happens that out of all those, one has come through that should pay us a healthy sum. But it's quite a ways off, and we'll be setting out within the next day or two." Ashal felt a dropping sensation in her gut as Gravel spoke.

"Where will you be going?" she asked. Gravel shrugged before responding.

"Turns out the Hegemony has a silver mine that they lack the manpower to dig. It's far to their south, near Golloch's Empire and fairly out of the way. Even with the Abyss being rather quiet these days, it's hard for them to justify setting up an outpost there that exposes them to attack from Golloch, should he decide to get frisky with them again." Ashal nodded, it made sense. Golloch was the king of the dwarven empire to the south, across the Sea of Suan in the realm of Abercarr. Gravel and his kin were not subject to him as they were part of a group made up a conglomerate nation of Free Dwarfs to the north across a great cataract of waterfalls that separated the two landmasses. Presently they had made their homes on the outskirts of a nearby Free Dwarf hold of Gars nestled in between the Halpi Mountains and the Sea of Suan.

The Hegemony of Basilea was not on friendly terms with Golloch and his empire. While outright war had not broken out, small skirmishes were common along their borders, and if the mine which Gravel and his troupe had signed on for was anywhere close to there, then the Basileans would be hard pressed to keep it protected if they sent their own miners to dig for the silver. However, if they hired Gravel's crew and simply took a percentage of whatever they mined, they could still exploit the resource without endangering their own people. As an added bonus, it would profit the Free Dwarfs, which was bound to antagonize Golloch in the process.

This saddened Ashal, however, as she'd come to enjoy Gravel's stoic presence. He'd taught her some metallurgy and was her regular contact when selling the supplies that she and Magdolon harvested off the coast. They were one of their biggest buyers and had supported them through the past winter by purchasing the skins and smoked meat gathered from their regular hunting forays. Beyond that, Ashal had come to recognize Gravel as a friend, or at least something as close to a friend as she could remember.

"I hope you were planning on at least saying goodbye to me before vanishing." Ashal glared at the dwarf, who wisely continued to avoid her gaze and stare at the ground. "Gravel?"

"Well, missy, I placed a large order with you and figured you'd be smart enough to figure it out." Gravel spoke slowly, his deep bass voice almost lost in his beard.

"Gravel! You were just going to leave, without so much as a nod in my direction?" Ashal planted her fists on her hips and leaned down to look into the dwarf's face, now tinged slightly red in the cheeks. A mortified dwarf! Ashal would have laughed if she wasn't so upset.

"Well… no… not exactly like that," Gravel grumbled.

"Then what?" Ashal demanded.

"Missy, I'm used to leaving people behind when I have to!" Gravel snapped. "My crew and I… we don't usually get attached because we know we're always only going to be temporarily in any given spot, so…" His voice trailed off.

"So you don't do goodbyes, is that it?" Ashal pursed her lips. She felt something in her chest drop. "Too much trouble for you? Don't get too close to anyone, cause you're just going to leave?" The words hurt more than she thought they would. What had she been thinking?! Gravel was a business contact! Did she think he was going to go all teary-eyed when they bid farewell to one another? Or maybe that such a goodbye would never come? This thought caused her to snort. *No, I just thought that I would be the one to leave first.* She realized now that she had been a part of this conversation before, but usually she was in Gravel's position, not the other way around.

"Ashal, you don't get it. I'm quite fond of you, but this is how our lives work! I didn't mean to upset you." Gravel reached into his satchel and pulled out a coin purse. He rooted around in it, pulled out a thick stack of coins, and thrust them in Ashal's direction. "Here, I threw in a little more for the extra skins and meat." Ashal stared at the money, clenching her jaw. *Why is this affecting me like this? What is wrong with me?* Ashal snatched the coins out of Gravel's hand, stuffing them into her belt pouch.

"A pleasure doing business with you, sir." She turned and walked stiffly out of the storehouse. Once outside, her pace quickened, and she did not respond to dwarfs who called out to her or waved as she strode past. She didn't stop walking until she cleared the camp, crested a small hill, and begun descending the opposite side. She stomped down the incline until she skidded on some loose gravel and almost toppled over, but she managed to catch herself and then fell to one knee, shaking.

"You'd think I'd be used to goodbyes by now, even the bad ones," she spoke out loud to the air as she took some unsteady breaths that rattled in her constricted throat. It was a lie, she told herself to help mask the pain. She hated farewells, and she'd never been able to follow through with them gracefully. But there was something more this time. The dwarfs were not known for their welcoming nature, but Gravel had been kind to her. In the world, she knew, kindness was a foreign concept. The world was a stark, lonely, and forbidding place, and she knew this firsthand.

Her mind drifted into a memory swirling in bleak clouds of ire. It was one of many such memories that persistently hung just outside of her perception, waiting to rush in and attack her present situation. In this particular memory, she was back at the edge of the Dragon Teeth Mountains where the great stony peaks gave way to the Ardovikian Plain. She and Magdolon had stood before the Great Wall that the fledgling kingdoms of man had erected. It stretched from one horizon as far as the eye could see all the way through to other without break. Ashal had marvelled at its construction. She and Magdolon had earned some much needed coin by fighting in the war there with the orcs who had threatened the Wall during its construction. The fighting had been lackluster, but Magdolon had wanted her to gain some real combat experience. They had nearly starved the winter previous due to lack of resources, and this opportunity had proven itself to be far too lucrative to pass up.

"Why must they build it so large?" she asked aloud. Magdolon had shrugged in response.

"Perhaps it is because they lack in some other part of their life and this is how they must live with that." His voice was gruff, but years of living amongst the land dwelling kingdoms had erased most of the traces of their Neritican accents from their words. Ashal had chuckled at his response.

"Come, the head king of the menfolk is speaking. Let us go hear him." Magdolon turned to walk toward where a large crowd was gathering, and Ashal followed closely behind. As they drew closer, many of the soldiers eyed the two fish-folk and gave a wide berth, whispering to each other as they stared. Naiads were a rare sight this far from the Infant Sea, and only a bare few had come to the fighting here in the Ardovikian Plain. Mostly the armies had consisted of men, ogres bought with coin, and the occasional regiment of halflings or dwarfs hoping to win some honor or test some new contraption of war on the unsuspecting orcs. Ashal and Magdolon were oddities, and the soldiers were always willing to remind them of this.

"Gods but do you smell that?" She heard a loud whisper in front of them. A man in riding leathers with a sword strapped to his waist was staring at her while he leaned on his companion beside him. "It smells like low-tide, doesn't it?

How a fish can rot so long out of water and not die is a mystery to me." The two men laughed and Ashal felt that same, familiar falling sensation grip her chest. She hefted her spear and took a step forward, but Magdolon's hand fell heavily on her shoulder.

"Don't. Sometimes a talking jackass is just that." The old placoderm stared pointedly at the offending soldier. The large reptilian guard was a good head and shoulders taller than the man and easily twice as broad with thick, corded muscle and a powerful tail behind him. The sneering soldier sniffed and turned around as some trumpets blared out for the crowd to grow still. Ashal lowered her eyes to the ground.

"Do not be disturbed, *Lueshwy'n*." Magdolon murmured as the crowd cheered for the man now standing on the wall before them. He used the Neritican word for a stingray as a pet name for her. "He is not worth sullying your honor." Ashal snorted at this.

"My honor died with my mother, remember? Unless our pilgrimage around Mantica is a farce and we can go home to the depths now." Ashal's throat tightened as she spoke. The human soldier was not the first to insult her thus, but it hurt worse each time. Magdolon shook his head at this.

"You are worth a thousand of that man. And your mother would have been proud to see how you acquitted yourself on the field. Do not fall to bandying crude insults with a swine when you are worth so much more than that." Magdolon released his grip on her shoulder and patted her back gently. Ashal simply shrugged and turned her attention back to the man standing on the wall addressing the crowd. There was an eerie silence from the rest of the spectators and something uneasy had stirred within her stomach. She listened to his words.

"Forget Basilea, forget the halls of Dwarfs or the Glades of Elves, Men are the true rulers of Mantica, and we shall make our presence felt throughout the land." The audience erupted into applause at his words, and Ashal felt the sinking sensation in her chest from before intensify.

"Oh, Kyron! I hope not. If this is the age of man, if this is their influence…" Her voice trailed off as she saw the soldier in his riding leathers staring at her again.

"What's that, fish girl?" he spat. "Don't like what you're hearing?" Ashal tried to ignore him, but soon he was in her face, his voice a low growl.

"Then maybe you should go back where you came from!" Spittle from the soldier's lips flecked onto Ashal's face, causing her to flinch backward. Magdolon stepped forward and shoved the man back forcibly.

"Stand back, *friend*." Magdolon's voice was low, but he put his own hooked beak within inches of the man's face. The soldier sneered and stepped back, eyeing Magdolon up and down as he did so. Then he smiled and began to take up a chant that Ashal had not realized the rest of the crowd had begun to shout.

She looked up at Magdolon, who motioned for her to follow him, and they retreated to the roar of the crowd behind calling up to the figure above them on the Wall.

"Darvled! Darvled! Darvled!"

The memory receded, and Ashal found herself back on the grassy hillside with her knees hugged against her chest. She exhaled slowly, her chest a war of emotions. She had hundreds of similar memories. That was one of the most recent ones, however, and it seemed to punctuate a growing problem in the communities where Magdolon had taken them. In the year following their time at the Wall, they had gradually retreated east, skirting around the Hegemony until finally settling here in the realm of the Free Dwarfs. Gravel had been the first contact they had made, and he'd always been polite in his dour, dwarfish way. He'd never made Ashal and Magdolon feel threatened, he'd made them feel like outsiders but that was to be expected regardless of where they went. Eventually that initial awkwardness had broken down and they'd become an outlier portion of the small community in this area. Apart, but welcome to stay. It was the closest thing to acceptance Ashal could remember from any of their fleeting homes they had tried to establish in the years since her family's betrayal, and now it was all going to fall apart, again. To top it off, Gravel hadn't even planned to say goodbye! The illusion of home was shattered by the weight of the coins now sitting in her pouch. Dismissed because her usefulness was at an end.

The sun was beginning to set in the west. Ashal sighed; her chest still hurt, but the shaking had subsided and so she pushed herself to her feet and began walking. It was about two miles until she reached the seaside hut that she and Magdolon had constructed to be their home during their stay here. They had also built a second, smaller shack that they used to smoke and dry the meat from their various hunts so they could sell it. Several pelts were stretched and drying in their cradles along the side of the smoking hut. The slight stink of tanning chemicals filled the air as she drew closer, and she wrinkled her nose at that. She didn't bother checking on the hides, they wouldn't be ready for another day or so.

Making straight for their living hut, she pulled open the heavy wooden door they had built to keep out the winter chill and stepped inside. The light of the outside world filtered in through a rather small window constructed from broken pieces of seaglass and filled the one room hut with a dingy, green light. The sun was nearly set and so the shadows were deep as she stepped forward and lit a small tallow candle on the small table at the center of the room. The orange light flared up and illuminated the sparse contents of their home. Besides the table, there was a small chest filled with various tools they needed to maintain their trade as hunters, and two cots piled with soft rabbit furs to keep them warm.

Ashal sank onto her cot. Magdolon was still away on one of his increasingly more regular journeys. He always made a pretense of it being something personal in nature, or that he was scouting out other potential places they could flee to, should the need arise. Ashal didn't believe that, at least not entirely. Magdolon had begun taking weeks to himself for these journeys and recently they had occurred at least once every month, sometimes more. Either he was preparing to move them again or there was something else he was doing that he didn't want Ashal to know about. She didn't care what he did, she was capable of hunting enough to keep their clients satisfied and their life was relatively easy from a menial standpoint. But it did bother her that he didn't feel he could trust her with what he was doing.

Tonight in particular, it stung. Gravel's indifference to her notwithstanding, there was another issue that pricked the back of her mind, something that she didn't want to acknowledge. Today would mark the annual spawning for her people if they were back home, or the time when new naiads would come forth out of their eggs in the spawning pools to be received by their families and parents. This was the day when newborns would be scooped up into the arms of their parents and given names. This would mark the eighteenth anniversary of her own spawning, and if she still lived among the Palaces of the Deep, it would have been marked with a week long celebration filled with gifts, food, and stories. This anniversary in particular would be the beginning of the next phase in her life and the end of her childhood. The humans had a name for this celebration, and she spoke it now to the darkness, her voice weak and strangled with emotion.

"Happy Birthday." She could not deny the tears that stung her eyes and ran down her cheeks. Nobody had known except for one person, and he was off doing something he couldn't trust her knowing about it. The silence answered back in the soft flicker of the candle. Ashal tilted her head back and swallowed the lump in her throat before standing and walking toward the table where the candle sat sputtering. She bent to blow out the sad flame, but as she did so, the door banged open and she gasped, spinning.

Magdolon stood in the doorway holding in one hand a silver spear mounted to a bone shaft. In the other hand, he held a piece of parchment with a broken wax seal and a blue ribbon attached to it.

Three

A BIRTHDAY SURPRISE

Magdolon stepped over the threshold, his face terse and his eyes scanning the room. Slowly he turned and closed the door behind him. Ashal watched all this with a twinge of curiosity.

"I saw the light," Magdolon said. "I did not see your cart and so I wondered who could be inside our home and reacted as I felt was necessary." Ashal's hand flew to her forehead. *The cart!* She used a single axle hand cart to help her haul the loads of supplies for her deliveries and she'd forgotten it at the mining camp! That would make for a very awkward encounter with Gravel tomorrow when she went to retrieve it.

"I left the cart with the dwarfs on accident." She responded, stalking over and sinking onto her cot. "I'll have to go get it in the morning." Magdolon tilted his head at this.

"I know! I made a mistake!" Ashal snapped.

"What happened?" he asked. Ashal turned to face the wall of the hut, scrubbing at her eyes to try and hide the fact that she was crying.

"Gravel and his crew are leaving, can you believe it?" She sniffed.

"I know." Magdolon said. This shocked Ashal so much that she sat up in her cot and twisted to look him in the face.

"You knew?" She struggled to keep the accusation out of her voice.

"I only just found out. It was the reason why I returned so quickly. I have…" He held up the letter, but his voice trailed off as he looked at Ashal's face. A storm was brewing between her brows and her eyes were narrowed at him.

"What is wrong?" He asked.

"The *dwarfs* are the reason you hurried back?!" She snarled. "Nothing else?!"

"You seem upset." Magdolon walked forward and placed the letter on the table, then turned to lean the spear against the wall. Some part of Ashal registered that he was wearing his old, steel spear on his back, but she was too furious and tired to think anything of it.

49

"I *seem* upset because I *am* upset!" she hissed, turning back to the wall. "Have you forgotten what today is?!"

"The anniversary of your spawning." Magdolon spoke while he pulled his old spear off of his back and placed it beside his cot. Ashal's eyes brimmed with tears, and yet her mouth hung open, furious words piling up in the back of her throat as she tried to process what he'd just said.

"You remembered?" she croaked after a long pause. Magdolon was smiling as he stood and moved to sit at the foot of her cot, laying a large hand on her shoulder.

"Of course I remembered, *Lueshwy'n*." He scooped her into his arms and she folded against him. Her face burned, but she soon found her arms wrapping around his massive bulk and a stubborn smile spreading across her face.

"I would not have missed this special day for anything." Magdolon stepped back from her and turned to grab the spear he had left leaning against the wall. Facing her, he held out the magnificent weapon. Ashal hesitated and then cautiously took hold of the bone shaft. She gasped in delight as she felt the balance, the smooth bone of the handle sliding through her fingers with practiced ease as if she had used this weapon for years. She twirled it through a few half steps of a spear dance before slapping the haft up under her arm and landing in a defensive stance with her off-hand extended in front of her. She looked at the spearhead. It glimmered in the weak light of the candle, shining from the high sheen of its polish. In the metal was worked the likeness of a stingray whose horns met at the tip of the spear and whose wings wrapped around the bone shaft below. It was a beautiful weapon.

"The spear is a silver alloy that will not rust, and the bone shaft is carved from a mammoth tusk from the Mammoth Steppe, stronger than any hardwood out there and impervious to water rot." Out of the corner of her eye, Ashal could see the sparkle in Magdolon's eyes as he watched her inspect the spear. His face fell somewhat as he continued to talk. "Normally there would also be given a set of armor for one who had begun the path of the warrior, but alas, we did not have the money for such a thing. I am sorry."

"No! It's perfect! Thank you so much!" Ashal threw her arms around his thick neck in another embrace and then once again took to staring at the spear. Out of the corner of her vision, she could see that Magdolon had not stopped watching her, his eyes still twinkling in the sad light of the dying candle while a mad grin played across his face. They sat for several minutes in that perfect moment before Magdolon harrumphed and walked over to the table, setting down the letter he had brought with him.

"That is not your only gift this year." He spoke with a thick voice, almost reluctantly. Ashal reverently placed her new spear on her cot and moved to stand beside him, her head cocked as she waited for him to continue. He opened and closed his mouth several times, trying to find the right words to say.

50

"I have been thinking of this day for so very long and yet have no words to say now that it is here." He held out his hand and gripped her shoulder affectionately. "*Lueshwy'n*, you have grown to be a fine warrior, and I know that your family would have been proud of what you have made of the life that was thrust upon you. I wish your mother was here to say so himself, but if only dreams were as plentiful as the sea's bounty and as easily caught. On this day, you leave behind your childhood and enter into your inheritance. I cannot give you all that you are owed, or even a portion of what rights your birth entitled you to receive. But I believe that I can give you some small measure of comfort." He tapped the letter sitting on the table.

"What is it?" Ashal asked, taking the letter into her hands.

"Justice." Magdolon replied. Ashal read through the letter quickly and then gave Magdolon a quizzical look. The letter had a relatively simple message scrawled across its single page:

My dear Mag,

I am so glad to hear of your continued success in planting the fields. I feel that the days when your harvest might finally bear fruit is not far off and that, together, we might soon enjoy them and their cold bounty.

Word has spread that we will have visitors, soon. Your friend, whom you've mentioned in previous letters, and several of his companions will soon be journeying here to begin their toil in our hills to the west of my home. Perhaps you should send some form of greeting through them to me, or to those whom I am ordered to serve.

I would urge you to consider reclaiming your vineyard here. As we speak, the olive trees which you planted so long ago have begun to bear fruit. But the head tree, whose care you entrusted to me, it has grown sickly and its disease is spread to the other trees. All are sickly, now, and soon I fear that the blight will spread to other vineyards outside of this one, perhaps even becoming a plague on the whole of my home. I beg of you to return and reclaim it so that this might not come to pass.

The time is ripe. This vineyard is prepared for its culling, and the seeds of its fate have been adequately planted. I would urge you to come and I shall tell you more upon your arrival.

Most sincerely,

-Y

"I don't understand. It seems a plain correspondence from someone who doesn't even bother to leave her name, and if you hadn't given it to me I wouldn't even think it had anything to do with us. What does it mean?" She held the paper out to him, something within her thrilled as she did, though. Some premonition hinting at its importance.

"After that first year of helplessness when we were first cast out, I began setting up a way to try and keep my eye on Sister Laurine who betrayed us." Ashal hissed at her name, anger causing the edge of her vision to blur at the mere mention of it. Magdolon held out a hand. "I began keeping tabs on her activities. I did this at great risk to myself alone, using whatever money we could spare to pass bribes when necessary, occasionally sneaking into the Hegemony to uncover what I could. Mostly, though, I sought out her victims which she left in her wake. Many of these were people who wished their own vengeance on Laurine and were thus easy to convert to our cause. Over the years I cultivated a fairly rudimentary, but effective, network of informants that were able to pass unnoticed into places where my physical presence could not go."

"Why go to that much effort? Why not just kill her and be done with it?" Ashal felt her cheeks growing hot. She knew Magdolon was no coward, she'd seen the terror that he could unleash with his spear. He'd taught her everything she knew about fighting, and she'd seen him unleash his abilities on the field of battle. It was obvious that fear held little sway over him. So why had he hesitated in bringing about the vengeance that was Laurine's debt to her?

"It was not my place, dear one. I reserved that decision to you, but I knew that a child could not make such a difficult choice. So I kept my informants and my contacts busy keeping track of her movements. I waited until this day, when you became an adult, to finally tell you of this. It is your family that was destroyed by her actions, your life that she ruined. While I was wronged, the greater debt is owed to you, and so you should be her judge and decide her fate as she so callously decided yours so long ago. Such is justice in the Coral Courts below, and while we may live in the squalor of the dirt, still we are subjects to the depths and will abide by its law so much as we are able." Ashal was taken aback by this response. So many questions were spinning in her head.

"None of this explains why that letter is so important." She spoke slowly, trying to organize her thoughts.

"This letter is from a contact who is very close to Laurine. The code we use is a crude one, but it delivers some very urgent news for us. The letter hints that Laurine is preparing to do something big, that her plans are bearing fruit and are preparing for harvest. Which means that Laurine is preparing to create more victims in her schemes." Magdolon took a deep breath. "Perhaps I should start at the beginning and explain what has happened."

"Perhaps you should," Ashal agreed.

Magdolon nodded and leaned back. His expression hardened and his gaze seemed to focus on something far away. He opened his mouth several times before he actually spoke, as if trying to decide where to start.

"Much of what you need to know began about two years ago."

Four

A CHANCE MEETING

Two years earlier…

Magdolon stared up the side of the cliff that rose before him like a great tidal wave of stone. At its crest, there sat a stone wall that extended the height by an extra fifteen feet or so, before ending in structured crenellations. The sunburnt rock glowed a dark amber in the light of the setting sun, forcing him to shade his eyes with his hand, despite the tree cover of the forest that extended up to the base of the cliff. Magdolon knew that a dirt pathway wound itself up the southern side of the inclines, and that was the main passage that lead to the gate of the abbey itself, but it also passed through a small town that had guards and many eyes that would be watching him should he attempt to climb that way.

However, the cliff face was even more imposing. The steep, granite peaks which formed this side of the Abkhazla mountain range were harsh and unforgiving in their slopes, and this was no exception. It looked as though the plateau which housed the abbey itself was man-made, likely blasted out of the rock by dwarven engineers in a time where the Basileans must have enjoyed friendlier relations with the mountain folk. The great placoderm was positive that few, if any, could make that climb and still be able to fight once they reached the top. This meant that the only plausible way to take the position was through an extended siege, something that required time, patience, and an army. Magdolon had plenty of the first two, but none of the last.

He grunted and lowered himself to a knee, still holding his spear erect and ready for action. He allowed his mind to wander. He'd been tracking the corrupt sister Laurine for the better part of a decade now. His search had dragged Ashal and himself across the lands of Mantica searching one lead after another. Magdolon had exhausted nearly all of his resources and most of his contacts he had established during his years of campaigning across the face of the continent before coming under service of Ashal's mother. He had traded coin, services, loot, and blood for the information that had helped him stay in

Laurine's shadow for the past eight years. He'd formed contacts in the seedy underworld of Basilea. Scraping for coin, he had hired spies to report to him specifically about the fallen sister who now sat in the abbey high above him.

Laurine's career had been an illustrious one, and wherever she'd gone, Magdolon had followed her. She had been sent to purify entire villages on the outskirts of the Hegemony's borders, and she had done so willingly. She had marched at the head of a column of battle sisters, urging them into the fray against demons, orcs, and dwarfs alike. Each enemy a supposed threat to the Hegemon and his goals. She was loyal to a fault in her orders and with every conquest, every purge, every battle, she grew in status.

Rarely did she use her necromantic gifts which she had displayed while trying to capture Magdolon and Ashal all those years ago in the Golden Horn, but this made sense. If she was caught using such dark magic she would be burned as a heretic and a necromancer. But then, what was her goal? She never did anything to undermine the Hegemon's authority, and when she did use her necromancy, it was done in such a way that any rumors of it that drifted back to her superiors could easily be dismissed. Indeed, Magdolon would have found it hard to believe she was capable of such dark deeds had he not been a victim to them himself so long ago. The rumors were usually outrageous, such as a whisper that she would occasionally march on a rebellious town by herself, not wanting to risk her men. She would return days later and march her soldiers into the said town to find it a smoldering ruin, the young women and children who had been spared her wrath cowering in the shadows at the army's passing. Some older woman would sometimes stumble out and accuse Laurine of her fell deeds, but these were easily dismissed as the ramblings of a grief stricken and aged woman. No one dared challenge Laurine openly.

Throughout all of this carnage, Magdolon followed. Her trail of broken bodies and destroyed lives was an easy one to see for Magdolon, who knew where to look. Everywhere she went, she had brought suffering. Yet she always spared younglings and their mothers. She seemed to have some sort of sense of misplaced honor in her workings. At nights, she was known to lead her soldiers in prayers to their Shining Ones, asking forgiveness for the heinous acts she wrought in their name and in the name of their Hegemony who sent them. Much of the time her missions were those of mercy, and oddly enough, there were even a few times that Magdolon had aided her from the shadows, seeing her missions as honorable or just. Those had been rare occasions, but Laurine had never known of his participation and had carried on with her orders. It was an odd picture that Magdolon had painted of their foe. Basilea was an enemy to the Abyss, and so many times he found her fighting on the side of the light to push back the demons and monsters that threatened the weak and innocent. At other times, her orders were clear, and she was forced to put entire homesteads, farms, and villages to the torch. She was nothing if not an obedient servant, though it was known that after the dark acts were accomplished, that she would retire to her tent in order to weep and give penance.

Magdolon shook his head; she was a conundrum, and one which he didn't care to understand. But, in order to hunt, one must know their prey. He'd watched Laurine rise through the ranks of the Basilean sisterhood, becoming more and more familiar with their structure. It was a complicated mess of ranks and titles, but he had puzzled out the majority of it in order to understand how much sway Laurine held by her title.

Ashal was quickly growing and soon she would come of age. Then the real hunt would begin, and there would be blood. The old warrior once again looked up at the towering cliffs. Laurine had come here, to this place, on the outskirts of Basilean lands, but for what? This was the longest she had ever stayed in one place that Magdolon could remember. What had drawn her here, and what did she hope to accomplish? How did this further her goals? He remembered Laurine saying she would tear down the Hegemon. So why, then, was she so loyal to him in her actions? Hers was the long game, as evidenced by her years of service and subtle subversions here and there, but what was her final goal? And how did this abbey fit into that scheme? It was obviously important, or else why had she come and why had she stayed so long?

There was one more mystery that Magdolon could not understand. A little over a year ago, Laurine had brought a seemingly random sister into her fold. Known only as Sister Rose, this beautiful creature had become an eager and willing servant to Laurine's plans, and the bloodshed that had followed her acceptance to Laurine's inner circle had increased tenfold what Laurine had ever accomplished. Where before there had been cold-blooded killing at times, it had always been calculated and contained to specific offenders. Once Rose had joined her, it suddenly became a bloody mess whenever a rebellion was put down or an enemy was defeated on the battlefield. Laurine stopped taking prisoners and began slaughtering her enemies to the last soldier. Her followers became a thing of fearful infamy, of quiet whispers that were never spoken in the daylight. If Laurine was the famine of conscience sweeping through the land to cull the Hegemon's followers, Rose was the dark flame that followed after and scoured the land and left a barren waste behind her of broken corpses.

A twig snapped behind Magodlon and he spun soundlessly to look at its source. He spied a hooded figure carrying a wicker basket darting between the trees. They hadn't spotted him, he realized, the individual was simply hurrying too fast and had grown careless in their haste. He looked closer and recognized that underneath the cloak he saw flashes of blue and white on cloth that looked like it was part of a dress. The figure carried itself with the steady steps of someone trained in combat, but their hesitance suggested they hadn't actually seen any fighting, yet.

He tensed, an opportunity had presented itself. He needed answers regarding the abbey and of Laurine's intentions here. The hooded figure was quite likely a young soldier, probably a battle sister. The speed of her flight marked her as either a deserter or a messenger, and the time of day suggested that whatever her role, her purpose was urgent. Magdolon made a quick decision and spread his webbed feet wide to help lessen the pressure of each step, hoping to avoid breaking any branches that might alert the person he was stalking.

Gradually he closed the distance between them, taking long strides with careful steps, and he was able to slowly creep up on the smaller figure who was shuffling hurriedly through the underbrush. When he felt he was close enough, Magdolon leapt out of the shadows and sprinted toward the cloaked person before him. His prey turned and dropped the basket; at this distance Magdolon was able to confirm that his suspicions were correct, it was a young girl he was charging toward. Her pretty face was framed by dark brown curls and her eyes were wide as Magdolon flew at her.

He stabbed his spearhead forward and was slightly surprised to see the young girl duck underneath where the blow was aimed. Magdolon had no intentions of killing her; the attack was merely a feint that he pulled back and whipped the butt of his spear out in a sweeping motion that knocked the girl's legs out from beneath her, causing her to fall to the ground hard. Moving quickly, Magdolon knelt and pressed his knee to her chest with enough weight to keep her down and make it slightly difficult to breath. He clamped a hand over her mouth to silence any screams she might make. The girl, however, was silent. Her eyes stared upward at him, unblinking, although tears trickled out of the edge of her eyes.

"You will not scream," Magdolon instructed her. After a few seconds, she nodded. "I will not kill you unless you give me reason." Magdolon slowly pulled his hand away and eased the pressure on her chest by leaning back slightly while still maintaining his center of balance. The girl did not scream, she simply stared up at him with her unblinking gaze. Magdolon reasoned that she was about sixteen years old, a little older than Ashal back home.

"What is your business in the forest this late?" Magdolon asked, motioning for her to speak. The girl licked her lips and her eyes flickered into the shadows of the underbrush and trees around them.

"I..." she began, her voice nothing more than a squeak that was strained under the pressure of Magdolon's knee. He eased back a little more. "I was running away." Magdolon's brow furrowed at this response.

"From what do you flee?" he asked, cautiously. The girl did not respond immediately, but instead took a few, sucking breaths. "I will not hurt you, child. But I need answers." His voice took on a gentler edge, but his knee stayed in place. The girl stopped wheezing and her eyes began to glisten in the fading light.

"They killed her!" she gasped at length, then the tears burst forth and Magdolon began to feel more and more uncomfortable as he knelt over her. He tried to make soothing sounds, but they felt hollow in his present position. After several moments had passed, she was able to compose herself somewhat and began speaking again.

"I am getting myself away from that forsaken abbey. There is a darkness that hangs about the necks of the new abbess and her retinue that will crush all who serve beneath them." At this comment, Magdolon arched his brow and stepped back, removing his knee from the girl's chest.

"What do you mean by that?"

The girl rubbed her sternum as she sat up.

"My mother is dead," she whispered. "I found her this morning when I went to wake her. She was lying in her bed, her eyes were closed like she was sleeping, but when I went to shake her, she was stiff and cold." The girl drew her knees to her chest and shuddered at the memory. Magdolon sighed and shook his head.

"She passed on in her sleep? This is a tragic thing, but it happens often. Why do you think she was killed?"

"I found a small cut on the side of her neck. It was very small, but there was no scab over it, just some dried blood around the edges. My mother was a strong woman, she was not sick or old! She would not have died in her bed like a weak and infirm hag!" The girl's voice rose accusingly and Magdolon flinched at its volume, glancing around at the quiet forest around them.

"I did not mean to offend." He raised his hands disarmingly before him as the girl stared daggers into his chest. "What would cause her to be killed?"

"She had the audacity to challenge the new abbess. Said she didn't feel what she was doing to the abbey was right. Especially with her second in command, her 'Protectorate' as she calls her. They've changed the way things are done here so drastically that my mother spoke out and was called an insubordinate for her pains."

"What were the new things commanded by the abbess?"

"They've started clearing away sections of the forest. Surely you've seen them? Great swathes of land that are dotted with broken stumps and charred grass?" The girl put her head in her hands. Magdolon nodded, he had seen some of the areas of which she spoke. He was about to question the motive behind this, but the girl spoke before him.

"Our abbey has always maintained an unsteady peace with the forest spirits in this area. We know that the dangers of this place are too great to begin fighting with the forest and its minions, as well as the potential threat of the dwarfs to the east!"

"Why would she do this thing, then?" Magdolon finally questioned.

"She wouldn't say! She holds herself above the rest of the sisters and doesn't speak to us of her intentions. Already we have seen the forest grow restless. My mother spoke out against the order, and so many others that were given, that it seems Abbess Laurine needed her silenced…" Her voice trailed off as Magdolon grabbed her hand.

"What did you say? *Abbess* Laurine?" The girl recoiled from Magdolon's strong grip, but her hand could not pull away.

"Y…yes. That is her name: Laurine." The girl stammered, her eyes wide with fear and her voice soft as Magdolon drew closer.

"She has attained the rank of abbess, then," he muttered, his eyes flitting to the growing shadows formed in the dying light of the setting sun. "What is she planning…? Why would she come here?"

"Do you know this woman? The abbess?" the girl's voice cut through his thoughts. He realized that his hand was still clenched tightly around hers and that he was standing rather close to her in a threatening posture. He quickly released her hand and stepped back, grumbling an apology.

"Yes. I know her," he responded gruffly. "She is the cause for much sorrow in my life."

"From her reputation, you are not the only one to suffer from her actions." The girl rubbed her hand softly as she spoke, it was already red where Magdolon's fingers had gripped. It was likely to bruise from the looks of it.

"I can see that you are one of her victims to suffer as well." Magdolon spoke slowly, a dangerous thought beginning to stir within his mind.

"I am, as I've told you already. Which is why I am running away. The prelates must know of what is happening here."

She moved to gather up her basket and its spilled contents from the forest floor. Magdolon eyed her as she stooped to pick up her supplies, the nagging thought becoming more persistent as he watched her straighten and begin to walk away.

"Wait!" He called out, hating himself for what he was about to suggest. "What if there is another way? A way that brings sweeter vengeance for your mother?" The girl stopped and turned back to face him again.

"What do you mean?"

Magdolon took a deep breath.

"If you go to your prelates, they will then send someone to investigate. Laurine will charm them away. She will have ready stories to explain all accusations you claim. I have seen it many times. This is not the worst thing that she has done. At the end of this, you will be accused for challenging an authority and punished, probably by being sent back to Laurine for her to decide your fate."

"But what of my mother? How could she…" The girl raised a hand to her mouth.

"You mean that mother who will be buried by the time you return? Her rites already performed and only your word that she died in a way that is not natural?" Magdolon arched a brow. "It may even be that you become the accused for this thing. Laurine will have many who will swear she did not do what you say she did."

"I would never…"

"No, you would not, but neither would Laurine according to your prelates." The sense of self-loathing drove itself deeper into Magdolon's stomach as he watched her shoulders sag.

"What can I do, then?" Her voice was a choked whisper, and Magdolon saw the red light of the evening reflected in her tears as they streamed down her face. He sighed and closed his eyes while he spoke.

"I and my ward are hunting Laurine. We know of the evils she has done." Magdolon's voice was a low growl that clawed its way from his throat, the girl took a step back from him even as she strained to listen. "But we cannot enter this keep. Not without her knowing of our presence. We need someone inside. Someone who can be our hands and deliver the justice that she deserves. We need information before we strike. We need someone like you." He opened his eyes and settled his gaze on her face.

"You want me to be your spy?" Her eyes met his, and she did not falter under his gaze. Eventually it was Magdolon who could not maintain her stare and looked away.

"Yes," he spoke, the sinking feeling in his gut grew deeper, and he felt that he might fall into it. He stared out through the trees at the horizon where the sinking sun had finally retreated behind the hills and the light of the evening had transformed into the cool blue of twilight. Even that was almost gone by the time she spoke, the silver moonbeams beginning to make themselves visible in the pollen and dust motes of the forest.

"I'll do it." She spoke quietly, but her voice held a firm edge to it, and she straightened her back as she spoke, lifting her head to gaze into the night sky which was just beginning to show its stars in the dark blanket which now covered the landscape.

"It will be dangerous." Magdolon's voice took on a pleading quality that he had not anticipated.

"I know."

Magdolon tried to explain to her all the various forms that danger might take, but her response was always the same. All the while, she continued looking into the stars as the darkness deepened beneath the boughs of the trees around them. Magdolon sighed, letting his shoulders drop. He should have been happier, but all he felt was guilt at what he was allowing this girl to do at his bidding.

"You needn't worry about me." The girl lowered her gaze, by now the cold of the night was settling about them, and her breath misted before her as she spoke. "I know what I am getting myself into. You are right in what you have pointed out to me, but I will not allow my mother's death to go unanswered. I do this of my own choice. Laurine will pay for what she has done, I swear it."

As she spoke, Magdolon felt a chill run up his spine which had nothing to do with the creeping cold in the air. The girl turned to face him.

"How will I be able to get a message to you?" She pulled her cloak tighter about her as she asked. Magdolon studied her for a moment before nodding.

"I will be taking my ward and myself to live among the peoples of the Free Dwarfs. Whenever possible, send word to the Free Dwarf embassy in the Golden Horn, in particular one Krathak Tabuur. He and I have... a history together and he will make sure that I receive your message. I will let him know to expect messages from you... Er..." He stopped suddenly.

"What's wrong?"

"I just realized that I never asked your name," he admitted, smiling somewhat ruefully. She smiled disarmingly in response.

"For my safety, I don't think you should know my actual name." She held out a hand to him. "But for correspondence, look for letters addressed from 'Y'."

Five

COLD CONSIDERATIONS

Ever since then, I have received letters almost every month." Magdolon sat back, looking across at Ashal. "She was willing to be my eyes. This allowed me to be at home with you. And to deal with… other things… to prepare for this event."

"Other things?" Ashal tilted her head at this. Magdolon gave a crooked smile and stretched his arms above his head.

"I have been engaged in giving small… reminders… to our prey. Reminders of her sins so that she may never forget what she has taken from others."

"You mean us? What she has taken from us?" Ashal said, her voice flat. Magdolon leaned forward, staring intently.

"Do not be so focused on your own pain that you do not see the suffering of others." He said quietly. "We are not Laurine's only victims, not even her worst ones. In fact, we were some of her first when she was far more squeamish about the consequences of her actions. Would we have met her back then as she is now, she would have left us to die in that dungeon." Ashal sat in silence at these words, a dark fury burning in her eyes as she stared across at Magdolon.

"When I kill Laurine, I want her to know that it was me who did it." Her voice was cold. "I do not want her last moments to be one of confusion as to who is holding the spear that has been thrust through her chest. I do not want her to be going through a long list of possible individuals who *might* be responsible for her downfall. I want her to stare into my eyes as the life fades from hers and know that I have come to avenge my mother for her treachery. I want her to regret ever having thought to manipulate us!" By the end, her voice had risen with each declaration to the point where she was nearly shouting. Magdolon sat and waited for her to finish.

"She will know your face when her time comes," he said after a moment of silence, "and she will remember what pains she caused you. But," he spoke as he rose to his feet, towering over her, "you will not make the mistake of thinking that you are taking vengeance only for yourself."

"Who else should I be concerned for?" The snarl that twisted her words with venom surprised even her. Magdolon closed his eyes and took a deep breath. His face was twisted into a mask of sorrow.

"Do not fall into this trap of thinking that your suffering is the ultimate ends of this world," he whispered at length, reaching out to her. She swatted his hand away and stormed past him, grabbing her new spear as she made for the door and out into the moonlit night.

The gentle rustling of the surf washing against the sand was incongruous with her present mood as she snapped her spear under her arm and settled into a starting pose that would lead her through various exercises. She dug her webbed feet into the wet sand and took several deep breaths to try and find her center. Why was she so angry? Why had Magdolon's words sparked such angst in her? These questions plagued her as she swept her spear up and made several quick, successive jabs into the air in a strict zig-zagging pattern before following up with a quick series of kicks that would hypothetically throw her enemy off guard and allow for a killing thrust which ended that stance and moved her into a second pattern of movements.

She became lost in the motions. This was *Lurquada*, a style of fighting that had been developed by the placoderms of Magdolon's tribe for spears and tridents and was meant for underwater fighting, but because not all battles the Trident Realms fought were under the waves, this particular style had also been adapted to be useful on land as well. Movements were precise, usually involving stabs and thrusts which would be easier to execute in the water but were equally deadly and twice as fast without the water's resistance to hold them back.

Magdolon had taught her this method of fighting. It had been a source of bonding for them over the years they had spent in exile. Now Ashal used it as a form of distraction. Focusing on the movements gave her a certain stillness of mind. She could not physically fight her anxiety, her fear, or her anger; but here in the practiced movements of her spear steps, she was in control. She decided what came next. She knew what was expected. For these reasons, she danced through the sandy beach and into the shallows, stabbing and sidestepping invisible attackers in a rhythmic dance that was both beautiful and deadly in its nature.

Ashal was vaguely aware of Magdolon's approach, but she knew he wouldn't interrupt her practice. Doing that would only aggravate her further and make any kind of discussion impossible. She knew that he would simply stand and watch, making mental notes the whole time that he would chastise her for later, waiting for the perfect moment to speak. She performed an aerial lunge that was designed more for aquatic battles as it allowed the fighter to push off and use their own buoyancy to rise up over their attacker and stab downward in a devastating plunge. Yet she performed it with an acrobatic twist that would be just as deadly on land, flying up into the air and crashing down to embed her spear in the sand to slay some imaginary foe. Her lithe form and graceful movements pushed her through the shallows of the sea without hardly a splash as every step was precise and purposefully placed. This was the true test of a master spearman, if they could fight waist-deep in the water without getting their chest and shoulders wet. She was not quite at the level of the legendary masters, yet, but she was better by far than any common soldier or thug with a spear.

With a final thrust that ended with her stabbing upward in a vicious surge of motion, she stood panting in the shallows, her face flushed with a sense of accomplishment. Magdolon clapped in appreciation and she turned toward him, eyes narrowing.

"Have you come to continue your lecture?" Her question came between ragged breaths.

"Only if you are willing to listen." Magdolon moved forward and pulled his own spear free of its holster on his back. He stabbed it down and leaned on the shaft, looking at her expectantly. She considered his stance and a vicious gleam appeared in her eye.

"If you can best me here and now, I will listen." Her lips twisted into a smile. Magdolon sat in thought for a few moments, then shrugged and took up a defensive stance with his body clenching the back quarters of the shaft and his spear extended out before him. Ashal whooped and dropped into a more aggressive position with her spear butt pressed into the ground beside her feet and her off-hand outstretched to help push her off toward her foe, the waves of the tide lapping against her forearm. Magdolon stared at her and she could see the spark of curiosity behind his gaze. The stance she had chosen was designed to allow her to propel off a surface toward her opponent in a quick surge that would be difficult to block, but on land it would be decidedly less effective. He had to wonder what she was planning. She didn't give him time to puzzle over it for long.

With a sharp cry, Ashal lunged forward and launched herself into the air, much like she had just done in practice. It was an intimidating feat and the placoderm was surprised at her tenacity, but the action was too dramatic and pronounced, giving him ample time to dodge to the side. She landed with a splash and rolled forward immediately. Magdolon watched her with interest, not bothering to strike just yet. She rolled onto her feet with the shaft of her spear held at an angle across her body, prepared to ward off any attack the placoderm might attempt. Magdolon simply stood where he was, his spear held loosely in his off-hand with his dominant held before him with his palm opened.

"You try too hard to impress me," he growled. "Stop dancing and start fighting!"

Ashal was taken aback by this, and in her moment of hesitation, Magdolon charged. Ashal gasped and deflected the first attack that was aimed at her shoulder, the force of the blow rocked her back on to her heels, and Magdolon pressed his advantage. He swept out the butt of his spear and caught Ashal's ankle with a sharp crack that reverberated up her leg. She muffled a cry of pain and fell onto her back in an attempt to roll away from Magdolon and his precise blows. Magdolon smiled and stabbed down, embedding his point right where her back would land moments before she hit there. He rose quickly, levering her weight to the side with his weapon. Ashal, caught off guard, rolled away from the upturned spear to land on her stomach. In a flash, Magdolon placed his knee in the small of her back and grabbed a fistful of her dreadlocks, pulling her head back until she cried out. He pulled a small dagger he kept strapped to his calf and placed the blade against her throat.

"I have bested you," he growled. Ashal bit back a childish accusation of him fighting dirty. Of course he did. What would she expect on the battlefield? What had she seen in the battles she had already fought? She closed her eyes and tamped down the feelings of embarrassment and irritation at her loss.

"I concede." She whispered the words, his knee in her back making it hard to breathe much less speak. Magdolon grunted and stepped off her back. She gasped and rolled onto her back, the night sky glittered back at her as if it were laughing.

"Why did you lose?" Magdolon was once again leaning on his spear as he stared down at her.

"Because I wasn't expecting you to fight dirty," Ashal responded, wincing as she sat up and touched her swelling ankle, knowing that she would have a decent sized bruise there in the morning.

"There is no such thing," Magdolon snorted. "'Fair' has no place in fighting. When you fight, you are fighting to live. You cannot fight 'dirty' because you must be willing to use any trick you need so that you might survive. 'Fair' is a thing for games and play. I have taught you this before, yet you still view our sparring as playing and not fighting. Perhaps I need to leave more scars for you to realize that I do not play when I fight." He punctuated this by slapping her arm with the butt of his spear. Ashal groaned and pushed herself to her feet.

"I'm going to bed." She grumbled and turned toward their small hut.

"No" Magdolon replied, staring out over the waves. Ashal paused, grimacing at his simple rebuke.

"What do you want from me?"

"Does your word mean so little to you?" Magdolon stared out over the moon-washed waves.

"I listened to your lecture on fighting versus playing. I have kept my word." Ashal turned and stared at him defiantly.

"You know that is not what I meant when I agreed to the match." At this, Magdolon blinked and allowed his eyes to rest on her. "A person who would use such trickery with words and promises is the same as a liar, worse because a fulfilled but empty promise is more foul than a false oath. For one is simply a liar, but the other is a *liar* and a trickster and thus a more painful wound to heal, and neither have any honor." Ashal glared at him, but she stomped over and sank down to sit in the sand beside him. They sat in silence, the only sound that of the waves breaking gently against the shore. The moon rose in the sky while they watched, and Ashal felt that she would burst from waiting.

"Are you going to speak?" she finally asked impatiently.

"I am choosing a time when you are not so angry and are willing to listen to my words." Magdolon continued to stare out over the water before them.

"Then we may be here all night and part of tomorrow," Ashal snapped.

"If that is what is necessary. But you *will* abide until I am ready to speak, if your word means anything at all to you. For I have words for you that you must hear." Ashal's face burned and words bubbled up into her mouth that she wished to scream at him, but she forced them down and made herself look back at the waters, trying to take in the calm of her surroundings. The silence spread out for several more minutes before finally she spoke again.

"I am sorry, Magdolon, I am ready to hear your words." She spoke with a neutral voice.

"That is good, I accept your apology." Magdolon nodded but did not speak further, and Ashal was forced to continue sitting in silence as the time ticked by. She realized that she was still angry, but she didn't want to stop the feelings of anger that burned within her chest. She felt justified in her mood, and she didn't care that Magdolon knew that she was still upset; in fact she wanted him to know. If he wanted to wait her out, then she was up for the challenge, and they would sit out here all night if the need was there for her to prove her point. She would not fold.

After another long period of silence, Ashal began to yawn. The fire in her chest began to fizzle out and her eyelids began to droop. She forced herself to sit up straighter and shook her head to ward off her drowsiness. It wasn't long, however, before she found her head leaning on Magdolon's massive shoulder, her breathing deep and steady. It was at that moment that he bucked her head off of him and rose to stand before her. She blinked blearily at him through sleep-starved eyes.

"Now I think you are better prepared to listen to me." Magdolon smiled down at her. "It seems your anger has abated and you are in a better mood to hear what I have to say."

"Wha...?" Ashal stifled a yawn, tears glistening in her eyes at the effort. Magdolon chuckled and reached out a hand to her. She took it and blinked when he pulled her to her feet. He reached an arm around her shoulders and pulled her close to him as they walked closer to the lapping waves of the sandy beach.

"Look out there." Magdolon pointed over the horizon where the sea stretched out to the edge of her vision. "Tell me what do you see?"

"Magdolon," Ashal sighed, "if this is another of your lectures about our home and our goals, I swear…"

"Just tell me," Magdolon cut across her complaints.

"The sea. Waves. The night sky. Stars." Ashal rolled her eyes as she spoke. "Are any of those the answer that you're looking for?"

"Perhaps." Magdolon smiled. "You are a strong swimmer, are you not?"

"I suppose." Ashal felt a sneaking suspicion trickling into her words. Where was he going with this? Magdolon nodded.

"Having lived above the waves of our people has given you different… strengths. Your legs are far stronger than the average naiad, allowing you to propel yourself in great leaping bounds both on the earthen shores and the watery depths. This makes you a very dangerous and unique fighter." Magdolon patted his ward on her shoulder and pulled away to look at her. "But when you swim with me for any great distance, you begin to tire much sooner than I." Ashal shook off his hand on her shoulder and glared at him.

"This is because of my upbringing! We couldn't always live near great bodies of water!" Rage and resentment, not at Magdolon, but at the hand fate had dealt her, gripped her as she snarled. "I have spent more of my days on land than what is normal for my people! You have said so yourself! Yet in battle, I will be strong!" Magdolon simply returned her glare with another of his nods.

"No one doubts your courage or your strength, *Lueshwy'n*. I bring up this only to illustrate a point." Magdolon turned and pointed out to the sea again. "Do you remember only a few years ago, when we first arrived and set up our home? You were so happy to see the great waters again that you dived in and swam far out into the sea, so far that you seemed but a small speck from the shore where I was busy building our shelter." Ashal's face fell and her eyes began to search through the dark sand before them, swirling her toes in the wet beach's surface.

"I remember," she whispered her reply. "I got caught in an underwater current without realizing it and was swept out into the sea. I fought against it and became too exhausted to swim any longer because of it. You had to swim out and retrieve me, but you only did it after hours of my own fruitless struggling. It was one of the most embarrassing moments of my life. A naiad having to be saved from the water! How pathetic." Magdolon brought his hand under her chin and lifted it so that she was forced to look him in the eyes.

"Your path has been difficult, *Lueshwy'n*, but you have strengths that many do not. These strengths will carry you in ways that no other Child of the Deep could manage. Yours is not the way of the Trident and the Conch. You have darker, more difficult roads to walk." Magdolon pointed back out to the sea again. "The current that took you out into the great waters is called the riptide by the land dwellers, and these currents have claimed the lives of many an unwary swimmer not born to the waves as you are." Despite Magdolon's kind words, Ashal still felt the sting of her own shame pushing silent tears from her eyes.

"Do not sadden, *Lueshwy'n*. You are stronger than you know." Magdolon replaced his hand on Ashal's shoulder, and this time she allowed him to pull her into an embrace. "But you must be careful, too. You have become so shortsighted with Laurine that you are willing to simply dive in to your quest for vengeance without being fully aware of that which you are doing. Just like you dived into the ocean that day and were pulled out to sea, so will this quest for revenge do to you if you are not careful." He pulled away and cupped Ashal's face in his giant hands, forcing her to look into his eyes.

"Beware the riptide of your emotions," he spoke softly and leaned in close, placing his forehead against hers. "If you are not careful, it will pull you out to sea and leave you to drown. Just like the riptide of these waters pulled you into the blue despite you being a stronger swimmer than any human or dwarf who might also have swam here. So might your desires for revenge draw you out into a place where you will be destroyed."

"Are you saying that I should not pursue Laurine, then?" Ashal pulled back in surprise at his words.

"No." Magdolon shook his head. "But I urge you to caution. There is little to be gained by simply fueling our desires and giving the lead to our emotions. This is what will bring about your death and Laurine's victory. Use patience in your quest. Be thoughtful. Do not give in to the idea that you have been uniquely singled out for suffering in this life, or that you are special because of your struggles. There are many who have suffered as much or more than you, even at Laurine's hands." He took a step back and looked once more into the lapping waves as they brushed against the shore. Ashal watched him as he stared in silence, both of them wrapped in the chill darkness of the night as the moon washed over them. At length, he sighed and turned back to her.

"Your anger is a tool, and you must use it. Your desire for vengeance must be equal to your desire for justice. You are not simply getting revenge for yourself. You are also avenging all the widows, the orphans, and the dead that Laurine and the others who have wronged you have left in their passing. You must be strong. You must control your anger, your desire. Do not let this quest change you into something less than you are."

"You think it will?" Ashal furrowed her brow at him.

"It is my greatest fear for you," he responded, nodding. "Long have you been my *Lueshwy'n*, my little stingray. But now you grow older. Age brings with it many good things. But also many bad. We choose which we will cling to. We choose if we hold to our memories of light or our scars from the dark. Vengeance is a dark road, and its end does not bring light of its own. This is my fear for you. That you will change into something that I cannot follow."

"I promise you it will not." Ashal stepped forward to lay a hand on Magdolon's shoulder. He smiled and laid his own hand over hers, but it was a sad smile that left his face covered in shadows. He patted her hand and turned back to the sea.

"Do not make promises of which you are unsure you can follow." His voice was tight, as if forcing the words from his mouth caused him physical pain. Ashal waited for him to say more, but he remained silent, staring out into the waves. After several moments of silence, she turned to go back to their hut, a mutual need for solitude driving them apart. She had plans to make, but she turned to look back at him from the door. He hadn't stirred a muscle and continued to stare out into the night. The light of the moon shimmered across his scaled body, causing him to glow with a silvery light. His words still swirled around in her mind. They terrified her. But the thought of letting Laurine go caused bile to rise in the back of her throat, and so she stamped down her apprehension, her fear, and began to bend her thoughts toward the future and the look on Laurine's face when she would drive her spear through that traitorous coward's heart.

Six

ROUGH PASSAGE

The sea misted as it splashed against the metal hull of the dwarven cog. The flat-bottomed ship was not the smoothest of passages through the sometimes choppy waves, but its utilitarian barges allowed for greater cargo capacity and the high sides made for better defense against potential boarders. It was exactly the kind of ship that Ashal had expected from the efficient and hardy mining company with whom they were sailing. It was one of three such vessels pushing its way south across the Low Sea of Suan, each one filled to the brim with some seventy-five dwarven miners, along with supplies and equipment to last them the duration of the early days of their expedition.

Together with Magdolon, they had approached the dwarven company about sharing passage with them to the outskirts of the Basilean Hegemony where the silver mine they had been hired to excavate was located. The foreman had been his usual dour self, but after they had produced a few extra furs and some coin from their hunting and trading expeditions, he had relented. He muttered something about how they shouldn't expect high quality accommodations but that he would find them a place to sleep and food to eat during their journey together.

Now Ashal sat on the deck of the ship with her legs thrust through the slats in the railing and held her hands above her head, letting her feet dangle over the edge so that the salty spray that came with each teeth chattering plunge could wash across her calves with its icy droplets. The sun beat down on her as she stared out across the flat horizon that was broken only by the lazy rolling of the sea as the wind played across its surface. Her mind was still puzzling over the sudden turn of events which had led her to where she now sat. The confrontation with Magdolon and his strange warnings echoed in her ears. What did he mean by telling her those things? Why would he belittle her suffering? Her brow furrowed the more she thought about it, and she found herself drumming her fingers across the corroded brass railing where she sat.

A small cough caused her to turn in surprise. She found Gravel staring at her, a sheepish expression on his face. He held in his hands what looked like a bowl of fish stew, brought up from the mess hall below. Gravel had been struggling with the jarring motions of the ship and his face looked a little green as he held out the pungent smelling dish toward her, his legs swaying unsteadily beneath him. Ashal suppressed a smile as she watched and forced herself to tilt her head quizzically in his direction.

"Yes, Gravel?" she asked sweetly. Gravel swallowed and his eyes rolled back into his head before he could speak. He staggered and gave another cough before focusing back on her once more.

"Blast you, girl!" he growled, once more thrusting the bowl under her nose. "I'm trying to give a peace offering and you are content only to give me heartache over it."

Ashal smiled and took the proffered bowl. The dwarven food was always seasoned a little too heavily with pepper and a strange powdered root called turmen that gave everything a strange, acidic flavor. But this was better than stale biscuits and grog for another day, and so she willingly forced the steaming concoction down as the ship continued to shudder its way through the waves.

"It doesn't seem as though it is your heart that's aching though," she said around bites of the steaming stew. The dwarf groaned and leaned hard against the railing beside her.

"I've never been the seafaring type," he muttered in between hiccups. "I always hate it when we have to travel across the waters. Try to avoid it whenever I can. But this was too good to pass up." He burped and his face screwed up at the taste of it, causing him to lean over the railing and force up the contents of his already empty stomach.

"I never understood how a dwarf could become a sailor." He groaned from over the side of the railing. "My father told me tales of his second cousin, King Billiam XXXVIII, who ate some strange berries and said that Fulgria appeared to him and told him to go west. I think of the amount of water that stretches from our home to the east and all that goes out to the west, and it makes my stomach turn with the effort of it all."

"Perhaps you should eat something to help calm it, then?" Ashal teased, although she was forced to hold her breath to avoid the smell of the dwarf's renewed retching. Gravel muttered something in his native tongue and pulled himself upright to stagger away from her. He clutched his stomach as he tottered back toward the quarters, his face pale and sweating as he went. Ashal smiled and finished her stew in a few quick slurps. She watched Magdolon approach, dodging around the seasick Gravel who didn't even seem to notice that the giant placoderm was in his path.

"Even for a people who hate the sea, that one is cursed by the depths to never set foot on its domain." Magdolon shook his head, looking in Gravel's direction as he came and sat next to Ashal, placing his back against the railing. "Have you not tortured him enough? He is obviously sorry for what he did."

He turned his gaze on Ashal, who was swishing the dregs of her stew around in her bowl.

"I'm not holding anything against him. He tortures himself! I've already told him that all is forgiven!" She set the bowl down on the deck. It didn't take long before the ship crested another small wave and shuddered back into the water, causing the bowl to tilt and skitter away from her to land in a coil of thick rope not far away. Magdolon sighed.

"Somehow I feel that your forgiveness for him is the same as it is for me." He leaned his head back against the railing and closed his eyes. "I may never find rest again for my offenses."

"You're the one who says that," Ashal grumbled. "Your suffering is not unique, remember?"

Magdolon shook his head but did not open his eyes.

"Have you given thought to my words? How do you wish to cause Laurine's suffering?"

Ashal was silent for a long time, letting the sound of the water splashing across the hull fill the void between them.

"I want to humiliate her. I want her fall to be a public display of shame. The whole world will know of her heartless treachery." Her voice was quiet, to the point where the wake of the ship almost drowned her out. Magdolon did not respond immediately.

"What will you do? Will you walk into the abbey and call her out in front of her advisors and her court?"

"Am I not living evidence of the terrible things that she has done? We both can testify against her. We can offer to take them to the Quarter of Woe in the Golden Horn and show them what we found there!" Ashal's whispers were heated as she spoke, but Magdolon did not turn to meet them.

"We are outsiders in a world of fanatics," Magdolon spoke slow, his voice level. "Others have tried the very thing that you suggest and Laurine has killed them. Swiftly. She does not toy with her victims and silences those who raise a hand against her. She is ruthless, and she will kill you if this is the route you choose to seek."

"Are you saying we should kill her quietly? Allow her to die a martyr to her people and be buried with honors?" Ashal hissed. "I will not allow her to depart this world without knowing that her death is brought about by the weight of her own actions!"

"She will be." Magdolon raised a hand to calm her, but she swatted it away.

"No! I will not be placated! You bring me news of my mother's killer, then you caution me to avoid vengeance because it will destroy me. Now you advise me to sneak into her room and steal her life like a thief, thus destroying my chance of clearing my family's name!" Ashal snarled under her breath, her words shocking even her with their vehemence. Magdolon reacted quickly and cuffed her soundly to the side of her head. Her vision blurred for a moment, and she struggled to think clearly as she regained her breath.

"If you speak like a spawnling, I will treat you as such." Magdolon's voice was quiet and level, devoid of emotion. It caused Ashal to shiver. She had only seen him this angry a handful of times, and each time she had regretted what followed. Her stomach flooded with embarrassment and she stared daggers into the deck, her tongue ached to spit insults at him, but she wisely kept her peace. Magdolon stared at her for several long instances then spoke again in the same quiet, level voice.

"I will not hold with your accusation that I did not love and serve your mother."

Instantly, Ashal's anger drained away, leaving a cold and uncomfortable sensation in her chest.

"But, I never said..."

"Do not try to hide your words with pointless explanations." Magdolon cut her off. "You accused me of wanting to take the easy path. You think that vengeance for your mother is a chore for me? Something that I wish to accomplish with as little effort as I can? *N'Cha!*" He spat the curse into the sea and turned to look at her again. "I have been patient with you and your tantrums while you have thought over this very difficult task. But if you *ever* think so poorly of me again, I will take you away from this and you will not be part of it. You are here because of your right as my master's daughter, but I am here to make sure it is done in a way that honors her and does not get you killed. *That* is my first duty. All else is at my will. Do you understand?"

Tears shimmered in her eyes as she nodded.

"I'm sorry... I..." She stammered and soon she found his big arms around her shoulders and pulling her into his chest.

"It is okay." He swayed his body in time with the ship, and the movement soothed her. "I know that you are young and that what has been given to you is more than you should have to do. I am sorry for what you have lost. I do not relish your suffering, but I will not stand to have my honor questioned, and I will not let you be killed because you are too angry or too young to fight in a smart way." He lifted her head up so that he could look into her face. "I too, am sorry. I should not have done that." He gently laid his hand across where it had connected with her head.

Ashal blinked and nodded, a sad smile spreading across her face. He had never reacted that violently before. Never, in all of their arguments, had he ever struck her before. Magdolon was the rock in her life. Calm, stoic, and dependable. Those were his traits. Now he was on edge. He was a warrior, and while he had struggled with raising a naiad on his own, he had never resorted to any kind of violence with her until now. What had changed?

For a moment, she wavered. Was it the nature of their quest? Was this the riptide that Magdolon had been warning her about? Was this the change that it wrought? Things were changing. A cold dread had settled in her stomach that would not shake itself from her; like weighted clothes that pulled her down while in the water, she felt an inexorable tug being exerted on her, pulling her further away. She clung to Magdolon's embrace as the waves continued to crash against the hull below them.

Magdolon obscured his face as they pulled apart, looking in the opposite direction, and the two sat for a long time in a troublesome silence where each of them struggled to find words for their discomfort. At long last, Magdolon pushed himself to his feet and turned to look back down at her.

"I would not confront Laurine directly. This will end only in your death and I…" His voice cut off for a moment and his eyes shifted from her face to the deck. "I could not live with that. Not again. Please reconsider." With that, he turned and walked away.

Ashal thought to chase after him and continue the conversation, but he moved with a speed that suggested he did not wish any company at the moment. She stared after him as he hurried below deck. The ship once again crested a small wave and slapped back onto the water, causing her to reach out and grasp the railing beside her, but she missed and almost tipped back into the sea itself. Only her frantic grasping saved her as she managed to catch herself on the edge of the deck before tipping forward into the water below her.

She shuddered and forced herself back from the edge. Standing, she moved toward one of the center masts of the ship. She began to climb up the rigging toward the crow's nest located at the top of the long pillar of wood. She had gained quite an aptitude for climbing in her years ashore, scrabbling through the wilderness and up trees. Something no naiad child would normally have done, would not have any ability to do. If she had grown up in the world her mother would have given her, she would not know such joys as the thrill of climbing a tree and standing at its height gazing out over the windswept hills. She would not know the rush of hunting a boar or of stalking a deer so that they might eat and survive another winter. Ashal loved the sea, there was no doubt of that, but she often found her thoughts wandering through the what-ifs of her life and how it would have been different and whether or not she preferred her alternate history to what had really come to pass.

With a last heave, she pulled herself over the edge of the nest and tumbled into its basket. The dwarf whose shift it was to keep watch grumbled as Ashal brushed herself off, but then moved to give her room. Ashal was well-liked among the crew, in no small part because of the grief she gave poor Gravel, and so the dwarfs of the company had learned to tolerate her eccentricities such as climbing into the crow's nest at odd times of the day. She straightened and looked out over the horizon. It was flat all around them. They were still some time away from their port, and they had left the shores of the Free Dwarfs several days behind. The horizon curved ever so slightly at the edges when she stared hard enough, but other than that there was nothing to be seen in any direction.

Up here, the world fell away. Even the dwarf standing next to her seemed to respect the isolation of the sea and did not disturb the reverie this particular spot on the ship allotted them. Up here, the only sound was the wind as it played across the waves. Up here, the rough passage of the ship seemed less abrasive as the mast was supple and prone to suppress the shudders of the ship grinding across the sea. It was quiet, and beyond that, time seemed to disappear here as well. Besides the sun's journey across the sky, there was nothing to mark the hours as they slid through her fingers. It was oddly disconcerting to be so disconnected to the world. She kept replaying her interaction with Magdolon in her head, and she felt the fins around her face deepen their crimson hue as she went over the exchange again and again. Something caused her to drum her fingers on the edge of the nest.

Why was she treating him like this? Her anger, she knew, was not directed at Magdolon, even though he bore the brunt of her temper. The sea rolled by beneath her as she stared out, the waves filling her with a sense of melancholy. She tried to call up memories of her home in the depths, but all that came to her was fuzzy, half-formed faces that spoke in muted tones. The colors that Magdolon described to her of the coral cities was dull and lackluster. Even her mother refused to answer her summons within her mind's eye. Her stern but practical mother, she remembered her more as a list of attributes than as someone who had brought her into this world. Most of her memories only came into focus because of Magdolon.

That was another issue that caused her stomach to twist uncomfortably. Magdolon and her relationship with him was an unorthodox one. In the Trident Realm, it would not have been allowed to exist. A placoderm raising a naiad would be considered the height of absurdity! What would become of them when they returned to the depths? Would he return to his life and leave her alone? She shuddered at this thought. Magdolon had been raised in her mother's court, as such his brothers and sisters were as much the other children of dignitaries and household members as any related by blood. His life had mainly consisted of his military service, first to the crown, and then to Ashal's mother when that duty had finished. When Ashal asked him of his family, his face filled with such sadness and melancholy that she had quickly learned to avoid the subject altogether.

The mast swayed underneath them; a wave hit the ship at an odd angle and forced the vessel to tilt precariously as it crested the wave at an uncomfortable pitch, the motion rippling up through the mast and causing the crow's nest to jag violently back and forth. The movement caused Ashal's already upset stomach to heave, and she nearly lost the spicy soup which Gravel had brought her. She swallowed a few times and took some deep breaths as the ship corrected itself on the water.

All of these worries and concerns were for a future that she wasn't sure she would live to see. The nausea threatened to overwhelm her again as this encompassed her thoughts. They were careening across the sea to face a powerful foe who Ashal was unsure they could defeat. Laurine had always been a looming shadow over Ashal's life. The reason they had moved around so much was to avoid being found by her and now, according to Magdolon, she was stronger than ever and with more influence within the Hegemony. Beyond this, she could control soldiers and issue orders now as an Abbess of the Hegemon. How could two outcasts, completely abandoned by their own people and any allies, ever hope to overcome what lay before them?

Her eyes scanned the southern horizon as these thoughts circled in her mind, when suddenly something seemed to jump out at her. She grabbed the small telescope that hung from the dwarf watchman's waist, who grunted in surprise and exclaimed in alarm as she pointed it toward her quarry.

"Do you see what I see?" She asked, handing the telescope to the dwarf again. "Isn't that impossible?" The dwarf took the scope and looked through it, twisting the glass to try and get it to focus. He grunted and shook his head.

"We must've had better wind than we thought we did, but it's still a good ways away." He turned and bellowed to the crew below them.

"Land HO!"

Seven
Morning Devotions

R Ruddy sunlight filtered through the gray cloud cover outside and penetrated the stained glass of the chapel where Yvette knelt, her hands clasped together in a supplicative position before a miniature diorama of Dominar casting the evil Oskan into the Abyss. The ruby light danced across the small carved images of the two gods frozen in an eternal struggle that to this day dominated the Basilean way of life. The rendition was a rather crude one, as the remote location of their abbey mixed with the frugal nature of those who kept it meant that what little art that did exist within the stone walls of its keep were generally locally sourced. The local scene had generally consisted of farmers and blacksmiths, and the diorama was sturdy and functional, but it was no great work of art. Yvette didn't mind, she liked the simple nature of the work, even if she felt no stirrings in her breast at its depiction.

Her prayers were the simple repetitions of memorized verse which she repeated over and over again.

"Mighty Dominar, he who rent the darkness and cast evil into the fire, hear my devotions on this morning of thy light and bless me with thy wisdom. Give me strength to fight the wickedness and overcome the temptations which assail me. Sanctify me with thy light and arm me with thy justice. Cleave away my impurities as thou didst cleave the earth in twain to seal away the Wicked Ones. Guide me in my mortal sojourn so that I may live with the Shining Ones in paradise when I come to journey's end."

Her lips continued to whisper this psalm as her mind whirled in nervous contemplation, the words failing to give the solace she had once felt from them. Her thoughts were focused elsewhere. She hadn't heard back from Magdolon, yet, and her gut twisted as her mind played out all the terrible scenarios that could have caused this lapse in communication. Another, much larger portion of her attention was dedicated to pouring over the revelations she had received in her increasingly frequent visits with Laurine. The abbess had taken to confiding in her, speaking about her frustrations with the abbey, and in particular, with Sister Rose, who was coming to dominate more and more of their conversations. In particular, their conversation from the previous night kept intruding on her prayers.

"Why do you allow her to show you such insolence?" Yvette had asked, interrupting Laurine as she handed the young sister another envelope for her to seal. The abbess's time was very valuable, and so she would have Yvette attend to her during times that were usually occupied with menial tasks. That night, the task was addressing missives to be sent out to the local magistrate who would convey their reports all the way up to the Golden Horn like a well-drilled military regiment. This allowed them to talk as they folded and sealed envelopes with the abbey's stamp that marked the communications as official business of the Hegemony. As was becoming increasingly more frequent, Laurine had been speaking of her frustrations with Rose. This interruption caused her to pause in thought.

"Rose controls so much of the sisterhood. She is essentially the mother of so many of you for all intents and purposes. If I were to disgrace her, it would likely only make her a martyr to the rest of your sisters and confirm what Rose has been preaching to them." Laurine sighed, once again taking up her quill to address a missive to the General Quartermaster under the Supreme Magistrate, detailing the use of their supplies.

"But you've said that you fear Rose is trying to get rid of you. Wouldn't dealing with her directly and publicly showing that you are the master of this place help cement your control?"

"No, it would only make her right. She has set me up as indolent and lazy. Shaming her would only make me a tyrant as well." Laurine stood up from her desk, placing her hands in the small of her back and stretching. They were quiet a moment, and Laurine turned to walk over to a window which had been opened to allow a view of the forest that spread out below the plateau, illuminated in the silver light of a full moon. Years of cutting and clearing had pushed the forest back several yards from the base of the mountain cliff over which the abbey loomed.

"All I want to do is make the world a safer place." The abbess leaned her head against the cold glass of the window. Yvette sat in silence. She had heard iterations of this speech many times already from Laurine and knew that the best thing to do was wait for her to finish before attempting to share her own thoughts. Laurine did not turn from the window as she spoke.

"I grew up on a border village much like this one. Up north, closer to the Abyss where raids from orcs and demons were far more common. I watched my mother butchered in front of me, her screams haunt me to this day. I watched those hulking brutes with their terrible blades designed to inflict pain cut her open while I watched from my hiding place. The beasts didn't even bother searching once they had finished with her, simply left her corpse on the floor and set fire to the hut where we lived. In the smoke and the flames, I somehow managed to escape as our village burned to the ground around me. I spent a terrifying week stumbling through the wilderness as I dreamed that the greenskins were chasing after me, enjoying the sport of my terror. When I finally stumbled on the local magistrate's manor, I must've looked like some creature of the woods, but his soldiers took me to the servants' quarters and fed me. I could barely speak, but I told them where I had come from, and they deduced what had happened from the burns on my clothes and arms. I heard the whispers from one of the younger maids as I ate, whispering that they had heard reports of the orc raiding parties in the area." At this, Laurine finally turned from the window and looked back at Yvette, her eyes alight with the fires of her childhood.

"They had known about the danger and done nothing!" she spat. "As I got older, I swore that I would never allow what happened to me become the fate of any other child. I fought tooth and nail to get to this position, and I'll be damned if I allow Rose to take it from me, now that I can finally use my influence to protect the people of this Hegemony!"

It always surprised Yvette at the amount of vehemence Laurine could press into her words, despite the many times she had repeated that same story and its accompanying vows to her. The silence stretched out for several long moments before Laurine sighed and moved over to sink into her chair once more, her fingers massaging her temples.

Far away in the Great Hall, Yvette could hear the choir of sisters beginning their midnight practices. The lilting melody was beautiful as it floated through the still night air, and it caused something to stir within Yvette's chest. It was a canto to Mescator, the god of justice, pleading for his righteous protection and singing praises to the story of when he struck down the hydras of the Green Woods so long ago. The song was beautiful and ponderous in its descriptions, its melody meditative and soothing. It wasn't until Laurine let out a mournful sigh that Yvette realized that she had been holding her own breath as she listened.

"It is a beautiful thing, isn't it?" Laurine had whispered, her voice thick as she spoke. Yvette did not dare speak at this sudden change in her demeanor, and so she simply nodded. Her own thoughts were far less generous than those of the abbess. She knew the sisters of the choir, and she knew the words they sang were vain repetitions and cruel lies meant to deceive. There was no worship in their prayers.

"I remember listening to the hymns when I was younger. I remember hiding in the turrets of the cathedral where I was small enough to escape and none would dare follow me or try to find me there," Laurine continued, closing her eyes and leaning back in her chair to rest her head against the padded backing. "Those songs filled something within me as I hid in the shadowed rafters of the chapel and listened to the angelic chords. I had so much anger in my heart in those days. I fear that this anger still plagues me to this day, but the one thing that can still lull me into something resembling peace are the blessed notes of our holy songs." The song reached the crescendo of its opening movement, and Laurine breathed another sigh. It was too much for Yvette, and she snorted in spite of herself. The abbess opened an eye to stare at her.

"You find my memory reproachful?" Her voice lost its huskiness as she spoke and instead grew hard like granite.

"No, Mother Abbess!" Yvette stuttered. "You know who those sisters are! You know *what* they are, and yet you say that the praises they sing are holy. I guess I do not understand how you can praise the very sisters who would seek to overthrow you for their pious nature, especially considering *their* true nature." Yvette shook her head and looked to the darkened windows.

Laurine did not respond for some time, and instead she stood and walked over to an ancient looking chest which sat on a table in the corner of the room. Quietly, she lifted the lid and rummaged around for a few moments before pulling out something wrapped in white linen and returning to her seat. Yvette slid forward on her chair and Laurine held up a hand, motioning for her to come closer. The young sister stood and circled around the table which separated them to stand at Laurine's shoulder.

The linens fell away to reveal a beautiful plaque depicting a tree sculpted from jade. Intricate branches snaked outward, intertwining and curling about each other. Every so often a tiny, glittering ruby was drilled into the green stone to make a likeness of leaves still clinging to the intertwined branches. At the center of the round plaque was inlaid the outline of a small bird, etched in gold. It was breathtaking.

"Where did you get this?" Yvette had gasped, leaning in closer. She saw Laurine smile out of the corner of her eye.

"Before I was granted the title of abbess, I was a missionary at the head of a Retributionary Task Force. I was sent to a small settlement on the northern border of the Hegemony to investigate rumors of a heretical sect that had supposedly taken root there." Laurine shook her head and turned the plaque over to reveal a cracked face of silvered glass. Yvette's instincts immediately took hold and she recoiled in horror, recognizing the mirror for the token that it was.

"They were Fenulian Cultists?!"

Laurine nodded slowly and began replacing the linen wrappings. Yvette's mind reeled at this. Followers of the Fenulian Cult were fanatical savages dedicated to suffering for the sins of their namesake. Calisor Fenulian, the elf who crafted the mirror which split the Celestians in twain for the forbidden love of a human woman. The Fenulian Cultists performed savage rituals on their bodies as penance for his sins. They carved mirror wounds on both sides of their bodies in parodic stigmata of that infamous mirror. They claimed it was to honor the dual nature of the Shining and Wicked Ones formed from the remnants of the Celestians who were torn in half by the shattering of the

Fenulian Mirror. They were also given to wanton lust as a way of satisfying the desires their patron was denied and were easily susceptible to the whisperings of the Wicked Ones, often times giving themselves willingly to their enslavement in the pits of the Abyss as a twisted form of penance. Many of the fleshling slaves which marched against the Hegemony to the crack of demonic whips were willing subjects of the Fenulian Cult. What Laurine now held and was carefully wrapping in its protective covering was one of their holy icons.

"I killed them all." Laruine's voice was flat and her hands paused as she caught sight of her own visage in the cracked surface of the glass. "The entire colony had been corrupted by their wicked teachings and required cleansing, or else they..." Her voice trailed off as she lifted a hand to touch her face. The angelic voices of the choir still filled the air, they were now coming to the final stanza and the ebb of the music was reaching a hushed stillness as the song began to fade into its conclusion. Laurine shook herself and quickly wrapped the linen once more around the mirror.

"Thankfully there were no children there. Small mercies, I suppose." Laurine coughed uncomfortably.

"Why would you keep such a terrible thing?" Yvette furrowed her brow as she spoke, her own voice quiet like the music that was receding down the hallway.

"As a lesson, my dear." Laurine turned in her seat and looked up at Yvette. "As a reminder, this mirror is beautiful and there is divinity in all that is beautiful. The artisan who crafted it was blessed to have such talent, even though he chose to use it for a wicked purpose. You see, Yvette, even evil can create something truly beautiful and wondrous, just like those sisters and their hymns. Sometimes the forces of light can bring much pain and suffering into this world, just as I did to that settlement of cultists. This mirror reminds me that I must find that beauty where I can, and it helps remind me of why I must continue the path that I have chosen."

Yvette stared down at the mother abbess sitting before her, her mouth dry and her throat choked. She took a small step backward in spite of herself. Laurine rose to her feet and Yvette felt that she towered over her now, the darkness in the windows behind her reaching out to grasp her from behind.

"I fear I have said something that has upset you, my dear," Laurine said.

"No, Mother Abbess... I... I appreciate your lesson. I am feeling rather tired, may I be excused?" Yvette almost sagged with relief when Laurine smiled and nodded.

"Oh, and Yvette." Laurine called out as Yvette opened the door. The younger sister looked back. "Just like those sisters, you, too, can create something beautiful if you try. You are not as far gone as you wish yourself to believe." The mother abbess smiled crookedly at Yvette, who nodded awkwardly and then rushed out of the room toward her own quarters.

81

What had followed had been a sleepless night spent pondering, and she still wasn't sure what had disturbed her so deeply about the conversation. She usually retired to this place in the small chapel when she felt distressed. Since Laurine had taken over the abbey, the chapel had become increasingly deserted as the Mother Abbess often held services in the great hall where petitioners to the Great Hegemon's court were greeted and their cases heard. Here, the stained glass was not arrayed in intricate patterns, nor were depictions of religious stories etched in them. Most were randomly adorned with whatever colors the glass maker could find, it seemed. The majority of the windows were red, or orange, with some yellow and the occasional blue that sprung up here and there. All of the windows were smaller and placed several feet above the ground in case the chapel needed to be used as a final stand against invaders. A sturdy, but unadorned wooden pulpit dominated the center of a small stage and some old, oak pews and a few prayer stations were the only other adornments of the small building.

The chapel itself, with its basic art and crude stained glass, was a relic of darker times. It hailed from an era where survival was more important than decadence, and the rough construction was a testament to the need for faith in an age where religion was a survival technique. The people who had built this portion of the abbey had done so out of a need to worship, in order that they might have some hope that the next day would bring with it blessings, and not more threats and further violence. While the danger of invading armies and roving bandits was still prevalent in the world, the vanity of its people had grown with the expansion of their empires. Basilea had grown wealthy, and with that wealth came a certain unrealistic sense of security. Even a remote abbey like this now sported thick, stone walls with several sturdy buildings and halls to hold off attackers. Not to mention the 'guardians' that Laurine employed who watched over both the abbey and the city below, and all of this on what was considered the 'frontier' of their kingdom...

Fingers traced themselves across the back of Yvette's neck, causing her to shudder and forcing her out of her meditations. She turned to see a tall, stately woman staring down at her. Cold, blue eyes and a thin set of lips sat etched into a statuesque face that seemed to drop the temperature of the room by several degrees simply by noticing it. Right now, the thin lips were curled into a tight, cruel smile.

"Sister Yvette." A smoky voice purred out from those cold lips. "How good it is to see you clinging to your traditions." Yvette winced, clenching her jaw.

"Sister Rose. I did not hear you enter." Yvette made to rise, but Rose put a hand on her shoulder to stop her. The older sister was not even really a member of the sisterhood, so the title was a moot point, but everything in this abbey was about hiding behind appearances and ceremony. She was another of Laurine's underlings who had snaked her way into the graces of the Hegemony under false pretenses. She was a serpent, yet many of the sisters at the abbey saw her as a motherly figure. Yvette could not fathom why, but perhaps it was because they had never been subject to her more particular 'attentions.'

"I have no idea why Laurine has not done away with that dusty old thing." Rose said as she looked over at the diorama of Dominar and Oskan locked in combat. She reached out and ran her finger along the base of the miniatures as if inspecting it for grime. She shuddered as she brought her hand away.

"I rather like it." Yvette found herself saying, wincing as the words left her mouth. Rose laughed, flicking her fingers to kick off the dust from her inspection.

"There's irony in that. Surely you can see it?" Rose lifted Yvette's chin with a slender finger. The younger sister was forced to stare into those icy blue eyes, repressing a shudder. Yvette did not answer and slowly the small smile slipped from Rose's face.

"You cannot pray your way into grace, little sister." Rose said sweetly. "Your hunger won't allow you to be forgiven. It would take a miracle for such a thing to occur." Rose bent over to place her lips inches from Yvette's ear. Yvette inhaled the smell of flowers as Rose whispered.

"And you know, better than anyone, that the age of miracles has long since passed."

Yvette closed her eyes, trying to drown out Rose's voice and the smell of her hair as it brushed against her cheek. The older sister smiled and straightened to her full height, once again staring down at Yvette with her cold eyes tempered, this time, with a small quirk of a smile at the corner of her mouth.

"What do you want?" Yvette spoke low and bitter. Rose's smile widened ever so slightly and she reached down to take Yvette by the arm, lifting her to her feet.

"I know that you went to Abbess Laurine's quarters again last night." Rose laced her arm through Yvette's and together the two began to stride down the side aisle of the pews toward the doors. Yvette felt her blood begin to cry out in her veins, and she scrambled in her mind to find any excuse she could manage that might save her from this steadily declining situation.

"She visits me from time to time," Yvette stammered. "You know this. I swear she hasn't said anything about you, other than how weary she is and wishes you would stop trying to turn others against her. I swear! She has said nothing more!"

"Calm yourself, little duckling!" Rose stroked Yvette's arm with her fingers, making soothing noises as she did so. "I am not here to chastise. Rather, I am simply checking in on you. I love our talks. They are so vibrant and full of new perspective!" Yvette stiffened as they stopped walking, and Rose placed her hand in the small of her back, pulling her closer so as to again whisper conspiratorially in her ear.

"Also, we found your letter." Rose's words cut through Yvette's stomach like a hot knife, twisting her innards as she spoke. "I am quite interested to learn who this 'Burning Man' is to whom the letters are addressed." Yvette's stomach fell further at the mention of one of her contact's names.

"I don't understand." It was a lie, but would Rose recognize it as such? Her answer came instantly as Rose's face split into a full grin.

"I was hoping you would say that, dear little duckling." She grinned. Rose stepped back and looked into the face of the younger sister. "Please, come with me now." She said, indicating toward the main doors that lead out into the common area of the abbey where the other buildings surrounded a large, grassy hillock. Yvette knew what was coming, it had happened before many times. She had grown used to the pain that was coming; even though she feared it, she realized it was necessary to maintain appearances. She made a token effort of resistance and Rose's hand snaked out and grasped her wrist, squeezing tightly until Yvette called out in pain.

"My dear sister! Please do not struggle. I will take you across the courtyard kicking and screaming if I must. No one will come to your aid, although it may alert Laurine to our arrangement, at which point I would have no further need of you. I have no use for a tool that has lost its ability to function as it should." Rose wrenched on her arm, pulling her close so that their bodies were pressed against one another. Yvette's eyes watered convincingly as she bit her lip to appear as if she wanted to cry out in pain, which part of her did. With her free hand, Rose reached up to stroke the side of Yvette's face.

"Control is such an intoxicating euphoria," she purred, twisting Yvette's arm and causing her to cry out briefly. The sharp agony flooded Yvette's senses and, for a moment, overwhelmed her caution. In that instant, her vision turned red and her face twisted into a vicious snarl. Her head snapped forward with her mouth open, prepared to bite. Her teeth were primed to rip out Rose's jugular. There was a blinding flash of white and a sensation of heat on the side of her face, and the next thing Yvette understood was that she was somehow lying on the ground with the metallic tang of blood in her mouth. She looked up to see a wavering image of Rose standing over her, the same smile still playing across her lips.

"Do not try such a thing again, little duckling, or I'll clip your wings so far back that you will never fly again." Rose leaned over, extending her hand out toward Yvette, who snarled and pushed herself backward. "Don't be foolish, take my hand." Rose's voice was a roll of thunder in the distance, threatening to grow closer if she was not obeyed. Yvette reluctantly seized hold of the older woman's arm and pulled herself back up to her feet. Her cheek ached and the skin stung when she touched it with a shaking hand. What was she thinking? She knew better than to attack Rose openly like that, there was no contest of strength with that woman that she could even remotely hope of winning.

"Let's walk, shall we?" Once again Rose snaked her arm through Yvette's and gently lead her through the door and out into the courtyard. Yvette knew the path well, though she occasionally allowed herself to stumble or whimper as they walked, noting the smile of pleasure her weakness brought to Rose's lips. She kept touching the sensitive skin of her face where Rose's strike had landed, each time wincing as she did so. They walked toward the larger building where Laurine held her court, and also where a good number of their sisterhood were housed. In particular, there was one room, dark, insulated, and painted with the screams of dozens of victims. The dark of that room haunted her memories.

"Now, about this 'Burning Man'," Rose spoke as they entered the shadow of the building. Their footsteps echoed through the stone corridors as they wound their way deeper into the heart of the abbey. Yvette felt that with every step, the shadows seemed to grow longer, her steps heavier. Her breathing became more frenetic, and while she knew that Rose was speaking to her, she pretended to be unable to focus on the words she was saying.

"My goodness, you still aren't listening, are you?" Rose's voice cut through her thoughts as they stopped before a large, oaken door with wrought iron splayed across its face and a heavy lock laid into its handle. "We shall have to work on your personal interactions, won't we? Perhaps I can give you a lesson in etiquette once we are through with our discussion, hmmm?" Rose produced a set of keys and quickly turned the lock. The door opened with an ominous creaking that sent tremors throughout the air. Yvette's mouth grew dry; even though she was prepared for what lay ahead, she did not relish the coming agony. Rose reached out and guided her inside, her feet moving mechanically as her mind grew numb in preparation for the pain.

Inside the room were a variety of strange furniture, including several tables with shackles rigged to their surfaces and rusty iron chairs that had ragged edges designed to bite into the flesh of any forced to sit in them. Beyond that there were several other pieces that, unless one was familiar with their purposes, were unidentifiable. One of the worst was a small, triangular piece that had cuffs built into each side of its peaks. Yvette shuddered as she remembered being bound to it in a way that kept her in a forced bent position over it, unable to rest her body on the peak due to its bladed edge that one could not see unless they closely inspected it. The pain of being left in that position for hours at a time whilst her tormentor took her time slicing her back open with various instruments was something that caused the old scars to twinge uncontrollably.

"You know what comes next." Rose had come up behind her and whispered in her ear. "Please, have a seat!" Yvette felt a delirious and confusing wave of relief as Rose pushed her toward a rough looking chair with straps for her feet and wrists, one of the less exotic instruments in the dungeon.

"Please!" Yvette whispered urgently. "Why do you do this?"

This caused Rose to pause with a simple paring knife in her hand. She cocked her eyebrows as she looked down at Yvette. The cold wind of her smile slowly turning to a neutral line indenting her face.

"You have never asked me that before." The older sister's voice was hushed as she spoke, and she seemed to be staring at something that was far behind where Yvette sat.

"I always assumed it was just part of your nature. But that doesn't satisfy me anymore. Why do you feel the need to hurt?" Yvette tried desperately to keep the worried edge from her voice. The longer she could keep Rose talking, the more likely she could avoid what followed. Rose laughed, but it was a dry sound like that of the wind rushing over a dead riverbed.

"It is not a need born within me, child. It is one that I have had to cultivate within myself. The need is not to hurt others, but to prevent hurt from falling on that which I protect."

"How does hurting me protect anyone?" Yvette hated the whimper that crept into her words. Rose shook her head and brought a finger under Yvette's chin, forcing her to lock eyes with her tormentor.

"The world does not understand monsters like us, little duckling," Rose said, and Yvette was surprised at the emotion that seemed to choke her words. "I have been around much longer than you, and I promise you that the world is cruel to the beautiful things of the dark. That is where your misguided duty causes pain to that which I love. That is why I will not let you endanger that which we have built here, this home we have crafted."

"What does that mean? What have I done?"

"You would bring pain to your sisters here. I must know the damage and to what extent you have wrought upon us here."

"I have no sisters here," Yvette spat. A sudden blur of motion was the only warning she received as Rose struck her across the face, sending flashes of light through her vision.

"I suppose in the traditional sense, you are right. We are not sisters under the false pretenses of the Shining Ones. We do not bow to Basilea anymore, at least not beyond the token superfluous lip service to deter suspicion upon us. But you must recognize family for what it is, little sister. On some levels, I am sorry for the pain you feel, my dear sister, but it is necessary for you to learn." Rose leaned down and wiped the corner of Yvette's mouth with a rag. It came away spotted with red. "The strongest of us all start out as you have. You struggle against the curse, clinging to the remnants of your humanity. Your past life and the promises it held. But that was your fleeting childhood in the youthful blossom of life. But those days are past for you, and for everyone at this abbey. You are the only one that struggles against this truth." Rose straightened and stepped back, sighing as she did.

"It is this reason that I feel that you are special, little duckling. The other sisters resent the time I spend on you. They see your rebellious nature as a waste of my time. But the strongest stock are always the toughest to break. But once they yield, they are always the best, most faithful. I do not enjoy bringing you pain, my child. Well, there is some pleasure in it, but that is not my purpose."

"You are a monster!" Yvette tried to recoil in her chair, but the straps held her firm. Rose shook her head and leaned down again toward her, the older sister's frosty eyes filling her world.

"Of course I am," she sighed, "but mark my words: you may not be able to pinpoint the exact moment, but eventually you will have to become *exactly* as I am in order to survive. You will find that you even enjoy it. Cruelty will become another tool, along with a pretty face, for you to protect that which *you* grow to care about. Even if that is only yourself.

"That was one of the first things that Laurine taught me, long ago when we first met, actually. She had been sent to kill me as I had taken to killing the peasants in the nearby town for sport. She stormed the manor where I had taken up residence with a full regiment of paladins. I was still a fairly newly brought into my curse and was unable to resist its allure, but after dispatching nearly all of the paladins I found myself facing our Mother Abbes alone. Do you know what she told me?"

Yvette struggled to form words as she pushed herself further into the chair, desperately trying to retreat from the beautiful smile before her.

"No," she finally managed to force out of her frozen lips. Rose laughed quietly.

"She told me that she regretted killing something so beautiful as me, but that I was an abomination and could not serve the light, and as such, I deserved only oblivion. She said that there were times that her position required her to be a monster in order to fulfill the will of the Shining Ones. Then she did what I had not expected, she extended her hands and the bodies of her paladins which I had already slain pushed off the ground and came at me again. It was hopeless after that, and I knew it. I pleaded for her mercy even as I ripped her minions apart again and again, each time I threw one down it would struggle back to its feet and rejoin the fight. I said I could help her with her duties, if only she would allow me."

Rose straightened and lifted a hand to her face to suppress laughter.

"Do you know that she asked me to repent? Me?! For being what I am, she asked if I would recant all of my evil actions and serve her as a divine emissary of the Shining Ones? Can you believe that?!" Rose shook herself and pushed the laughter from her eyes.

"Of course I agreed, because survival is always paramount to those like us. Laurine introduced me as a victim she had found at the manor and that I would be joining the sisterhood as her personal assistant. She was respected enough that this was barely questioned, and so I became a subject of the Hegemony. At first I plotted how I might rip her throat out in her sleep and thus win my freedom, but she was too cautious, and so months went by while I plotted against her. Then something miraculous actually did happen.

"I realized that I wasn't afraid of being caught any longer. Laurine showed me how our curse was actually a blessing, and how I could spread that blessing to others and help them. I still took my vengeance out on those that Laurine sent me to hunt, and I relished this. But Laurine created something truly special for me, and then for you and our sisters here. She created a buffer of safety. She saved us from the prying eyes of those who would do us harm."

Yvette gasped as Rose's knife sliced across her upper arm, a stinging pain radiating out from the wound like rusted nails pushing their way through her veins.

"And you would threaten that with your thoughtless machinations!" Rose snarled and dug her nails into Yvette's fresh wound.

Yvette cried out. There was something different about this wound. Normally Yvette could block out the pain of her sessions with Rose to some extent, but this agony grabbed hold of her senses and refused to let go. She heard a scream which she eventually recognized as her own. The fire that flooded her veins forbid her from focusing on anything else.

Time became a relative matter, and she was unsure how much of it had passed before the pain began to dim. She did know that her throat was raw, but the darkened stone had swallowed her cries for mercy and fed her the pitted sounds of her agony back to her. She felt something wet on her back and realized that her shoulders were bare, her habit had been pulled away to reveal the skin underneath. Her arms were likewise stinging and she was able to make out little rivulets of scarlet leaking out from under her forearms. Her head was light and she felt as though she might pass out, but her body had become blessedly numb.

"Oh, my child! What a tangled web of deceit you've drawn." Rose sighed beside her. The older woman walked into Yvette's field of vision which continued to come in and out of focus. Her frazzled brain scrambled through the bits of agony in her memory. What had she said in her delirium? What had she revealed? What lies had she told just to make the pain stop? She grasped upon whatever shred of memory she could hold, biting down the revulsion of the hurt that came with each piece she held.

"I am so sorry, sister." Yvette's voice came out in a croak, her throat torn ragged by her shrieking protests. She felt something cold press itself under her chin, forcing her head upward, the muscles of her back screaming in protest at the movement. She saw that it was the short paring knife that was held in Rose's outstretched hand, red traveled up her hand almost to her elbow, and it took Yvette several moments to realize that it was her own blood which stained Rose's arm. Rose wore a broad smile and reached up with her other hand, surprisingly free from stain, to stroke a stray curl out of Yvette's sweat-stained face.

"Oh dear, sweet, Yvette. What are we going to do with you?" Rose cooed gently as she knelt down in front of her victim. Yvette recoiled, pushing herself into the hard chair in which she sat. Her arms strained against the restraints that held her involuntarily, and as she pulled, she felt something... her left hand moved a little bit more than it should have been able to do. The rough leather pressed painfully against her wrist and the rusty metal buckle bit into her skin, causing her to bite her lip to keep from crying out; and yet as she tugged experimentally, she could feel the aged leather giving way just a little and the cuff began to loosen ever so slightly as the leather began to tear.

A sharp slap forced her face to the side, and for a moment, all she could see was whiteness, all she could hear was ringing in her ears. She once again tasted the salty tang of blood in her mouth, and as her eyes began to come back into focus, she saw Rose standing before her, rubbing her hand.

"You'll not be escaping me that easily, little duckling. No hidden rooms in the back of your mind for you to escape to. Perhaps later," Rose smiled and leaned in close to Yvette's face, who whimpered and pressed herself back once more, "I will let you escape into your imaginary safe place, but not before I have my answers." She brought her hand up and softly traced the contours of Yvette's now swollen cheek. Yvette flinched at the touch. She was tempted to focus on her discovery with the leather cuff, in order to escape the terrible present which bore down on her with Rose's beautiful face and terrible hands. Hands that could cut so deep, and a face that smiled wonderfully while those hands ripped and tore at her victims' flesh. Yvette shook her head to try and clear the cloudy waves of pain and delirium which washed over her like a rising tide. This was not the time to utilize her discovery. She needed a plan before she acted.

"Please, dear sister! I am parched! I cannot speak!" Her voice was a cracked whisper. Rose stared down at her for a moment, as if considering her request, then nodded and walked over to a table where a goblet sat next to a pitcher of iced wine. Beads of perspirations streaked the side of the clay pot and Yvette licked her lips as Rose poured the crimson liquid out into the goblet and took several long swallows from it, sighing with pleasure as she lowered the vessel from her mouth. She then refilled the goblet and walked over to stand beside Yvette, who forced herself to look straight ahead, away from her tormentor. Rose reached up and snaked her fingers through Yvette's hair as if she was playing with it. Yvette tightened her shoulders and closed her eyes.

"I do enjoy our time together, sister." Rose's hand tightened into a fist, clutching strands of Yvette's hair and wrenching backward. The younger sister cried as her head tilted back to slam against the back of the chair, forcing her to look straight up at the ceiling. Rose smiled and tipped the contents of the goblet over Yvette's lips, and she quickly opened her mouth to try and capture as much of the cold liquid as she could to soothe the fire in her throat. The bitter wine stung as she swallowed what she could. The vast majority of the drink weeped out of the corner of her mouth and down her neck to her back.

"Now, dear duckling." Rose spoke as she walked back over to the table and set the goblet back on the table next to the pitcher. "I know of your hatred toward Laurine, and I know of your manipulations of her. I can understand why you feel this way and the treachery you practice, it just…" Rose took a deep breath and sighed contentedly. "It warms my frozen heart. Perhaps that is why I take such pleasure in your company, dear Yvette, because you remind me so much of myself." She turned at this and walked over to sit in a simple, wooden chair close to Yvette's.

"You think I am trying to get rid of Laurine, and you are probably wondering why I care so much about your machinations. Why would I want to hurt you so badly for doing something that you think I would want done in any case?"

"I don't…!" Yvette began, but Rose placed a finger on her lips and shushed her soothingly, shaking her head as she did so.

"There, there." She smiled. "We are past lies, you and I. We have passed through the crucible together. I have seen you at your absolute lowest. I know you better than any parent, for I have walked you through the halls of suffering as no one else could do. Pretense has no place in a sisterly companionship like that which we now share. Do not insult our bond, or me, by thinking that I do not know when you are lying." Rose leaned in close, the icy chill of her breath causing goosebumps to rise on Yvette's neck.

"Do not anger me, child," she whispered. "I am the only friend that you can rely on. I am the only one who knows the full extent of your sins and will not kill you for them alone. But you are on thin ice. To anger me with half truths and naked lies." With that, Rose leaned back and crossed her legs into a comfortable position. "Now then, shall we try again? Do you wonder why I take such an interest in your activities, even though they seem aligned with my own goals?"

"Y…yes, please tell me." Yvette stammered, realizing that her answer and its request were sincere. This revelation caused a dull ache to form in her stomach. How much did the older woman see? Were her lies that transparent to her? Rose smiled one of her small smiles and leaned forward conspiratorially.

"It is because I do not wish Laurine dead, or to be rid of her for that matter." Rose laughed; it was a cold sound devoid of emotion. Yvette frowned at this.

"Then why do you persecute her so much?"

"Laurine is prone to becoming complacent if there are no threats at her proverbial door. Besides, we all have our diversions, and I would grow rather bored here without you and Laurine to torment, each of you in your own special way. No, she is an excellent shield to us here in this remote abbey. She is good at deflecting any interest that is shone toward what we do here. She is far better at that than I. I am more focused on securing our power here and ensuring that our goals are met for those plans which we have in the grander scheme of things. If Laurine were out of the picture, then we would have to deal with more than a few… uncomfortable questions being asked. But her stirling reputation protects us from that. So you see? Why would I want to be rid of her? She is an extremely valuable resource."

With that, Rose stood and walked back over to the pitcher and poured herself another portion of wine. She raised the goblet to her lips and took several long pulls on the dark liquid. Yvette watched her in abject fascination, her terror momentarily forgotten. Rose set the glass on the table and sighed again before turning to address the younger sister.

"Which is why I am so disappointed that you would bring others into our wonderful establishment and risk what we have built here." Rose held up a piece of paper, one bearing a blood red seal of a shark tooth and hasty, if precise, writing scrawled across its length. "This arrived for you the other day, I took the liberty of opening it, but it seems as though you don't trust the author to speak plainly. Based off of our previous… conversations… I know that you have been in contact with individuals who would do our safe haven harm." Rose walked over and opened the letter so that Yvette could see what it said.

"Now," Rose said, "what songs have your little birds sent for you to hear?" Yvette scanned the page quickly, trying desperately to think up something that might placate the vengeful sister standing over her. Magdolon had received her message! He was coming! Rose's cold smile broadened as she watched Yvette's face.

"It will take time for me to decipher it. He is using a difficult code!" Yvette's voice tripped over itself to respond. "Give me a few days and I will be able to give you what you seek."

Rose ripped the letter away from her and cast it to the ground.

"Wrong answer, little duckling." Rose magically produced the paring knife from somewhere and her face fell into its frigid mask. "I warned you not to lie to me again…"

It wasn't long until Yvette's ragged screams once again filled the small chamber.

Eight

A MEETING IN THE WOODS

So this contact of yours, will she know that we are coming?" Ashal asked as she ducked under a low hanging branch.

"I sent a message when we landed ashore, two weeks past." Magdolon stooped under the same branch as he responded. "She will know we are coming and likely meet us before we make it to the abbey or the town below it."

Ashal nodded at this and continued moving forward.

"How do you know that we can trust her?"

"She is another of Laurine's victims." Magdolon grunted. "She has just as much cause to hate her as you do, and if she betrays us, then she will have lost her best chance at revenge."

"That's assuming she really wants vengeance and this isn't just some sneaky ploy."

"I doubt that such is the case. Our meeting was too fateful to be such."

"Almost as if it was orchestrated, even?" Ashal quipped as she stepped around a small sapling that was struggling to stay erect in the shade of the bigger trees around it. She almost tripped over one of its exposed roots which tore itself out of the ground with a wet crunching sound as her foot made contact with it. Ashal grunted and kicked the small tree, causing it to shudder, before moving on. Magdolon stared after her as she walked, stumping through the forest's undergrowth.

"There are times I worry for you," he said, reaching out to touch the leaves of the small tree. They broke away in his hand. "You have such a hard time seeing good in this world." Ashal snorted at this.

"What good, Magdolon? The only good thing that has remained good in my experience has been you. Everything else has always spoiled under prolonged contact with me." Ashal stopped, looking down at the small plants and underbrush that covered the floor of the forest. "Maybe I'm the thing that makes other things spoil. After all, even you leave me from time to time. Maybe I'm the reason things are so bad."

Magdolon came up behind her and placed his big, heavy hands on her shoulders.

"Or maybe it is how you see this world that causes you hurt." His deep voice rumbled as he spoke. "Maybe you have been hurt so much that all you see is the bad. There are many who do this, and it can be easy to give in to that darkness. There is a comfort in despair. In casting off our better parts for bitterness. Be careful that this thing does not happen to you. This is what happened to the woman you seek vengeance against. Bitterness, despair, anger. These things cause pain, and if you hold them tightly enough, then they overflow onto others so that you are a new pain for them. Is this what you want? To cause hurt?"

"You are so confusing, Magdolon. You bring me the tools for vengeance, but you deny me the satisfaction of enacting it!" She turned around to face him. "Do you want me to kill Laurine, or not?" The words fell from her mouth and filled the empty space between them, stretching out so that it seemed to cover the entire forest in a blanket of tense silence.

"I want justice for you," Magdolon said at length. "But justice given in anger is a dangerous thing. You must see this through, I think, but you are the only one who can choose how this will be. If you are not wary, this quest will drag you to the depths, and the Ashal that I love will die as surely as any spear may pierce your heart."

"We have had this conversation before!" Ashal sighed in exasperation, brushing his hands from her shoulders. "You refuse to give me a straight answer, and so I will refuse to continue this talk!" She turned and stomped away from him.

* * * * *

They walked in silence for several hours, the only sound between them was the occasional snapping twig or brush of wind through the tree branches above them. This had become a common pattern in the weeks that they had been traveling since arriving on the northern shore of the border between Golloch's Empire and the Hegemony's outer provinces. A brooding shadow hung over them like a yoke that grew heavier with each passing day. They hardly ever spoke at this point, and what conversations they did have usually devolved into one form of argument or another.

Magdolon tried to take in the beauty of his surroundings. While it was no coral city like those of the Trident Realm, he had grown to enjoy the verdant forests of Mantica. He had learned to enjoy his walks through the trees. The sound of wildlife as it chattered and moved about him in a strange and exotic dance expressed as creatures that sought to survive in the natural chain of predator and prey. This had been one of the reasons he had suggested they make their way cross country toward the abbey. He had thought that the natural splendor and quiet might give them time to talk and reconcile the widening gulf between them. The other reason was the fact that the road that lead to the abbey had a long stretch where there were no turn offs, and a pair of Neriticans walking along its dusty lengths might raise suspicions. They had made good time, almost as good as what they would have made on the road; but even so, the quiet and lack of distraction had only served to drive the wedge more firmly between them, he felt.

He came to an abrupt halt as his senses called out to him in quiet alarm. Part of him had been listening for the pleasant birdsong that had accompanied him throughout the morning. He had no idea what kind of bird it was that made such a sound, but it had been a pleasant distraction to his own frustrations, and he had welcomed it. Now, that sound was gone. A voluminous void filled the space where the noise had occupied, magnified further by the lack of any other sounds in the area. Magdolon had noticed this before when he had traveled to the abbey. The wildlife here were either extremely quiet, or they avoided the area entirely. They must have made very good time if they were already at the edge of the forest that surrounded the abbey with its town.

Moving quietly, Magdolon advanced and tapped on Ashal's shoulder. She spun angrily to stare at him, but he simply held a webbed finger to his beak and motioned for her to listen. She cocked her head and her fins fanned out around her ears to hopefully catch more sounds in the air. They stood in the almost absolute silence until there came a sound, so faint that neither was really sure they heard it. But when they looked at each other and nodded, it confirmed that neither was hearing incorrectly. Someone was crying.

They made their way toward the source of the sound. As they walked, the treeline started to thin and then, in the distance, the blue sky began to peak its way through the branches, tinged orange ever so slightly as the sun had begun its descent toward evening. Eventually, even the mighty oaks of the forest gave way to smaller aspens and less hardy trees. Magdolon could even make out the abbey sitting on its plateau, nestled against the mountains in the distance.

The weeping grew louder as they pushed through the trees, trying to move as silently as possible. They came upon a clearing, and the source of the sound became evident as they saw the bent figure of a woman sitting on the ground facing away from them. Her shoulders shook as she wept into her hands, small gasps escaping here and there as she drew breath before devolving into another round of sobbing. Her clothes were torn and ragged and her skin an alabaster white in the light of the evening sun which was hidden behind a sudden onset of clouds. As soon as he saw the woman, Magdolon rose to his full height and moved toward her.

His eyes widened as he recognized her, his feet moving of their own volition forward. Magdolon heard the sound of branches breaking as Ashal also broke cover, running after her mentor. The woman, shocked out of her tears by Magdolon's exclamation, turned to look at them and then shook her head, recoiling from them with a look of terror on her face.

"No! Don't! Run!" She cried out. Magdolon noticed there were some fresh bandages on her arms, and her face hid more than a few purple bruises beneath her long hair. Ashal pulled up short.

"Magdolon! Stop!" Ashal pulled her spear free from her back and looked around the clearing. Magdolon hesitated at her warning.

"Y! What has happened?" He asked, his hands going to his own spear. The young woman scrambled to her feet as there came the sound of rustling from the brush surrounding the glade. About eight or nine men came into view, their forms were bent and their clothes ragged. All were bald except for a few oily strands of hair that fell from their scalps like cobwebs, and their skin was a pale gray, like that of a long dead corpse. The biggest one smiled at them, displaying broken and rotted teeth that still held chunks of his last meal visibly evident clinging to the shards of teeth. The rest of the poor souls spread out to surround Ashal and Magdolon. The big placoderm's eyes flickered between their ambushers and his contact.

"Still think this wasn't a setup?" Ashal growled at him, taking up a position with her back to his. Magdolon simply grunted, falling into a similar stance. His eyes once more focused on the young woman, who stood with her hands covering her mouth across the way.

"I'm sorry." Her voice was almost a whisper, and Magdolon had to strain to hear her. Then the woman turned and fled back into the trees, heading toward the abbey. The biggest of the wretches that encircled them smiled an even broader smile, then howled into the sky in a disharmonious voice that scratched at Magdolon's ears, causing him to wince. That seemed like a signal to the others as they launched themselves forward, a feral hunger reflecting in their eyes as they scrambled toward them.

The big brute who lead the gang waited at the back of the initial assault, and while Magdolon had killed the first wretch to launch himself at the great reptilian guard, he now found himself ducking under the blows of the leader of the group while two more of his cronies circled around his sides. Thankfully, with Ashal at his back, they could not get a good enough position to flank him entirely, and so he had managed to keep them at bay with a few well placed attacks. But they were getting closer. Magdolon could feel the attack coming, could sense the tension in the air.

As if on cue, the three men lunged forward, starting with the two smaller ones at his sides before the larger one followed up close behind them. Magdolon flung his fist out and connected with the first attacker, he felt the bone in the man's jaw give way under the blow, and the attacker crumpled under his fist to land on the ground. The second attacker was a bit luckier and was able to dodge

Magdolon's hasty spear thrust. Ducking under the blow, the man clawed at him with his dirty nails and managed to score a few superficial cuts on Magdolon's arm. Magdolon swung wide, knocking the foe back, out of immediate reach. He readied for the next attack, searching for the bigger ghoul, but it was too late. He turned just as the lumbering creature came upon him and knocked him onto his back with such force that it winded Magdolon.

Magdolon pulled a knife from his waist, and as the small man leapt at him, he held it against the foe's chest. The feral light began to die in his eyes and the wild man reached out with his filthy hands, pulling himself closer to Magdolon's throat. His mad jowls chomped and saliva flecked over the placoderm's face as Magdolon pressed his head into the dirt to avoid the rotten teeth of his attacker. Warm blood washed over Magdolon from the wound he had inflicted on the man writhing on top of him and quickly the struggling body grew still, the sounds of his teeth clacking together in desperate attempts to latch onto his throat stopped. Magdolon breathed a short sigh of relief.

Magdolon heaved the dead body from on top of him and rolled to his feet. The brute of the group threw a clawed hand at his exposed side. Magdolon dropped his shoulder down and the blow hit against the scales there, causing the man to recoil, clutching his fist. Magdolon smiled and grabbed his spear, thrusting upward in a vicious strike that impaled the larger man through his stomach. His opponent reached down and grabbed the shaft of the spear; with a smile, he viciously snapped the wooden haft. Magdolon stepped back in surprise, clutching the broken portion of his now useless weapon. He glanced over to see how Ashal was fairing.

He watched as she spun about trying to fend off the crouched form of her attackers on either side. They locked eyes and Magdolon shook his head, he couldn't come to her aid right away. It was obvious that Ashal's arms were beginning to tire as she constantly swung her spear from side to side. Each spin was slower than the last, and every time she turned, her opponents scurried closer. She couldn't keep this up for much longer.

"Magdolon," she cried out to her mentor, "we need to go!"

The large placoderm nodded at her words before ducking under a blow from the large man before him. The brute howled in the air, and as he did so, Magdolon sensed other shapes rustling in the forest as more of the strange wild men emerged from the underbrush and began making their way toward them.

"We need to run! There's too many! We're going to be overrun!" Ashal's voice rose in pitch when she saw the newcomers to the fray. Magdolon grunted in agreement.

"On my signal, run toward the abbey. If we can get to the town, we may be able to lose them in the streets and alleys. Laurine might know that we're here, but at least we'll avoid capture this way." The placoderm reached into a pouch at his belt and removed a small, round capsule. He danced out of range of his opponent's arms and hurled the sphere at the ground just in front of the brute's surprised face.

"Now!" he shouted. The capsule ignited with a sound of thunder and everyone besides Magdolon fell to the ground in surprise as a thick cloud of black smoke filled the air. He ran over to Ashal's prone form and wrenched her to her feet. "Move!" he bellowed, and together the pair sprinted out of the clearing and back into the forest, headed toward the abbey in the distance.

"What was that?!" Ashal gasped as they ran.

"A smattering of black powder with a touch of firestone and a bit of steel shavings," Magdolon replied, his voice even and calm as he ran. "A small thing I picked up from some dwarven scouts, it will not hurt anyone but sometimes it makes for a good distraction."

"What were those things?" Ashal's breathing was even, but Magdolon could hear the ragged edge that burned on the tips of her words.

"I do not know," he said, "but I fear they are a warning of what is to come. Save your breath, now, we have a long ways to run, yet."

With that, the two warriors ducked into the shadows of the trees as the sounds of their pursuers drew closer and closer behind them.

Nine

A Deathly Quiet

A shal stared out at the city gate that stood open before them. One of the
gate doors hung askance from a massive broken hinge that caused it to lean
away from the wall at a precarious angle. The first rays of a morning sun were
just peeking over the horizon, tinging the world in the twilight blue of change
between night and day.

They had evaded their pursuers quite easily. While the crazed maniacs
were faster than her and Magdolon, they were not as experienced foresters as
the pair were. Their attackers had plowed through the undergrowth with such
a ferocity that Ashal and Magdolon had no problems knowing where they were
and were able to slip into smaller thickets or climb trees in order to avoid being
seen. Eventually the sounds of pursuit began to fade as either they got too far
ahead or gave up on their chase. Either way, Ashal and Magdolon had made
their way toward the abbey unmolested, despite the journey having taken the
majority of the night since they had to move so slowly in case any other pursuers
happened upon them.

Now they stood before the open and somewhat dilapidated entrance to
the town where their enemy sat, waiting for them. The attack from the previous
day proved that Laurine was aware of their approach and was expecting them,
and this changed everything.

"What should we do?" Ashal asked, her voice still a whisper in the calm
quiet of the sunrise. Magdolon shook his head in response.

"I do not like this," he said slowly. "If she knows that we are coming,
she will be ready. I do not think it is wise that we continue with our original plan.
Maybe we should wait for a week or two in order to throw her off our scent."

"Are you sure that you don't want to scout the town and such before we
tuck tail and run?" Ashal snorted impatiently. "The element of surprise is lost,
what will giving her a few weeks to wait do for us?"

"For one, it may convince her that we have abandoned our attempts on
her life. I will cut off communications with Y, and if we have any luck, she will
believe that we are dead in the wilderness. At the very least it will give us time to

consider a new strategy." He turned toward her, his large eyes searching her face. "Patience is our best choice at this point."

"I have been patient these past ten years!" Ashal snapped. "Now that our goal is within sight, you would have me wait even longer?" Ashal stood and made her way toward the gate. She felt Magdolon's hand grab hold of her arm as she walked away, and she spun around to glare at him.

"I am not going to the abbey up above," she growled. Her eyes met his and read the pleading in them. Slowly, her features softened and she sighed. "I'm sorry, Magdolon. I know what you suggest makes sense. But I can't come this close and then turn away. Even if it is the smart thing to do. I can't come close to my goal only to be told that I need to wait even longer. My mother's murderer is in that keep at the top of this plateau! I know this for a fact, and I know what I want to do to her! I want to rip her heart out of her chest and watch her eyes as it slowly stops beating! I want to burn her alive and dance to the tune of her screams as they slowly fade away. I want her to suffer as she watches everything she has built come crashing down while my spear rips through her body!" Her eyes shone with a mad light as she spoke, and Magdolon reached out to place a webbed hand on her shoulder. She sagged under the weight, and tears welled up in her eyes, cascading down her cheeks. Magdolon pulled her close to him. She protested weakly but allowed herself to be gathered in and pressed against his massive chest.

"I know, *Lueshwy'n*, I know that you desire this. I desire this as well. But we must be careful or else it is her that will dance to the tune of our screams, and then your mother's vengeance will forever remain incomplete." He stroked a finger across her cheek, and she took a shuddering sob into her body, her lungs crying out for air as she pushed the tears back down into the black parts of her chest. The feelings would not release their grip on her so easily, however, and she looked imploringly up at her placoderm defender, eyes wide and filled with salty tears that spilled down her face. The older Neritican smiled sadly and lowered his face so that their foreheads touched. Under this onslaught of emotion, Ashal felt the crumbling debate in his voice when he spoke.

"Let us go into the town, then, and see what we can see. Let Laurine see that we are not afraid and that her thugs can not force us to run." Ashal's face split into a smile that was tainted only slightly by the falling tears that clung to her lips.

"If we do this thing," he said, standing back up to his full height, "we do it wisely. We go quiet and do not bring attention to ourselves."

"But how will Laurine know that we were here unless we call attention to ourselves?" Ashal asked, her voice still somewhat shaky.

"I do not think that this will be a problem. She will know." Magdolon glanced up at the abbey walls high above them. "She has made herself into a queen. She seeks power, and power sees everything it can."

He returned his gaze down to Ashal.

"I…" he began, but his voice caught in his throat. "I fear what is to come. There is some dread that fills me at the prospect of what we face."

"I have never known you to be afraid." Ashal smiled, but there was worry in her eyes as she spoke.

"I do not feel fear for our enemies that we must face. I am afraid of how this thing will change you. I know that this is not a fair thing, but it has given me pause in the past weeks as I have thought of you going through with this. Such a thing is not fair, and I am sorry for this." Magdolon sighed. Ashal smiled sadly at him.

"It is unavoidable that I will change, dear Magdolon, but I will never leave you behind!" she stared up at Magdolon, a sharpness in her gaze that mirrored that in her voice. The big placoderm simply shook his head.

"We will see, *Lueshwy'n*."

They did not speak further and instead made their way toward the town, passing through the aging archways and into the village proper. The buildings were constructed from a crumbling type of mud plaster splashed with a fading coat of whitewash and thatched roofs that looked as if they were ready to collapse under their own weight, bowing down in the middle. The buildings were tightly packed together, so close that many shared roof awnings, and lacked doors that instead stood open to reveal all inside to the world.

They passed a gaunt beggar who sat with glazed over eyes and pale, gray skin as they walked through a side street. The man reached out to them with grasping hands, his lips moving as he stretched his arms toward them, but a dry whisper was all that escaped as he muttered something unintelligible at them. They hurried on.

"That man looked as if he were half-dead!" Ashal whispered as they dodged around the beggar's clenching hands. She glanced back as they neared the end of the street and saw the mewling wretch was trying to crawl toward them! She shuddered as they rounded the corner, leaving the stranger behind them as his dry whispers grew into a ragged moan that followed them for some time before being lost in the twisting streets and alleys.

After a few more turns, they stumbled into what looked like the village center. A few faded and torn sunshades sat propped over dusty tables which were scattered around a square that was formed by the husks of buildings on all sides and was large enough that the sun's weak morning light was able to touch the cobblestones in some spots. On each of the merchant tables was scattered an assortment of objects in various states of disrepair and decay. In nearly every stall sat a hunched figure covered in rags with tattered cowls pulled down to cover their features. The entire place was deathly quiet with the exception of the distant moaning of the beggar which Ashal could still hear faintly in the distance.

The hooded figures all turned to stare at Ashal and Magdolon as they drew near, their silent heads turning in unison to fixate on them as they approached a row of stalls. There were no other sounds besides the two Neriticans stepping across the dusty cobbles and the slight whistle of a sharp breeze that had begun to blow as the sun had risen above the edges of the buildings. There was no chatter or bartering in this marketplace, no shouting or even the sounds of people milling around merchants and their wares. Even the whistling wind seemed to be an unwelcome intruder on the chilly silence.

Ashal stopped at a vendor's table and picked up a strange, rusted piece of metal which sat there. It looked to be some kind of child's toy, a fabrication made up to look like a bird of some sort. Rust caked it on all sides, and even as she picked it up, a portion of its left wing crumbled and fell onto the stones at her feet.

"I'm so sorry!" Ashal exclaimed as she put the broken toy back on the table. "I will pay for that! I promise! How much do I owe you?" She turned to look at the vendor, her hand going to one of her pouches where she kept some of the few coins she had saved. The stall owner stared out from beneath a shaded cowl for a few moments before muttering something in the same kind of dry whisper that the beggar had used earlier. Ashal's stomach clenched as the vendor struggled to its feet to stand unsteadily before lurching toward her. Ashal took a step backward as the figure drew closer and her hand went to the spear on her back, but as she moved to grasp the haft of her weapon, a shriveled hand leapt out from the tattered folds of the vendor's cloak and grabbed hold of her forearm.

Ashal cried out and pulled her arm free of the figure's grasp, and the vendor staggered forward, toppling the table with its dubious wares onto the ground. The shrouded figure tripped over the prone table and fell onto the ground, a raspy moan rising up from beneath the shadows of its cowl.

"Ashal!" Magdolon called out, and her head snapped up from the wretched sight of the figure pulling itself across the flagstones at her feet. She gasped as she realized that several other cloaked figures were now standing around them. Each of them shuffling forward slowly with raspy whispers emanating from under their hoods.

Ashal took a quick step back and her spear leapt into her hands. The hooded figures pressed in closer and the dry, rasping whispers grew to a chorus of moans which cascaded upward into the still morning air. Ashal felt a dry, withered hand wrap itself around her ankle and she looked down to see the fallen vendor grasping her foot. She kicked out and connected with the head of her assailant which snapped back and caused the hood to fall away, revealing a face that was covered with dried and cracked skin with milky blue eyes that stared at nothing.

"More are coming!" Magdolon's voice showed only the barest hints of the panic that was starting to claw at the edges of Ashal's mental state. She wrenched her foot free and glanced at the various streets that lead into the square where they stood. Other shuffling figures had appeared. The shadows of the early morning light still hid their features as they staggered forward, but Ashal could tell that they were all the same skinny, shriveled creatures that raised their hands toward them hungrily.

"What is wrong with these people?" Ashal cried out.

"I do not know," Magdolon responded, his own spear out and in his hands. "I will say that I believe Laurine is behind whatever it is, though."

Ashal nodded, looking into the hood of the closest figure.

"I'm sorry, then, for what I must do."

She reversed her grip on the spear and stabbed the butt of her weapon into the face of the closest creature. The bone shaft cracked against her attacker's skull and the figure staggered backward. Ashal was already turning to stab at the next one when she realized that the first foe was not toppling to the ground. Another dry moan escaped the thing's lips before it once again began staggering forward. The blow she had delivered would have knocked an orc to its knees! Yet this creature was only momentarily stunned! A chill rippled through Ashal's body.

"What do we do, Magdolon?"

"I am thinking." Magdolon's head whipped around the square desperately. Ashal also scanned the growing threat as more and more abominations filled the common area with their grasping limbs, each one looking as aged and decrepit as the village in which they stood. Fighting wasn't an option. Even though these things didn't show an aptitude for combat, their numbers would quickly overwhelm them. Running was their best chance. But where? Behind them already held more villagers than in front, and neither direction was overly promising.

"Follow me!" Magdolon barked and took off running to where the crowd of hooded figures seemed to be thinnest. Ashal turned and followed, swinging her spear in wide arcs to try and ward off their pursuers. Magdolon lowered his massive shoulder and used his bulk to plow into the first of the moaning wretches in their way. The first of them went flying as the placoderm made contact, the creature's body crumbling to dusty debris as the placoderm's armored shoulder slammed into its dried sternum. Ashal heard a rotten crunch as he pushed forward, ramming into another attacker and pushing several more back.

Ashal followed in the wake of his passing, her spear flashing out to push any stubborn pursuers further back. Together they punctured through the ring of cloaked figures and instantly began running. Magdolon made for a small side street which was darkened by the early morning shadows. Behind them, the villagers raised a cry that sounded like the din of a wounded animal multiplied by several dozen dry throats rasping through the chill air. Ashal shivered as she ran, the haunting sound ran up her spine and caused her to continually glance over her shoulder. The figures were pursuing them at a very slow pace, and by the time they rounded a bend in the small street, Ashal lost sight of them. The dry moaning hounded their steps, however.

So focused on what was behind them, Ashal did not see that Magdolon had stopped in front of her, and she ran full speed into his back. The larger placoderm grunted but did not move as she pitched backward onto the worn stone. Ashal was about to question why he had stopped when she spotted what lay past him. More of the shrouded creatures were shuffling up the street toward them, their arms outstretched and a whispering moan already beginning to force its way from beneath their darkened hoods.

Scrambling to her feet, Ashal cast another quick glance behind them and felt a chill clutch the blood in her veins. The vendors from the square were already behind them and quickly closing the distance on them. Her head whipped back and forth as she looked from one of the hordes to the other.

"Magdolon!" she cried out. The placoderm gripped his spear tightly and stepped into a defensive stance. The sounds of the moaning were reaching a deafening level at this point.

"Prepare yourself, *Lueshwy'n*." He glanced over his shoulder at her and gave a small smile that was not reflected in his flat gaze. "I am sorry I could not protect you. Also that together we could not avenge your family."

Ashal reeled from this response. *No, no, no! This is not how this is supposed to go!* Her eyes frantically searched their surroundings for some form of escape. The street which they had run down was really more of an alleyway, there were no doors on either side of them, the only entrances to the buildings that flanked them were already behind the line of shambling bodies. She was about to suggest that they try to charge through one side of their opponents and force their way to one of those doors, when a sudden flash of red light caused her to flinch.

Shaking her head, she looked up at the source of the light and saw a window a few feet directly above them. The red light was the morning sun finally peaking its way through the dark streets of the village and reflecting off one of the glass panes. A spark of fire ignited in her chest.

"Magdolon!" She shook his shoulder and pointed upward. He turned and followed her gaze. Seeing the window, he quickly fell to one knee and cupped his hands before him. The shambling figures were getting close now. In the light of the rising sun, Ashal could make out some of their withered features twisted into howls beneath the shadow of their hoods. She quickly stepped into Magdolon's hands and the powerful warrior shoved her up. Using the tip of her spear, she easily broke through the aged glass, shattered pieces flying all about her in a shower of glittering red as it reflected the morning sun like sparks falling from a smithy's hammer.

She threw herself forward and grasped the edge of the windowsill, grimacing as some remnants of the window pane bit into her hands. Ignoring the pain, she quickly pulled herself up and toppled into the room beyond, landing rather ungracefully in a heap on the ground. She struggled to her feet and took stock of her surroundings. An ancient bed sat in the middle of the room with an equally aged blanket covered in dust sitting rumpled over the straw sack that served as a mattress. Ashal whispered a quiet mantra as she gathered up the blanket and threw one side out to Magdolon.

The large placoderm had turned his attention back to their attackers, some of which had already staggered forward into range of his spear. He stabbed outward, impaling one of them through the head. The figure dropped, and he brought his weapon back for another stab. As he did so, one of the figures clawed at him from behind, raking a withered claw across the defender's exposed arm. Magdolon winced and flung out a clenched fist that connected with a sickening crunch beneath the folds of the creature's cowl, causing it to crumple to the ground.

"Magdolon! Catch!" Ashal lowered the dusty blanket down so that he could grasp the end. Quickly placing his weapon in the sling on his back, Magdolon kicked out with his feet as he pulled himself upward with his powerful arms. The blanket immediately made a ripping sound, and Ashal cried out as it began to give way. But the window was not that far off the ground, and Magdolon had only needed a little bit of leverage. Before the blanket could tear completely away, he lunged forward and caught hold of the edge of the window, wincing as the shards of glass there also bit into his hands.

The cloaked figures milled around below them with their heads cast upward, the motion had caused some of the hoods to fall away to reveal horrific faces that snarled and moaned as they reached hungrily upward. Dried skin stretched and cracked across rotten teeth and yellowed skulls. Sunken eyes stared blankly upward and broken fingernails scratched and groped for Magdolon's feet as he pulled himself up and into the room with Ashal.

"What are those things?!" Ashal exclaimed as she helped Magdolon stand, still staring down into the milling swarm below them.

"I feared for this place, that such a thing would happen when Laurine came here." Magdolon grunted, trying to catch his breath. "They have been turned into husks, just bodies with no life in them but the desire to feed and maim. They are mere puppets on the end of Laurine's strings. She has grown stronger in her necromancy to have such power to control an entire village worth of corpses."

"How is she able to get away with this? Why hasn't the Hegemony sent armies to burn this abomination to the ground?"

"I do not know." Magdolon shook his head. "Perhaps it is because no one ever comes here and she is able to keep it a secret. Perhaps the Hegemony does not like to look in its darker places and would rather the infection fester than take the effort to cleanse it."

"I have a hard time believing that they would be willing to ignore something like this."

"It is amazing what we can ignore if it means we are not forced to change ourselves. The level of sins we are willing to allow increases with the magnitude of what would be required of us to hold them accountable."

"That is terrible!" Ashal turned from the window and stared at Magdolon.

"It is, and perhaps this is what separates a hero from someone who simply accomplishes great things. One can do great things and still be comfortable with evil things. A true hero cannot see injustice and allow it to be out of a sense of convenience or justification." Magdolon stepped forward to stand beside the window and looked down at the scrabbling, moaning group of undead below them. "What Laurine has done with her life has made her a minor hero in the Hegemony. She has brought safety to many villages and destroyed many enemies of Basilea in her deeds. But she has taken shortcuts. She has allowed evil to enter into her life, and she has embraced it and given it purpose in her own desires. To us, she is a villain. But there are many children and villages who are waking to this rising sun who would not have without Laurine's intervention, maybe not in this village, but in others. In their eyes, she is a hero. But which of us is right?"

"How can you ask that? Our own wrongs against her aside, what she's done to these villagers is horrific! She cannot hide her sins in a guise of holiness by simply holding up a few examples of convenient righteousness!" Ashal's didn't realize that she was shouting until she stopped to draw breath. Magdolon smiled, but it was a small smile devoid of mirth.

"I agree. Such fake righteousness is worse than outright villainy. It is so easy to call this out in others, and so easy to ignore it when we are the ones justifying." Magdolon turned and placed a hand on Ashal's shoulder. "Be sure that you apply the same strong standard to your own life that you are requiring of your enemies."

With that, Magdolon turned and walked over to another side of the room. Ashal stood, staring down at the evidence of Laurine's sins. Her own thoughts a hot coil in her stomach that kept expanding.

Ten

WITHERED MEMORIES

The morning passed along quietly as Ashal and Magdolon hid in the shadows of the rundown building. A thick layer of dust sat on everything within reach, and they both learned very quickly to sit as still as possible or else the ensuing cloud from even the slightest of movements caused a fit of coughing from the offender.

Ashal watched the shadows lengthen as she sat on the floor, dozing in and out of wakefulness. The sounds of shuffling and the occasional moan from the street below reminded them that the swarm of undead were still waiting for them. At a little past midday, she realized that trying to sleep was futile and so rose up to try and explore the small building that was their temporary prison. Moving carefully in a mostly unsuccessful attempt to not to stir up dust and cause herself another coughing fit, she stalked quietly into one of the back rooms. Here she found the dry remains of another tattered straw mattress and a desiccated wooden bed frame, both of which had been devoured by various rodents and insects and had been long out of use.

In the corner of the room sat a crumbling wooden chair, and on its seat lay a small leather-bound book. Curious, Ashal picked it up and thumbed through its pages. It was a business ledger, small enough to fit easily into a satchel, and with numbers and lines scribbled furiously throughout its margins, tallying profits and losses. Ashal sighed and was about to put the book back when something fell out from its center and landed with a dry rustle on the ground. Looking down, Ashal discovered that it was a wildflower, something that she had learned was called by several names but most prominently was referred to as an Autumnal Paintbrush. It received the name because the petals were a vibrant orange with streaks of brown cascading outward so that it looked like the many leaves which fell from the trees as the onset of winter approached. She reached down to pick it up and noticed that a small note had been folded, and the long time of being pressed together in the pages of the ledger had caused the paper and the dried flower to stick together. She carefully unfolded the letter and read the writing within.

> *My dearest Kalessa,*
> *I am longing for the days when I see you again. Until then, remember our harvest days and the promises of future kisses.*
> *Forever Yours,*
> *Griegos*

Ashal felt something catch in the back of her throat as she read and then reread the note. The ink was somewhat faded, suggesting that it was much older than even the ledger from which it had fallen. Who were these unfortunate people? They were obviously in love, but had they had the opportunity to wed? Was theirs a doomed romance? Had they escaped this cursed place, or were they another of its victims?

A sudden creaking of the floorboards behind her caused Ashal to spin around, her hand instantly moving to grasp the haft of her spear on her back. Magdolon stood before her with a rather sheepish look on his face, and Ashal breathed out a sigh of relief, her hand falling back to her side, only to rise again to stifle a small coughing fit.

"I apologize," Magdolon said. "I merely wanted to check in and see what you had found."

"Love letters, apparently." Ashal shook her head, smiling, and handed over the now crumpled note and the dried flower attached to it. Magdolon took them and read the note, his eyes taking on a melancholy light as he did so.

"This is a sad thing," he said at length. "I wonder what happened to them?"

"Me, too. I hope they got out, for all the good hoping does. It seemed like they were in love, so they had something that not many others have enjoyed."

"Oh, now." Magdolon's smile turned mischievous. "You were once quite smitten as I recall."

"What?" Ashal balked.

"Back before, when we lived in the Coral Cities. I remember you chasing after a certain young spawnling a little older than yourself. What was her name... Ah! Chrossum! Yes! That was her name!" Magdolon chuckled and Ashal felt the red deepen in her fins surrounding her face. "Yes, I remember, she was the spawn of Captain Chro'ean, your mother's personal guard. I distinctly recall one afternoon where she fled down the halls of the palace, screaming that she did not want your kisses. And you chased after her with arms outstretched." Magdolon's chuckle turned to a full belly laugh at this which he tried unsuccessfully to still, and Ashal found herself unable to resist his good spirits, either.

"We were merely spawnlings!" she snapped playfully, though her smile betrayed her as she did so. "I wanted to play at court, and she refused to be the dutiful confidant that stood by my side!" Picturing it now in her mind's eye brought with it a flood of other similar memories, and before long, Ashal and Magdolon were covering their mouths to hide their laughter as they traded stories of home back and forth.

Ashal sat down on the floor as she fought back tears of mirth while Magdolon recounted one of her favorite stories of when he had accompanied her mother on a diplomatic mission to a small human kingdom on the coast of their realm. The human representative had tried to greet the Neriticans in their native tongue but had butchered the pronunciation, and instead of stressing the third syllable in the word *cuer'yal* which was the Neritican form of address equivalent to 'Your Honor' in the human language, he had stressed the first syllable, and swapped the l sound at the end for a j, so that it was pronounced much like the human word 'courage.' However, this made it sound like the title given to a prized beast of burden in the Trident Realm. Without breaking stride, her mother had fired back by calling the representative a 'kind ass' and thanking him for his attempt to speak their language but asked that he refrained from doing so in future interactions.

Ashal leaned back, putting out her hand to catch herself from falling all the way to the ground while she choked on a laughing fit that threatened to draw attention to their location. As she did so, she heard a crackling sound and looked over to see the crushed remains of the dried flower from the ledger, its orange petals turned to powder under the grinding weight of her palm. Instantly the mirth died in her throat, and she found herself staring blankly at the remains of the dried plant.

"Ah, *Luesh'wyn*," Magdolon spoke while he rubbed his eyes, sensing the change in her mood. "I hope I will see the day when you are given back your crown of pearls and your place in the courts below."

"Could that ever happen?" Ashal whispered, her eyes still on the ruined flower. "Could we ever really go back home?" Would I even want to at this point? She added to herself. After all, she had lived longer out of the depths than she had while growing up in the courts of the Trident Kings. Would she even enjoy it, now? Was it really her home?

"First, let us deal with Laurine. Then we will see what can be done about going home."

"Do you still miss it? The Depths? The cities beneath the waves?" Ashal whispered, finally turning her gaze back to him as she brushed the crumbled remains of the flower from her hands. Magdolon hesitated before he responded, regarding her eyes for several minutes before speaking.

"I do. It is my home. It is a place where my family has lived and grown. It is where I wish to die and be given to the Dark Currents. I wish desperately to return to my home."

"That is the most I have heard you speak of your family." Ashal's voice was soft, distant. "Did you have a mate? Are there spawns of Magdolon swimming through the ocean?" She regretted these questions immediately as she watched Magdolon's smile fall, and he shifted to look back out into the room where they had crashed through the window. She had tried asking these questions before, and each time they had brought this same kind of response. There was another long pause before he spoke.

"The only family I have now is you. The only family that yet lives is in this room." Before Ashal could say anything else, Magdolon turned and walked quickly out of the room, leaving her to look after him and to wait in silence once more.

Finally, when evening was starting to spread its dusky light across the streets, the moaning of the undead quieted. Magdolon crossed the room and peered out of the broken window through which they had entered. He motioned to Ashal, and she moved to join him beside the jagged shards of glass. She saw none of the huddled and cloaked figures pawing at the sides of the small street below them. He turned and motioned to Ashal, and together they descended to the door that led back out into the night. They had learned that noise attracted the monsters, and so they moved with practiced stealth through the darkening light of the evening.

Open flames atop lamp posts lit the gloom and cast an orange hue across the stones of the streets. Ashal wondered who it was that would have lit them, adding to the curious horror building within her chest. Magdolon held up a hand and pressed her into the wall behind him, his head looking down a small alleyway where Ashal could hear the sounds of someone shuffling and groaning slightly. The sounds diminished as it seemed as though the creature was moving away from them, and after a few minutes, Magdolon released her and they moved forward again.

Ashal also noticed that lights were appearing in some of the windows which they passed, not all, but about every third house seemed to be illuminated by what appeared to be gentle blue candlelight that was barely noticeable. She tapped Magdolon's shoulder and motioned to one of these windows and also to the torchlights atop the lamp poles. Magdolon nodded, acknowledging that he had seen them, but he shrugged as well. He quickly signed to her.

I. Don't. Know. He motioned around them. *Keep. Your. Wits. About. You.* His hands flashed before he turned and once again began moving through the darkened streets. As they rounded a corner, Ashal nearly slammed into Magdolon's back. The placoderm had his hand raised to signal her to stillness, and as she glanced past his hulking form, she saw the reason why. Several robed figures lay sprawled out in the small street before them, the closest of which was already beginning to stir, a whispering moan escaping into the night air as it struggled to stand.

Magdolon and Ashal turned in unison and ran back down the street which they had just exited, searching desperately for a place to hide. A stronger groan came from the creatures behind them. Ashal quickly spotted a door on a smaller building that looked like it had been someone's home at one time. She motioned to Magdolon and they hurried over to it, but when she tried to open it, the door refused to budge. She pushed on it, throwing her shoulder against the dried wood, but it didn't move. Magdolon motioned her out of the way and threw a vicious kick against the door, which cracked under the weight of the blow. The low moan of the undead was growing louder, the ones they had stumbled upon seemed to be calling out to the other zombies. As if in response, there was another series of low moans from the other side of the street. The wood cracked wider, this time exposing the interior of the house and creating a hole wide enough that Ashal's arm could fit through.

Ashal quickly reached through and felt for the the lock on the opposite side. Her fingers grasped what felt like a wooden bar that braced the other side. She fumbled to find a less awkward position as she pushed upward to try and dislodge the beam, but Magdolon's kicks had fractured it at an angle which made it difficult to move. After a few moments, and with the sounds of the undead drawing closer, Ashal gave a small cry of triumph as the wooden brace fell to the floor and the door swung inward. The pair quickly ducked inside and closed the door behind them, replacing the brace in its holds that were mounted to the frame surrounding the entrance and grabbing what looked like a mostly empty bookshelf to slide in front of it.

The sounds of the moaning grew louder as the creatures approached their hiding place, but as they drew level with the door so that the noise of their passing had reached a nearly deafening level, the creatures stopped. Ashal braced herself against the bookshelf, waiting for the inevitable sounds of the creatures to begin pounding against the entrance. But it never came. Ashal waited, holding her breath for several long minutes, until finally she realized that the moaning had ceased. The night was still and not even the rustling noises could be heard from the outside. Pulling the bookshelf to the side of the door. Magdolon watched as Ashal peered out into the darkened street through the hole they had made to get inside.

"They're gone?!" Ashal's voice could not hide the question in her voice.

"What do you mean, they are gone?" Magdolon said, kneeling down beside her and glancing through the hole as well. Ashal stood up nervously and took a step backward to give him the room he needed. She glanced around the room where they had entered. A chill traveled up her spine as she turned to a table beside a large window that looked out into the inexplicably empty street. On the table sat a single, black candle with a blue flame glowing at the end of its long wick. The light it emitted was cold and no shadows formed from its flickering tendrils. Instead, the darkness seemed to deepen the closer one looked at it. It caused the glass of the window to glow with the eerie light they had seen in various buildings they had passed in the streets. Ashal had not realized they had been trying to get into one such building as this.

111

There came a small cough from behind her, and Ashal cried out as she turned to face it. She gasped as she beheld a little girl who could not have been more than five or six summers old. She looked up at her from a sunken set of eyes that looked almost silver in the flickering blue light, her whole face and body seemed skeletal, and a bandage was wound around her left hand which clutched a dirty sackcloth doll with only one eye. The little girl looked up at Ashal and held a finger to her lips.

"Daddy says you mustn't make so much noise or the monsters will come again!" she whispered.

Eleven

A LEGACY OF CRUELTY

Ashal gasped in surprise and Magdolon turned to see what she had discovered. The small child stared up at them with large, imploring eyes. Wisps of greasy brown hair poked out from a hastily gathered bun on the back of her head, and she was clothed in a dirty, cornflower blue dress that exposed shoeless feet sticking out from under its hem.

"Where did you come from, little one?" Magdolon spoke in a low rumble. The child turned her gaze on him and swayed back and forth with a small smile playing across her lips as her tattered dress swayed back and forth around her. She brought her doll up to hug it against her chest.

"This is my home, silly!" She gave a quick glance behind her. "Daddy is asleep right now, but we don't get many visitors here. My name is Sasha!" She held out a dirty little hand toward the giant placoderm, who smiled and took it. Sasha giggled as she watched her hand disappear into his, and then she turned to Ashal and extended a hand toward her as well. Ashal hesitated a moment then reached out to take the child's extended palm.

"My daddy says the monsters won't hurt us in here, so long as we're quiet, but you guys were pretty loud." Sasha brought one of her dirty fingers up and stuck it in her mouth as she spoke, she danced from one foot to the other causing her ragged skirt to sway back and forth with her movements and rested her head on the tattered twine that made up the doll's hair which she held. She glanced behind the two Neriticans and shrugged. "But it looks like they left anyways. Lucky!"

"Aren't you scared of us?" Ashal asked. The little girl shook her head and smiled.

"Daddy says the monsters protect us from the bad people, and you are much prettier than the monsters, and they left you alone, so you must be okay!" Her mouth split wider into a big grin before her fingers quickly found their way back to it. Ashal felt her fins redden at the earnest compliment.

"Where is your father, Sasha?" Magdolon knelt down so that he could be level with the child. The little girl pulled her fingers out of her mouth and pointed behind her into the back rooms of the building.

"I already told you, he's asleep. He's always really tired when he gets home from the fields." Her hand went back into her mouth.

"Your father is a farmer?" Ashal couldn't hide the surprise in her voice. Sasha nodded her head vigorously.

"Uh-huh. It always makes him really tired. And dirty. But I don't mind. He leaves me here to tend Mommy and Baby Jackson."

"How old are you, little one?" Magdolon spoke softly, a smile hiding in his eyes. Sasha didn't respond verbally, but instead held up two hands, one splayed open with all fingers and another with just the thumb sticking out.

"Six?!" Magdolon exclaimed. "And already caring for your mother and baby brother? You must be very smart for this." Sasha grinned and nodded.

"Sasha?" A gravelly, tired voice came from the back room, followed by the sound of footsteps. "Who are you talking to?" A man with a disheveled mop of brown hair and a scraggly beard stumbled through the doorway and blinked blearily at the unexpected guests he found before him.

"Who..." he stuttered. "Who are...?"

Ashal stepped forward quickly, raising her hands in a disarming way, and speaking quickly.

"We are simply travelers who stumbled upon your village. We were attacked by these creatures that are roaming your streets and stumbled into your home in order to find refuge." The man blinked suspiciously, pulling Sasha behind him.

"We are in the absolute end of nowhere. Nobody just stumbles on our village. And the guardians only attack those who don't know our ways. Who and what are you?" The man edged backward even further, pushing his daughter back as he went.

"We mean you no harm." Ashal took a step backward. "We only wish to spend the night, if that is okay with you. In the morning we will depart, but you cannot ask us to face those creatures in the dark. Doing so would be consigning us to our deaths." Ashal brought a hand in front of her. "My name is Ashal, and this is Magdolon. We are from..." She paused for only a moment as the weight of this statement settled on her shoulders. "We are from the Trident Realm. We are simple travelers who have been sent to study the lands around the coasts of the seas which are in our domain." The man did not seem to relax and instead shifted his gaze to Magdolon.

"Why do you look so different from each other if you're both from the same place?" he asked. Ashal felt herself bristle, and the fins around her head shifted uncomfortably at the question. She opened her mouth to answer, but it was Magdolon who responded first.

"We are a different breed. She is a naiad, and I am a placoderm. We call the Trident Realm home, but it is home to many different species."

"That seems odd." The man seemed to relax a little. "I've never been out of my little home town here, though. Can't even read or write. Never heard of the Trident Realm, or fish people for that matter. But, we've seen talking trees, centaurs, and other beasts from the forests, and all of them have done nothing but try to kill us and take our food." He looked questioningly at the pair before him.

"I assure you we have no interest in your food, and no desire to kill you." Magdolon rumbled calmly.

"Unless we could trouble you for a small bit now?" Ashal added as her stomach growled at the mention of food. "We will gladly pay you for it." She produced a small, silver coin covered in dwarven runes from her trading with the mining company. The man eyed the coin hungrily, the blue light from the solitary candle in the window reflecting dully off its surface. After a few moments of consideration, the man nodded and motioned them into the back room.

"I have a bit of pottage left from our dinner. Probably still warm if you hurry." He held out his hand and Ashal dropped the coin into his outstretched palm. He snatched the silver and quickly caused it to disappear into a pouch at his belt, his eyes never leaving his unexpected guests as he did so.

They walked into the back room where there was a simple, wooden table and three equally simple wooden chairs around it. In the corner was a hearth where a black pot was hung over some glowing embers that were the remains of a fire long since extinguished. The man quickly produced a pair of bowls and ladled some thick concoction from the pot into each, handing Ashal and Magdolon a bowl each. Ashal wrinkled her nose as the mess smelled of overcooked vegetables and some kind of burnt grease. It was still warm, though, and the gruel filled the void in her belly so she ate it quickly, trying to ignore the taste on her tongue.

During their meal, Ashal occasionally heard some thumping coming from above them, and she noticed a small, spiral staircase in the corner of the room opposite the hearth. She quickly finished the last few bites of her food and wiped her mouth.

"Your daughter told us that she helps your wife with your baby during the day while you're out working. I hope we haven't disturbed them with our rude entrance," she said, her voice cutting through the silence. The man grimaced at these words, his eyes darting to the staircase.

"Oh, I'm sure they're fine," he muttered. "The baby probably just needs feeding is all."

"But we already fed Jackson today!" Sasha smiled as she spoke. "Remember? You brought back a crow and we..."

"That's enough, Sasha!" The man hissed, cutting his daughter off mid-sentence. He smiled at Ashal, though it was a crooked smile that did not reflect in his eyes. "Children sometimes do not understand what they see." He explained, shrugging. An awkward silence fell, broken only by the occasional slurp from

Magdolon as he finished his lukewarm meal. Finally, Ashal could stand it no longer, and so she broke the quiet.

"So, what are those creatures outside? You seemed to know about them. You called them the 'guardians,' I think." She watched his face as she spoke, and he didn't seem perturbed by the question.

"Those are a gift from Abbess Laurine," the man replied, his eyes still refusing to meet Ashal's. "She summoned them shortly after taking command of the abbey above us. The guardians ensure that our village is safe. If anyone is out of their house at the wrong hours, or if they enter the village without the abbess's permission, then they attack them. A couple weeks back, a group of beastmen tried to make their way through the village. They didn't get far before the guardians were on top of them, surrounding them. Do you know the sound of a centaur screaming in agony? I always thought they were monsters that didn't feel any pain, but those beasts kept up a right old chorus of howls throughout the night. Then the abbess took what was left of them and added them to the ranks of the guardians. Same thing she does with anybody who doesn't keep the rules of our village. Thieves, killers, anyone who makes it less safe to live here, they end up as one of the guardians and go back to contributing to our community."

"How is it that they don't attack you?" Ashal asked, trying to conceal the horror in her voice.

"The blue candle out there marks this as a safe place." The man shrugged, motioning to the front room. "During the day there are specific streets and ways that the guardians are forbidden to enter, these let us do our work in the fields, and every fourth day, Abbess Laurine comes down and clears out the market square so we can buy and sell our goods." He lifted his head as a sudden realization dawned on him. "You were the reason that the guardians were in an uproar yesterday, weren't you? I had to work especially late cause of that!"

Ashal bit back a response as Magdolon laid a hand on her shoulder.

"We apologize for any inconvenience we may have caused you." His voice was devoid of emotion. The man shrugged again in response.

"Nothing for it, I suppose. You didn't know about them, nobody ever does. We are so out of the way that, thankfully, travelers rarely, if ever, stumble in here unannounced. Sometimes someone will turn down the wrong street if they aren't paying attention and the guardians will take them, but those instances are rare." He shuddered then as if a cold breeze had whipped through the room.

"That sounds horrible!" Ashal finally burst out. "How can you put up with this?" Magdolon made to shush her, but she shook him off, giving him a glare as she did so.

"The guardians keep us safe!" the man shot back. "Besides that, Abbess Laurine brings other blessings with her that are divine gifts from the Shining

116

Ones! She performs miracles!" His eyes flickered to the ceiling as he spoke where the thumping sounds from earlier were growing louder.

"These things are an abomination!" Ashal responded. "Think what would happen if Sasha were to wander down one of those wrong streets! What if she wandered out while you were in the fields one day?"

"She knows better than that!" The man snapped, but he glanced nervously at his young daughter who had stopped playing in the corner with her dolly as the conversation had escalated to nearly shouting levels.

"She's a child! What would happen if Laurine suddenly decided that you deserved to join the ranks of these 'guardians'?" She stabbed an accusing finger into the man's chest. His eyes widened in horror.

"She wouldn't! I obey the laws!"

"Laws mean nothing to a monster like Laurine." Ashal was surprised to hear Magdolon's calm voice cut through the argument. "We know this for a fact. We have witnessed her cruelty."

"I think it best if you leave." The man's voice quavered as he shakily rose to his feet.

"We will leave in the morning, as we discussed." Magdolon did not rise from his chair but instead fixed a level stare at the father. The man seemed to shrink back under that gaze. Ashal felt something move inside her. She saw the dirty, disheveled appearance of the father and his daughter standing before them. The man's unkempt hair hadn't been washed in weeks, his patchy beard was the result of inattentiveness on his part. His eyes were sunken beneath heavy lids that looked as though they hid terrible visions behind them. This man had lived with fear for so long now that she wasn't sure he knew how to exist without it. Even the daughter, so innocent as she appeared, now looked up at them with shimmering tears hidden away in her eyes. She crouched behind a brave smile, but it was a thin facade that was only as thick as the grime which lay over her like a second skin.

"If you answer some questions, we will go," Ashal said quietly. Both the man and Magdolon turned to look at her in surprise.

"What questions?" As the man asked, Magdolon cocked his head, his eyes narrowing.

"First, am I correct that this street is safe from your... guardians?" Ashal took a deep breath as she spoke.

"Yes, it is." The man nodded.

"Second, you said that Laurine comes down every fourth day to clear the market for you to trade?" The man nodded again. "When is the next market day?"

"Tomorrow." The man did not even stop to consider his response.

"No it's not, Daddy!" Sasha's small voice caused everyone to turn toward her.

117

"Sasha! Be quiet!" the man hissed, but Sasha just smiled and kept talking.

"No! The market was day before yesterday, I know cause you sent me to buy onions! That means that the market will be day after tomorrow." Magdolon growled at this, and Ashal turned to the man.

"You tread on thin ice," she warned. "Do not lie to us again."

"Or what?" The man sneered, his voice rising in pitch as he spoke. "You'll kill me? Hurt me? Some simple travelers you are! You're no better than the beasts who Laurine protects us from!"

At this accusation, Magdolon rose and turned toward Ashal.

"I think it best if you leave this to me." He spoke low, his voice was flat. Ashal had seen him this way on only a few occasions previous to this. She turned quickly toward the little girl who had returned to her toys in the corner.

"Sasha!" She called softly. "Can you show me your room? Maybe I can meet your mother and baby brother?" Sasha turned and beamed at this request, nodding vigorously. She skipped over toward Ashal but was intercepted by her father.

"You leave my daughter alone!" he snarled. Above them, the thumping sounds grew louder, and there came the sound of scraping, like something was being dragged across the wood. Magdolon crossed the room quickly, placing his face inches from the man's, so that his breath washed over his face as he spoke.

"Your daughter will come to no harm and neither will you," he growled. "However, I think that you would rather she not be in the room while we discuss these… delicate things." The man shrank before the placoderm's impressive bulk, his face turning pale in the wan light of the darkened house. A groan came from the rooms above them as the thumping became more insistent.

"Daddy!" Sasha's fragile voice was quiet, her eyes wide in terror at things happening that were beyond her understanding. "I think we woke Mommy!" The man froze, his breathing shortened to quick gasps, and he turned slowly toward the stairs.

"What does she mean?" Ashal asked.

"Mommy is scary when we wake her…" Sasha whimpered.

"She doesn't know what she's talking about. My wife has been sick for some time and…" The man was cut off as there was another loud thump above them, and the groaning grew louder. Magdolon's eyes narrowed and he stormed toward the small staircase that wound toward the upper floor.

"No!" The man cried out and scrambled to intercept him. Ashal easily reached forward and shifted his momentum against him to throw him gently against the floor. "Please! Leave her alone!" His voice was choked as he lay on the ground. His tone was imploring now, not threatening.

Ashal hurried after Magdolon, climbing up the stairs as the large placoderm reached the top and found a sturdy door blocking their passage. A few kicks easily forced the door from its hinges and it toppled inward to reveal a surreal image. A rocking chair sat in the middle of a destroyed room, beside it sat a small cradle that rocked back and forth on its curved bars. A shriveled hand extended out to rest on the edge of the crib, its fingernails torn and bloody, stained with a dark, viscous liquid that extended up onto the white cuff of the clothing.

Ashal covered her mouth as they entered, the stench of rotting meat almost overwhelming her. The room itself had been ripped to shreds, torn pieces of a straw mattress lay strewn about, and a ruined bed frame lay in pieces in one corner. A boarded up window was positioned in the middle of the far wall, and bits of glass reflected from the broken moonlight that penetrated the gloom. The hand that rocked the crib stilled as they moved inside the room, and a rasping moan rose up from a dry throat as another of the undead creatures like the ones they had encountered outside rose and turned to face them. It took a few shuddering steps toward them before being jerked back by a leash that bound it to the floor by its foot. The creature rasped and screeched as it lifted its hands, clutched in their direction while gnashing its broken teeth. Patches of blonde hair still stuck to its decayed scalp, but its eyes had already faded to a milky white above sunken cheeks and a mouth that were stained with fresh blood.

"Do not touch her!" The man pushed himself between Ashal and Magdolon and stood between them and the zombie of what Ashal could only assume had been his wife. "You will not touch my Mariett!" His voice was half pleading sob, half vicious snarl.

"What is this?" Magdolon spoke in a whisper. The man held out his hands to stop any advances as tears streamed down his face.

"A little over a year ago, my wife died giving birth to my son Jackson, who never even took his first breath before his little spirit was spent. The Abbess Laurine gave them back to me! She brought them back! Please! Leave us in peace!" Despite the man's warding arms, Ashal took a few steps forward and her breath caught in her chest as she gazed down into the small crib. A withered husk sat there, writhing with its undeveloped muscles and staring through the rotted lids of death with milky white pupils. A mewling cry escaped its lips, a sickening parody to its mother's groans beside it. Ashal turned away and walked back to the door where she looked down to see little Sasha climbing up the stairs, her eyes glistening with tears that streamed down her cheeks. Ashal felt her stomach coil within her gut.

"We cannot allow this." Magdolon's voice cut across Ashal's thoughts. "This is an affront to the natural order of things. You would keep this here? Your wife is dead, and you would defile her memory by allowing this…this *thing* to inhabit her corpse?!" The placoderm pulled his spear from his back and moved forward toward the undead creature who sat reaching for him, tugging at the leash that bound it.

"Please! No!" The man sobbed as Magdolon pushed him to the side, crumpling to the floor as he lifted his hands weakly to protest. Magdolon moved forward to stand just out of reach of the zombie's outstretched arms. He took aim with his spear. It would be a precise strike, likely planted through the mouth and out the base of the skull so as to be a quick dispatch of the abomination. Ashal felt something brush past her.

"Are you going to hurt my mommy?" Sasha's voice was so brittle that Ashal feared it would break at any moment and never reshape itself. Magdolon's eyes closed and he lowered his spear. Stepping back, he turned to face the small child.

"Yes, little one. Your mother left a long time ago. This thing that stands here now is not your mother. It is something else, and it is dangerous. So I must deal with it."

"I don't want you to hurt Mommy. Or Baby Jackson!" Sasha's pinched voice cut through the placoderm, and Ashal saw his resolve falter in his eyes before a steely resolve forced itself to stabilize him.

"I am sorry little one. It must be done."

"But why? Mommy hasn't hurt anyone."

"But she may."

"That's not fair!" The girl's voice finally shattered and she threw herself at Magdolon, wrapping her tiny arms around his spear. The room grew still with the exception of the zombie of Mariett in the background straining against her bonds. Sasha's small frame waivered like a reed in a windstorm as terrible sobs tore themselves from her throat. Magdolon stared down at her for a few moments before reaching out a massive hand and began stroking her hair.

"I know... I know..." He kept repeating it as if it were a mantra, whispering it into the child's dirty hair as her father sat in a heap on the floor. Ashal stared at the scene, her own mind reaching far back into her memory to replay the horrific events of a night spent in a dungeon so long ago. She had barely been older than little Sasha at the time. That had been the night her world had ended, her childhood ripped from her with the cold realization that her family was gone. Taken from her by the woman who sat in the security of her abbey that loomed over this small family before her. This poor, wretched, broken family that could not release the tragedy that had begun to define their relationships. Ashal looked up as Magdolon shook Sasha off of his spear and took up the position he had held before in preparation to end the zombie's misery.

"Magdolon! Stop!" She heard her voice cry out. The large placoderm hesitated and turned once more, this time to stare at her. "This is an abomination. This whole situation is. But I will not have this child's only memory of us being the one that took her mother from her." Magdolon maintained his gaze at her for a few moments before inclining his head.

"If that is your order," he said softly.

"It is." Ashal's voice was steady. "Our lives have enough tragedy in it without this being added to it." The broken man shuffled over to her on his knees, grasping for her hand as he sobbed his gratitude into it.

"May the Shining Ones bless you for your mercy!" He kissed her webbed fingers, but Ashal pulled her hand away and stepped back.

"Do not bless me just yet," she said, scrubbing her hand against her leg. "You said that Laurine will be coming down for the market in two days?" The man nodded. Ashal sighed deeply and fixed her gaze on Magdolon. He nodded in approval.

"Then that is when we will strike. She has caused too much harm to worry about her suffering for her sins. She must be removed and may your gods sort out her penance. In two days, Laurine will die!"

Twelve

MARKET DAY

The only thing that alerted Yvette to the fact that morning had arrived was the lighter gradient of the gray stone in her cell where she lay. Her eyes were dried and bloodshot, they hurt when she tried to move them. The bandages that covered her arms and hands were dyed a rusty red color tinged with yellow at the edges. Her every movement felt sluggish, and she could feel the poisons clogging her veins from the now several days old wounds that Rose had given her in the darkness of her dungeons. She was lying on her side in a pile of dirty straw that rustled with her feverish movements. It hurt to lie still and it hurt to move, but they were different kinds of pain so she would alternate between frantic spasms and moments of motionless whimpering in order to try and find whatever relief she might.

She kept replaying the scene in the forest. Seeing the betrayal on Magdolon's face when she had fled, weeping, to abandon him to the ghouls that Rose had sent after them. She wondered if he and his ward had been able to escape. She had run for so long in the woods that when she stopped, the sun had already disappeared in the sky and the stars had begun to emerge. Her wounds from Rose's torture had burned unnaturally under their already foetid bandages. She had come to the conclusion that the wounds were likely poisoned, based off the smell and the tingling sensation that spread throughout her limbs. For a time she considered just laying down and letting the venom do its work, it would be nice to simply go to sleep and leave these nightmares behind. She had lost her hope of Magdolon working for her, and Rose would be able to control all aspects of her life if she returned to the abbey. It would be much simpler if she were to just lie down and disappear into the aether. She *was* so very tired.

It had been a struggle to force herself to her feet and then to turn back toward the abbey. She buried the anxiety which clawed at her stomach and instead focused on the memory of her mother's smile which had been taken from her. If she died here, then Rose and Laurine would win and would never know the punishment they deserved for what they had done to her. That anger, that hatred, had carried her through the gates of the village below the abbey.

Several of the shuffling guardians had seen her, but they hadn't stopped or let out the hue and cry of their duties, recognizing in her a kindred spirit. They knew what she was, and so she had staggered up to the abbey. By now the feverish visions had begun to plague her, and she was waving away ghosts that hovered before her eyes that only she could see.

There was no way for her to tell how long she had lain in the cold prison cell where they had deposited her, but she suspected not much time had passed. The part of her brain that wasn't controlled by the fiery poison reasoned that she hadn't seen anyone in her rare moments of lucidity, and she knew that if Rose wanted to keep her alive then she couldn't wait too long before administering the antidote for her poison. If she didn't, then the venom would likely soon claim her in any case, and she would then be dead and beyond the cares of this world. At this point, she welcomed either outcome.

There came the sound of metal clinking against metal as a key was inserted into the door to her cell. Yvette didn't bother pushing herself up, she doubted that she had the strength. She felt more than she could see the shadows of two figures hovering over her. After a few moments, one of the figures bent to touch her shoulder.

"Get up, little duckling."

Rose's smoky voice echoed against the hard stone. Yvette stifled a groan and rolled onto her back, her bleary vision barely registering the outline of Rose's face. Even clouded in the haze of a fever, she could tell the older sister was smiling.

"You're probably wondering how a poison could affect someone like us so effectively, I'd wager?" Rose chuckled. "It's my own special concoction. A touch of silver, a bit of sanguine leaf, a bit of this and a bit of that. It wouldn't affect a normal human being hardly at all, apart from some possibly minor infections. But someone living under our affliction, well, it won't kill you but it will make you supremely uncomfortable. You may wish for death at times, however." Rose tilted her head back and gave a full throated laugh.

"The best part," she continued, "is that the only way to push the poison out is to feed. Because of our unique blood condition, our bodies don't process toxins in quite the same way they used to." Rose reached down and grabbed Yvette by the arm, wrenching her up into a sitting position, and pulled her over to rest against the wall. Yvette's vision swam as she slumped against the cold stone, she couldn't even muster a baleful stare at her tormentor's face.

"You're a monster," her dry lips managed to whisper. Rose's face once again appeared before her eyes, and the older sister reached out to press her hand against Yvette's chin.

"Yes. I am. We all are here, and that includes you, little duckling. Do not act so above us that you would forget that." Rose stood up and took hold of the figure who had accompanied her into the cell. Yvette recognized the middle

124

aged man whom Rose forced to his knees and pushed toward Yvette's slumped form. His name escaped her memory, but she knew he worked in the kitchens, not as a full chef but as one of the helpers there. She could see the wide-eyed terror he felt as he was pushed closer and closer to Yvette's face.

"This will take care of the poison. Our little pet is eager to please, aren't you?" Rose reached down and stroked the side of the man's face; he flinched aside and licked his lips nervously. Rose smiled and leaned down to rest her chin on his shoulder.

"Aren't you hungry?" The older sister smiled.

Yvette felt herself reaching out as if to embrace the man. She tried to resist the movement, but her arms refused to obey her commands and twined themself around the shaking man's form, pulling him closer. A smell filtered through Yvette's swimming senses, a smell that had reminded her of when she was younger and her mother had been cooking a stew in the abbey kitchens. Yvette had been so hungry in her memory, and she couldn't tell if the rumbling of her stomach was from her past self or emanated from her present situation as she pulled the man closer. One hand snaked up to grab his short cropped blond hair and slowly pulled his head to the side, exposing the gentle nape of his neck.

"Hurry up, we don't have time to delay, as much as your predicament amuses me and I enjoy watching your moral dilemma unfold." Rose's voice cut through the fevered fog around Yvette's vision, and she realized that she sat hovering over his neck, her mouth already opened wide, her whole body willing her to close the gap except for one small part of her that was crying out in protest. Yvette could hear the man quietly sobbing as he hung on the verge of anticipation, waiting for the pain. Yvette closed her eyes and willed the protesting voice in her mind back into the dark recesses where she could ignore it more completely. Then, she sank her teeth into his bared skin.

As soon as the salty tang of his blood touched her tongue, Yvette felt a release within her body. Instantly the cuts in her arms and shoulders began to close, and the sense of nausea and fever fell away. Her senses returned and her mind let loose the bands of fog that had clouded her thinking. She drank deep, her parched lips greedily sucking at the crimson liquid. She heard her victim whimpering as she pulled again and again, gulping greedily at his blood. The voice in the back of her mind called out for her to stop, but she silenced it, far easier than she felt comfortable admitting.

Yvette couldn't tell how long she had been drinking when finally there was nothing left when her teeth bit into the man's neck. She pulled her head back and wiped the blood from her mouth. The bandages that had been covering her hands had already begun falling off, and she could tell that there would not even be scars underneath them as she flexed her fingers. The older man's desiccated corpse fell forward as she moved and slumped onto the stone floor.

"You didn't need to take all of his blood, you know." Rose's voice startled Yvette as she stared at the body before her. Rose's voice sounded infinitely loud and sharp without the clouding influence of her poison. Yvette turned, her eyes wide as she stared up at the older sister who sat with her arms crossed staring down at her with a small smile on her full lips.

"I... I'm sorry... I didn't mean to..." Yvette stammered. She suddenly realized that her hands were crimson, and she began to rub them along the hem of her ragged dress. There was a small part of her that wished she felt some form of revulsion or disgust with herself for what she had done. Instead, the only thing that dominated her thoughts was a terrible desire to feed even more. She trembled because she felt wonderful! The cool stone of the ground beneath felt breathtaking after the fires of her fever. The slight breeze that entered the cell through the open door behind Rose stirred against her skin and caused exultant goosebumps to rise from her flesh. The absence of the pain and discomfort from only moments before relaxed her muscles, and she barely had the presence of mind to keep a pleased sigh from escaping her mouth as she sat scrubbing her hands in a theatrical mimicry of humanity.

"I know you didn't mean to, little duckling, and I don't blame you that you did. However we are running low on stock and his loss will be felt this evening at dinner. But there's nothing for it at this point, and what's done is done." Rose reached down and picked up a new dress that she must have brought in with her and slid the clothes over to Yvette who blinked at how loud the sound of it moving across the stone felt to her. "Change your clothes. It's Market Day down in the village, and Laurine has requested that you accompany her." Rose walked toward the door where she stopped and turned to look back at Yvette.

"It is good to have you back with us, little duckling." She said before walking out. Yvette glared after her.

* * * * *

The gray sunlight filtered through the overcast sky and caused Yvette to shift uncomfortably beneath its rays. The light seemed unnaturally bright so soon after a feeding, and her skin felt uncomfortably hot underneath the sunbeams. She knew that it was just a part of the heightened senses that came with ingesting fresh blood, but still she itched regularly at her collar which seemed to chafe against her skin. From the looks of her companions, several of them had fed recently, too, as evidenced by their constant shifting and itching. There was a reason that most of their kind preferred to dress in silks and fine linens as opposed to the wool habits of the Sisterhood. But there was no arguing with the practicality of their lives under Laurine's guidance. Rather than hunted, they were revered, and there would never be a shortage of fresh blood, even if there would also never be an excess for that matter. Pragmatism and restraint were holy attributes, after all, and very fitting for the sisters of the abbey to strive after.

They walked through the drab streets of the village, pushing the reanimated 'guardians' before Laurine as she willed her undead servants away from the marketplace and the surrounding streets where they would wait until the villagers had finished their business for the day. It was always a bizarre scene to behold as Laurine worked her necrotic powers. Yvette watched as she willed the corpses to stand up and shuffle into the deeper shadows of the dark alleys, their stifled moans slowly fading away as they left.

Once all the robed corpses had been dealt with, the villagers emerged from their homes with wary looks on their faces. Each one carried various bundles that they would either take to their assigned stalls and begin arranging their wares or would be tucked under arms or on shoulders as they walked from merchant to merchant inspecting what was for sale. There was an unnatural hush that prevailed over the whole affair. No vendors called out their prices, there were no singers or performers that played in order to receive the odd coin from a passerby. Any haggling was done in hushed whispers, bent over the table where the prices were being negotiated. Even this was usually done quickly with one side prevailing or walking away with little more than a few whispered words and a nod of the head before coins or goods were exchanged.

Many times, vendors would leave their goods unattended and do some trading with their neighbors or some other transaction with others at the market. No one worried that their items might be stolen, because everyone dreaded the price that such an ill-gotten prize might cost them.

Yvette stood beside a wicker chair on a wooden dais set up so that Laurine could watch as the villagers took their turns at the various stalls. They hurriedly went about their trading, knowing that it would be several days before they would be able to do so again. Yvette looked at the other four sisters who had accompanied Laurine, each of them part of Rose's inner circle. A short and brutish looking woman named Thera was the leader of their small retinue. She was one of Rose's most loyal of pets. They both shared a delight for the same devious diversions, and Yvette had felt Thera's cruelty cut into her skin on various occasions. She lacked the finesse that Rose exhibited, but it was effective nonetheless. The other three sisters were ones that Yvette knew only in passing.

A blonde sister who appeared to be in the middle years of her life stood close beside Yvette and did not seem to move from her position. Yvette had decided to name the older woman 'Leash' in her head, a little on the nose but it was an apt description.

Laurine sighed and stifled a yawn at the same time. Yvette couldn't blame her, this was not a very exciting affair. This market day was nothing like the ones found in stories full of exotic smells and goods. The people here did not shout or greet each other enthusiastically, and the only things for sale were basic goods of local produce and dried meats. Their existence was about as gray as the overcast sky above them.

Yvette found her mind wandering as she stood waiting for Laurine to decide that the market day was over. She wondered what had happened to Magdolon and that other creature he had brought with him. Had they been able to escape? If so, they were likely already leagues from here. Although, there had been a disturbance in the village while Yvette had laid in her cell, suffering from Rose's poison. The other sisters had been talking about it as they had descended from the abbey that morning. Could it be that Magdolon and his ward had stayed and were still planning to attack Laurine? The abbess did not seem overly concerned, as she hadn't even brought additional guards with her. Perhaps she didn't know everything that Rose did and therefore wouldn't know the goal of the interlopers? Or perhaps if it was Magdolon, maybe the 'guardians' had discouraged him from his attack.

She shifted her weight uncomfortably from one foot to the other, her thoughts interrupted by the scraping of the woolen skirts against her legs. Why had Rose allowed her to live? The question nagged at her like a sliver of wood that had burrowed under her skin. She had proven herself to be a liability, so much so that Rose had assigned her a chaperone. Perhaps she thought that Yvette had more spies that could be dug out of her, more plots to be uncovered. Yvette wished that there were, but besides Magdolon, her only other contact was her 'Burning Man' who likely didn't know what else was going on since Rose had intercepted her last letter to him. He would probably abandon her, too, if he had any sense. She knew that she would if their positions were reversed. Yvette didn't dare try to send any more letters to him, and it was doubtful that Rose would let her out of her sight long enough to rendezvous, especially with Leash attached to her shadow.

Something shifted in the movements of the villagers, and Yvette felt the hair on her skin raise up. She shivered and looked out at the crowd moving between the stalls. She could feel someone's eyes staring at her from the clutch of bodies moving around them. Her gaze stopped on a hooded figure standing several paces away from the dais where she stood. She could sense the intensity of those eyes peering out through the shadows of that hood, locked on her face, glowing with a heat that struck Yvette like someone had grabbed her stomach and twisted it around their fist. The figure simply stood there, allowing the villagers to flow around it, everyone who passed by gave the strange person a wide berth. With a start, Yvette realized that the figure was waiting for something, but what?

There came a crash and the sound of shattered glass hitting the cobblestones behind them and Yvette turned with a startled look on her face. Her shock increased when she saw the massive form of Magdolon standing before them, his spear in hand and a look of determination on his face. The shattered window of what looked like an abandoned shop behind him and shards of jagged glass at his feet.

"Laurine!" He bellowed, moving to close the distance between himself and the abbess. "Your time of evil has come to an end. I call you now to answer for your sins!"

Laurine's eyes widened as she looked upon the large figure charging toward her. Immediately, two of the guard sisters charged off the dais and toward the large creature before them, a coil of chain with a cruelly spiked ball at the end of it uncoiling from each of their hands. Yvette waited a moment and saw that her Leash stayed put behind her. Thera also hesitated, casting her eyes about warily, and Yvette knew she was looking for other ambushers. She smelled a trap. Yvette cast a quick glance behind her and saw that the hooded figure was still standing there, staring at her, unmoving even as the cries of the villagers raised bedlam around them.

Making a snap decision, Yvette turned and charged toward Magdolon, arms outstretched and a snarl on her face. Magdolon's face registered her sense of betrayal for only a moment before his spear lashed out, the flat of its long blade slapping against the side of one of the sisters that was closest to him. The blow caused her to stagger and fall to one knee, but she was quickly up again and charged once more. Magdolon took a step backward as both sisters launched themselves at him, their flails whirling at their sides as they came.

For a creature so large, the placoderm moved well and stepped smartly between them, throwing the butt of his spear out as he did so and tangling one of the sister's weapons. He sent her sprawling to the ground and then lashed out with a vicious kick to her jaw, spinning in the same motion to his remaining opponent. By now, Yvette was nearly on top of him, and she screeched as she jumped into the air. The fresh blood in her system gave her an extra boost that sent her sailing above his head. Once again Magdolon's face registered surprise and hurt as he watched her come. He stepped smartly to the side and Yvette landed harmlessly on the flagstones, rolling forward to get out of reach of his spear.

The sister who had taken Magdolon's kick to her head was pushing herself to her feet, wiping blood from her mouth and spitting a few teeth out as she did. This caused Magdolon to stare for a few precious moments and almost cost him his life as Yvette's Leash charged up behind him and threw her arms around his neck. Magdolon's eyes bulged as she pressed down on his windpipe, and he reversed the grip on his spear to stab behind him with the blunt end which connected to Leash's eye. She cried out and fell back, releasing her hold on him. He coughed as she let go and turned to face her, his shoulders heaving as he gulped for air.

He thinks he's fighting regular Basilean Sisters! Yvette realized. *He has no idea what he's actually up against!* Yvette looked around and saw that the sisters had surrounded the still gasping placoderm, and their intent was obvious. Magdolon's back was exposed to her, and a wild plan caught her as she sprinted forward and latched onto Magdolon's shoulders.

"You are in over your head," she whispered urgently in his ear as he thrashed about trying to dislodge her. He paused briefly at her words, which allowed one of the other sisters to run in, her flail whirling around her head as she charged. Magdolon slammed the shaft of his spear into her gut, causing her to grunt and double over. The placoderm guard then brought his spear haft up to slam into her throat, throwing her to the ground in a dazed heap.

"That won't work against us," Yvette hissed as she tried to make it look as though she were trying to dig her fingers into the side of his neck. "We are undead! We do not falter under non-lethal blows! You are not fighting innocents here. You must strike to kill!" Magdolon bellowed and reached back to grasp Yvette by the hair. She cried out and released her hold, allowing Magdolon to haul her over his shoulder and onto the hard cobblestones.

He doesn't believe me! She realized as the air rushed out of her lungs. She couldn't blame him, she had betrayed him already, albeit unwillingly. She would have to show him irrefutable proof of what he was dealing with. She rolled away and sprang to her feet, her hands spread into vicious claws before her. She dug deep down into the violent, animalistic part of her mind, dredging up the beast that dwelled within her. Her vision turned red and a primal rage bubbled into her chest. She knew what she must look like to those around her. Her pupils would have dilated and the whites of her eyes would have turned blood red, glistening like a predator seen in the moonlight. She felt her jaw pop as new, sharper teeth emerged from her gums that were useful for tearing flesh and letting blood flow freely from victims so sadly caught in its grasp.

No villagers were around to witness this transformation, but it would only have added to the chaos of their flight from the market square. Magdolon's eyes were wide, but his jaw was set as he watched her change and then braced himself. The other sisters, seeing Yvette's change, decided that they would unmask their true nature as well. Each one hissed in turn, baring their newly protruding teeth. Yvette felt a new hunger emerge in her gut and she longed for the cold blood which stirred in Magdolon's still thrumming veins. She resisted this urge with everything she had left, thankful that Rose had allowed her to feed before coming to the market. Only that stopped her from charging headlong at him to suck him dry. The other sisters, however, had no such restraint. They attacked as one, closing the gap quickly.

Yvette struggled to think clearly as she watched the vicious assault. Magdolon stabbed with his spear at the first of the sisters to reach him, no longer trying for non-lethal blows but now using the tip of his spear in earnest. The blonde sister ducked under the blow, moving with inhuman speed, meanwhile the sister behind him had abandoned her flail in her animalistic hunger and instead raked her claws across his back. Magdolon arched away in pain, using the movement to dodge around Leash's attack and stab out with his spear to take the last sister through the throat. She gurgled as the point of the weapon nearly took her head from her shoulders, and she fell to the ground in a pool of blood. Her face relaxed and the animalistic qualities of her features disappeared, leaving the shocked expression of a young woman in their place.

Yvette knew that she needed to help Magdolon or else the other three sisters would quickly finish him off, and he was moving so that his back was to a row of buildings so that he couldn't be surrounded again. Yvette's Leash stood in the middle of the other two vampiric sisters, all three hissing and moving to close the distance between them and their foe. Yvette saw an opportunity and charged forward, a dire cry escaping her lips as she ran. She saw Magdolon's eyes flick to focus on her, and he braced his spear in his hands in preparation to strike when she came within range. She aimed herself carefully, seeming to stumble and collide with her Leash as she reached her. Together they fell forward, the older sister pushed forward by Yvette's momentum. Magdolon saw an opportunity and stabbed his weapon forward, the spear tip speeding toward Yvette's face.

At the last moment, Yvette threw herself to the side, pulling Leash with her, and instead of taking Yvette's head off like it had the other, less fortunate sister, the spear impaled her Leash through the chest. The impact was so forceful that it threw the older woman back despite her forward momentum. However, the spear stuck between her ribs and wrenched it from Magdolon's hands. Caught up in a tangle, Yvette tumbled backward with the already dead body of her Leash, landing underneath the weight of the cold corpse where she lay still, forcing her mind to clear and the vampiric features to relax on her stunned face.

"That is enough!" A voice bellowed from across the square. Yvette vaguely registered that it was Laurine who was speaking. She turned her head and saw the Mother Abbess standing there with her hands stretched out at her sides, a purple mist emanating from her downward facing palms and passing down into the ground.

"This ends now!" Laurine snarled as the mists began to coalesce into her hands, forming strange balls of mystical energy that crackled with power. Yvette saw a shrouded figure running up behind Laurine, and the hood fell back to reveal a feminine face with shining fish scales and deep red fins surrounding her strong features, a magnificent spear held in her hands.

"Laurine!" The figure called out, startling the abbess who turned just as her attacker reached her. Yvette watched in disbelief as the newcomer's spear stabbed deep into Laurine's stomach, causing her to grunt and stagger back. The naiad caught Laurine with her arm and pulled her close. Together, the pair sank down onto their knees, and it looked as though the naiad was whispering something to Laurine as they knelt there.

"I am Ashal, daughter of Ai-ellain, I have come to avenge my family and end your evil reign," Ashal yelled. Laurine looked at her as hot blood spilled from the open stomach wound in her midriff. She reached up with a crimson hand and cupped the side of Ashal's face, the naiad did not flinch away but instead continued to stare balefully at her enemy's dazed expression.

Then, Laurine began to laugh.

Thirteen

INTO THE WOODS

A blank stare was all that Ashal could muster as she stabbed her spear into Laurine's stomach, blood immediately spattered as the wound penetrated her habit. Laurine reacted quickly and grabbed the shaft of the weapon, causing Ashal to grunt as her forward momentum was suddenly stopped by Laurine's grip. The abbess gasped in pain as she looked down at her bloodied midriff, she coughed and specks of crimson sprayed out of her mouth. Ashal floated in a void of emotions. She knew she had to say something in the last fleeting moments of Laurine's ebbing life. She had to let her tormentor know who she was, force her to remember what she had done.

"Here is the reward for your treachery. May you find nothing waiting for you on the other side of that veil." Ashal whispered, grinding her spear against Laurine's vice like grip with each syllable. "I am Ashal, daughter of Ai-ellain, I have come to avenge my family and end your evil reign." By the end, Ashal was practically screaming.

Laurine's face was puzzled, but she reached up a scarlet hand to touch the side of Ashal's face, who felt the sticky warmth of fresh blood on her cheek but did not flinch away. Then Laurine began to laugh. It started out as a low, wet chuckle that bubbled out through the blood in her mouth and then grew in volume until it was almost a full throated howl of mirth. Ashal blinked and stepped back. She tried to pull her spear free, but Laurine's hands held it firmly in place. Laurine's laughter cut off suddenly and she glared at Ashal.

"You think that this will be enough, my little sea flower?" Laurine cackled and pulled the spear from her stomach and flung it away from her. Ashal spared a moment to stare at it as the weapon sailed away to land on the flagstones several yards behind the bloodied abbess. Laurine staggered, and her eyes rolled up into her skull. A sickly violet light began to emanate from her hands as she placed them over the still gushing wound. Ashal recoiled in horror at the sight, pulling a knife from her belt as she did so, but beyond that she stood transfixed by what she beheld.

Laurine hugged her glowing hands around her wound, and Ashal watched in horror as the bleeding seemed to stop immediately. Laurine groaned and then straightened her back as if she were in great pain. The blood on her chin gave her a monstrous look, as if she had just fed on some grisly meal. As quickly as it had appeared, the glowing light vanished and Laurine let out a long sigh before opening her eyes to stare levelly at Ashal.

"I've improved my healing abilities since last we met." Laurine grinned, raising a hand in front of her. "You are not the first to seek me in hopes of taking vengeance. I learned long ago that there would be many misguided souls that would try to stop me from achieving my goals out of a poor choice to seek revenge rather than look at what I have achieved!" With that, Laurine raised her hand and purple fire exploded out from her palm and slammed into Ashal's chest, throwing her backward to land in a dazed heap on the cobbles of the market square.

Her body numb with pain and crackling with arcane energy, Ashal could barely move other than to writhe in agony. Her vision was unfocused and her limbs refused to do as she told them. Some part of her was vaguely aware of shapes moving about her. The sounds of fighting seemed to come from somewhere near her head, and there were several hot blasts of purple light that shot around the square followed by Laurine's irritated screeches. She felt a hand reach down to grab her arm, and then she felt the ground slide underneath her as that hand tugged and pulled her along the rough stones of the cursed city.

Her body jostled along the cobbles and gradually she was able to focus her eyes on the person who was hauling against her arm. The person was dressed in the Basilean blue habit of a sister, and she was carrying Ashal's spear in her other hand! Ashal pawed weakly at the hand that was holding her, but her captor simply brushed her aside and continued to drag her away. Her head spinning from the effort of moving, Ashal closed her eyes and unwillingly succumbed to the darkness that followed.

Visions danced before her as she tumbled through the shadows. She saw stone walls that turned to trees and a sun that became a bloody moon hanging over her head. She could sense something hiding in the dark, stalking her. She couldn't see the beast, but she knew it was there, and it was hungry. Ashal found herself unable to move, yet the world spun past her at a steady rate. She felt strong arms bearing her up, but her body was too tired to move itself. Every time she tried to resist or move on her own, a stinging pain cut through her flesh and caused her to cry out. Throughout all of this, the beast in the shadows continued to creep closer.

Ashal could sense the monster more than she could see it. It hovered in the periphery of her vision, always bent over and always snarling with viciously long teeth. She had no idea how she knew that its teeth were long, but in a way that only made sense in a dream, she knew that it was so. The beast never appeared to come close enough to really make out any details, but it was persistently there, and Ashal could feel its hungry eyes roaming across her wounded body.

Suddenly the world stopped spinning and she felt the arms shudder as Ashal was lowered to the ground. She felt a pleasant coolness slip over her tired limbs and then her body. The chilling sensation climbed up to almost cover her face but stopped just shy of her chin. The stinging pain she had felt while moving began to fade, and she found herself able to look around. She glanced upward to see if she could spy the person who had been carrying her. She cried out as her eyes fell on the beast that had been stalking her with its large red eyes and long, sharp teeth. The creature snarled and opened its mouth wide. Ashal's cry became a scream as the fanged mouth plunged downward at her, its teeth seeking her throat.

Ashal's eyes opened and she sat bolt upright, her body screaming in protest at the movement. Water splashed all around her as she looked about, adrenaline pouring through her. She found herself breathing hard, and the effort of sitting up caused the world to tilt and blur a little. Her stomach muscles ached from the strain, and she slumped backward against her will. A shadow fell across her face and she forced her eyes to focus on a dark figure standing over her.

"Relax, you're safe," a voice said soothingly. The figure bent and Ashal felt a hand being placed behind her head and lifting her up into a sitting position once more and then supporting her. Ashal looked around her again and realized that she was in a cave, sitting in a shallow spring that bubbled out of a small pile of rocks to her right. The cave itself wasn't much bigger than an average sized room and had moss and lichen growing on the walls. Small, white flowers growing among the mossy rocks seemed to glow in the reluctant light coming from around a bend in the cave walls where Ashal assumed sat the mouth.

Finally, Ashal glanced up at the figure who held her upright. She gasped when she saw the pretty face of Magdolon's informant, the girl who had betrayed them! Ashal struggled to stand, but she only succeeded in pulling away from her helper's surprisingly strong grip and gasped as her muscles gave out on her and forced her to lay back, weakly propping herself up on her elbows.

"You!" she spat, trying desperately to fix her with what she hoped was a withering glare.

"My name is Yvette," the young woman raised an eyebrow as she spoke. "And you are safe, as I said before. I was able to get you both out of the village, and Laurine will not dare send troops here. Not into the forest."

"Where is Magdolon?"

"He's off gathering some firewood. The forest here does not mind if we are careful and only take those branches that have already fallen to the ground for our fires."

"Where are we?"

"This is one of several enchanted springs in the Forest of Edin-Thuur, as the fae folk call it in these parts. Officially on Basilean registry, this place is simply labelled as part of the Abercarr Woods as it juts up against the mountain range by the same name."

"Enchanted springs?" Ashal hated that she was speaking only in questions, but her mind was blurry with half-formed thoughts, and the questions fell naturally from her mouth as she tried to piece together what had happened.

"You're sitting in water blessed by the Green Lady herself. This natural fountain produces waters that have certain healing properties as a result. The Hegemony would love to know that little tidbit, I'm sure." Yvette sat back, shaking water off her hands and then massaging the palms of each in turn. Her face grimaced as she did so. "Laurine really did a number on you, and that's why I had Magdolon bring you here. The water should help you heal quickly. Especially since you are a naiad, the process should be even faster. I imagine you'll be up and moving in the next day or two at the latest."

As Yvette spoke, the air seemed to grow colder. Ashal gasped as the images of her encounter with Laurine came crashing back. She groaned as a wave of nausea washed over her and she felt one of her arms slip, causing her to splash as she fought to keep herself upright. Yvette cringed and pulled away from the droplets of water that Ashal sent flying in her direction as she struggled to right herself.

"What happened with Laurine? Why didn't my blow kill her?" Ashal sputtered. Yvette laughed, but it was not a happy sound.

"Laurine is a skilled necromancer and undeath has become a part of her. Beyond that, she is unique in that she was trained as a sisterhood cleric before being granted the title of Mother Abbess. It will take a precise and deadly blow indeed to kill her. Next time, aim for the head, or the heart." Yvette's hard stare caused Ashal to shift uncomfortably, another wave of dizziness hit her and she found herself fighting back the urge to close her eyes. But the image of the beast from her dreams waited behind her eyelids, and she snapped her eyes open to stare at the crouched form of her rescuer. A creeping suspicion gripped Ashal's chest as she spoke.

"You serve Laurine, don't you?" This elicited another hollow laugh from Yvette who shrugged.

"I serve that which keeps me alive and brings me closer to vengeance."

"Then why are you helping us? If Laurine saw you helping us, then you are surely as good as dead, right?" Yvette was silent a long time before responding.

"Because they took everything from me." Her voice was small when she responded, and it seemed as though it was difficult for her to speak.

"I saw your transformation when you were fighting Magdolon... what...?" Ashal struggled to find the appropriate words.

"We call ourselves vampires, but there are many names for us throughout the known world. Soul Reavers, umpyr, Nocht Sanger, shadowmen, some of the more superstitious and less educated cultures even refer to us as Blood Kin, thinking that we are a cursed type of elf. It all depends on what version of the stories you've heard." Yvette shook her head and Ashal barked an awkward laugh at this.

"But those are just stories! You mean the boogeymen who drink the blood of the innocent and live forever in the shadows of mankind's sins? That's ridiculous!" Ashal snorted.

"Innocence doesn't matter for our food. Good, bad, innocent, or vile it makes no difference, so long as it is red and comes from a living creature's veins, it'll satisfy our hunger for a time." Yvette's eyes lingered on Ashal's neck for a few moments. "It doesn't even need to be warm." She licked her lips and Ashal felt herself pushing backward into the water.

"You can't be serious!"

Yvette's gaze fell at this, and she folded her legs up into her chest as she spoke.

"I wish I wasn't," she said slowly. "But they took my mother from me, and then they made me into this... this thing!" Yvette practically spat out the last word. She sighed and laid her head on her knees.

"When Laurine and Rose first came to the abbey, we were under the command of a real beast of a man. He had been named Dictator Prelate of the area, and we had not had an actual cleric appointed over our abbey since before I was born. All the sisters had suffered under his egotistical rule, but my mother was one of his worst victims. She always said that the only good thing that came of that Dictator was me. Of course, later on I learned that my mother was not the only one to receive such... *'special'* attention, and that there were others who... anyways. When Laurine and Rose arrived, and Laurine learned of the vile acts he'd committed, abusing his authority and causing terror among both the village and the sisterhood, she made him disappear." Yvette sighed before continuing.

"When that happened, I felt for sure that things would improve for everyone, and at first they did; no more lascivious Dictator looking over their shoulders, rationing restrictions were eased, and the villagers were given more freedom. But then, gradually, little things began to pop up. Sisters began getting tired and sick. Some taking to their beds for weeks at a time. Laurine began ordering weekly bleedings for these sisters. She claimed it was a medical procedure that would cause the blood in their bodies to push out the sickness and give them a fighting chance against the disease. Several sisters succumbed to the wasting illness, and those that did survive it came back changed. Kind, loving sisters became cruel and angry. Devout members of the divine rights became lax in their responsibilities, preferring to drink their dark wine and play games than see to their devotions.

"My mother sensed that something was wrong and spoke out against Laurine and Rose, and shortly after that, she fell prey to the wasting sickness herself. She didn't last long, only a few weeks, and then one morning I came in and found her cold body in her bed, two small punctures that were still weeping scarlet drops of blood on the side of her neck. It was that day that I decided to run. As fate would have it, that's the day I met Magdolon and he convinced me to stay." Yvette gave a dry chuckle here. "I guess you could say it's because of him that I am what I am today. Laurine wasted no time in having Rose turn me after I returned from my escape attempt. She said she wanted to bind me close to the sisterhood, and that we would be seeing some grand changes coming along that she wanted me to be part of. At the time, my knowledge of vampires was as superficial as your own and I had no idea what was going on, only that I was convinced that Laurine was behind my mother's death. I was working with Magdolon, so I agreed to become part of her inner circle and unwittingly also agreed to be reborn as a vampire with Rose as my sire."

There was a long pause before either of them spoke. Yvette was the one to finally break the awkward silence.

"I hate what I have become, and the only thing that has kept me going is the knowledge of people like Magdolon who remind me that Laurine and Rose will have to pay for their sins. For what they have done to me. For what they have taken from me..." Yvette stared into the far wall of the cave for several moments, Ashal watching her the whole time. Finally Yvette stood and walked toward the entrance of the cave.

"You need to rest in order to regain your strength. You're going to need it if you plan on killing Laurine. I will go and keep watch outside so you can get some sleep." She disappeared around the bend in the cave wall, and Ashal stared after her. She was confident that she wouldn't be able to sleep, not with the knowledge of what sat just outside of the entrance to where she lay. But after another wave of dizziness hit her, she decided to lay her head back, and within moments she had succumbed to the bone deep weariness she felt creeping through her limbs.

Fourteen
FAMILY TIES

Magdolon bent under a low branch as he stalked quietly back toward the cave where he'd left Ashal and Yvette. In his arms he carried enough deadwood sticks he'd gathered from the forest floor to make a small fire. He'd left the cave with his excuse of gathering fuel for a fire, but his hands still shook when he stood and replayed the scene in his mind of what had happened in the village market. He'd watched Ashal tumble through the air after Laurine had blasted her with infernal magic. He'd also watched before then with horrified eyes as she'd pulled Ashal's spear from her gut and then stand to deliver her blow to Ashal. His eyes had misted over in red as he'd stared at his ward's crumpled body on the stone cobbles and after that was a flurry of memories, each of them violent. He knew he'd killed the other two sisters with their warped and hungry faces, the details of how were a bit fuzzy to him, but he knew that it had involved a lot of blood.

Yvette had been what snapped him out of his frenzy. She'd managed to get his attention and pointed at Laurine. She'd climbed on his back and had whispered in his ear, using the same tactic she'd tried before, but this time it had worked. This time she had clung on harder and her urgent whispers found purchase in his ears as she spoke.

"If you want to save your child, you must listen!" she had hissed, and the words had stopped him cold. *If you want to save your daughter, you must distract Laurine!*

Yvette's voice echoed in his brain, her words hanging around his neck like a sack of stones as his focus drifted back to the present. She had called Ashal his daughter, and that label sent thrills of adrenaline through his veins. Families in the Ai-ellain's household were a different affair than among the surface dwellers Magdolon had observed. In the Depths, Ai-ellain could spawn dozens of children over the course of her lifetime, just as her mother before her and their parents before that. Birthing offspring was not as laborious as it was for humans, where the female would carry a single child in her belly for the better part of a year before finally freeing their spawn. While the head of their household loved

139

each of their offspring, they were less emotional about their children, out of pure necessity. It was difficult to form lasting bonds between so many children. Many spawnlings would be raised as much by servants as their own parents, and the kingdom which they would be raised to serve would act as something of an extended family in many instances. This was a good thing as it bred loyalty into their children and a sense of duty to their kingdom.

Placoderms in Ai-ellain's household were similar in how they were raised, although there were some significant differences. Magdolon remembered much of his younger days spent playing in the household nurseries where he was taught proper etiquette, the histories of his people, and other studies important for a proper education. His brothers and sisters were all equal in that regard, and Magdolon knew his parents by name more than by sight, and in all honesty, he felt more fondness for the nurses and instructors who had been more involved in his upbringing. In many ways, he had felt that kind of closeness with Ashal.

Ashal's situation, however, had been very different from his own. She had been hand selected as a potential heir to her mother's estate among her assortment of siblings. She had been the rare one among the many who would be raised more directly and uniquely by Ai-ellain in order that she might inherit the station her mother had held. As such, she would have enjoyed a much closer relationship with her parents, something more similar to that enjoyed by human children here on the surface. Even so, her mother was an important member of the courts below and had not always had time to care for even her elected child. That was where servants like Magdolon came in to help ensure the child's safety and upbringing were completely taken care of, even when her mother was unable to provide it directly.

The title of daughter was a complicated one for Magdolon to fully accept. He had never spawned children of his own. It hadn't felt right for him, and he'd always thought he'd die without any offspring. Ashal was the daughter of his lord and commander, yet Magdolon did feel that there was something unique in the bond that they shared. He had never presumed to call her *daughter* before, however. The thought of it made him uncomfortable and yet awoke a deep yearning within him that urged him to embrace the title. It was very confusing to the giant placoderm, and he found that his mind would not let the idea rest, no matter how many times he tried to push it away. That and the anger and fear he'd felt when he'd seen Ashal thrown to the ground, fearing that she'd...

Magdolon's ears suddenly pricked up the sound of voices ahead of him, and he fell into a silent crouch. Creeping forward, he began to make out words coming from two different people. One voice he recognized as Yvette's, the other was a strange voice that had an interesting lilt to it that sounded almost familiar.

"Why be there two strangers within our woods?" The stranger's voice was cold, flat, and betrayed no emotion. "Bitter Bark will be very angry when he comes to know of them. He will take your head. Perhaps mine, too."

"I told you why they are here!" Yvette sounded impatient. "They are enemies of Laurine and the other 'abominations' you detest so much, and they are hunting them! I know it is difficult for you to understand that these two are not enemies simply because they did not crawl out of the same pond as you, but they need your help!"

"This is not my problem. There are many who are wanting Laurine's life. We do not be saving them. Why should we do different things for these two?"

"Because these two have gotten the closest of any who have tried before them!" Yvette sighed.

"And why should I take you at your word?"

"Look, just tell Thistle about the situation and he'll take care of it."

"Thistle is the reason that I be not killing you already and been done with this thing!" The flat voice finally broke its monotone and took on an edge of violence. Magdolon crept forward and peered through the trees, trying to catch a glimpse of the two. He spied Yvette quickly, her pale blue habit and white undersleeves were easy to make out in the quickening gloom of the forest at sunset. The other voice's owner was a bit harder to spy, but Magdolon almost gasped in surprise as he recognized the outline of a naiad standing beside her. The lithe form of the newcomer was a pale emerald color, and Magdolon could just make out a kind of armor fashioned to look like leaves covering her shoulders and chest.

"Then remind me to thank him when he gets here." Yvette pushed past the naiad and stalked over toward the mouth of the cave where Ashal was resting.

"What make you think he is to be coming?"

This caused Yvette to stop and turn back toward her.

"Shesh'ra, do not play this game." Yvette's voice developed a hard edge, and Magdolon tensed his muscles unconsciously as he watched. "Where is Thistle?" Yvette growled. Silence hung in the air between them for several long moments. Finally, it was Shesh'ra who broke the quiet.

"He is to be coming, I am sure of it." She shook her head as she spoke. "But you speak about the abominations that be living in the abbey, you say these things as if you were not an abomination, also."

"What did you say?" Yvette snarled.

"You heard the words I speak." Shesh'ra shot back.

"How dare you!" Yvette stalked forward and Magdolon made to rise, but he felt a sudden pressure on his shoulder and looked over to see the end of a wooden staff resting there. He whirled around and found himself looking

141

into the clear blue eyes of a man. Golden hair fell in gentle waves from his head, matching the beard that grew out from his jaw. He was dressed in simple linens and held an equally simple staff in his hands. As Magdolon met his gaze, the man raised a finger to his lips and shook his head.

"I wouldn't interfere, my friend," he said, smiling. "Those two always get after each other whenever they meet. Thankfully they don't see each other very often, so we rarely have to worry about it; but when they do, it can be a truly catastrophic event. Best to let them sort things out on their own, then we can head over and take care of what's left."

Magdolon looked at the man quizzically. There was something odd about him, his face and arms were smooth, and his voice gave the impression of belonging to a youth. But the beard gave him the appearance of being much older than that.

"You must be the Thistle of which they spoke." Magdolon spoke slowly, still measuring the newcomer. The man's eyebrows shot up and he gave a small laugh.

"Indeed I am. Which gives you an advantage. You know my name, may I know yours?"

"I am called Magdolon." This response caused the blonde man's eyes to widen.

"*The* Magdolon? The one who convinced Yvette to stay and spy on Laurine?" There was something strange in his tone when the bearded man spoke.

"Uh... yes...?" Magdolon stammered.

"Yvette has spoken at length about you! I am... glad... to finally meet you face to face!" The man eyed Magdolon up and down with a scrutinizing gaze. "May I say that you speak our language very well! You even lack the heavy accent that Shesh'ra and the others struggle with. From what I understand, your language has a lot more syllables to it and there's a certain rhythm and cadence that you have to follow in order to convey your meaning?" Magdolon blinked as the man's voice began to speed up while he talked, and his head began to spin at the sudden change in topic.

"Yes, I have had much practice, more than most of my kind would have with your tongue." Magdolon responded uncertainly. "I used to have her accent, but it has faded with time."

Thistle nodded enthusiastically.

"Of course! Of course! I have so many questions for you but I... Ah!" He cut off abruptly. "We should probably go over as it seems things have elevated to a certain level of physicality, and the spirit of the forest would likely be unhappy if anything were to happen to his favorite naiad." He stepped to the side and walked briskly toward the cave. Magdolon turned, his head still fuzzy with the sharp topic changes. He saw that Yvette and Shesh'ra were now rolling around on the ground, with Yvette having the apparent upper hand.

"Ladies!" Thistle called out and the two struggling combatants paused, glancing up at him with gazes that threatened further violence upon whoever was interrupting them. Magdolon sighed and hurried to follow Thistle in case they followed through with that threat.

"Why this fighting?!" The blond man's voice seemed very loud as it bounced through the trees of the forest. "Haven't you two found some kind of solace in your ongoing feud?" He smiled broadly, but the angry gazes did not change. Finally Yvette grunted, pushing herself off of Shesh'ra, who she'd pinned beneath her.

"Be quiet, Thistle," she growled. Thistle's smile faded and he backed away from her. "Where have you been?"

"I... I was on the other side of the wood, Bitter Bark had me checking on the saplings there to ensure the forest was recovering from the recent fire. But I came as soon as I heard the bells tolling at the abbey! I figured there might have been something that happened, and Shesh'ra's messenger met me as I was on my way here."

"Yes, something happened!" Yvette stopped herself from stalking forward and closed her eyes, taking several deep breaths before opening them again. "Magdolon is here." She said at length, motioning behind Thistle to him.

"Yes, we've met!" Thistle grinned again, then grimaced when Yvette glared at him.

"His ward is inside the cave, healing from one of Laurine's spells. She's taken quite the beating, but she should be fine with a long soak in the spring." Thistle opened his mouth as if to say something but then seemed to think better of it and closed his mouth with an audible click of his teeth. Yvette rubbed her temples.

"What do we do now?" Magdolon asked, his voice causing Thistle to jump slightly and Yvette to look at him.

"You stay here and rest up with Ashal. I have to go back to the abbey and convince them I'm not a traitor." Yvette rubbed her wrists, and for a moment her exasperated expression slipped into that of a terrified child. Magdolon was taken aback, but as soon as it appeared, the haunted expression fled and was replaced with a neutral stare.

"Are you sure that is wise? Will Laurine not know that you helped us to escape?"

"I doubt it." Yvette shook her head. "There was so much going on when you two attacked that she probably thought I was dead. I'll just say I chased you and followed you as far as I dared before coming back. I'll try to get them to believe that you ran away. After things have died down a bit, I will reach out to you and we can try again. This time with a better plan, I hope."

"You wish to leave your peoples with us?" Shesh'ra growled.

"Not with you!" Yvette glared. "With Thistle."

"This is an impossible thing to ask," the naiad sputtered. "Bitter Bark will not allow this thing!"

"Bitter Bark doesn't need to know right away," Thistle protested.

"You would tell untruths to him?" Shesh'ra exclaimed.

"No! Just wait a few days to report, at least until the younger one is healed up!" Thistle countered.

"We do not wish to be a burden," Magdolon tried to interject.

"You're not, well, you are, but it's okay." Thistle nodded at him while looking at Shesh'ra.

"You are burdens," Shesh'ra growled, "but you are needing the rest and are enemy to Laurine. I will give three days before I will be reporting this thing to Bitter Bark. But he will be knowing the whole truth this time, Thistle. You will not be hiding *her* being here from him again." She said this while thrusting an accusing finger at Yvette, who rolled her eyes but kept quiet. Shesh'ra grumbled something under her breath and then stalked off into the growing shadows of the evening. Magdolon stared after her with a pensive look on his face.

"Don't worry about her. She's the leader of a group of naiads in the area that swore allegiance to the Green Lady a long time ago. They hate the undead who've taken over the abbey as much as anyone and will do just about anything to cleanse it. She'll keep her word." Thistle patted Magdolon on the arm, and the giant placoderm looked down at him with a cocked eyebrow. The druid cleared his throat and turned to Yvette.

"No offense about the hating undead thing. I'm afraid they view you as collateral damage in most cases," he said, reaching a hand out to pat her shoulder. Yvette twisted away and growled at him.

"Why did it take you so long?"

Thistle's face fell at this reaction.

"I told you already... I..."

"Why do you let him order you around like that?" Yvette cut him off. "I haven't been able to get a communication to you in weeks! And you go about your life as if there's nothing different?! Am I just collateral damage to you, too?"

Magdolon flinched under the stinging tone in her words, and they weren't even directed at him. Thistle shrank visibly under the onslaught.

"What do you expect me to do?" Thistle straightened his back and set his jaw as he spoke. "Bitter Bark won't even launch an attack when I tell him that you'll open the gates for us! What do you think he'll do if I say I need to rescue you? You're an abomination to him, remember?!" Yvette's face froze as if she'd been slapped, and she stared at Thistle with an intensity that broke whatever resolve he'd built up.

"I'm sorry," he tried to say, but she cut him off with a wave of her hand.

"It's fine. You're right." She turned and began walking away. "I need to get back before it becomes too suspicious. I've already been gone too long." She disappeared into the trees and Thistle watched her go with a strange look on his face, something of a mixture between anger and sadness. Magdolon waited patiently for the moments to pass until Thistle shook himself and turned to look at him.

"Yvette mentioned you had a friend in the cave who was healing up in the spring, then was it?" Magdolon nodded in response and Thistle smiled again. "Excellent, let me have a look at her and you can fill me in on the details as to why Yvette is mad at me while we do. How does that sound?" Magdolon nodded for a second time and together they walked into the cave where they found Ashal still asleep in the small stream which bubbled up from the rocks below and trickled out of the mouth of the cave. Thistle blew his cheeks out when he spied her.

"Yes, it looks like Laurine did a number on her, that's for sure. Not much light in here and I can still tell that." Thistle snapped his fingers and a small column of fire appeared above his open palm, casting orange light across the dimly lit cavern. Magdolon started at the sudden use of magic, and Thistle snickered at his reaction.

"Sorry! I should have warned you I was going to do that. We all learn healing as part of growing up a druid, but I picked up a few tricks along the way from various salamander priests who've passed through the woods and found that I had an affinity for fire magic. Comes in handy when dealing with forest fires and summoning fire elementals and whatnot. Also helps for those of us who aren't born with good eyes for the dark, right?"

Thistle walked over to where Ashal lay and held out his free hand over her body. Green light gathered under his outstretched fingers, and Magdolon watched in awe as the light washed over the naiad, flickering shades of emerald and teal that pulsed and rippled over her. After a few seconds, Thistle gasped and fell backward, the green light flickered and then disappeared with a flash. In the remaining light of the small column of fire in the druid's other hand, Magdolon could see a thick sheen of sweat on the man's forehead.

"That's the best I can do, I'm afraid," he gasped. "She'll be fine by tomorrow morning, worst case tomorrow afternoon if she doesn't stay in the water the whole time." Magdolon walked over and knelt beside Ashal. Her breathing was even and she seemed to have slipped off into a deep sleep, her eyes moving rapidly behind their lids.

"Thank you," Magdolon said honestly as he met the man's eyes.

"It's nothing. Though if you want to tell me about what happened today, and how you and the younger one came to be here, that would be a grand start of repaying me!" Thistle chuckled at his own cleverness. Magdolon nodded; moving to sit beside the druid, he began their long tale.

* * * * *

Yvette's boots echoed dully against the stone walls as she all but ran down the hallway toward Laurine's door. The abbey was suspiciously quiet this night. No choirs singing in the Great Hall, no whispering sisters in the corridors. Torches flickered gloomily in their sconces along the wall, but that was the only activity to disturb the stillness. Yvette paused before the door, her mind racing as she tried to sort out the story she'd cobbled together on her walk back to the abbey, giving it one last inspection before she would have to deliver it. She took a deep breath and then rapped twice on the wooden door.

"Come in," a weak voice called from the other side. Yvette pushed the heavy oaken door and stepped into Laurine's quarters. She gasped at the sight that greeted her. Laurine lay on her bed, her face pale and her hands covered in blood. Laying beside her were a pile of bloody bandages and open bottles that made the room smell of sharp medicinal ointment.

"Ah, my child." Laurine smiled weakly. "So good of you to return." She held out a shuddering hand and beckoned Yvette closer.

"Mother Abbess!" Yvette cried, hurrying to take the outstretched hand. "What happened?"

"Weren't you there?" Laurine started to ask, but a fit of coughing overtook her and she was forced to press a fresh scrap of bandage to her mouth. It was stained a ruby hue when she took it away. "I was attacked today, or don't you remember?"

"I remember, Abbess, but I thought you were able to heal the wounds from your attack?" Yvette examined Laurine's face. It was stretched thin, her eyes were tired and slightly feverish, her skin pale and clammy.

"Healing magic was never my strongest talent." Laurine coughed again. "Besides that, I think the dark arts are taking their toll on me. Thankfully, I had enough pluck to bluff my way through it at the market square. Managed to make it all the way back to my room before collapsing." Another coughing fit and Yvette moved closer to the abbess, her eyes lingering on a nearby cushion, her fingers twitching as she began leaning slowly toward it, a dreadful thought entering her mind.

"Let me make you more comfortable, Mother Abbess. If you can prop yourself up a bit, I can get this pillow underneath your back. It might make it easier to breath."

"Do not worry so, my child." Laurine smiled. "My mission here is not over. The Shining Ones will not take me just yet. There is so much more work left to do."

"I never doubted for a second, Mother Abbess." Yvette gripped the pillow in her hands, smiling at Laurine as she leaned over her, the cushion hovering a few inches from the abbess's face. "I just want to make sure that you can rest easier."A hand clamped down on Yvette's hand, cold as ice. Yvette spun around and found herself staring into Rose's frosty eyes.

"Hello, little duckling." That cruel smile filled Yvette's vision. "Where have you been, I wonder?"

Fifteen

MEMORIES OF THE DEEP

Ashal awoke with a start, the visions of her dream already fading into the recesses of her mind. She remembered bright green lights flashing and a sensation of warmth spreading throughout her body. Then it had all vanished and she had fallen into the dark void of her dreams that appeared as an endless pit. Screams had risen up around her. Screams of pain, some of them her own, filled the empty void accompanied with the pleading cries to stop the agony. Vague images that were sliding through her memory like sand through a sieve flashed across her eyes. She saw faces looking up at her with betrayed expressions, a hand reaching out of the flames, and an image of a shadow that was disappearing in the distance that brought with it feelings of immense sorrow.

As soon as she thought of these images, they disappeared from her memory. But there was one image that struck her and stayed with her into her waking moments. A beautiful woman with emerald eyes stared down at her. She whispered something that filled Ashal with dread for some reason which she could not explain.

"Betrayal is not a thing reserved only for the wicked. It is also the domain of the zealous, the cruel, and the inexperienced." Her voice was not angry, nor did she seem to chastise with her words, but Ashal knew that they were meant for her. The words became muddled in the blaring reality of the waking world, but the sensation of an impending weight loomed over her head in a way that caused her heart to pound quickly against her ribs.

"Magdolon!" She cried out.

"I am here." The large placoderm seemed to materialize out of the wall, his scales and their patterning blending in well with the dimly lit cave. Around the bend that lead to the mouth of the cave, Ashal could just make out the blue light of dawn pushing its way through the night sky. Her breathing came easier as she felt the steady presence of Magdolon kneeling beside her. She moved her limbs and was surprised at how well they responded. The heavy cloud that had hovered over her senses also seemed to be lifting. When she tried to lift her head, however, she found that her muscles screamed in protest from her neck down to her stomach, and she flopped backward with a splash.

"The druid said that you would feel the soreness for a time, but that it would fade by this evening. He said that you must stay in the stream for this to happen, though." Magdolon patted her shoulder then stood and returned to where he had been sitting. Ashal groaned as she lay in the cool water. She had to admit that the stream did feel good as it poured across her body. There was an ache deep in her muscles, but it was the ache of healing; and while it was tiring, she felt the difference between that and the pain of injury and was oddly comforted by it.

"What am I supposed to do for the day, then?" she asked. "I'll go crazy just lying here!"

"I do not know." Magdolon said with a shrug. "Perhaps you could practice with your meditation?" Ashal shot him a glare, and he chuckled in response.

"You could be a bit more helpful than that," she snapped. Magdolon continued chuckling. Finally after a moment or two, Magdolon sighed deeply and smiled at Ashal.

"What would you have me do to help?"

"I don't know… tell me a story or something to help pass the time?" She closed her eyes as she asked. "I know! Tell me about my mother! How did you come to join her personal household?" With her eyes closed, Ashal did not see the look on Magdolon's face, but she heard the melancholy steal into his voice.

"That was a very hard day. But I think that a story that would be better is the tale of the day you spawned." Magdolon forced a smile onto his face. "Lucky that they are the same story, too."

"Really?!" Ashal turned her head toward him, her eyes wide with surprise. Magdolon nodded.

"I will go back many years to tell this tale. This is also how your mother came to choose you as a potential heir. For you see, on the day of your spawning, there came a dark creature to the borders of your mother's domain…"

* * * * *

Magdolon gripped his spear tightly as he stared out over the field of battle. A gentle spring of warm salt water flowed from the depths of the deep underwater ravine and washed over the placoderm and his companions who stood arranged in a long battle line against the ridges of the abyssal trench that spread out before them. Behind him were lined several of the large harpoon guns that had been aptly named the Leviathan's Bane, as they were used for hunting large game beneath the waves.

All of the placoderms gripped either barbed spears or cruelly spiked tridents, the preferred weapons for fighting underwater where it took less effort to stab than it did to swing a blade or other heavy weapon. Glittering fish scale armor covered each of the placoderms, and the front few ranks carried heavy shields which they held close to their bodies.

A bitter anticipation had settled upon Magdolon. He was still considered fairly young for the cohort in which he found himself, but he was big for his age and the other soldiers were grateful for his extra strength. He was big even compared to other placoderms and stood a good head taller than any of his brothers beside him. This would be his first real confrontation since returning from his time in the Royal Army, and while that filled him with a type of excitement, he lamented that it would not be against an enemy army but something far more bestial in nature.

Reports had been filing in from the border stations of the other principalities of a creature making its way along one of the many trenches that split the ocean floor and passed directly through Ai-ellain's domain. The monster was reported to be several times larger than that of even the most hulking beasts of the deep and had earned the catch-all title of leviathan. At random intervals, the creature would rise up out of the trench and attack nearby settlements, often wiping them out with little to no survivors. No one understood the purpose of the attacks. Some reasoned that the leviathan was feeding on the villages, but that didn't seem to be the case as the bodies that were discovered never appeared to have been molested after being killed. The creature was not eating its victims, but there was no other logical reason for the senseless violence.

It had been determined that the creature was headed in a direction that threatened their waters, and so Ai-ellain had dispatched her troops to prepare for its arrival. She had also sent scouts to watch for its approach, and if they saw it to try and draw it to this indicated spot where they had prepared an organized defense. The scouts soon reported that the beast was nearly there and that they were luring it as had been planned. The troops had been assembled and dispatched to the designated location. Now came the waiting game and Magdolon was tired of it. He was also feeling a bit hurt that their liege had not shown herself that day. But Magdolon needn't have worried about his lord's absence, for even as he sat sulking, he heard a ripple of cheering from further down the line which caused him to look up.

There he saw a sight that both lifted his spirits considerably while at the same time filling his belly with shame for having doubted. Ai-ellain was parading down the line of her soldiers atop an armored sea turtle, standing on its shell like it was a battle platform and leaning against one of the Leviathan Banes that was attached there. The naiad noble was clad in overlapping plates that gleamed in the flickering blue light of the ocean in a way that made her appear to shimmer where she stood. In her right hand she gripped a large trident, which she waved about and called out to her soldiers, her diaphragm pushed the song of her words through the water to wash over their gathered ranks. The prolonged syllables of her speech allowed the water to carry their meaning further and made it possible that even those in the back of the battle line would understand them.

"My Neriticans which dwell with me this day! This day is a day for which we will sing to our spawnlings who now rest in our homes! This day have we been given to celebrate with festivities!" Her words caused a confused ripple of conversation among her troops. She laughed at their response.

"Do you not see the sense of my words?!" She smiled. "Our trophy is to be coming to us through the dark of the trench! I will be for mounting the head of this beast in our hall, insomuch that all who visit our waters shall know of the prowess of our warriors! This day we hunt! We hunt the big game that threatens this our kingdom and our home waters! This day will we put down a terror of the deep! Be proud that you are among our company as a warrior!" A cheer rose up among the gathered soldiers as they clapped each other on the back and bellowed their approval of their leader's words.

Magdolon felt himself smiling in spite of himself. His shame at doubting the nerve of his liege mingled with the pride and anticipation he felt at being present at this event, at having been selected as part of the companionship that would defend their home. The two emotions left him with a bittersweet melancholy. But he didn't have long to dwell on his feelings.

A deep, keening screech echoed up from out of the trench. It sounded distant, but then the sound repeated and Magdolon saw the silver flash of something shooting out of the deep chasm. It took him a moment to realize that it was the armored figure of one of the naiad scouts that had been sent ahead to try and lure the leviathan to their position. From the sound of the creature's cries, they had been successful, but Magdolon was quick to note that no other scouts were seen escaping the trench, either.

"*Placoderms!*" The commander of their unit cried out beside Magdolon. Instantly, he snapped to attention, as did the rest of his unit, and as one they raised their spears and tridents above their head.

"*Quoi' nakena?!*" The commander bellowed out his challenge in the placoderm's native tongue.

"*Hai nam!*" They responded with a simple phrase: *I stand ready!*

"*Quoi' nakena?!*" Again the challenge came: A*re you prepared?!*

"Hai nam!"

"*Soi'fala nakena?!*" The commander bellowed, and the placoderms began stamping their feet in response to another challenge: *Are your feet prepared?*"

"*Fala nam!*" *My feet stand ready!*

"*Soi'het nakena?!*" *Are your hands prepared?!* The placoderms began slamming their fists into their chest in a slow, rhythmic thump.

"*Het nam! My hands are ready!* The commander let out a deep, growling cry and launched straight into the battle prayer.

"*To're tefee!*" He chanted to the rhythm of the stamping feet and the thumping fists. The placoderms repeated the simple phrase: *I call out my challenge!*

"*To're tefee!*" Again it was repeated. Several of the members of the back called out loudly as well, the adrenaline causing them to cry out more individualized battlecries. All of the placoderms began shaking their weapons toward the trench.

"*Ca'ohm namena!*" Their hands all shot up above their heads as they cried out in unison: *Come to me!*

"*Sao'nete y manutahu et folah!*" *The water's light is bright, it shines upon the sand.* The placoderms chanted while bringing their hands down to their sides.

"*Com'rah nete onwei upan et co'pah!*" *We are they who call upon the tides of the deep.* The placoderms leaned forward and extended their hands out, shaking them back and forth.

"*Et mohet, iri tamateen neturufar!*" They repeated this phrase twice, the second time louder than the first. *If death is my end, let it come!*

"*Hai nam! Hai nam! Hai nam!*" They chanted this last part slowly, taking a step forward each time it repeated.

"*Ca'ohm onwei nah!*" *Let the wave come!* The placoderms threw their hands above their heads on this last syllable and erupted into a series of cries, hissing, and cheers. Some banged their weapons against shields, others slapped their tails or stamped their feet into the sand which threw up golden clouds of water dust. All around them, the other warriors of Ai'ellain's army echoed their cheers, caught up in the thumping rhythm and anticipation of the battle prayer.

Gulping down air through his gills, Magdolon steadied himself for the coming fight, his heart hammering in his temples. Then there came the sound of cracking rocks from the trench and the ground seemed to ripple under his feet. Another screech, this time the sound was nearly deafening, as if the monster was already in front of them. Magdolon winced under the pressure of the sound and his vision blurred. When it cleared, he had to shake his head to make sure what he saw was real. The edge of the trench appeared to be moving! Magdolon squinted and looked closer; no, it wasn't the lip of the trench that was moving, but rather dozens of creatures that were clawing their way up from the depths!

Magdolon recoiled as he saw great fanged beasts whose mouths covered half of their bodies. Great, finned limbs that stretched to impossible lengths ended in claws and milky white eyes darted back and forth as the creatures scrambled frantically up out of the trench and began running toward the line of placoderm defenders that separated them from the leviathan's bane harpoon guns behind them. What were these things? They couldn't be the source of the screeches from before, and they surely weren't the leviathan they had been sent to hunt!

"Hold fast!" Ai-ellain's voice cut through the reverberations of the leviathan's keening down below and helped steel Magdolon's nerves. He allowed

153

the practised discipline that had been drilled into him and his fellow defenders to control his movments. He stepped forward to lock his bone shield together with the others to form a wall with their spears and tridents resting on the edges of their shields pointed outward toward the oncoming swarm of their new foe. Behind them, the second rank of placoderms raised their shields to form a type of shell around the whole unit so that none of their attackers could simply swim above them and bypass their defenses.

The horrific creatures charged forward and the chittering noises they made grew louder as they approached, which grated against Magdolon's nerves. He tensed his shoulders and braced against the impact as the first creature slammed against his shield, and he gasped as others hit the defensive wall further down the line. This caused a ripple of pressure against the defenders and pushed them back a few inches. Magdolon bellowed his defiance and stabbed outward with his trident, feeling a satisfying squelch as the tips of his weapon pierced the scaly flesh of the beast before him and caused it to go limp and float away.

Another creature immediately replaced its fallen companion and thrust its claws toward Magdolon's face. He brought his shield up to block and the attack was forced wide. Instead of hitting him, the twisted limb twitched sideways and scored a deep wound in the placoderm standing to Magdolon's side, and his brother fell back screaming in pain. Magdolon quickly moved to try and plug the gap, but it was too late. The trained movements of the defenders were being overwhelmed by the sheer numbers of the creatures throwing themselves uncaringly at their lines, and already several holes had opened up in the shield wall. The beasts wasted no time in exploiting these, and the battle lines quickly devolved into frantic skirmishes of two and three placoderms forming up to stab at their attackers while trying to guard each other's flanks.

Magdolon found himself alone and he kept stabbing outward at the beasts as they surrounded him. It was a whirl of dark scales with the occasional flash of sharp claws and fanged teeth. Magdolon felt stinging wounds all over his body, but still he continued to lash out with his weapon, and when that was torn from him, he drew the long knife from his belt and continued to fight. He didn't know how long this continued, but eventually even his knife spun out of his nerveless grasp as the creatures continued to surge over him. He then he felt the bulk of a monster slam into his shield and he fell to the ground in a dazed heap.

His assailant stood over him with its blind eyes glistening. Its enormous mouth seemed to unhinge as it prepared to bite down. Magdolon was exhausted and pinned under the creature's weight and his own shield. He closed his eyes and prepared for the pain, but it never came. Magdolon opened his eyes and was surprised to see the gleaming form of Ai-ellain standing over him, her trident flashing about her in glorious arcs. Each stab took one of the beasts through its eyes or another's throat was torn out by a masterful thrust. The naiad lord was a wonder to behold, and as Magdolon hauled himself to his feet, he saw the corpses of dozens, if not hundreds, of the horrors laying about him. His brothers had fought well, and while their bodies also littered the ocean floor, there were at least four of the beasts for every placoderm that lay dead. What's more, the harpoon guns had remained safe despite the monstrous onslaught.

Another keening cry pierced the water and the dying sounds of battle, accompanied by a massive limb the size of one of the great warships that Magdolon had seen the humans command on the surface. The limb shot out of the trench to plant an enormous claw into the sand of the ocean floor. Next appeared a great, beady eye that was easily the size of Magdolon's entire body, also milky white like that of the beasts that had come before. It rolled in its socket and focused on the remaining warriors who stood on the blood-soaked lip of the trench. A gaping maw appeared and another piercing screech tore through the water. This time it was deafening and forced Magdolon to his knees as the sound washed over him in a painful wave of noise. The fanged mouth was attached to a great, bulbous head that towered over the Neritican warriors.

The leviathan swung a massive claw across the gathered figures before it, and Magdolon quickly swam upward to try and avoid its reach. He was one of the fortunate few who managed to clear it, and the wake that followed in its passage sent Magdolon spinning through the water. When he re-focused his eyes, he gasped at the carnage that the creature had so quickly visited on his brethren. The entire field leading up to the lip of the trench was obscured by the swirling sand as it tumbled through the open water. Inside this cloud, Magdolon could see hundreds of bodies and disembodied limbs spinning; the sand was darkened in places by clouds of viscous liquid that Magdolon assumed was blood. Around him, Magdolon saw a few dozen other survivors who were reacting with similar horror to the sight of what lay before them.

"Fire!" A voice carried out through the water and shook Magdolong from his stunned reverie. There was a loud series of cracks and Magdolon looked down to see all of the great harpoon guns firing their shafts into the bloody cloud of sand, toward the colossal beast responsible for the carnage. Magdolon held his breath as he watched the projectiles soar past him, and though it was difficult to see the beast itself, the keening cry that followed gave a distinct impression of a wounded animal. Magdolon smiled grimly. The beast could be hurt!

Casting his eyes about, Magdolon spotted his liege once again astride her giant sea turtle. The harpoon gun mounted to its back was loaded, and as the sand began to settle from the Leviathan's rage, Magdolon watched Ai-ellain take aim with the large weapon. The beast reared up and its eye fixed on the naiad and her turtle just as the harpoon shot forward. Ai-ellain's aim was true, and the barbed metal shaft embedded itself deep within the creature's scarred iris. The leviathan thrashed wildly, and Magdolon saw one of its massive claws swinging toward Ai-ellain who was busy reloading her harpoon gun.

"My lord!" Magdolon cried out and flicked his massive tail to shoot through the water. He collided with the naiad lord moments before the claw connected with the giant sea turtle. The concussive blast of the blow sent both Ai-ellain and Magdolon spiraling through the water, tumbling end over end, and turned the turtle into a bloody red mist. The monster screeched out its pain as it continued to lash out blindly.

When he finally stopped spinning, Magdolon looked around him for Ai-ellain, and for a few panicked moments was unable to locate her until he cast his eyes upward and saw the golden glint of her armor. He swam toward the outline of the naiad lord until he was level with her. Ai-ellain had a dazed look on her face and there was some blood on her cheek, but beyond that she didn't seem to be hurt.

"My lord?" Magdolon shouted, and Ai-ellain blinked in response, her eyes focusing on the placoderm.

"You... saved me..." she said, and Magdolon simply stared in response. "By what name are you called?" The naiad spun in the water so that she was fully facing the other warrior.

"I am he that is called Magdolon, my lord."

"My gratitude is given to you, Magdolon." Ai-ellain grimaced as another screech from the leviathan wrent their ears. Glancing back at the giant creature, she frowned and then turned her attention back to the placoderm. "It is the eyes where this creature bleeds the most. Go and give counsel to the Leviathan's Bane down the flank that is furthest, I shall also do this but with those ones who are closest. Be swift! The creature is angry now, but sorrow will follow if we are not swift, and the beast will do harm to our families and our homes if we do not bring its death here and now."

Magdolon nodded his understanding and then sped off through the water, his powerful tail pushing him toward the weapons' crews ahead of him. The monster wailed its pain and he watched in horror as it brought one of its massive claws down to crush a harpoon launcher and several of its crew who were unfortunate enough to get caught beneath the titanic weight of the creature's limbs. Magdolon tried to ignore the wails and cries of the wounded and dying as he swam around the destruction left by the leviathan's strike, closing on the nearest launcher.

"The eyes! You are to shoot for the eyes!" he cried as he drew closer, and the weapon's master gunner turned a quizzical look at him. "Lord Ai-ellain says to shoot for the eyes!" Magdolon yelled breathlessly as he came to a halt in front of her.

"That target that you request is too small, and we are too distant from it to make a shot such as this," the master gunner yelled back.

"But no other shot will do what is needed!" Magdolon replied, still gasping. "Please! It is not myself, but our liege who demands this thing!"

The master gunner shrugged and began bellowing orders to her crews. Soon, all of the harpoons were flying at the leviathan's face. The creature screamed its rage at them and threw its massive claws at their lines. The carnage was great, but Magdolon could see no reward for following Ai-ellain's orders; and so he swam to find his liege and see what other plans she might have. He found the naiad lord on the edge of the line of weapons, near the wreckage of one crew, where she sat holding one of the heavy harpoons that the Leviathan's Bane fired from its powerful recurves.

"My lord!" Magdolon called out. "The weapons are firing as you did request, but the distance is too great and they cannot claim the hits that you wish."

"This thing I know," Ai-ellain replied, her voice was quiet. "Did you know that this day my spawnlings are hatching back at my rookery?" The question caught Magdolon off guard.

"No, my lord, I did not know this thing. So you are to be a mother today?"

"Yes," Ai-ellain spoke softly, a small smile spreading across her lips, the red fins at the sides of her head swishing back and forth excitedly. "I was to choose my heir this day."

Magdolon's eyes widened.

"Then should you not leave the battle, my lord?" Ai-ellain shook her head at the question and looked up at the placoderm.

"How would I speak to my child of courage if I did such a thing as this?" She stood slowly, lifting the end of the large weapon's harpoon she held with her. The other half of the projectile remained buried in the recently disturbed sand. She hefted the heavy shaft in her hands and looked at Magdolon.

"Will you help me in this thing that I must do?" Her voice was low, and a small smile spread across her face as she spoke. Magdolon was taken aback by the request, but he did not hesitate and stepped forward to dig out the back half of the harpoon. It was heavier than he expected, but he quickly pulled it up to his chest and nodded to his liege. Together they kicked off the ocean floor and ascended.

The leviathan was screaming its rage and pain at the remaining war machines. What guns were left were not significant enough to really cause any lasting damage to the beast. Most had already fallen to its scaled claws that were even now raking down another team who had been too slow in abandoning their position. Their screams of terror were drowned out by the bellowing of the leviathan as it moved on to its next target. Ai-ellain held up a hand to stop their ascent, and Magdolon could see what she was planning. They were level with the beast's head, more specifically they were pointed at its massive eye which was still spinning in its socket, trying to dislodge the harpoon that Ai-ellain had lodged there previously.

"We have but one shot to kill the creature." The naiad kept her gaze fixed forward as she spoke. "If we do not strike with trueness, then we will be cast down into the depths." Magdolon closed his eyes and nodded before responding.

"*Hai nam*, my liege." His voice was steady despite the trembling he felt in his stomach. Together they began pushing themselves toward their target. The creature screamed once more, but its wounded eye could not see them, or at least if it did, it thought that they were nothing more than floating detritus from the massacre below. Magdolon snapped his powerful tail back and forth to gain momentum, kicking his webbed feet in time with Ai-ellain ahead of him. They gained speed as they flowed through the water, bubbles began to fall away from them as they moved faster and faster toward their prey.

They were within feet of their target when the creature sensed the danger. Desperately it reeled backward and brought a massive claw up to defend itself, but it was too late. Magdolon watched as the tip of the harpoon buried itself in the soft flesh of the leviathan's eye. He grunted as the shaft encountered resistance and ground to a jarring halt in his hands.

"Release! Get away!" Ai-ellain commanded and Magdolon obeyed, swimming swiftly away from the creature as it bellowed in pain. He barely put enough distance between himself and the eye before a scaled hand cleaved the water that separated them, and he struggled not to be carried away in the wake of its passing. The creature screamed again in rage and pain, but it was obviously not dead.

"It will not go to the dark so quietly," Ai-ellain yelled over the noise of its agonized cries.

"What else is there for us to do?" Magdolon responded. Ai-ellain shook her head. Magdolon looked back at the injured eye, blood was filling the water around it like some red cloud in the skies above the surface. The leviathan reached its claw back up and rubbed at its wound, and Magdolon watched in dismay as the harpoon dislodged and went spinning down into the darkness of the trench. This caused the red haze to deepen its intensity as the wound was torn open further and more blood poured from it.

"It has stopped its destruction of our soldiers, for a time at least," Ai-ellain said slowly, and Magdolon looked about to discover that it was true. The monster was concentrating on its wound rather than the remaining Neriticans still standing on the battlefield. Magdolon's eyes widened and he turned to his liege.

"Perhaps it is not necessary that we send this beast to the dark," he spoke quickly. "Let us blind it and may it be that the creature will descend to the depths on its own!" Ai-ellain smiled at this and nodded.

"It may suffice, it may do nothing, but we have nothing better for our time, and we must attempt one thing or another. This is better than most plans." She nodded and together they swam back down to the ocean floor. It was a simple matter to find a discarded and serviceable harpoon buried in the sand from the myriad of shots that had failed to penetrate their target's armored scales. Hefting it onto their shoulders, they swam up quickly to return to eye level with their monstrous foe who was still thrashing about wildly and howling in pain. Its wounded eye trailed a crimson cloud behind it as it moved through the water.

"We will have only a single attempt at this," Ai-ellain said over her shoulder. Magdolon grunted in response and together they kicked out, aiming for the uninjured eye rolling madly in its socket before them. As they sped through the water, Magdolon felt a sudden weight settle in his stomach, twisting his innards with a sense of foreboding. He cast his gaze about, trying to see what his premonition was trying to warn him about. He looked straight ahead and almost cried out as he saw the beast's eye, their target, was fixed solidly on them, and it was angry.

Magdolon winced as the leviathan screamed its pain at them; he tried to call out to warn his liege, but the sound was too loud and their target so close that Ai-ellain pushed forward heedless of the danger. It was likely that she wouldn't have heeded Magdolon had she actually heard him. Magdolon glanced to the side and saw the creature's massive claws speeding toward them, and in a moment's thought he twisted his torso, throwing Ai-ellain's aim off and sending her spinning away at the jolt of Magdolon's sudden movement.

Ai-ellain shot away from the harpoon and Magdolon found himself holding the weapon by himself. It was immensely heavy and the momentum of their charge was almost spent. Magdolon could feel the metal rod pulling him down and he watched the beast's claw as it drew closer, preparing to swat him away like some annoying school of fish that might hover about its head.

Magdolon heaved the massive harpoon up to clutch it against his chest and kicked his massive tail upward. The claw drew closer, and for a moment he was afraid that it would catch him before he could reach the appropriate height. But the scaled limb passed beneath him by several feet, and Magdolon felt the pressure of its passage as bubbles washed over him in waves. Turning, he looked down at the beast that now lay beneath him. Its uninjured eye was rolling around, searching for him, but the beast never looked up. From his vantage, Magdolon noticed that the creature's back, over which he currently floated, was rigid and covered with a hardened carapace. He realized that the creature *couldn't* look up! Its massive bulk and carapace prevented it from doing so!

Safe in his new discovery, Magdolon quickly looked about for signs that his liege had been thrown clear by his actions. He couldn't see her anywhere, but he knew that she would not live long if Magdolon did not act quickly. Taking his time to line up the shot appropriately, he took several deep breaths to steady his nerves. Below him, the creature screamed and again began its rampage. Magdolon dove, allowing the weight of the harpoon to lend its momentum to that generated by his own limbs. The placoderm sped toward his target.

The leviathan never saw the harpoon until its point penetrated the soft flesh of its eye. Magdolon slammed all of his weight into the blow and gasped as another cloud of ruby blood washed over him to mirror its sister wound in the creature's other eye. The beast screamed and Magdolon kicked backward, leaving the harpoon embedded in the beast's pupil. He swam upward again, knowing it was the best chance for safety.

Above the creature, Magdolon watched its violent lashings and heard its terrible cries of pain. Part of him pitied the beast, but it had come to their home and they had responded in kind to its destructive advances. This creature would likely die from its wounds. The salt water would cause the metal from the harpoon to oxidize eventually, and that would poison the beast's blood, likely killing it in a slow and very painful way after it retreated back to the depths to wallow in its own eternal darkness. It was not a good death, and Magdolon wished that he had the means to end it sooner for the beast, but this was all that they could do at this point.

Eventually the creature began to descend as its cries turned to whimpers. It stopped flailing about with its limbs and instead pulled back into the depths of the trench from whence it had come. Below Magdolon, he could hear the ragged cheering of his brothers and sisters in arms. Slowly, he began his descent toward them.

He saw how terrible the price had been for his fellow warriors. Almost a quarter of those who had gathered that morning were now scattered across the sand or suspended in the water with blank stares plastered on their faces. The dark stain of gore and blood hung heavy in the otherwise clear blue of the ocean floor. Magdolon felt pangs of sadness at this. However, the cheering masses of his surviving family of soldiers buoyed him up, and he swam anxiously toward them, searching for familiar faces amongst the crowds.

"Magdolon!" He heard an imperial voice cry out and he stopped to turn toward it. Ai-ellain hovered in the water above him. Blood from the beast had stained parts of her armor, and she clutched her ribs protectively as she swam down to meet the placoderm.

"My liege!" Magdolon bowed before her, but the naiad lord shook her head and motioned for him to rise.

"The bones of my side are broken because of you." Ai-ellain's voice held no malice, and a smile played at the side of her mouth. "But we are alive because of it. Because of you. You show great promise with your bravery and the speed of your thoughts."

"I thank you, my lord." Magdolon smiled in spite of himself.

"I am about to leave for my home spring. My children await me there. But I will send for you in time so that we may speak of your actions this day. I feel that you have shown your worth, and such will be written in songs that this was the beginning for you." Ai-ellain smiled and placed a hand on Magdolon's shoulder for just a moment before turning and swimming away. Magdolon watched her go and then moved to join his celebrating comrades at the defeat of the leviathan.

* * * * *

"That was the day that you were spawned." Magdolon ended his story. Ashal was now sitting up in the pool, flexing her arms to test their strength. Several hours had passed, and in that time, Magdolon had stopped a few times to discover that food had been left for them at the entrance of the cave. Usually berries and roots, but occasionally some nuts and acorns were also left. Ashal felt strong, and only small scars touched her skin where the magic had burned the hottest, and she marveled at her progress, she had accomplished a month's worth of recovery in the space of a day.

"I remember my mother telling me this story," she said, rising from the pool and walking over to retrieve her spear. "She said it is where I got my name."

"You were the first of your brood to emerge, and thus you were named firstling and given the honor of being made heir. That also meant you received the name that your mother had picked for her heir." Magdolon smiled.

"I understand that." Ashal shook her head, smiling as she fell into a defensive stance and felt the stretch of her newly healed muscles. "But she never told me what my name means, or if she did, I was too young to remember."

"Your full title is *Ashal Thuun Leviatum*," Magdolon said, his rumbling voice taking on a gravelly quality as he spoke. "It is a relic of the ancient tongues of the deep. It translates, roughly, to 'The Wake of the Leviathan'." Ashal stopped and turned a quizzical stare at him. Magdolon chuckled at her response.

"Your mother had a special style of humor." He laughed. Ashal shook her head but then quickly joined in the laughter. She felt something inside her begin to uncoil, a sense of calm that wrapped around her like a blanket that lay just above her skin. The laughter felt good and it continued far past what mirth Magdolon's revelation warranted. But, like the healing spring which tumbled over the rocks of the cave floor, the bubbling waves of laughter soothed the stinging reproach of their failure, and after the laughter had subsided, Ashal found herself in the fuzzy warmth of an exhausted sleep.

* * * * *

Outside the cave, the sun set on their second day inside the cave. The sunlight changed from bright yellow to vibrant red until the sky was punctuated with a muted blue and the stars began to emerge. Beneath those stars sat shadowy figures who sat watching the mouth of the cave. Fanged teeth and ancient steel sat waiting to tear flesh and drink blood. Finally as the moon began its climb into the night sky, they advanced toward their prey.

Sixteen

WHERE TO GO FROM HERE

Ashal couldn't sleep anymore. After the comforting warmth of her rest following Magdolon's story, she had awoken to the darkness of the cave, and the terrible prospect of what lay ahead of her clutched her gut and refused to allow her to relax. She pulled herself up and out of the pool of water, finding her strength renewed beyond her expectations, and began to pace the small space. Ideas and thoughts ran through her mind as she walked. She stretched her muscles as she moved, feeling a pleasant soreness there like she was recovering from a hard day of training. It was a welcome distraction to the difficult scenarios that whirled about in her head.

What were they going to do about Laurine? Ashal had delivered a blow that should have killed her, and she laughed it off before almost burning her to death with necrotic flames, and even tried to do the same to Magdolon. What would it take to finish her? Ashal shook her head, her lips moving as she muttered to herself while she walked. She formed ideas and discarded them as quickly as they came. Nothing seemed to work in her mind. There was always a fatal flaw. There were too many unknowns, and as she pondered, a sick feeling began to settle in the pit of her stomach. She felt the sensation spread outward, first to her chest, then to her throat, as a damp feeling of panic slowly began to overcome her.

"Magdolon," she whispered urgently, gently shaking him. "Are you awake?"

His eyes flashed open and she felt his body stiffen as his mind sprang into the waking world.

"What is it? What is wrong?" he hissed. Ashal shook her head.

"Nothing, I just wished to talk with you." She stood up and walked away, words already pouring from her mouth before Magdolon could respond.

"I don't know what to do. Our plan almost got us both killed before, and now it seems that Laurine is impossible to kill. How can we hope to defeat her?" She looked down at him, waiting for an answer. He simply lay there, returning her stare with an implacable one of his own.

"I do not have the answers that you seek," he said at length. Ashal growled in frustration.

"What are we going to do?!" She all but screamed it. Magdolon stood and gripped her by the shoulders.

"Gather your spear and practice your forms." His voice was flat to match his face.

"I don't want to practice forms right now!" Ashal snarled.

"You will do as I tell you!" Magdolon roared, and Ashal flinched in surprise. Numbly, she walked over and picked up her spear. Falling into a practiced defensive stance, she began flowing through her different poses that were meant as the baseline of so many fighting styles. She felt the cool bone shaft beneath her fingers and the reassuring weight at the end of the shaft. Yvette had managed to recover the spear for her during their flight from the village, and Ashal was surprised at how comforting it was to hold the magnificent weapon in her hands again. She would have to thank Yvette the next time they crossed paths.

As she moved through her practice movements, the familiar motions settled around her and caused her vision to focus. Thrust upward, pull back to a defensive position with the spear haft crossways across her body. Low thrust, retract, twin body stabs in quick succession, followed by another low thrust. She felt herself beginning to calm, her heart rate now elevated due to exertion rather than panic. Her breathing came in deep gulps of air which fed the blood now pounding in her temples. As she finished the last sweep of her spear and pounded the butt of it into the rocky ground at her feet, she took a deep breath and rolled her shoulders.

"Have you reached a better place in your mind?"

Ashal sighed and turned to face her mentor. Magdolon nodded and motioned for her to sit beside him on a large stone that sat half-buried in mud and pebbles.

"While you slept, the druid Thistle and I spoke concerning this thing for which you worry." Ashal walked over and sat beside him. "Thistle told me many things that will help you decide what you must do next."

"Such as?" Ashal brought her knee up to her chest and rested her chin on it while staring sideways at him.

"This forest is under the protection of the Green Lady, and she has placed an ancient herder of the woods to guard it. The name of this guardian is Bitter Bark, and Thistle has begged him many times to lead the forces of nature here to cleanse the corrupt abbey."

"Why has he refused? Is the guardian a coward?" Ashal snorted. Magdolon growled a warning at her, and she gave a short sigh. He glared at her for a short moment before speaking.

"Do not think that because he has not attacked that he is a coward," he rumbled. "He has not attacked because he is a guardian first and foremost.

He worries that the Hegemony would retaliate against the forest here. The fury of Mother Earth is only so strong and with all the threats it must face. The destruction of a small forest such as this would be tragic but not something that would be avenged. The Basileans would be foolhardy enough to burn the trees down in their anger, and Bitter Bark would be a poor protector indeed if he were to provoke that. At present, the corruption of the abbey has not spread to his domain, and so he waits for the day when his hand will be forced one way or another."

"So he is useless to us, then." Ashal gave a frustrated grunt. "How does this help us?"

"Information is never a bad thing to have, and there is a potential ally that might come to our aid if the situation is turned just right."

"Great!" Ashal rolled her eyes. "What other information do you have?"

"Tomorrow we will go before this Bitter Bark and plead our case." This pushed Ashal to her feet. Magdolon's eyes twinkled mischievously as he watched her.

"What do you mean, tomorrow?!"

"Exactly what I have said." Magdolon smiled. "Bitter Bark has learned of our presence through Shesh'ra, as she promised that he would. The guardian has demanded that we present ourselves before him."

"How is this a good thing?!"

"Remember that we have a possible ally in this creature, and he commands an army capable of storming Laurine's defenses."

"And he is already angry at us for coming uninvited into his lands."

"Yes, but he has already granted us an audience. How very convenient of him!"

"But what are we going to say to him?"

"You must convince him that attacking the abbey is vital to the protection of his forest."

"And how do you suggest we do that?!"

"Me?!" Magdolon opened his eyes wide in mock surprise. "I will not be doing anything! This is *your* task." Ashal gave an exasperated grunt and turned away from him.

"Fine!" She growled with a hint of exasperation. "Then what do you suggest that I do?"

"Convince him by any means necessary." Ashal turned and glared at Magdolon, who smiled in return.

"You are awfully cavalier about what may end up costing our lives," she said. Magdolon's smile only deepened.

"I have absolute faith in you and your ability to do the right thing." He stood and walked over to her, pulling her to his chest and squeezing her affectionately around her shoulders. Ashal sighed but pushed her face into his arm and returned the embrace.

"How sweet!" A voice came from the entrance of the cave, and both Ashal and Magdolon spun toward it. Ashal's eyes glanced over to where her spear lay propped against the cave wall. Magdolon quickly drew his weapon from where it had been strapped to his back.

Standing before them was a beautiful woman clad in Basilean armor. Gilded steel with golden filigree work along its edges covered a blue battle skirt that extended down to her shins, which were covered by more exquisite armor and steel sabatons. At her hip was strapped an ornate sword with a handle that was worked in a likeness of an angelic warrior whose wings formed the crossguard. She held a steel barbute against her other hip. Her face was a ravishing mask of cruelty that held two empty, cold eyes and a smirk on her full lips as she eyed them up and down.

"I am terribly sorry to interrupt," she sneered. "We would have tried to finish you in your sleep, but this one," she motioned toward Ashal, "she refused to close her eyes all night. With morning fast approaching, we figured we should just end this and be done with it."

"We?" Ashal narrowed her brows. As if in response to the question, two more armored figures stepped around the bend in the cave to stand behind the original speaker. They had their helmets in place and their swords were drawn and held ready.

"We have been betrayed!" Ashal hissed, glancing over at Magdolon. He did not respond but simply lowered the tip of his spear at the closest of their attackers. The woman who stood in the middle and seemed to be the leader of the trio laughed. It was a lilting sound that was at odds with the mood in the air.

"Ah, yes! But do not be too harsh with the little coquette! She did not betray you willingly, and she lasted far longer than she should have before giving you up."

"You will suffer for this!" Magdolon's voice rumbled.

"I'm sure I will." The woman smirked a final time before her face contorted into a howling visage. Her mouth opened wide and she shrieked at them as her teeth grew longer, sharpening into points. She cast her helmet to the side and drew her sword with long, claw-like fingers and lunged forward. Her companions followed her lead, and before Ashal could think, they were upon them.

Ashal dodged to the side as the nearest of the two attackers slashed at her, aiming for her midriff and missing by inches. Almost too quickly to follow, the blade reversed its direction and came back at her, this time slashing upward, and Ashal was forced to topple backward to avoid it. She tripped over a rock and landed on her back. Rather than fighting the momentum, she used it to roll backward. Springing to her feet she sprinted toward her spear that was still leaning against the wall. Glancing across the darkened cavern, she saw that Magdolon was fending off two of the vampires as they danced around him, throwing a whirlwind of attacks which bounced off the haft of his spear or cut through empty air as he dodged.

Ashal leapt forward to grab her own weapon, snatching it as she landed and turned to face her attacker. The undead warrior hissed as she lunged toward Ashal, who performed a quick parry that was more reflex than skill. The vampire's sword glanced off the haft of her spear. Ashal riposted with a quick jab which managed to score a glancing blow to her opponent's shoulder. The vampire was stunned by the hit and staggered backward. Ashal pressed the attack. She executed a flurry of thrusts that was part of her exercises that she had practiced so long in the shallow tides of the sea. Her muscles carried her through the familiar motions with an ease that kept the vampire wary. Ashal's spear tip flickered and blurred as it stabbed outward again and again.

The vampire tried to retaliate and gave a sloppy swing of her sword. Ashal easily ducked under the blow and thrust her spear up to embed itself in her attacker's side. The strike bit deep and the undead creature screeched in agony. The vampire reached over to grasp the haft of Ashal's spear while it was still embedded in her side, and Ashal watched in horror as the Basilean vampire wrenched her body sideways and swung her blade at Ashal's head. Ashal released her grip on the spear and fell to her knees to avoid the blow, moving back in anticipation of vampire's next strike.

Ashal kicked her assailant in the stomach and the blow threw the vampire to the ground. Ashal jumped forward to pull her spear free as it was still buried in her attacker's side, and in one smooth motion she tore the weapon free and whirled it above her head. She held the vampire's sword arm down with one foot and braced herself with the other. She took half a breath to steady her aim before stabbing downward for the small gap between the vampire's helmet and her breastplate. Her opponent tried to ward off the blow with her free hand, but Ashal's strike was too quick, the spear tip's aim too true, and the vampire was soon choking on its own blood.

Ashal wrenched her spear free and looked up toward Magdolon, who had not fared as well as her. She could see blood on his arms, shoulders, and legs from a multitude of little cuts which weren't fatal by any means but were enough to slow him down. Magdolon had no time to attack, all his energy was being spent in deflecting the tireless blows raining down on him from the two vampires. She knew that he could not win by only defending, however, and she moved to help him. But even as Ashal watched, he pushed off the ground in a lunge which caught the helmeted sister off guard and allowed him to drive his shoulder into her chest, causing her to double over in pain. Magdolon took advantage of this by drawing his dagger from his belt, and in one smooth motion, he drove the blade down into the base of the vampiric sister's skull. The woman dropped to the ground instantly.

Magdolon's attack didn't come without its cost; even as he finished the blow, he turned desperately back toward the leader of the vampire attackers.

It was not enough. Ashal tried to run and intercept the blow, but she was not quick enough. The sword of the leader pierced Magdolon's thigh clean through, and the placoderm cried out in pain. The beautiful woman smiled in triumph for a moment before Ashal slammed into her side, sending her crashing to the ground.

"Magdolon!" Ashal cried out.

"I am fine, child! Focus on your fight!" Magdolon cried out through gritted teeth as he gripped the handle of the sword now piercing his leg. Ashal nodded and fell into a defensive pose with her spear pointing toward the vampire who was already on her feet again and snarling. Even without her sword, she still had her claws which were deadly enough to finish Ashal and Magdolon both. Ashal advanced cautiously, knowing that the vampire had the speed to deliver the first blow. There was no way a quick strike from Ashal, even with her longer reach with the spear, would be able to end this fight that easily. She was proven right as her foe rushed her quickly, her movements a blur as she came on, her hands clawing at Ashal's face.

Ashal tried to use the haft of her spear to block the blows, but she still felt a burning pain sear across her forehead and down her cheek as clawed fingers tore across her face. She stabbed out blindly with her spear and the undead warrior danced to the side. Blood was running into Ashal's right eye from her wound, forcing her to close it. She could also see blood dripping from the vampire's claws as she raised it to her lips and licked the crimson liquid from her fingers.

"I've never been one to favor seafood," she snarled, baring her pointed teeth. Ashal took a deep breath and lunged at her opponent, stabbing desperately with only her one eye to guide her blows. The vampire laughed as she swayed from side to side, avoiding Ashal's strikes with ease. Ashal's arms burned with exertion, her attacks becoming more and more sluggish. The practiced discipline of her training dissolving in the heat of the vampire's laughter as she danced around her attacks.

Finally, the creature surged forward and slammed her fist into Ashal's stomach. She doubled over and coughed, sending a bloody spray across the rocky ground of the cave. The vampire extended her hand and lifted Ashal's gasping face by placing a single finger under her chin.

"I think we've waltzed long enough, little fish." She raised a clawed hand. Ashal stared up in horror, waiting for it to fall. The vampire suddenly stiffened and cried out in pain. She threw Ashal backward to slam against the floor, knocking the breath from her lungs. The undead sister turned, and Ashal saw Magdolon's dagger protruding from the small of her back, with the placoderm kneeling on the ground with a pained expression on his face.

"You miserable hulk of wretched sorrows!" The fallen paladin screamed with her back to her. Ashal watched as she grabbed Magdolon by the throat with one of her clawed hands and lifted him into the air. "I'm going to hurt you just enough that you can't move, then make you watch as I drain the naiad dry in front of you. Your suffering is only just beginning!" With that, the vampire snapped her head forward and bit deep into the side of Magdolon's throat. He cried out weakly but could not pull away from her terrible grip.

Ashal struggled to clear the gray clouds away from her vision. She felt pain in every part of her body and couldn't open her right eye. Something screamed inside of her that she needed to get up. She needed to move! To do something! She took a deep breath and focused on the horrible sight before her. Magdolon's struggles were growing weaker as the vampire sucked greedily at his blood. The bodies of their other attackers littered the floor of the cave.

"No!" she cried, surging forward from an unbalanced crouch. The vampire did not turn, too engrossed in her feeding to notice Ashal's staggering charge. It wasn't until Ashal ripped Magdolon's dagger from her back that the vampire arched backward in pain, tearing a huge chunk of flesh from Magdolon's neck as she did so. The creature screamed, but it was already too late for her. Ashal raised the dagger over the vampire's head and slammed it down into her chest, cutting her scream off in one bloody movement. The vampire coughed and then collapsed onto the floor. Magdolon stared at Ashal in stunned disbelief before also crashing to the ground.

"Magdolon!" Ashal cried, falling to her knees. She reached for her mentor's face. His eyes were unfocused and rolling slowly in their sockets.

"Magdolon!" She cried his name again, pulling his massive bulk closer to him. Magdolon's eyes seemed to lock on hers for a moment and he smiled, then his eyes closed and his head slumped backward.

"No! No, no no no no!" Ashal stood up and heaved on his arms, pulling his body toward the spring. Blood on her hands caused them to slip, and she fought to find purchase on his scaled limbs.

"Magdolon! Help me! I have to get you to the water! Magdolon!"

He didn't respond. After several long moments of pulling with no success, Ashal ran to his other side and began pushing against his shoulders. Gradually, he began to slide, his blood slicking the stones and making it easier for her to make some progress. Eventually he slid down and into the small stream, turning the water a rusty red color as it flowed over him. Magdolon gave a small gasp and then lay still in the flowing waters. Achieving her goal, Ashal ran to the mouth of the cave.

"Somebody! Help! Please!" She screamed into the dark, pre-dawn air. It was the only sound to break the silence. Not even the insects or the wind dared to disturb the deathly quiet that had fallen on the forest. Ashal continued screaming until she was hoarse, but nobody answered.

Part Three
BLOOD IN THE WATER

Seventeen

A BITTER DAWN

T histle knew that something was wrong the moment he stepped into the cave and saw the discarded Basilean helmet laying on the ground. He rushed further into the dark and was met with a gut-wrenching sight.

Ashal sat with Magdolon's head cradled in her lap, the gentle waters of the spring lapping over his chest. Three bodies wearing Basilean armor were strewn about the cave in pools of blood. Ashal herself was rocking back and forth, her breathing shallow and erratic. Thistle feared the worst.

"Ashal?" The druid whispered and her head snapped up, her eyes focusing on him. Dried blood covered her face and hands.

"Thistle! Please help!" Her voice was cracked like a shattered plate. "Hurry! Maybe you can save him! Maybe it's not too late!" She stood and rushed over to him, pulling on his arms impatiently. Thistle hurried forward and placed a hand on Magdolon's shoulder and then shook his head.

"Ashal. I'm sorry," Thistle said, looking down at Magdolon's frozen face. "The spring won't help him now." Ashal stared at the floor, her gaze a thousand miles away from her focus.

"I was afraid of that," she whispered. Her eyes were red, and the scales on her face were flaxen and wane. Thistle opened his mouth to say something but realized he didn't know what words would fit the moment, and so he closed it again. Ashal slid down to sit on the floor, hugging her knees to her chest, an aching sound escaped her chest that continued to grow. It was the sound of a wounded creature crying in the woods. The wordless void springing up to give sound to her pain.

Thistle stared at her awkwardly for a moment before shifting back to Magdolon's still face. The giant placoderm's shoulders seemed to stir, and Thistle's heart leapt into his throat. Summoning his magic, he began to probe the extent of the wounds with invisible tendrils. He felt a spark of life, like a small candle burning in Magdolon's chest. He breathed mystical air onto that spark and it flickered a little, then seemed to catch. Thistle continued to ease power into the still form of the nearly dead warrior, not daring to stop or tell

171

Ashal what he was doing for fear that any hesitation would cause Magdolon to fade into that final oblivion. Magdolon had lost a lot of blood, and his heart was weak, but it was still fighting to keep him alive. Thistle drew on the healing properties of the spring and pushed that magic into the wound at Magdolon's neck. He felt the muscle and skin there beginning to knit together, and the pain of that seemed to jolt the patient back from the edge. With a deep, sucking gasp, Magdolon opened his eyes and a sharp cry tore itself from his throat.

Ashal ran over to them both and placed her hands on the sides of Magdolon's face, crying his name over and over again. The giant placoderm's eyes were blurred and unseeing, but his chest was heaving up and down as they watched. Finally exhausted, Thistle tumbled backward. With a deep sigh, Magdolon's eyes closed and his head went limp in Ashal's hands. At first, Thistle was worried that he had succumbed to his wounds a second time, but a quick glance saw that his breath was still rising and falling in regular intervals.

"I've done everything I can, Ashal. His spirit wants to live, but now it is his fight to see if he will come back to you," Thistle said to calm her as she'd begun to panic after Magdolon's body had grown slack again.

Thistle stumbled over to sit against the wall. In a few moments, his strength would return, but he needed to rest first. In the back of his mind, he knew that Bitter Bark was waiting for them. He would send someone before too long if they did not return promptly. But it seemed too cruel to force the young naiad to deal with such matters while her mentor lay on the edge of death.

An idea struck Thistle, however, and he stood up unsteadily to walk over to one of the vampire's corpses strewn about the cave. He picked up one of the discarded Basilean swords and gripped the dead body's head by its hair. After several imprecise and messy hacking cuts from the sword, he managed to dislodge the head from the body in a bloody splash of gore that almost caused him to be sick.

Ashal had stopped crying by the time he finished, but now she simply sat beside Magdolon's head with a blank look on her face. Thistle shifted uncomfortably and wiped his bloody hands on the skirt of the newly decapitated body.

"A-Ashal…" She stiffened at the stammering of her name and turned bleary eyes to stare at him. He swallowed before continuing.

"Ashal, Bitter Bark has sent me to fetch you. We need to go or else he will send others to retrieve us, and they will not be gentle."

"I don't care." Ashal whispered and turned back to stare at Magdolon's chest as it rose and fell raggedly. They sat in silence for a long time. Thistle kept running different things that he might say through his mind, but nothing seemed appropriate or likely to motivate her to move away from her spot. The dawn light of morning began to filter into the cave as the sun began to banish the terrible night. At one point, there came the sound of movement from the mouth of the cave and Shesh'ra appeared.

172

"What is this that has happened?" she barked, her eyes focusing on the bodies that lay strewn about the cave. Then her gaze fell on Magdolon's body and at Ashal who still sat rocking back and forth. "Oh! *Spraw'nielt'ati!*" The word tripped off her tongue almost involuntarily, and in moments she was across the distance of the cave and kneeling beside Ashal, placing a hand on her back. Two other naiad warriors appeared, having followed their commander to the cave. In their hands they held alien looking heartpiercer harpoon guns, and they gazed about the cave with shocked looks on their faces. Thistle gave a sad smile at them and shrugged.

Shesh'ra continued speaking in a low tone, using the strange language of her people to talk with Ashal, who stopped rocking and stared at the newcomer with those same muted eyes that couldn't seem to focus. Then, just as suddenly, she seemed to break into tears and once again began to wail.

"What did you do?!" Thistle asked, leaping to his feet. Shesh'ra turned a furious gaze at him as she stroked Ashal's head gently.

"This one has felt the blow of a great pain. I am telling her that this is a good thing for to sadden. That she must shed water for the pain that she feels and that this is a good thing to do."

"But she's already done that!" Thistle declared, rubbing his forehead.

"No! She has not. She has only felt pains of not helping her loved one stay from harm. She has not dared to shed water for his hurt."

"But what about Bitter Bark?"

"He will wait on this. Bitter Bark has trust for me. I have never given him a gift of deception to make this trust fall from me."

"Since when have you decided to care for these outsiders so much?" Thistle's brow furrowed.

"This child, she has lost her home. If she is here to fight Laurine, then this will not be the first time that she has grieved such a thing. She is alone, now. The first thing she must need is to feel that it is okay to express this grief. On some things, the world must wait. On this thing, our world will wait."

"Why do you care, though?" Thistle's voice was a cold gust of wind, his face a stone cliff as he spoke. Shesh'ra motioned to the room around her before she replied.

"Because there is no other to do so for her at this moment." The cave had grown very still except for the ugly sobs that ripped themselves from Ashal's throat. Shesh'ra leaned over her and continued soothing her while using the Neritican language. Ashal gripped the rough rock of the wall as she wept. Thistle sat there, waiting patiently, sifting through the confusing tangle of emotions shooting through his veins. He felt relief that Shesh'ra had arrived and that she was able to help with Ashal, but another part of him was fuming at... something. Exactly what this heat rising in his chest was meant for, he couldn't say, but unconsciously a scowl formed on his face while he sat staring at Shesh'ra's back.

Finally the crying subsided, and Ashal's gaze focused on the body of her mentor still laying in the wake of the small spring. By now the bleeding had stopped and the water was no longer tinged a shade of ruby. Shesh'ra followed her eyes and then said something in their odd tongue. Ashal glanced back at her with red-rimmed eyes and nodded before standing and walking toward the mouth of the cave.

"What did you say to her?" Thistle asked, unable to keep a sullen note from his tone.

"I tell her we will be watching over him til she returns. That he will be seen to until she can do so herself. But now, it is to be her duty to seeing that his revenge be his for his wounding. She must be speaking to Bitter Bark to do this thing. That she must go now. The saddenings will come again, but now is time for purpose."

"Are you sure she will be able to convince Bitter Bark of anything? Especially in this state?" Thistle asked, staring after Ashal who stood now at the mouth of the cave with her eyes closed as the orange sunlight of the late morning washed over her.

"She is now more fierce than ever before. *If* Bitter Bark is to listen to her, there is no time that better it may be."

They left the two naiad guards to deal with the vampire bodies and to care for Magdolon before they began the walk to the sacred meadow where Bitter Bark held his court. It took a little more than an hour to make their way there, and when they stepped into the clearing, the sun was already high overhead.

The meadow was beautiful. Wild flowers grew in heaps and mounds throughout the clearing, and long grass rippled in a gentle breeze. Insects buzzed lazily through the air, mostly bees flitting from flower to flower in their quest for pollen. In the middle of the clearing sat a huge weeping willow. Its roughly striped bark was a stark contrast with the vibrant green that sat about its long, whippy branches which stirred in the slight breeze that played through the grass. The tree stood easily thirty or forty feet high, and its trunk was a massive series of twisting, thick cords of vines that seemed somewhat unnatural.

As they watched, however, the willow began to move. The odd vines seemed to sway in a way that suggested they were more tentacle than wood, pulling on the larger branches much like the muscles of an arm. The tree shifted to have a rough approximation of a man with long arms that nearly brushed the ground when he stood upon the massive legs formed from a split trunk at his base. The thin, whippy strands of branches that made up the signature appearance of the weeping willow gathered at a high point of the tree's rapidly changing shape in a way that suggested long hair spilling off from its head. Lastly, a pair of glowing green eyes snapped open on a long piece of thick trunk that sat just below the willow's "hair." Below those eyes, a crooked mouth appeared that seemed permanently set in a frown.

Thistle looked around the edge of the clearing to confirm that things were moving in the shadows of the trees there. Four-legged, majestic centaurs stamped around, some with bows that had arrows already nocked and ready to fly at the slightest sign of danger. Though they were harder to spot, there were more naiads and even hulking salamanders, along with other woodland creatures that were far too interested in what was happening, beyond what an animal should be. A bear sat back on its haunches and stared at them, and a herd of large deer sat pawing the earth next to that. The court had been assembled to learn the fate of the interlopers who the abomination had brought to their forest.

The giant willow marched its way over to them, its frown deepening as it came. Shesh'ra lowered herself to a knee and tugged on Ashal's arm to indicate that she should do the same. Thistle lowered himself slowly as well but did not move his gaze from the tree's face.

"I am he that is called Bitter Bark." The hulking willow's voice rumbled like thunder.

"I thought as much," Ashal's tired voice responded. Shesh'ra's head snapped to the side to give her a disapproving look.

"Indeed," Bitter Bark growled. "And why have you come to my forest?"

"I never meant to have anything to do with your forest, ancient one." Ashal inclined her head as she spoke. It was stiff and awkward, but Thistle could see the approval in Bitter Bark's mostly impassive face. "I came for the necromancer named Laurine."

"Yes, I know of her," Bitter Bark grunted. "It seems you have failed in that quest, more's the pity. Now you have brought her anger to the shadow of my woods. What have you to say of that?"

"Only that I am grateful for the refuge you have granted me." Ashal's voice continued to be flat and devoid of any emotion. Bitter Bark narrowed his eyes at her response.

"You don't seem overly grateful. You seem angry. Tell me why I should spare you for your intrusion to these woods? My people have been greatly upset by your coming."

"I have no great reason, mighty sir." Ashal's whole body quivered as she spoke. "I merely plead that you will spare me so that I might seek vengeance and possibly rid you of a threat that resides in the abbey to the east of here."

"You've already had one attempt, I've heard," The tree herder harrumphed. "What makes you think another will be more successful?" Thistle breathed out slowly at this response. If Bitter Bark was asking that question, then that meant he was interested in what she had to say; she had a chance to convince him!

"Because I would ask for your aid in helping to ensure that it is." Ashal raised her head to stare into Bitter Bark's eyes. The tree herder laughed in response; it was a hollow sound that caused the gathered masses at the tree line to shift and whisper among themselves.

"I am sure you would ask that. But why should I give it?" Bitter Bark motioned toward Thistle. "This one has been trying to convince me for years to attack the abbey and burn it to the ground and has yet to accomplish the task. What do you bring to his case that would add weight to it?"

"I have nothing, great one. Laurine has taken everything from me except a very little. I can offer up my rage and my righteous indignation at what she represents. Give me your strength and I will lead your forces to victory. Laurine must be stopped, her abbey is an abomination by your standards and by my own. This is all I can give you as argument as to why you should help me." Ashal once again lowered her eyes, and Thistle could see her shoulders sag.

No! He shouted in his mind. *Don't give up already! You have his attention!* Think of something! Bitter Bark let out another laugh, this one was less threatening in its tone, however.

"You are audacious, little naiad. But I would not risk the wrath of the Hegemony for your vengeance, even if the contamination that sits inside that abbey is something that we should see to." Bitter Bark shook his head. "No, that is not enough reason for me to attack. Even if we were able to destroy Laurine and her coven of undead that reside there, the Golden Horn would see it as an attack on them and would send an army we would not be equipped to deal with to burn our forest to the ground as repayment for our actions. I will not risk the lives of my creatures for that."

"You would cower in your forest for fear of a possible retribution!" Ashal's body shook and she clenched her fists, rising to her feet. She pointed accusingly at the great willow standing before her. Bitter Bark's frown returned, and his eyes deepened into a scowl.

"How dare you speak to me in this way, child!" The skies above his head seemed to darken. Shesh'ra leapt to her feet.

"Mighty lord, do be forgiving her! She has had much grief given to her by Laurine. One who is dear to her lies close to death even this day at the order of the cursed abbess! She is filled with the sadness and the regret that is being the cause of her poor words!" Bitter Bark stopped and turned to look at her.

"You speak for this one?" Thistle tensed as he felt the ground rumble beneath his feet with every word Bitter Bark spoke.

"Only from a place of sympathy, Ancient." Shesh'ra kept her head bowed, but her voice was level and firm.

"What do you propose should be her fate?"

"To be giving her of supplies and to be sending her away, once her mentor be healed or dead." As the words came out of Shesh'ra's mouth, Ashal fixed her with a glare that could cut ice.

"That is not my wish!" Ashal did not look away from Shesh'ra as she spoke. "I will kill Laurine, and I will not leave this place until I have done so, or until someone or something kills me first."

Bitter Bark considered her for a moment before he spoke.

"Be careful with your words, child." He spoke softly, or what would be softly for someone of his size. "I am not disinclined to simply ending you here and now for all the trouble that you have caused."

"My mentor taught me of the Green Lady and the Mother Earth that you swear to serve!" Ashal did not hide the disdain from her voice. "Magdolon said that you fought to balance the world, to keep it in its natural state. The Cycle of Life! The Eternal Hunt! The Bounty of Eternity! Death is an essential part of what you serve. Yet you have something that literally breaks everything that you preach and you are content to let it sit just at the edge of your forest because you are afraid of the destruction wrought by a mortal empire?!"

"Do not speak to me of our tenants, foolish girl!" Bitter Bark took a step toward her, his hands clenched into fists at his side.

"Ancient One!" Shesh'ra began to speak, but Ashal cut her off.

"No! She does not speak for me. I speak for myself," she said, stepping in front of the other naiad. Thistle fumbled at the small sack he held, now soaked through with blood.

"My lord," he cried out. "The child is not without merit in her argument! See here that your mutual enemy, Laurine, did send her minions into the woods. She has broken her promise of neutrality!" Thistle finally pulled the vampire's head from the sack and tossed it before him. Bitter Bark stared at the gruesome sight, and if anything, it made his countenance darken further.

"You have brought evil to my children." Bitter Bark seemed to whisper, but his words were lashed with such a heat that they caused Thistle to cringe. Only Ashal did not waver under the intensity of his speech.

"I brought you nothing!" Ashal sneered. "You have brought this evil upon yourself by doing nothing while it festered in a protected shell within throwing distance of your beloved trees! You..." Ashal cut off as Bitter Bark's fist slammed into the ground beside her, throwing her to the dirt.

"Enough!" he bellowed. "Do not speak to me as if morally superior! You would use my family, my children, to do your bloody work of revenge. You feel as though because you have suffered that this justifies your callous actions. Do not speak to me as if you are better because you have visited violence on your enemy more readily than I!"

Ashal stared daggers up into the face of the massive willow tree before her. Bitter Bark's features were rigid with fury. Shesh'ra stood off to the side, a look of shock on her face. Thistle was rooted to where he knelt.

"Do you think that your mentor is worth more than the lives of my children?" Bitter Bark's voice was ragged, his face was still twisted with anger, but there was a tired edge to his words. Ashal flinched under his gaze, and her glare fled from her face. Bitter Bark pulled himself back, and the darkness that had accompanied his rage shifted slightly.

"I know that the answer to that question, for you, is no. How could the lives of strangers mean more to you than a loved one you already hold dear? Know this, however, were it not for my servants here, I would have killed you where you lay even now." Bitter Bark spoke slowly, and Thistle thought he saw Ashal's eyes glisten, even though her face remained hard, her jaw clenched. Ashal and Bitter Bark stared at one another for some time before the Tree Herder spoke again.

"I am sorry for your grievances," he rumbled, "and if I thought that storming that abbey with my warriors would do us *any* good, I would do it without further thought. But I will not put the life of my family, my children here, as collateral for your bloody vengeance." Ashal's head drooped and she stared at the ground for several long moments while Bitter Bark turned and began to walk away.

"If there was any way that we could accomplish this task, I would do it gladly," the treeman said over his shoulder. Ashal reached out and scooped up a handful of small pebbles. She held out her hand and watched the small rocks spill through her webbed fingers, a strange look on her face.

"What if there was a way?" She called out after Bitter Bark, who stopped mid-stride and turned back to face her.

"What do you mean?" he asked.

"What if the Basileans thought it was somebody else who attacked the abbey?" Ashal slowly pushed herself to her feet, wiping the dust of the pebbles from her legs as she rose. "What if the Basileans thought that someone else ransacked their abbey and killed their abbess?"

"But who would do such a thing, especially to such a remote place such as this?"

"Are we not almost on the border of Golloch's empire? Are the Imperial Dwarfs friendly to the Basileans at present? Last I heard, they were all but at each other's throats. I think the Hegemony is just looking for an excuse to attack them, and vice versa." Bitter Bark's eyes widened at her words.

"You would risk starting a war between Golloch and the Hegemon just to win your vengeance?" Ashal looked away, her eyes hard, but remained silent. After several long moments passed, Bitter Bark moved forward so that he was standing over her.

"What did you have in mind?" he asked. She still refused to look at him as she spoke.

"I know of a dwarven mining camp about two days' journey to the northeast." Her voice choked, and she was forced to speak in a whisper as she laid out her plan.

Eighteen
FIRES OF CONVICTION

A gentle rain began to fall over the forest as the group of strange creatures pushed their way through the undergrowth. The gray sky overhead drizzled over the verdant limbs and caused a slight mist to arise that drifted through the trees like lost spirits. Ashal felt herself shiver. Autumn was approaching and the rain was frigid as it pelted her scaled skin.

Beside her walked Thistle with the hood of his cloak up to mask his features and ward off the rain. Beyond him, Ashal could make out shapes of various beasts and creatures of the forest. Centaurs stamped impatiently as they walked alongside the slower human and naiad. Some of the centaurs were armed with bows, others with large spiked clubs or repurposed woodsman axes. Behind them, the hunched forms of the massive salamanders stumped along, the rain sizzling as it touched their heated skin.

Ashal kept casting sideways glances at Thistle. The druid hadn't been talkative of late, and the approaching task before them likely was captivating all of his energies. The plan was fairly straightforward: go to the dwarf mining camp and retrieve enough weapons and armor that they could leave at the abbey so that the Hegemony would think that the dwarfs had sacked the settlement instead of Bitter Bark and his people. The tree herder had been skeptical of her ability to accomplish her plan, and to be honest, so was she. How was she going to convince Gravel and his company to give up their equipment? Even if they managed to accomplish that goal, how would they pass off what they did get from them as weapons from the Dwarven Empire instead of their free counterparts? There were so many variables to her plan that the more she thought of it, the more she began to question her choices. What if Gravel refused to go along? Bitter Bark had agreed to it, but he'd argued that it was a crazy plan despite sending with her a small army to see it accomplished.

She glanced around at the small army that moved to either side of her. Why had Bitter Bark sent so many? They were prepared to fight if the dwarfs proved uncooperative. Was Ashal willing to spill the blood of people she knew in order to accomplish her plan? Thistle had beaten this thought into her head during their fireside chat last night.

179

"The only reason that Bitter Bark went along with this insane plan is that he wants those dwarfs out of the forest almost as much as he wants the undead out of the abbey! He knows that you will be able to get close enough to them that we can attack before they are able to man their defenses!" Thistle had sighed and shook his head. "You'd best hope your tongue is made of silver, girl, or else there will be bloodshed, and that will be on you."

This information had put even more weight on her shoulders; simply getting weapons and equipment from the dwarfs wouldn't be enough, she also needed to convince them to leave. How was she going to do that? Not for the first time, she wished that Magdolon was at her side to help her think of a solution. But he hadn't woken up before she had been forced to leave. Shesh'ra had agreed to leave guards at the cave and had already sent for healers to help Magdolon fight his way back from the brink of death. Ashal hadn't wanted to leave him, but both Thistle and Bitter Bark had insisted that they must act quickly, before Laurine could figure out that her assassins had failed and send more to finish the job. Shesh'ra promised that she would move him at the earliest possibility, but now the healing spring was what was keeping him alive.

"What is Shesh'ra's story?" Ashal asked, breaking the quiet of the misty morning and causing Thistle to start suddenly at the noise. After recovering, he brushed invisible dust off his forearms and turned to look at her while they continued walking forward.

"She's an odd one, but you already knew that. She comes off as a bundle of raw anger the first time you meet her. She seems like she's more likely to chew your face off than talk to you. But in reality, she's probably the most mothering creature I've ever met, such an odd combination. Her fiery disposition coupled with a nurturing soul seems so at odds with each other." Thistle shrugged. "She is herself, a unique oddity as any I've ever seen." The young druid looked like he was about to say more, but stopped himself, and they continued walking on in silence. Ashal made a few more attempts at small talk that were less than successful before finally blurting out in frustration.

"Well, it seems as though you're not in a talkative mindset right now. What has you in such a sour mood?!" She gave him an accusing look which he didn't seem to notice. At first, she thought he wouldn't respond, but then after a few moments of silence, he sighed.

"I'm worried about Yvette. I know there's no way of knowing, but she usually sends some signal, or communication, or something to let me know she's okay, and I've received nothing."

"That might be because she's dead..." Ashal shrugged. "Which is not good, as we could use her information when we storm the abbey."

"Don't say that!" Thistle said quickly. Ashal give him a sidelong glance.

"What? That she might be dead? Why?" Ashal raised an eyebrow. "She's a vampire, and she betrayed us, twice now! And her second time almost killed Magdolon! It still might!"

"Not of her own will! She has been under duress, I'm sure of it!" Thistle glared at Ashal, and she had a sudden memory of the bandages that were on Yvette's arms when she first saw her in the forest.

"Still, it doesn't excuse what that has cost us!" Ashal replied.

"I'd like to see how long you can go with a knife carving your flesh up like a chicken at the market!" Ashal was surprised by the venom in Thistle's voice, and she pulled back from it.

"But she's a vampire! Why do you care?"

"That just means that it's easier for her to heal up after a session of torture so they can start again and the pain can be fresh!" Thistle snapped. The look of confusion on Ashal's face must have jogged something in Thistle's mind because he shook his head and sighed.

"Just because she's a vampire doesn't mean she's not a good person," he muttered.

"I think that is exactly what it means!" Ashal replied. "From what I've seen, vampires subsist on the life blood of others. They are parasites and should be destroyed with prejudice."

"No!" Thistle's voice was loud, and the moving party of warriors all stopped to turn and stare in his direction. He closed his eyes for a moment and then waved at them to keep them moving.

"No," he said again, this time quieter. "I have to believe that she is still a good person!"

"Why do you need this?" Ashal fired back, a growing sense of unease in the pit of her stomach.

"You wouldn't understand." Thistle shook his head, staring forward.

"Maybe if you helped me, then?" Ashal spoke softly, she couldn't have him closing up on her again. Thistle's agitation clung to the air like the thin mist around them. The druid continued walking for several minutes until Ashal thought that he had ignored her before finally breaking the silence once more.

"Did Magdolon ever tell you about Yvette's mother? Her situation? Why Yvette is still at the abbey despite all that's been done to her?"

"He told me that Laurine killed her mother, or at least it was heavily implied," Ashal replied.

"That's only part of it. That abbey has been a terrible place long before Laurine came along. Granted, it's become a bit more ostensibly so since her arrival, but it was never a happy nor peaceful place."

"What do you mean?" Ashal kept trying to look at Thistle without making it obvious that she was doing so, but it was becoming increasingly difficult.

"The head priest and commander of the abbey treated her mother and her like they were lower than the scum that lays atop the surface of a pond." Thistle paused here to take a breath. "He treated everyone like that, though. He

181

was prone to trysts and kept an orphanage in the village to house all of his little bastards that he sired with his… indiscretions." Ashal nodded in response to this. She knew because of her time among humans and other surface dwellers that this kind of behavior was… frowned upon. But Thistle was a druid of the forest, monogamy was not something the beasts of the woods practiced very frequently.

"So he was a man of a certain prowess, then?"

Thistle barked an acidic laugh at this.

"That's certainly one way of saying it." He narrowed his eyes and stared out amongst the trees.

"I don't understand where your anger comes from, though. Why does his treatment of Yvette bother you so much?" Ashal continued to watch him from the corner of her eye.

"It wasn't just her. Like I said, he treated everyone like this. He forced himself upon people, both physically and emotionally, and when they fought back, he would throw them out to the wilderness." Thistle spat to the side. Ashal kept quiet, waiting for him to reveal more.

"That's what he did to my mother. That's how I came to live here in the forest. My mother was one of his victims, and when she demanded he pay for his crimes, he threw her to the wilds before she could make too much noise or draw too much attention to his actions. He called her a sinner, saying she had tempted him and that he had resisted her to the best of his abilities, at least that's what he said publicly. Everyone knew different but were too afraid to say anything. And so they killed her by letting him have his way."

Thistle's whole frame shook as he spoke, and his steps grew slower as he walked. Ashal listened intently, not daring to interrupt or ask questions, but when several more moments went by without him saying anything, she voiced her thoughts aloud.

"So Yvette is your sibling through your father."

"My mother was younger than me when she was thrown into the woods. The priest swore that she would not find refuge in any city if she should try to run. She was already to the point of bursting from carrying me. She must've lasted only a few days before giving birth, all alone amidst the trees and the howls of wild animals. I oftentimes wonder how scared she must have felt. The pain and anguish mixing with the anger and fear to create a terrible beast that hung at the periphery of her fevered vision as she slowly washed away into oblivion…" Here, he paused a moment before shaking his head.

"Bitter Bark says that the forest was drawn to my infant cries. He says the Green Lady guided her servants to me. My birth mother became food for the forest, and my new family was born here. I grew up among the verdant undergrowth. Raised by wolves and sylphs." He took a shuddering breath. "I never felt like I belonged, though. I was too slow to be a hunter, too large to be a nimble sprite, too human to kill with my bare hands, and unable to grow my own food due to the nature of my circumstances. I lived off the bounty of the forest, eating roots and berries and the occasional scraps from a predator's kill.

"Often times I would sneak up to the village edges to watch the children and other townsfolk going about their lives and wish that I could join them, but who would take me? A poor, dirty wharf? Bitter Bark had told me of what had happened to my mother, and she had been beautiful. What would the people of the abbey think of me, a dirty little orphan? So I hid and watched and grew." At this, he stopped and turned to face Ashal.

"Please don't misunderstand, the denizens of the forest were kind to me, in their own way. I never went without food, I never froze in the winter, and I had friends among the various members of the woodland folk. But I was always regarded from a distance."

"I understand, perhaps more than you may know." Ashal gripped her forearm and felt a familiar sensation wash over her, causing her throat to constrict. Thistle regarded her for a moment before starting to walk forward again.

"Yes, I suppose you would," he said before continuing his story. "Yvette and I met by accident when we were just children. I know I don't look it, but I'm only a few years older than you. The beard does wonders for making me look older than I am." This caused Ashal to narrow her eyes in surprise.

"You are?"

"Yes, I'm only about three years or so older than Yvette, and I figure that you two are about the same age, roughly." Thistle gave a melancholy smile that seemed out of place with his worn face. "Of course, when I met Yvette when we were younger, those three years were extremely important for establishing my dominance as an Alpha to her. She never really bought into the idea, though."

"How did you meet?" Ashal smiled in spite of herself.

"She'd come out to pick berries with her mother and they'd been separated, really she'd accidentally wandered off and lost track of where she was. I had been watching her from a distance, it was rare for humans to enter the woods, even the fringes, and so her presence that day fascinated me."

"How old were you?"

"I must've been about eleven or twelve years old, which would've made her about eight or nine." Thistle smiled and looked up into the drizzling rain that was beginning to slow. In the distance, the clouds were beginning to break up and mirky shafts of sunlight were pushing through the misty air.

"What did you do?"

"I tried to scare her by rustling branches and making strange noises in the undergrowth, things of that nature. But when she sat down on a stump and began to cry for her mother, it broke something inside of me. I knew those cries, I'd heard them from pups whose mothers had abandoned them in the woods during hard winters. I had made those noises myself on those rare nights when my own emotions turned inward to my thoughts of loneliness."

"So you helped her find her mother?" Ashal ventured. Thistle nodded without looking at her.

"I must have been a strange sight. I was a wildling. Barely clothed and long hair. I moved more like an animal than a man, and the only human language I knew were the broken scraps that Bitter Bark had taught me in those rare moments he would spare me a second thought." Thistle made a strange noise in his throat at this comment, as if he were clearing it, but then spat to the side. "Yvette didn't get scared of me, though. When I emerged out of the shadows of the trees to stand before her, she simply looked at me and asked: 'Can you help me find my momma?' She didn't regard me with fear, she didn't cry out and run from me like I thought she would. She simply asked for my help. Something that no one had done, ever, in my life. So of course I helped her. I was a decent tracker even among the creatures of the wood, and it was an easy task to help her back to her mother." Thistle took a deep breath.

"From then on, Yvette would occasionally come to the forest to visit me. She brought me books and taught me to read. She gave me a connection that no creature of the forest had been able to do. I loved those books. When we found out we shared the same father, it deepened our bond in our united suffering, and many times we would spend hours plotting how we would make him pay for what he'd done to us.

"Then Laurine appeared at the gates one day. I knew as soon as I smelled her that something was wrong. By that time, I had become a full-fledged druid and could sense the corrupted magic's taint upon her. I'm surprised that her beloved priests hadn't sensed it before me and burned her as a heretic or something like that. Maybe they didn't want to know and so ignored it. Or worse, they didn't care so long as she produced results. Maybe she knew their ways so well that she was able to hide her activities from the rest of the Hegemony." Thistle shook his head, his smile from before long gone.

"I tried to warn her, but she wouldn't listen. Laurine publicly executed our father, but it was a hollow victory. She replaced him as the tyrant of the abbey. Then she killed Yvette's mother and everything fell apart. I knew she was going to attempt to flee, and a part of me died inside because I knew I would be alone again without her. I knew she needed to leave or else she would be killed, too, so I didn't object when she told me of her plan." Thistle's voice suddenly choked off and he stopped walking so abruptly that Ashal almost walked past him before realizing it. She looked at him and saw that his fist was clenched at his side and he seemed to be shaking.

"I was surprised when she told me she was staying. She said she'd met someone that would help her get revenge for her mother. I didn't care. I was selfish and I didn't care. I should've insisted that she run away! But I didn't. I told her I would help her. I said everything that I could that I thought would help convince her that staying was the right choice. That we would overthrow Laurine and make her pay. All the things we promised against our father, all the plans, all the hate, all of it that had brought us together shifted from his dead figure to Laurine. And I was glad for it." Thistle lifted his gaze to stare at Ashal, and she nearly gasped at the fierceness in his eyes.

"I wanted to blame Magdolon when I found out that she'd been turned. I wanted to lay all the fault on his shoulders for convincing her to stay, for manipulating her into this impossible situation that cost her soul. The cold revenge that awaited us was not worth what she was willing to give. What she willingly gave. I didn't even know his name and I wanted to kill Magdolon because of what he'd done in stopping her escape. But I slowly came to the realization that I was just as guilty. I'd made the same promises of revenge, and pleaded the same case but from a different position, which makes me even guiltier because I was her brother! I was supposed to protect her!" Thistle's voice was a cracked whisper. His red-rimmed eyes twitched as he fought to control tears that threatened to fall at any moment. Ashal swallowed in an attempt to wet her dry throat before speaking.

"You discount her own choices and devalue her own sacrifices with that thought," she said. Thistle gave a choked laugh and blinked several times before opening his mouth to respond. Ashal cut him off before he could speak.

"Furthermore, you make it seem as if it was your choice that she would stay. From what I know of Yvette, your approval or disapproval of her choice would have had little to no impact on what she eventually chose to do. Even Magdolon's words didn't convince her of that, they simply gave her another perspective to consider. Yvette is a creature of her own creation, and that is both assuring and terrifying at the same time." Her words seemed to slap Thistle across the face and it twisted into a snarl.

"You sound just like Bitter Bark," he sneered. "He said something very similar when I went to him to try and convince him to march on the abbey. He called Yvette an abomination, too, and said that the forest would not intervene until it was necessary for him to do so. That he would not risk his *family*," Thistle seemed to spit this word from his teeth, "he wouldn't risk them to save an abomination from the error of her own choices. He said that my sister was gone and that I should see to my family still left around me."

"I see, now, why that would make you angry." Ashal spoke slowly, choosing her words as she went. "I have felt something like it in these past days as I feared to lose Magdolon. He is my one connection in this world. I have no one else on whom to place my care and my affection. If I were to lose him, I don't know how I would react, or how I would recover from that loss. The thought of him lying in that cave so close to death fills me with a fear that I have never felt on any battlefield." Ashal took a deep breath to calm the quaiver in her voice.

"I do not think your anger is wrong to exist," she said at length, the words coming to her mind and leaving her tongue almost without her realizing it. "However, I hope you do not let that anger be the driving force behind why you fight. Magdolon once told me that anger is a hungry magic; it requires a great deal of sacrifice for a hollow result, and you must make payments to it long after it has wrought what you wished of it."

Thistle paused at her words, and his face grew smooth. The snarl disappeared from his lips, and he straightened from a crouch that Ashal hadn't even realized he'd taken.

"You're right, of course," he said, brushing some invisible dust off his shoulder. "I'm sorry that I let my emotions get the best of me." He started walking. Ashal watched him go, and as he passed her by she, held out a hand to stop him. He shied away from it and turned to look at her.

"I find it odd that you cling to your humanity so feverishly when it has brought you nothing but pain," Ashal said, a sad smile crossing her face. "You were raised by the wilds beside a village that neglected you out of fear, and now you seek revenge against someone who is also a human. I do not understand why you seek this so eagerly. Why did you connect with Yvette when she represents that which has caused you the most pain in your life?"

"In many ways you are right, Ashal." Thistle sighed and looked past her for a moment before fixing his eyes on her once more. "But let me ask you this, why are you seeking your vengeance?"

The question caught her off guard, but she was ready with a quick answer.

"Laurine killed my mother and forced me into exile. She took away my home and my family. Apart from that, she is evil and deserves to die." Thistle nodded at her response.

"How old were you when she did this?"

"By your reckoning, I was about eight years old."

"And how long have you been traveling and living with Magdolon since then?"

"A little more than ten years." Thistle bit his lip at her response and stared intently at her as he spoke. Ashal saw flickers of the fire he had shown earlier in their discussion dancing in his eyes.

"I find it odd that you would cling to your naiad heritage so... *feverishly*... when it has all but forgotten you and left you to rot in a world that is so cold and indifferent. Especially since you were raised by what seems like a very kind individual such as Magdolon who obviously loves you like a daughter and has dutifully given you such a strong connection to a family that died while you were still a child. Why are you seeking this vengeance when it has very nearly cost you the exact thing that you are seeking to avenge? I mean of course, your last remaining family member currently lies mere inches from death because of the choices that *you* have made."

Ashal's eyes widened in shock at his words. Thistle gave her a bland smirk before stepping around her and continuing forward to catch up with the column of salamanders ahead of them.

Ashal turned to stare after him. The sky above had melted into a golden afternoon as the light drizzle of rain finally gave way to the relentless sun. Ashal paid no heed to it and instead stumbled numbly after Thistle to try and catch up as the world pulsed around the edges of her vision.

Nineteen

GRAY FRIENDSHIPS

The rain was still calm as it fell from the sky, but the drop in temperature as the day had moved on was causing a gentle mist to rise out of the tops of the nearby mountains, and a gentle breeze pushed its way through the branches of the trees. Ashal crouched beside a large pine and stared out at the smoke rising from the campfires of the dwarven encampment. It was nestled into the side of a cleft in the ground where the foothills and forest began to give way to the granite rocks of the nearby mountain. The trees stopped abruptly at the rock line, and the entrance to the old silver mine gaped like a massive sore in the side of the mountain.

"You know your part of this, eh?" Thistle grumbled in a low whisper. Ashal gave him a quizzical look as they were still some distance away and it was highly unlikely that the dwarfs could hear them. She could make out several moving shapes going in between the tents and the makeshift buildings in the dying light of the day. But they were all preoccupied and there was no indication that the dwarfs even knew that a small army was positioned so close to their encampment.

"My job is to convince the dwarfs to retreat, give up their weapons and tools, and leave the forest," Ashal responded. Thistle snorted.

"If that's what you think, then that'll work, I suppose." Thistle shook his head. "The real job you're to do is to keep them occupied while the rest of us get into position. Unless you really think you can talk them into surrendering everything and just walking away?"

Ashal ignored him. The plan had been hackneyed to begin with. It was born of desperation, but that was all Ashal had at the moment. Bitter Bark had laughed at the idea when she had proposed it, but when Ashal said that she knew the dwarfs personally and could get inside the encampment to talk with them, he had changed his stance.

Ashal swallowed in an attempt to purge the sick feeling in her gut. Beside her, Thistle pulled some strange rocks from his pouch. There were three of them, each black as midnight and about the size of a fist. He placed them on

189

the ground and began muttering under his breath. Ashal gasped as sparks flew from his fingers and engulfed the wet grass beneath each of the stones. After a few small tongues of flame emerged from the undergrowth, Thistle sat back and wiped his brow. He turned his head and saw her staring at him.

"It's obsidian," he stated, as if that explained everything. He sighed when he saw the confused look on her face. "I'm summoning some fire elementals, but they need something to bind them in place so that they can focus their powers into this plane, otherwise they would simply run about lighting things on fire and be of no help whatsoever. The obsidian acts as their focus, kind of like their heart. There are other ways to summon them, but this is the way that I learned from the salamander clan that lives in our forest, some of which have come with us tonight."

"Won't that give away your position?" she asked, but Thistle shrugged.

"Not if you hurry. It'll take a bit of time before enough of their power can be gathered into each stone for them to manifest fully. Until then, they'll just smolder, and I doubt the smoke will be that noticeable." He nodded toward the encampment. "You'd best hurry, though. Your time to talk is fading fast. If you haven't worked your wonder with them by the time these things are active, then we'll have no choice but to attack."

"It's all bravado though, right?" Ashal asked, a sudden tightness in her voice. "You won't really hurt them, will you?" Thistle chuckled dryly.

"You don't get it, do you? The dwarfs are not our friends, they are very much the enemies of the forest. They cut down our trees to feed their fires, and they cut through the rock of the mountains, carving their very bones away and leaving them to crumble under their own weight. Bitter Bark will lose absolutely no tears for any stunted beard child who falls tonight. Our orders are to either escort them out of the woods, or purge them from it. So you'd better be good at talking, my dear, because your friends' lives depend on it."

Ashal stared in horror, and the druid motioned toward the encampment again.

"You'd better get going. I'd hate it if you were still inside there when the fighting gets started." He turned back to his smoldering obsidian glass and began muttering under his breath, more sparks jumping from his fingers. He had apparently forgotten that Ashal was even there. Ashal scurried out into the red light of the evening, moving quickly toward the edge of the encampment.

There was a rough cut wooden fence that marked the edge of the camp. Not even really a wooden palisade but rather a three-poled cattle fence meant to keep livestock from traveling outside the bounds of a landowner's territory. A dirt path lead up to a small break in the fence where two dwarfs in cloaks leaned against it, crossbows at their sides. They were talking with one another and didn't notice Ashal until she was nearly upon them.

"Hold there! Who's that?!" As the dwarf spoke, both sentries raised their crossbows and took aim at Ashal.

"I am a friend." The words felt bitter in Ashal's mouth, but she raised her hands above her head and smiled as best as she could.

"What's your name?" The second dwarf spoke this time, and Ashal was surprised to hear a female's voice! She hadn't realized that women dwarfs were part of the advanced mining party. She took a few steps closer and raised her face to catch the last few rays of the setting sun.

"My name is Ashal, I'm a friend of Gravel, he can vouch for me." This caused the male dwarf to relax, and he lowered his weapon.

"Ah! You're that naiad girl that came across the sea with us! Used to sell us furs and provisions at our base camp! I remember you!" Ashal looked closer as recognition slowly dawned on her. She remembered the old dwarf, too, his name was Threddik or something of that nature. He motioned to the other dwarf.

"Go and fetch the foreman's apprentice, he'll want to see her, I'm sure." Threddik turned and looked at his companion, who still had her crossbow pointed at Ashal. "Hurry up!" The old dwarf barked at the younger, who started abruptly before turning to jog off toward the tents and odd building. Threddik turned back to Ashal.

"It'll only be a few minutes, hopefully. What brings you here?" The dwarf lifted a pipe from beneath his cloaks and clenched it between his teeth. Ashal waited for him to light it, but he never did and instead simply chewed on the stem as he looked at her intently.

"It's… uh… rather private, actually," Ashal stammered. The dwarf sighed and simply continued to maul the end of his pipe as they waited in awkward silence.

The sun had fallen behind the horizon, and the hazy blue light of twilight was upon them when Ashal saw two shapes moving toward them from the encampment. It didn't take long for her to recognize the stout outline of Gravel and the smaller form of the other dwarven guard.

"Ashal!" A smile spread across his face as he spoke. Ashal's mouth was suddenly dry.

"Gravel," she responded, stepping forward to greet him.

"What brings you to these parts?" Gravel grasped her hand and shook it. Ashal stared at him for a few moments, her mind racing for the right words to say.

"I wish it were for a better reason, but I've come to warn you that you're in danger." The words fell from her mouth all too easily, she felt. The smile slid from Gravel's face.

"What do you mean?"

"I think it might be better if we spoke in private, preferably with the foreman," Ashal said, glancing at the two guards. Gravel gave her a sideways glance and then nodded slowly. He motioned for her to follow him, giving another nod to each of the guards, and the two of them set off toward the encampment.

"How big of a threat is it?" Gravel asked as they drew closer to the campfires and standing torches spread out between the various tents and makeshift shelters scattered about.

"Rather large," Ashal replied. A sudden thought struck her and she stopped dead in her tracks. "Have you already sent for your families to join you here?" She asked, her voice fraying at the edges.

"That we have!" Gravel smiled. "They'll be here in about two weeks' time, give or take. Unless this threat of yours tells us that we should have them wait longer?" He turned to look up at her, and Ashal felt a small amount of her panic ebb away. The cold sickness in her stomach still sat like one of Thistle's obsidian rocks.

"That might be best," she said slowly. Gravel's eyes narrowed at her.

"What is this that you've brought us?" He eyed her closely. She bore his scrutiny in silence for as long as she could.

"What do you mean?" she finally blurted out.

"What's wrong with you?" Gravel's voice was strained. "You're shaking like a cat in a tree surrounded by dogs! Is it really that bad?"

"Let's get to the foreman, but yes, it is bad." They walked the rest of the way in silence, picking their way through the narrow lanes between tents. Eventually they came to a small log cabin that had been hastily constructed and looked like it maybe had a few rooms at most. Gravel walked up and knocked on the door.

"Enter!" a crackled voice said from within. Gravel sighed and pushed the door open to reveal a small room, inside of which were positioned two small tables arranged against the back wall with chairs behind them and stacks of papers were strewn about their surfaces. Seated behind one was the foreman, his white beard practically concealing his face.

Standing in front of the other table was a man whose presence caused Ashal to stop cold in her tracks. It was not the man's physical appearance that caused her mouth to dry up, his features were normal for a man of his middle years. He had a balding scalp and a short cropped beard with flecks of gray spread through the brown. His eyes were also a pleasant brown and did not appear unfriendly. The part of his appearance which caused Ashal distress was the simple blue tunic the man wore over a chain hauberk. It bore the symbol of Basilea across his chest.

"What is it?" the man asked as Gravel strode into the room.

"Constable Fierence, Master Foreman," Gravel inclined his head and ushered Ashal inside, closing the door behind them. The constable raised an eyebrow when he saw the naiad. "This is my friend Ashal of the Trident Realm," Ashal winced at that, "she says she's brought us a warning of great danger."

"Oh?" The Basilean officer eyed her up and down, his eyes resting on her spear strapped to her back. "What kind of danger?"

Ashal hesitated, her tongue cleaving to the roof of her mouth, her lungs suddenly bursting as she realized that she was holding her breath.

"It's okay, girl," the foreman's wheezy voice coughed from underneath the eaves of his beard. "The constable is here to protect us. The Hegemony wishes to protect its investment and so has placed a contingent of men-at-arms and other soldiers here under his command. Thus, he should know of any threat to us."

Again Ashal swallowed, the room seemed to be spinning and her vision began to pulse in time with her racing heart. She opened her mouth several times and closed it again, strange sounds cringing from her throat each time.

"What is wrong, child?" Constable Fierence stepped forward, his eyes searching Ashal's face. "Are you okay? Is someone trying to hurt you?" Ashal's breath caught in her throat as she heard his words.

"Why would you ask me that?" her voice was a whisper that crept from her constricted throat.

"You seem distressed, scared even," he nodded toward her hand which, she realized, was grasping the haft of her spear over he shoulder. "We can help, my child, but only if you tell us what is going on."

This caused Ashal's attention to snap back to the present. She remembered what kind of help the Hegemony could provide.

"There is no easy way to tell you this, so I should just say it." Her eyes fixated on the worried gaze of the constable. "There is an army of nature at your doorstep. They are here, in the woods as we speak."

"What is the meaning of this?" Gravel's voice broke through hers, but Ashal refused to look at him. "Why didn't you say something so we could raise the alarm, then?"

"There is no need, because they won't attack…" Once again her words caught in her throat, but she forced them out. "T-They won't attack until I tell them to," she stammered, her voice quivering as she spoke. She watched the constable's face fall and a shadow pass over his brow.

"You mean to threaten us, then?"

"I mean to give you a chance to live, sir," her voice was strained, but she forced it to be steady at least.

"Ashal… I…" Gravel sputtered beside her, but she cut him off.

"These forces are intent on storming this encampment and killing everyone here. I have reasoned with them that if I could get you to leave, that you would be spared your lives, but you must leave *tonight* and take nothing with you but the clothes on your backs." Ashal glared fiercely at the Basilean man as she spoke. She knew that if her gaze wandered from his face that she would lose her nerve, so she fixed her anger and her frustration on his frowning face, willing the heat of her words to melt his eyes from his head.

"And what does a servant of the Green Lady want with a small mining camp?" Constable Fierence raised an eyebrow at her.

"I am no servant of..." Ashal began but bit her reply off and took a deep breath. "That is none of your concern. But I would have your decision now. Know that if you kill me here, then the army will attack and slaughter everyone here."

"I have no desire to kill a young one such as yourself," he straightened his shoulders, "but I cannot stand by idly while your kind threatens people who are under my protection."

"Ashal! What is the meaning of all this? Where did this come from?" Gravel broke into their conversation and grabbed Ashal's wrist. She shook it away but refused to look at him.

"I'm sorry, Gravel, but you must leave here. Tonight. Or the forest will rise up and kill you and everyone else in this camp."

"You can't be serious! Ashal!" Gravel's eyes pleaded with her from the periphery of her vision.

"I think you are wasting your words, Master Gravel," the constable's hand strayed to his sword that hung from his hip. Ashal tensed.

"Please! Stop this!" the foreman's gruff voice scratched from beneath his moustache.

"The foreman is correct, young miss, there is no need for violence. But if you insist on attacking the people whom I've sworn to protect, I promise you that I will not shrink from it." The look in the constable's eyes snapped something deep inside Ashal. It was a look of pity, but greater than that was a dismissal of her as a living being. She'd seen that look on countless opponents on the battlefield. She had become an obstacle to him, something that stood in the way of his survival, or his dogma, or whatever other reason he'd convinced himself of in order to make the coming bloodshed easier.

"You protect nothing but lies!" Ashal spat, the choler rising to the back of her throat. She wrenched her spear free of its bindings and dropped to a stance with the point directed at the constable.

"Your Hegemon hands out death as it suits him. Your holy veneer is nothing but a sham! Even now, corruption sits a few days march from here, masquerading as a pious sanctuary for your sanctified garbage and you will do nothing about it!" Ashal's vision was tinged red as she spat her accusations. "You do all this in the name of your damnable Shining Ones! You bring suffering and misery to those who worship differently than you, or who look differently from you, or who challenge your entitled sense of authority! You know nothing of protecting those who suffer, or lifting up the hands of those whose hope has been stolen!"

Constable Fierence's face was clouded over, his expression difficult to read. Ashal felt hot tears building in her eyes, blurring her surroundings. She was shocked when she heard Fierence's voice cut through the angry blackness that stretched through her chest.

"It is apparent that you have suffered some great injustice, dear child." He began to speak, but Ashal cut him off.

"You know nothing of my suffering!" she spat. "You took everything from me! You took my home!" The words hung in the air, and Ashal found it difficult to control her breathing as the moment stretched longer and longer. Blinking away the tears that now fell freely, Ashal was surprised to see a pained look on the man's face.

"I know that the Hegemony is far from a perfect place…" He began to speak, but he was never able to finish his thought as the sounds of yelling and the clash of fighting began to echo through the cabin walls.

"I thought you said they wouldn't attack unless you told them to!" Gravel groaned as he rushed over to an open window and glanced out. Ashal held her position, but she felt a sinking sensation in her stomach. Thistle must have started the fight earlier than he'd said he would.

"Throw down your weapon and we will grant you clemency, child. Call off this futile attack and we can discuss means of a more peaceful coexistence." Fierence's sword point dipped ever so slightly, a pleading expression on his face.

"It is too late for that now." Ashal took a deep breath and lunged at the constable. Her spear flashed forward and the seasoned soldier took an instinctive step backward, his sword coming up to catch the bone haft of Ashal's spear. She grunted and changed stances, whirling the butt of her weapon around to try and club he opponent's skull. Once again, the human evaded her blow, and this time he threw one of his own. Ashal easily ducked under the somewhat clumsy swing and looked around for the real attack. When none came, she stood quickly and threw a quick series of jabs, none of them lethal, but quick and precise. Several of the blows found home and pierced the constable's shoulder, hip, and cut along the exposed knuckles of his sword arm.

Anger flooded her vision. Red was the only color she could see, and she saw it in abundance as scarlet blossoms appeared on the soldier's arms and legs. Ashal felt the weight of years of injustice resting on the tip of her spear, driving each cut deeper into her opponent's flesh. She thought back to that day at the Golden Horn so long ago when soldiers just like him had taken her mother away. Punishment, she reasoned, not just petty vengeance ruled her spear that night. The soldier before her was a capable swordsman, but Ashal had youth and fury on her side, besides her own experience and training.

The Basilean officer fell to his knees as he clutched his fresh wounds, and with a quick riposte of her spear, Ashal had quickly disarmed the man who looked up at her face with a gloomy sadness that almost pierced Ashal's red haze of adrenaline. She raised her spear above her head, preparing the final blow.

A blur of motion from the corner of her eye caused her to pause at the last moment. She shifted her spear to block a two handed swing of what looked like a miner's pickaxe, the blow jarred the joints of her arm, but she reflexively turned her body and dropped the point of her spear. She pulled her new attacker's momentum with her, and in her bloodlust, she felt the satisfying sensation of the tip of her spear parting flesh as her opponent impaled themselves on her weapon.

Time seemed to slow as Gravel's shocked expression loomed large in Ashal's vision. His eyes and mouth both opened wide. She watched as he grimaced and his jaw attempted to work, to push some words out of his lips, but there were only senseless grunts. Then his focus seemed to shift as if he were looking behind her and he toppled to the side, the weight of his body tearing Ashal's spear from her nerveless fingers.

She stood slowly and looked around the room. The Basilean officer was still kneeling in his former position, his eyes still focused on where Ashal had stood moments before. He wore a similar expression on his face that was also painted across Gravel's sightless gaze which stared through the ceiling above them and out into the night sky.

"What have you done?!" The crackling voice of the foreman cut through her stupor. She turned her head and found the older dwarf standing over her. He held no weapon, but even if he had threatened her, she doubted whether or not she could have mustered up the nerve to defend herself.

"I…" she began, but no other words would come. She simply stared while her hands began to shake.

"Get out." The foreman grumbled. Ashal didn't move.

"GET OUT!" The foreman roared this time. Ashal shrunk back and grabbed the haft of her spear reflexively. The tip of the weapon remained buried in her friend's corpse. She rose shakily to her feet under the intense gaze of the elderly dwarf before her and unceremoniously pulled her spear free before staggering toward the door.

She looked back at the bloody scene which she left behind her. Constable Fierence's slack jaw was more evident now, the wounds she had visited him were ceasing their weepings as death cooled the blood where it lay in his veins. Gravel was sprawled out on the ground, his crimson stain also rapidly cooling on the wooden floor. The foreman was bent over his body and was pressing his forehead against the younger dwarf's in a wordless grief that was only just beginning.

The image branded itself on Ashal's mind. She forced herself to step out into the night.

Fire was everywhere. The cold night sky had turned red and orange from the bonfires that had been set to the makeshift shelters throughout the encampment. Ashal stared with her mouth open as she saw centaurs charging down dwarfs where they stood. She saw groups of miners gathered together, holding their heavy picks in front of them while the hulking forms of salamanders threatened with their large flint axes. Ashal ducked through the flickering lights of the various fires and the shadows they cast along the ground. She ran, looking for Thistle; she wanted answers as to why they had attacked so prematurely.

A figure stepped out of the shadows as she dodged around a few tents which had yet to be set ablaze. It was the stocky form of a dwarf, and Ashal was forced to dance to the side as her attacker lunged at her with an upraised axe. The blow went wide and Ashal brought her spear up to a defensive position.

"Stop!" Ashal called out, and the figure paused and squinted to look at her squarely. In the light of the burning encampment, Ashal recognized the face of the female guard who'd met her on the outskirts of the encampment.

"You!" she cried out. "What's going on? Is this what you came to warn us about?" With a jolt, Ashal realized that she didn't know what part Ashal had played in all this.

"Yes!" The lie came quickly to her lips, and she grabbed the young dwarf and began running to the edge of the camp, away from the fighting.

"You have to run!" She panted as she ran. "The enemy is too great a number for your guards to defeat, and they mean to kill everyone here." The young dwarf had a bewildered and terrified look on her face as they ran, but she did not resist Ashal's insistent pull on her arm. As they approached the edge of the woods, Ashal heard the sound of hooves approaching, and her heart sank.

"Naiad!" A deep bass voice challenged her. "Where are you going with that dwarf?! Thistle has ordered all captives be brought to the entrance to the mine."

"Don't stop! Keep running, no matter what!" Ashal said before turning to stand before the owner of the voice. A large, muscle-bound centaur stood with a confused look on his face as he stared at her, his front hoof pawing at the ground as he considered the situation.

"What are you doing, naiad?" The centaur looked behind her at the form of the retreating dwarf. "We cannot let any survivors escape, or else they will tell of what they saw."

"I did not agree to this slaughter!" Ashal cried, her voice caught in her throat as she spoke.

"Our Mother Earth did not agree to them cutting a hole in her side and burrowing deep into her bones, either, but they did that without a second thought." The centaur advanced slowly, hefting a large woodsman's axe in his hands. "Why should your agreement mean anything against her orders?"

"I don't care if it means anything to her." Ashal shook her head. "I will not agree to it, nor will I allow you to kill this dwarf." The centaur raised an eyebrow at her and then shook its head.

"I do not need your permission, naiad." The centaur charged forward, covering the ground between them so fast that Ashal almost didn't react in time. At the last moment, she planted her spear and aimed for the center of the heavy mass hurtling toward her. The centaur couldn't alter his course and crashed

197

straight into the tip of her spear. The force of the blow jarred her bones and pushed her back while her feet dug into the soil. Several hundred pounds of centaur toppled to the dirt and tore Ashal's weapon from her hands.

She stared down at the second corpse she had created that night. The centaur's dead eyes seemed to stare off in the distance after the escaping dwarf. A sudden tightness gripped Ashal's chest. How had things gone so wrong? Why had they attacked instead of letting her offer the deal to leave? Images of Gravel's dead face floated up in her vision and she felt again the stinging pain of unshed tears threatening to overflow. She quickly scrubbed her eyes and reached down to pull her spear free from the centaur's body, wiping his blood off on the nearby grass. She looked around to make sure that no one had noticed their encounter and then took off running toward the entrance to the mine, where the centaur had said they were taking the captives.

The mine had been built around the mouth of a natural cave that already lead into the mountain and gaped before them like an open mouth. Thistle stood before it with his staff in one hand and a torch in the other. Huddled in a circle before him were roughly about two dozen miners and six Basilean soldiers, all in various states of abuse ranging from being sprawled out on the ground in the midst of their own death throes to simply being beaten and bloodied from the fight. All of those who weren't wallowing in the dirt had been forced to their knees and made to look up at Thistle, who seemed to be waiting for something.

Ashal gave a small gasp as she recognized the face of the foreman kneeling at the front of the assembled captives. She walked forward and broke through the ring of warriors who sat with their weapons pointed toward the prisoners, intent on helping the foreman to his feet. As soon as she did this, however, Thistle's voice echoed out through the night.

"Ashal! Good of you to join us. I see you managed to wet your spear tonight?" The druid motioned toward her weapon which still had traces of blood and gore on it even after her hasty cleaning. Ashal swallowed hard, hoping her guilt would not show on her face.

"Why are these captives here? What are you going to do with them?" Ashal blurted the first questions that came to her mind. She had so many more, but her thoughts were coming as if they had to swim through a pool of honey to reach her. Thistle smiled in response before speaking.

"Interesting question!" The druid descended from the mouth of the cave until he stood before her. The fires lit in the encampment still burned and cast him in a devilishly red hue as he walked. "We are here to cleanse this place and heal an old scar in our Mother's flesh! And since these pests were the ones to cause her such pain, I feel that an adequate punishment is due for their insolence, don't you?"

"And what punishment might that be? Surely Nature's warriors have more honor than to kill their captives in cold blood." Ashal shifted uncomfortably under Thistle's intense gaze.

"Of course!" Thistle responded, his eyes never moving from hers. "Let them be placed inside their beloved mine where they can have all the silver there is to be found, but we cannot allow this open wound to sit here and fester. And so, like any good healer, we must cauterize it and seal it up so that it might recover." Ashal gave a start.

"You mean to bury them alive?" Her voice quavered with disbelief. "That's worse than simply executing them!" Around her, there was a confused buzz of activity. Several of the salamanders and centaurs looked befuddled at Thistle's words. Others nodded their approval.

"Is it? Let the Green Lady decide if they deserve life, we will not take that judgment from her." Thistle turned and motioned for the captives to be taken into the mine. Ashal was happy to see that the majority of the salamanders and the centaurs did not move. However, enough did respond to Thistle's command that soon the dwarf and Basilean captives were herded forward into the cave mouth.

"You can't do this!" Ashal cried out. "This is savagery!" She moved toward the cave entrance, but Thistle caught her arm.

"How did you think this would end?" He hissed in her ear. "If your ruse at the abbey is to succeed, then there must be no witnesses to tell of what we took from here!" He wrenched her back. "Did you honestly think that your plan would have worked in any other way than bloodshed?"

"I never meant for this to happen!" Ashal cried. She couldn't stop the trembling, nor the intense beating of her heart. The world spun, and she felt as if the ground might open up to swallow her as well. Her throat tightened as she fought to establish some semblance of control over her emotions. But this sudden, unfair turn of events loomed over her like a dark shadow that pulled her along like a marionette on its strings toward the ugly resolution that had spiraled so far out of her control.

"Of course you didn't. You're still a child in so many ways. This is war. But don't worry." Thistle motioned to someone behind her, and Ashal felt strong hands clasp both of her arms. Thistle released his grip and stepped back to look at her. "This mine would have been cleared regardless of whether you had suggested it be attacked or not. It is an open sore for the earth and needed to be cleansed. You just provided us with a more convenient way of accomplishing that."

The salamanders that had herded the captives into the cave were now emerging from the shadows. Several of them were also placing small casks and barrels along their path of retreat. One of them came to stand beside Thistle.

"Did you give them the supplies we gathered?" Thistle asked, and the salamander nodded. "And the black powder is in place?" Another nod.

"What do you mean supplies?" Ashal asked.

"We aren't without any compassion, Ashal," Thistle said without turning to face her. "We've left them enough food and water to last a few weeks or so, perhaps the caves will have another way out for them, if the Lady deems it their fate to live." This was followed by a hollow laugh.

"Why would you do that?"

"I just told you. The Lady's will demanded it. Besides, anyone who comes across this encampment would be suspicious if they found random supplies and food stuffs that the survivors hadn't carted off. It's all about crafting the narrative we want people to believe, dear Ashal." Thistle lifted a hand and began chanting. He pointed his fingers toward one of the nearest casks that had been left at the mouth of the cave.

"No!" Ashal cried out, feeling more helpless than ever in her life. "Please stop! We don't have to do this!"

A blast of fire leapt from Thistle's hand and connected with the nearest cask. There was a thunderous explosion that knocked everyone, including Thistle, to the ground and set off a series of fireballs that tore into the very rocks of the mountain and threw up a massive cloud of dust and debris. A heavy ringing settled on Ashal's ears as she slowly regained her senses. She looked at her surroundings but couldn't see anything in the storm of dust that swirled about her. Slowly she became aware of the sounds of small rocks and bits of wood hitting the ground and of individuals moving clumsily around her.

Finally, her vision started to clear as the dust began to settle. Ashal looked up at the side of the mountain where the cave had been. Now all that remained, illuminated by the dying fires of the encampment, was a wall of broken and cracked rocks that had tumbled down the side of its granite face. It seemed as though the mountain itself had collapsed downward on them and had even crushed several of the salamander and centaur warriors who had been standing too close to the cave.

Thistle was laying on the ground before her, and for the briefest of moments, she held out the hope that maybe his plan had backfired and resulted in his own demise. Then the druid coughed and began to roll about on the ground while holding his head. Ashal sank to her knees and stared at the terrible destruction that had been wrought on the mountainside. She thought of Gravel's dead eyes staring accusations at her from beyond the smoky haze that filled the night air.

Twenty

THE NATURE OF DISAPPOINTMENT

There was an impossible wind that tore through the stone pillars and pushed at Ashal's back, willing her to move forward. She resisted, willing herself to step backward as she stared out into the darkness surrounding the pylons. Something was hunting her out there, but she knew that the stone was keeping it at bay, and if the wind had its way, it would push her right into the open arms of her own death. She couldn't explain where this certainty came from, but she knew it as surely as her next breath that if she left the protection of the pillars, she would die.

The columns were scattered all around her in a type of loose circle, each one the deep bluish gray of living stone used in the great fortresses Ashal had seen in the dwarven cities of Aberkhal. She could see nothing past the edge of the closest one, except for a shroud of darkness that appeared to writhe as it waited for her, and she knew that it was patient.

The wind seemed to sense that it would not move her with force, and so it switched tactics, instead weaving in and out of the stone columns to create a whistling sound that screeched at her ears. Ashal clamped her hands to the side of her head, but the sound did not diminish, instead it grew louder and words began to form. Words that whispered beneath the screaming whistle and forced themselves into her mind while the stout cacophony of breathy shrieks continued to buffet her, driving her to her knees.

Why would you do this? The voice was familiar within her head, and through stuttering gasps of exertion, Ashal forced her eyes open against the torturous sound. She thought she saw glimpses of faces appearing in the dark.

"I don't know what you mean!" She tried to force the words through the increasing intensity of the whistling. A mounting pressure seemed to press from behind her eyes.

My blood cries from the rocks for you, and you have forgotten me so easily? Suddenly, in a moment of clarity, Ashal understood what was happening. She opened her

201

eyes and stared out into the darkness. The figure of Gravel stood staring back at her, his eyes had been replaced with empty holes and his mouth was frozen in a wordless howl.

"I'm sorry, Gravel. I never meant for this to happen." Her words felt hollow against the backdrop of the howling pillars. She knew, on some level, that she was dreaming, but that she had no control over what was happening even with that knowledge. The twisted face of Gravel shook its head and suddenly the wind died away; in its absence there came the sound of the columns cracking. The thing that pretended to be Gravel pressed itself against the invisible barrier that separated him from Ashal, and the young naiad recoiled as the sound of crumbling stone intensified.

Ashal looked around in horror as the columns began to shift, each one sending out small showers of dust as great spiderwebs of decay appeared on the face of the blue stone. As one, the mighty giants toppled to the ground, and Ashal knew with that same, dream-like clarity that Gravel could reach her, and the thought filled her with terror.

She fled into the darkness, willing herself to wake up, knowing it was a dream but finding herself unable to escape. She came upon the edge of a ravine where a thin, stone bridge stretched out into the murky shadows to reach the other side which she could not see. The bridge was barely wide enough for her to place one foot in front of the other, and she feared as she stepped onto it that she might fall if her balance faltered. She grasped onto a thin wooden railing that was loosely attached to the bridge to prevent herself from toppling into the void below. She hesitated as the wobbly railing trembled under her grip. Then came a sharp gust of wind that howled at her back, and she pushed herself onto the narrow stone passage, fearing the whispers that she could hear beneath the gust of rage that propelled her forward.

She inched herself precariously out and away from the precipice, balancing on the stone beam which shuddered beneath her. She thought she could hear the sound of running water coming from far below. She did not dare look for fear of losing her balance, or her nerve, and so she continued forward. The shaky railing to which she clasped so desperately shook in her hands, and in a moment of vertigo, it suddenly seemed to give way from the stone bridge and fall away completely, dissolving into the darkness.

Ashal teetered for a few seconds and looked behind her. She could see a pair of boots stumping confidently across the stone beam and knew to whom they belonged. She tried to move forward, but her balance betrayed her and she toppled over the side. She only just managed to catch herself on the side of the thin stone bridge which seemed to sway under the sudden motion, her feet dangling in the open air.

The boots had changed to webbed feet by the time they arrived above her, and she was shocked to see the hulking form of Magdolon staring down at her from above, holding her spear in his hand. The swaying of the bridge did not seem to affect him as he looked down at her with saddened eyes.

"Magdolon!" she cried out, feeling her fingers beginning to slip. "Help me! Please!" The giant placoderm regarded her for a moment before opening his mouth to speak. When he did so, a gust of wind burst forward and swallowed his words, but the message was carried clearly into her mind by the howling gale.

Why would you do this? Magdolon spoke with Gravel's voice, and she watched in silent apprehension as he reached out with her spear and stabbed downward at her face. She cried out and released her grip on the bridge to tumble down through the darkness. The sound of rushing water became louder as she fell until the icy cold water enveloped her in a sudden rush of pain and shock.

She twirled in the dark undercurrents which pulled her deeper and deeper into its embrace. She tried to swim to the surface, but in her spinning, she had completely lost her sense of direction. She tried to inhale, but the water choked her instead of granting breath. She tried to cough, but her body would not respond. The darkness surrounded her and pulled her deeper into its embrace where somewhere, far below, there came a red light which flickered and focused its energy on her.

Ashal looked down into the red light and screamed as it drew closer. All that came out was a muffled flood of bubbles as more of the dark water flooded her lungs instead of her gills which should have given her the air that her body so desperately craved. Ashal's vision grew blurred as the red light filled the darkness and pulled her further and further down into the depths.

* * * * *

Ashal opened her eyes and found herself staring up into Thistle's face illuminated by the flickering orange light of the campfires. In a half-awake stupor, she recoiled and rolled onto her feet, coming up in a defensive crouch with a dagger in her hand. The druid retreated quickly, his hands help up in front of him in a sign of surrender.

"You were calling out in your sleep," he said, slowly lowering his hands. "The rest of the troops were getting spooked by it, some of the more superstitious ones were muttering things about bad omens and such. It took me quite a bit to rouse you, and you kept making whimpering noises and sometimes outright screaming. It was really quite terrifying."

Thistle sank down onto his haunches beside the dying fire that Ashal had been tending before falling asleep. It had been reduced to some glowing embers which suggested that she had been asleep for only an hour or so at most, as it hadn't been that big of a fire when she'd started it. She also hadn't remembered falling asleep, either. Thistle reached into his robes and pulled out a couple of small, hardtack biscuits that looked like he'd stolen them from the mining camp. He offered one to Ashal, who shook her head.

"You need to eat." He insisted, tossing the dry bread into her lap. She simply stared at it with a blank expression on her face. "If you don't eat, the nightmares will only get worse, I promise."

There was something in his tone as he spoke that caused Ashal to look up at him. He prodded the fire with a stick and threw a couple smaller pieces of wood on the embers which quickly caught fire. The crackle of burning wood and its accompanying warmth washed over her. Ashal took the cracker-like biscuit and broke a piece off, considered it for a moment, then put it into her mouth. There was a crumbly texture and a bitter taste of something Ashal could only describe as 'earthy' before the biscuit dissolved into a formless mass in her mouth.

"Never a good idea to go to bed with an empty stomach after something like last night," Thistle said, eyes fixed on the fire. "Especially if it was your first time doing anything like that."

"Like what?" Ashal glared.

"The first time killing someone in a battle," Thistle said, shrugging. "It does something to you, changes you, and the absolutely terrifying thing is that you can't ever pinpoint exactly what effect it has on you. Others might be able to tell you, later on and if you choose to believe them."

"That was not my first time killing someone." Ashal continued her glare, and it seemed to her that Thistle pretended to be oblivious.

"It was, however, my first time betraying a friend." She spat and turned her gaze on the fire.

"If it helps any, I hope it's the last," Thistle said, taking a bite of his own biscuit, chewing thoughtfully. Ashal blinked back tears that stung the edge of her eyes.

"Why did you have to do that?" she asked, her voice a husky whisper. "The dwarfs in the mine? Why did you attack when I was still in there? You never had any intention of letting them leave in peace even if they agreed to my offer!"

"You're right, that was never my intention, or my orders, either," Thistle said, still chewing. "Bitter Bark made it clear that we were to push them out using any means I thought necessary and to make sure that they would not come back." He took another bite of the biscuit.

"I saw a way for us to accomplish that with minimal loss to his precious family that he sent with us. Thanks to you and your distraction, our losses were minimal. We only lost half a dozen of our troops. Among the dead there was only one unusual case of a centaur scout killed some distance outside of the camps, away from the fighting." He glanced at her meaningfully as he said this last part. "We had a few casualties that weren't fatal and some that may not live much longer, but overall it was much less than if we had met them on a fair battlefield or given them time to prepare for us after you'd left the fake negotiations, which were never going to be successful in any case."

"It was a cowardly trick!" Ashal growled, throwing her half-eaten biscuit into the fire.

"Cowardly or not, it kept the warriors on our side alive." Thistle took another bite of hardtack and looked over at her, returning her fiery gaze with a bland one of his own. "Don't sit there and dare to lecture me about honor. This isn't your underwater kingdom, or the halls of the dwarfs, or the Hegemony. What good does being the best fighter in a fair fight do for those of us who live in the wilds? Cowardice and trickery are the labels that we give to natural selection and survival out here. Honor is useless in a society like this where the stakes are much higher than how little everyone else thinks your dung stinks."

"What was the point of killing the hostages like that at the mine, then?" Ashal growled. "What could that possibly have gained for you?"

Thistle grew quiet at this and his chewing stopped.

"You don't know they're dead." He spoke quietly. Ashal snorted.

"Of course they are! Half of our own casualties are from that pointless and cruel display of yours at the end there!"

"That was a miscalculation on my part." Thistle shook his head slowly. "If your ruse is to succeed at the abbey with the Basileans thinking the dwarfs were the ones to attack, then there can be no reports of a dwarven mining colony being raided by a bunch of wildlings, and their weapons and armor being stolen making their way back to the Hegemon. I thought that if we collapsed the mine entrance, it would take them a couple weeks to dig their way out or so, and by that time, the Hegemon would already have retaliated. Even if their story got back to the right people, it would be too late. But I misjudged how strong their black powder was and..." his voice trailed off.

"That's a rather big mistake." Ashal's voice was a knife's edge.

"I know, and it's one I'll own when we get back. Bitter Bark will be furious with me, I'm sure. I've already sent ahead a messenger to give him the news so that maybe his head will clear some of the anger before I see him in person." Something flickered across Thistle's face so fast that Ashal wasn't quite sure whether it was fear or anger, but as soon as it appeared it was gone. He looked at her and gave a small smile.

"You said you had a friend in that group? You knew them better than you let on, then, I take it?" His voice was soft and the question caught her off guard.

"Y-Yes," she stammered, unsure of what else to say. "I knew all of them, or at least most of them. We lived next to their last settlement for over a year before coming here. They..." Her voice broke as the image from her dream of Gravel's eyeless gaze howling at her cut across her mind's eye. She sucked in a deep breath and closed her eyes, willing the image away. When she opened them, she saw Thistle looking at her.

"I'm sorry for that. I know that is a hollow apology coming from the man responsible for their deaths, but it is never easy losing a friend. Especially if you feel in any way responsible for it."

"What is that supposed to mean?" Ashal's voice turned hard, and Thistle again held his hands up in surrender.

"I mean, even though their blood is on my hands and the hands of my fighters, I'm sure that you can't help but feeling guilty for the part you unwittingly played in it. Take solace in that they haven't died in vain." He stared at Ashal, who didn't respond.

"The centaur scout, the one I told you about that was the only casualty of the skirmish, yesterday. His name was Reddin and he had a mate, and a colt who is barely a few seasons old, and that's the kind of solace I will be offering them when we get back." Thistle had a strange smile on his face as he spoke. "It was such a strange thing. They found him almost a hundred paces from the edge of the encampment. His wounds were odd, too, like he'd been run through with a polearm or a spear of some sort. I don't know what he was doing that far outside of the battle, but I'm sure he had his reasons."

There was a long, drawn out silence between them before Thistle finally rose to his feet, brushed himself off, and began moving away from the campfire which was already starting to burn down again. He stopped at the edge of the firelight and turned back to give her a last look.

"Don't worry in regards to your friends. They didn't die without a cause," he said before moving off into the night. "Eventually their faces fade and you won't see them every time you close your eyes."

* * * * *

Part of what Thistle said was proven right soon after they returned to the sacred grove. Ashal squinted against the harsh light of the late afternoon, her eyes were tired and she barely heard half of the angry words that spilled out of Bitter Bark's mouth, but what she did catch was that he was furious with his druid.

"What would possess you to act in such a way?" The forest rumbled around the mighty treeherder as he spoke. Thistle was almost pressing his forehead to the dirt at this point, but Ashal was too tired to care. She just wanted to return to the cave and speak with Magdolon, hoping beyond hope that he could help soothe the headache that was building in the back of her skull with some calming words of advice. A sudden change in the atmosphere caused Ashal to look around. It seemed as though someone had asked her a question as everyone was staring at her.

"Forgive me, I didn't sleep well last night and my focus is shattered because of it." Ashal coughed politely. "What was the question?"

"I asked if you were still prepared to follow through on your promise to destroy that abomination of an abbey?" Bitter Bark's voice was tense, the anger he had vented on Thistle still evident in his tone. "Although after that response, it does worry me about your dedication."

"No!" Ashal straightened her back, her attention springing back to the present immediately. "I am prepared to do what is asked of me, I promise!" Visions of the stone pillars and Gravel's hollow eyes staring out of the darkness at her flashed before her vision, and she shuddered. Bitter Bark regarded her for a moment, then did the tree's equivalent to a nod which caused his long, whippy branches to sigh as if moved by a breeze.

"Very well, then. I have spoken with my commanders and they agree that the abbey must be dealt with. It has always been an issue that we knew we would have to take care of. But because of your ploy and this success, such as it was with the dwarven encampment, it is generally accepted that this will be our best chance. I have sent out a cry to my children throughout the forest, and our strength is gathering. If you are ready, child, I would have you join us in the assault."

Ashal's head was spinning as she responded. Her words sounded far away and tinny in her ears as she spoke. But whatever words she uttered, they seemed to satisfy the treeman and he stalked away without another glance in their direction. The young naiad rose from her kneeling position and attempted to walk out of the grove, almost into Shesh'ra, who had stepped in front of her. She waved a hand in greeting, but the older naiad's face was as impassive as ever, and when she spoke, her voice was equally as stony as her face.

"You should be the hastening to the cave," she said as Ashal came to a halt. "Magdolon is to be waiting on you." Before Ashal could respond, Thistle was standing beside her and cut off their conversation before it could even begin.

"Did you receive a message for me? Did you check the usual spot?" There was an edge of panic in the druid's voice. Shesh'ra glared at him for a moment before producing what looked like a letter that was sealed with red wax and a black ribbon. The wax was imprinted with a skull shedding tears.

"It were being in the place to which you did say," she grumbled, handing it across to Thistle who took it greedily and hastily broke the seal. His eyes scanned the page and his shoulders seemed to relax as he read.

"It's from Yvette." He sighed at last. "She says that she is okay and that she has been biding her time to try and gain Laurine's approval once more. She says she is waiting for us to attack, and that when we do, she will make sure the gates to the abbey are open to us!"

"That is good news!" Ashal said, her own excitement caught up in his relief.

"That abomination be not worthy of the trusting," Shesh'ra grumbled, and before Thistle could respond, she turned and stumped away from the other two.

"This is a relief," Thistle said after Shesh'ra had left.

"I am glad that she is okay." Ashal was surprised at how earnest she was in saying that. "Did she say anything else?"

"Not really," Thistle said, folding the letter up and putting it in a satchel at his belt. "Just that she's waiting for the attack and she hopes that it will come soon."

"How did she know that there was going to be an attack?" Ashal asked, the thought striking her suddenly. Thistle's smile faltered.

"She's always ready for an attack," he said quickly, but the smile did not return and the druid spun quickly and walked off before Ashal could question any further. Sighing, she began making her way back to the cave where Magdolon was waiting.

It took her longer than she expected, probably because she was having to make her way from a memory that was already sleep addled. That, mixed with the effect of the past few days, which felt like an entire lifetime, combined to make it a difficult journey. Eventually she found it, but when she stepped inside, she found Magdolon sitting beside what looked like a pack of supplies and his spear was holstered on his back. Newly healed white skin was puckered around Magdolon's throat where his wound had sealed up, resulting in an ugly scar. The waters of the fountain must have done their work quickly, Ashal observed.

"Are we going somewhere?" Ashal asked, eyeing the pack with a raised eyebrow.

"I am." Magdolon rose to his feet and pulled a small piece of paper from his belt. "I thought about leaving before you arrived, it certainly would have made this easier, but I could not bring myself to do it. I felt that you deserved better. Either way, I was going to leave you this note explaining why I left." He handed her the piece of paper. Ashal's stomach made her feel as if she was falling, and she stared at Magdolon as she unfolded it. Inside, she saw his careful, neat handwriting.

My dear Ashal,

I am going away. There is no way to tell you this that is easy, but when I heard of your plan that you gave to Bitter Bark, the plan that you would be the one to lead harm to our friends who gave us passage and friendship for so long. The ones who did hide us and purchased goods from us. That their blood would come upon your hands has led me to my choice to go.

I fear the riptide has pulled you out to the bitter waters in your search for vengeance, and this time I will not save you, for you have gone where I will not follow. Your quest is no longer holy nor just. You must find your own way. I wish you well in your path, Lueshwy'n, but it is a path that I can no longer accompany you on, and that you must achieve yourself. Forgive me for my weakness, but you have done something in spite of what I believe to be right, and I will not support it.

I give you all my love. I have faith that you will return to the way that you know is just and true. When that happens, you will find me waiting where your journey leads.

Tier'nawa et nuievin Lueshwy'n,
-Magdolon

"What is the meaning of this?" Ashal whispered as she read through the letter one more time. "What do you mean that you are leaving?!" She looked up at her mentor, his icy gaze returned her own, but he said nothing.

"We are on the edge of attacking Laurine with an army at our back, and this is *because* of the decisions I made!"

"Therein lies the problem." Magdolon's words cut across her thoughts as she took another breath. "Your ambition has claimed the lives of innocents in your pursuit of vengeance. The dwarfs had no part in your vendetta."

"But I had no idea what Thistle was planning! I…" Ashal began, but Magdolon roared at her, cowing her into silence.

"Do not try to feed me your justifications!" Magdolon yelled, his booming voice echoing off the rock walls of the cave. "You cannot tell me that you had no misgivings! What did you think was going to happen?!" Ashal felt heat gathering in her face, and she suddenly felt that she could not lift her head from staring at the floor.

"You mean to tell me that you had no idea that bloodshed would come from your actions when Bitter Bark sent a small army of warriors with you?! When the basis of your plan was you threatening our friends with violence if they did not surrender their equipment and leave the forest?" Magdolon took a step closer and his voice became an intense whisper.

"Tell me your lies again and see if they work this time!" He put his face within inches of hers. Ashal's throat constricted, and she found it hard to breath.

"Gravel was my friend, too," she replied, her voice a hoarse rasping noise. Magdolon's eyes closed slowly and he took a step backward, sighing.

"Why would you do this?" he asked, and Ashal started as he spoke, his words echoing her dream.

"You asked me how dedicated I was to getting revenge against Laurine for my mother," Ashal responded in between shuddering gasps. "I suppose now I've proven that."

"I also warned you against being blinded by your desire for revenge. That it would pull you out and change you, and not for the better if you let it." Magdolon returned to his pack and threw the straps around his shoulder. "Do you even think that what you did was wrong?"

"I know that I shouldn't have suggested the plan," Ashal's voice was still forced, "but it was the only way that I could get Bitter Bark to help us! You weren't there to help me! What should I have done?!" Magdolon shook his head and stared at the cave wall as if it held some kind of secret information.

"You should not have gone after our allies, or the people who have helped us. Even as a bluff, you do not hunt those that are your friends." He shifted his gaze back to her. "We could have found another way. Maybe without Bitter Bark's help. Perhaps it would have taken longer, but there was no need for what you did, Ashal. Gravel and the others are all dead now because of you."

"That's not true!" Ashal cried out, the image of Gravel's dead face flashing before her eyes. "Thistle says that they would have attacked the camp anyways, in time! It was not my fault."

Magdolon sighed and began walking toward the entrance to the cave.

"If that was the case, little one, then why did they wait for you to present them with an opportunity before attacking? If that was the case, why have you allied with those who would kill your friends so ruthlessly and would use you as if you were merely a tool in their plans?" Magdolon did not pause until he reached the mouth of the cave.

"Where are you going?" Ashal asked. Magdolon answered without turning.

"I grow weary of this life above the waves. I am going home. Come and find me when this task is finished so that my soul may rest and this wound might heal."

"But they will kill you for refusing your exile!" Ashal gasped.

"Perhaps they will. But much has happened in the years that we have been gone. If I am careful, if I beg to the right individuals, then maybe they will let me in. And if I die, then at least it will be in a place that I call home, even if it is a home that does not want me to be there." Magdolon turned and looked back at her.

"Perhaps after this affair is finished you will come and find me there to see what has become of me, and of your home as well?" Magdolon gave a sad smile, and when Ashal did not answer, he nodded and walked out of the cave, leaving Ashal alone. Her mind raced as she tried to convince herself to chase after him, but her legs would not respond. Her chest felt hollow, and she sank to the floor. She pulled her knees to her chin and rocked back and forth as tears pulled her into a tired oblivion.

Twenty-One

A COLD SUNRISE

The yellow light of dawn spread swiftly across the forest once the sun had crested the peaks of the Abkhazla Mountains. Ashal sat at the edge of the woods, where the shadows of the trees stubbornly refused to acknowledge the new day. She stared out at the Abbey of Danos that lay nestled against the mountainous backdrop with the village that lay just below it. Her breath puffed in front of hear, leaving ghosts of frost in the chilly air. She refused to notice them, just as she refused to concede to the cold that hung over her like a damp cloak.

A dewy mist clung to the forest floor and gave the trees an extra layer of mystery that was lost on Ashal, who stood waiting on the edge of her own anticipation. Bitter Bark had decided that today would be the day, or rather that evening would be, about an hour before sunset so that the light would work in their advantage. Besides, Thistle had advised that this would be when the majority of the vampires would still be sleeping.

Thistle had also said that Yvette was alive and that she would be listening for the battle to commence. Once it did, she would ensure that the gates to the abbey would be open for the forces of Nature's warriors to quickly press their way inside. The druid had spent the better part of the previous evening summoning as many elementals as he had obsidian to do so, which included a rather massive creature that was still coalescing somewhere in the depths of the wood, being fed by entire trees and bits of coal. Ashal felt uneasy about Thistle's trust in Yvette. She had already betrayed them on various occasions, so how could they trust her now? Also, how had she been able to earn the trust of her fellow vampires so suddenly that she could control the gate to the abbey?

Something ached at the back of Ashal's mind, her head throbbed in time with the constant stream of adrenaline that ebbed and flowed on the edge of her awareness. There was a part of her thoughts which she consciously avoided, that of her last interaction with Magdolon, and it sat like a black spot, spilling off waves of sadness and shame which mingled with her stressed anxiety and made everything worse.

Ashal sighed and closed her eyes, listening to the various birds sing their songs as they cautiously woke in their chilled nests. There was an abnormal stillness to the woods right now, as all the denizens of the wood were gathering themselves for the attack. Ashal supposed that she could count herself among the citizens of the forest, now, as with Magdolon's departure, this became the closest to a home that she could remember.

She winced and shook her head. No, she couldn't think about him. The sudden jolts of shameful lighting that the look on his face dredged up out of the pit of her stomach were still too fresh. That was a complicated puzzle that she would have to wait for another day to solve. Today, her goals were clear, and they sat right in front of her, about halfway up the mountain across the divide between the forest and the mountains. Today was the day of Laurine's reckoning, and Ashal began to focus all of her energy toward that one goal. It helped take away the edge of the rolling emptiness and dread within her stomach.

"What thoughts pass through your mind?" A voice came from behind and caused her to whirl around. She spied Shesh'ra standing there and gave a sigh of relief. How had she moved so silently?

"So many things," Ashal answered, turning back to her view of the mountains and the abbey which seemed so small in comparison. "Mainly I am anxious to see justice done to Laurine and am shocked that after all these years it is finally going to happen."

"Laurine has many acts that are to be avenged by us this day. I do not feel as if this is all that is in your thoughts." Ashal looked the older naiad up and down as Shesh'ra moved up to sit beside her. She was wearing a type of armor Ashal remembered from her childhood. It was all pearlized brass built to resemble various types of overlapping shells and was a masterwork of blacksmithing.

"I did not know that you could get such a fine suit of armor outside of the Trident Realm." Shesh'ra smiled.

"This thing is true, you cannot," she replied. Ashal gave her a quizzical look for a few moments before realization dawned on her.

"You used to live there?" Ashal blurted out, her eyes widening in surprise.

"Long time, but yes, that place was my home. Now it is to being the forest where I claim." Ashal looked closer at the armor and recognized a stylized conch shell worked into the shoulder pauldrons.

"You were a centurion?" Ashal gasped. Another smile from Shesh'ra.

"Still am. All Neriticans are to be giving their lives to Mother Earth. I gave response to her call. This call did bring me to this place here. The Mother sees fit that I stay and now I have no more wish to be leaving it."

"I had no idea!" Ashal couldn't help but stare. Then a thought came to her.

"I am technically a fugitive of the Trident Realm, though," she said hesitantly. "Shouldn't you take me in or at least report to your higher ups?"

"This thing have I done," Shesh'ra responded casually. Ashal felt a moment of panic and rose to her feet, gripping her spear. "Ah! Sit down little hatchling! They do not be wanting you now for long time so long as you stay away. Also, I serve higher power than any queen under the waves, and she did tell me that you are not to be taken away. That you are a necessary thing for what is to happen here. I do not go against commands such as this." Ashal did not relax her stance, and Shesh'ra snorted and stood up.

"Spawnling, I do not be misunderstood. If I did be told to bring you in, you would not be stopping me." She leaned closer to Ashal's face as if to whisper some kind of secret, but instead she said, "come now. Bitter Bark is to be calling the reunion in the glade. We are to attend."

Ashal watched, bewildered, as Shesh'ra turned and walked back into the forest before shaking her head and following.

* * * * *

It took some time to reach the glade which was brimming with creatures of all sorts and sizes. Wolves prowled around the edges of the assembly with occasional snaps and howls. Large bears rubbed up against living trees which slowly pushed aside the furry beasts who looked around befuddled as their back scratchers walked away muttering to themselves. Ashal could see a large grouping of fire elementals which Thistle had summoned, including a towering one that appeared as a whirlwind of flame that dwarfed over all the others. Centaurs and salamanders made up the bulk of the army that had been gathered, but there was also a large contingent of naiads, Ashal was surprised to see, that were lined up holding their strange harpoon guns and wearing mismatched and individualized pieces of armor. A group of large water serpents lay coiled up behind those naiads. There were only a few of them, but the sight of their finned bodies and elongated heads was terrifying to Ashal, who had only heard of their ferocity in the stories that Magdolon had told her when she was younger.

Ashal felt a curious sensation come upon her as she was drawn inexorably toward these strangers who looked so much like her, and it wasn't long before she was standing beside them with a squeamish sensation building in her stomach.

"*Maheen'wei!*" A voice startled her, and a naiad stepped into her view. She was wearing a single pauldron that looked like it was carved from wood, oddly enough, along with a few other bits of armor that seemed wildly inadequate, and she gripped one of the heavier looking harpoon guns. Most startlingly of all, though, was the fact that she spoke in the Neritican tongue; it had been so long since Ashal had last heard it, that it seemed foreign and strange to her. She realized she'd greeted her in a traditional, formal way, and Ashal tripped over herself trying to remember the correct response.

"Er... Hello?" she finally said, feeling her fins deepen in their crimson hue as she replied in the common tongue she was so comfortable with these days. The naiad looked surprised by this response, then her brows furrowed in what Ashal hoped was concentration.

"You no to speak the tongue of us peoples?" The naiad's mouth seemed to be full of food when she was speaking.

"Yes... I am sorry to speak the tongue of the land dwellers." Ashal switched over to the awful sound of her own Neritican, it grated across her ears like a goblin trying to sing. The other naiad laughed at her response and held up the back of her hand toward her, giving a slight nod as was the custom among certain parts of her people.

"This is good, for I am not having the knowing of how those who walk the land speak their stumbling tongues." Her voice lacked the stuttering starts and stops of Ashal's rusty accent and the language flowed from his lips like water over river rock. "I am called Onwei. What is it that they call you?"

"I have the naming of Ashal, spawn of Ai-ellain," Ashal replied, her stumbling words causing the sinking feeling in her stomach to deepen further. Onwei tilted her head at Ashal, her eyes thoughtful as she considered her.

"You are the one for whom all this began?"

Ashal nodded in response.

"I..." she started then realized she did not remember the right words for what she wanted to say. "Forgiveness I beg you. Do you speak the way of the hands?" She moved her hands in a series of signs which Magdolon had taught her as part of the silent language that Neriticans used to speak in the heat of battle when water could become clouded with too much sound. Besides using this form of communication when she and Magdolon did not want others to understand them, it had proven helpful when she was learning to barter and trade. Onwei pursed her lips and replied in kind.

I. Speak. A. Little, she signed. Ashal grunted and then spoke again in her halting Neritican.

"This will then be enough. I am she who brought herself to Bitter Bark to seek holy revenge on Laurine of the abbey for the death of my parent. I..." She trailed off then signed.

Come. With. My. Parent. M-A-G-D-O-L-O-N. She stopped, realizing that she had signed the word 'parent' for Magdolon without thinking, and the realization tore an empty hole in her chest. Onwei looked at her quizzically.

"I thought you did say that your parent was to be avenged for his wrong death at Laurine's intentions?"

Ashal blinked and looked up at her. How could she answer that? Luckily, she didn't have to, as Bitter Bark's loud voice rolled across the glade.

"Silence!" The voice of the tree herder boomed, and the various growling, snapping, and whispering all fell away. The only sound that could be heard was the wind whistling around those trees which were still stationary and not moving about of their own free will. Ashal strained to see the giant tree herder as he walked around the glade, addressing his troops.

"My children!" he bellowed, his voice stern and his face impassable with its perpetual frown. The great willow tree was a grand sight to behold. "Today is to be a great day! Today we cleanse the land of a taint that has long been a festering wound in our Mother Earth's sight! Long has the abbey plagued us by cutting down our trees, harvesting our plants, killing our brothers and sisters! But no more!" He paused for what seemed to be dramatic effect.

"Fate has delivered into our hands an opportunity, and we shall not squander it! An outsider has come, and she has brought with her the tools for our attack. Remember the plan! We are to go inside and we will kill every single deathless abomination that resides within their walls!" Ashal searched the crowd for Thistle and found him across the glade standing beside the fire elementals. He was too far away to read his reaction to this declaration, but Ashal found herself wondering what was passing through his mind at that moment.

"We will leave no survivors," Bitter Bark continued. "We cannot if our plan is to succeed. We will plant the dwarven weapons and bodies which we have gathered so that the Basileans will not blame us for the loss of their abbey! We will burn it to the ground in order that our forest might heal!"

This caused a cheer from the assembled warriors as claws, fists, and branches were thrust into the air. It took several minutes for Bitter Bark to restore order and resume his speech.

"You all have your orders! We will start with the village and cleanse it first! Then we will move on to the abbey, where we will tear down their proud walls and dash their fanged lips against the uprooted stone! We are strong enough to accomplish this, and they do not know that we are coming! They have grown complacent living in the shadow of our Lady's displeasure. For too long have we allowed this affront to continue existing at our borders. For too long have we slept and waited for the right time. For too long have we suffered these abominations to find sanctuary when we should have destroyed them so long ago!

"But our apathy has gained us an advantage! Because they do not know that they have woken the sleeping beasts at their door! They sit sleeping in their coffins, unaware of the judgment that is preparing to fall on their heads! They will burn, and we will be the spark that ignites them! We will be the inferno that buries them under a mountain of ash so that their terrible lives will finally come to the end that they were meant to have!"

This caused another roar of approval. Bitter Bark once again calmed the ensuing war cries before continuing on.

"Form into your packs, your hunting parties, your clans, or whatever groups you will, and let us march to the Abbey of Danos, so that we may tear their walls down and send these abominations back to the dust where they belong! We attack today! Gather on the edge of the woods and await my command!"

After Bitter Bark concluded his speech, he turned back to an assorted collection of what Ashal could only assume were the leaders or chieftains of the various groups assembled. Bitter Bark's limbs moved animatedly as he spoke. He gestured toward Shesh'ra, which caused a small amount of yelling from the rest of the group, and the naiad herself seemed surprised by what was being said. Whatever it was, Bitter Bark was adamant, and the rest of the leaders quickly fell into what looked like a sullen silence. They were then dismissed with a wave of Bitter Bark's branches, and they each walked back across the glade to their assorted parties.

Shesh'ra approached Ashal with a puzzled expression on her face. Ashal moved toward her, but by the time she reached her, Shesh'ra had smoothed her features and was beginning to issue orders.

"Naiads!" She barked in a heavily accented Neritican tongue. The assembled warriors with their harpoon guns snapped to attention with a military discipline that surprised Ashal as they formed up into organized ranks. Looking around at the other creatures that had gathered, she saw that most of them were grouped into loosely organized mobs in some cases, while others seemed to have some form of order to their chaos, even if it was not one that Ashal could identify. Shesh'ra called out marching orders, and the naiads turned in unison and began marching in the direction of the abbey. Shesh'ra walked over and leapt into the saddle of one of the monstrous sea serpents, accompanied by two others who followed suit with the remaining serpents.

"You are to be marching with us then, child," Shesh'ra called out to Ashal, who shook herself as she watched the massive creature that was Shesh'ra's mount rise up. The huge eel-like creature's scales glistened with an unnatural wetness as it reared up and began to slither quite rapidly into the woods to keep pace with the naiads on foot. Ashal blinked quickly a few times before she took off after them.

Twenty-Two
THE BATTLE BEGINS

Ashal stood at the edge of the wood beside Onwei and looked out across the treeless expanse that separated the forest from the base of the mountains. She could see the dilapidated walls that stood around the village at the foot of the path leading up to the plateau which held the abbey proper and its much stronger fortifications. All around her, creatures of the forest shifted with anxious energy, awaiting the call to charge. The sun was beginning its descent behind them, but proper sunset was still at least an hour away, which meant that the time was fast approaching. Ashal could taste the anticipation in the air.

Finally, she watched as Bitter Bark stepped out from the massed ranks. Ashal took a deep breath as one great, gnarled limb rose to the heavens and then dropped back to his side. It was the signal that they had all been waiting for, and with a host of howls and war cries, the forest surged from its boundaries and rumbled toward the broken gates of the abbey's village. Hooves and claws and wooden limbs all churned in an effort to be the first to reach the goal. At the back of the force, there followed great spouts of burning heat from Thistle's summoned fire elementals. The flames lit up the evening air so that it appeared that the creatures of the wood were being chased by a massive forest fire.

Ashal sprinted to try and put herself out in front of the others who surged toward her vengeance, but she quickly realized that her legs, though strong for a naiad, were nothing compared to the swift pace set by the centaurs or the swooping dives of the eagles overhead. The slow pace of the shambling tree creatures and the fire elementals was the only one she was able to beat in their race to the walls. However, a problem quickly became apparent as the small gate proved to be a choke point for their forces as beasts and warriors argued and pushed to make their way inside. Ashal began to grow nervous as long minutes wore away and the army was still fighting to get inside the walls.

But it all seemed to be a wasted fear, as she eventually was able to flow through the gate and found herself running along the broken cobbles of the village streets. Something pricked at her mind as she ran, though; she realized that the streets were abandoned. Shouldn't they have encountered the shrouded

217

creatures that she and Magdolon had found their first time entering the village? If the creatures who had first entered the village had already fought and defeated them, there were no signs of it that Ashal could see. No pools of blood or broken bodies that would indicate a struggle had occurred. Where were the defenders? The monsters that had pursued her before were nowhere to be seen, and their absence caused a sinking feeling of dread to form in the pit of her stomach. She slowed her pace and allowed the other naiads to flow around her.

Then she heard the screams.

She ran toward them, but when she rounded a corner, the windows of an old shop shattered. A large group of cloaked monsters pushed their way through the building's wreckage with their grasping hands held outward in ravenous supplication. Dry, rattling moans escaped their lips, and Ashal shuddered at the sound. The staggering figures fell upon the unsuspecting warriors who were caught by their sudden appearance. The living turned desperately toward these new attackers, and even as they did so, there came another muffled moan from behind them. More aged doors and windows of the buildings came tumbling down to reveal another group of the cloaked figures grasping with decrepit hands and with terrible cries upon their withered lips.

Ashal turned to the various naiad and salamander soldiers who were caught in the street around her. Their confusion and surprise was almost as deadly as the dry husks which tore down several of those closest to the edges of the street before they could even understand what was happening. Various pockets of warriors had banded together to face one side of the ambush or the other, but none of them seemed like they would last long. It dawned on Ashal that this had been Laurine's plan all along. It was why they hadn't had any trouble getting into the town. With that realization came another, more terrifying one. Laurine had known they were coming!

One of the cloaked figures grabbed Ashal's arm, and in her dazed shock, she almost fell into her assailant before stabbing upward with the point of her small knife beneath the jaw. The blade seemed to sever whatever magic held it upright, and the corpse toppled away. Ashal took a deep breath to try and steady herself and took one more look around.

"To me!" She forced her voice above the din of battle. Several naiads and a few salamanders looked at her in surprise, but none seemed willing to respond to her command except a few of the naiads who held harpoon guns. Ashal grunted and pointed at the nearest group of warriors fighting against a swarm of milky eyed corpses.

"Concentrate your fire there, keep those troops alive and they will return the favor!" Ashal barked at the small squad of shooters that had responded to her order. They were all young, even though most were probably still older than her. The first of them nodded and took aim. The others were encouraged by being given orders and quickly followed suit. Ashal watched for a few moments as they slung their heavy bolts into the flank of the attacking husks before moving forward to assist the knot of warriors that were struggling against them.

She sprang into the air and landed heavily on the back of the nearest undead creature. It was screaming scratchy grunts while trying to grasp at the salamander who was desperately trying to keep the thing at bay with his obsidian axe. Ashal thrust downward with her spear and removed the creature's head from its body; the corpse immediately fell to the ground. Twisting, she then thrust her spear sideways and cleared a second undead creature before falling into line beside the salamander whom she'd just saved.

"We need to form a battle line!" Ashal cried out, desperately trying to pull up every memory of combat she could recall. All the lessons that Magdolon had taught her tumbled about her thoughts, like sand falling through a sieve. But one thing that both battle experience and her lessons had drilled into her was the necessity for a battle line with clear distinctions between friend and foe. They needed to right this massacre so that they were facing the undead straight away down the street, rather than trying to push them back on two fronts.

"Pass the word along!" Ashal yelled to the salamander at her side as she thrust her spear through the jaw of another rotting dead thing. "On my command, we step to the left. Every time I call out, we step to the left! We need to shift the lines!"

The salamander nodded and turned to press himself back into the rabble-like squad of soldiers who were fighting a losing battle. Ashal waited for a few moments, her spear flashing out to strike down the enemy periodically. The press of undead flesh began to alleviate a little before Ashal felt a cold hand grasp her ankle and pull her to the ground from behind. She gasped as she rolled and stabbed quickly down to sever the hand. The creature didn't react to its wound, and where it was laying prostrate on the ground, it simply attempted to push itself closer to her leg. Ashal snarled and thrust downward through the top of its skull before taking a quick survey of the skirmish. Her assailant had been the only one who had pushed through their rear flank, but it wasn't looking promising that the line would hold much longer as it currently stood. She looked sideways and saw the salamander return; he nodded to her and she raised her spear.

"Soldiers," she cried, "left step!" The strung out assortment of warriors obeyed, crying out "LEFT!" in response to her order. Ashal watched the line visibly shift as they re-oriented themselves to face the common threat together.

"Left step!" Ashal cried out, again the line shifted.

"Back step!" The line moved back.

"Form up," Ashal yelled, "to me!"

This time the warriors responded, and those with shields on the front line gave a unified push which caused the foremost of the undead to stagger backward. In that interim, the remaining soldiers retreated a few half steps and formed a new line in front of Ashal.

"Shooters! Open fire!" Ashal's words cut through the grimy moans of their enemy, and the naiads who had harpoon guns quickly responded by sending a volley of heavy metal shafts into the army of corpses before them. Some of the missiles found their targets and a few of the undead toppled to the ground, others struck withered limbs or into useless stomachs. The zombies joined together in a cacophony of moans that caused Ashal's skin to crawl before surging forward into the makeshift shieldwall of living warriors.

"Hold fast!" Ashal braced behind one of the salamander shield bearers and pressed against his warm scales as the crush of undead bore down on them. The initial momentum pushed them back a few feet. Ashal gritted her teeth and shoved harder against the salamander as together they fought to give room for the heart piercing harpoon guns behind them to find targets. Desiccated arms tried to grab at Ashal over the salamander's shoulders, and she heard several cries of pain from further down the line as the animated dead tore two of the warriors from their shields and enveloped them in a humming pile of dead flesh. Their screams did not subside for several minutes as the wet sound of tearing flesh and breaking bones punctuated their cries for help.

Ashal could feel the morale of the rest beginning to falter as they pushed desperately back at the undead swarm before them. Abruptly, one of the screams from the dying who had been pulled into the zombie's embrace cut off. The ensuing silence was filled with the sounds of chewing and other wet sounds before blood-soaked limbs fountained out of the mound and eagerly rushed toward the living soldiers behind the shield wall. One of the naiads behind her screamed and began running away. Her departure caused the others to begin to falter, their eyes darting about them like horses who've been spooked by a rabbit darting across their path. Ashal knew that if they broke now that a gruesome death awaited everyone.

"Hold the line!" Ashal barked, her body tensed against the constant pressure from the undead. She called out encouragement to the troops, but it was pointless. Another naiad turned and ran, followed by a salamander holding a two handed sword. This was just the beginning trickle, but it didn't take long before the fear took hold. Ashal gripped her spear close to her chest and prepared to step back and begin stabbing, bracing herself against the coming painful death that she was certain was mere moments away as more and more of the outnumbered naiads and salamanders turned to flee.

A sudden beam of light soared over her head, the heat of which caused Ashal to wince as it passed within a few feet of her face. Fire erupted among the dried and withered corpses calling out for her blood, orange tongues licking hungrily among the dry cloaks and exposed bone of the dead villagers. Soon, the fire spread to the buildings on the side as red-hot warmth crawled through the evening light, casting everything in a crimson hue. The dead did not seem to notice at first, but the smell of cooking meat and the sound of sizzling fat reached Ashal's senses. She watched as the burning undead began to stagger and fall while the devouring flames melted their muscles and turned their bones to ash. A few of the remaining living soldiers helped to quicken the task by cleaving through the remaining corpses that still remained twitching and moaning as the fire subsided and only the buildings remained alight.

"We must hurry to the abbey." Thistle's voice startled Ashal from behind, and she turned to look at him, his face set with a grim determination that was given a sinister twist in the flickering light of the fires behind her. "We have already wasted too much time. My fires will deal with these poor wretches. Everyone! To the abbey!" The druid made a few abrupt motions with his hands, and the remaining flames that still burned in the street where they stood slid to the buildings on either side, creating a sort of corridor of fire through which he walked as if it were a palace hallway.

Ashal stared after him for a few moments and then glanced behind her and motioned to the remaining warriors who still stood and followed after Thistle. The fires closed behind them as they hurried to catch up.

* * * * *

Yvette watched as Rose laid the small paring knife on the wooden table and picked up the bloodstained rag beside it to wipe her hands. The older vampire took a deep breath and exhaled slowly as she looked down at the slumped figure strapped to the chair before her. Yvette returned the gaze through blurred vision as she tried to steady her heartbeat. The poison that Rose used forced Yvette to remain conscious and aware of everything around her, but the myriad of small cuts all over her arms and across her shoulders and legs were excruciating and demanded all of her attention.

"I told you, my little duckling, that we had much to discuss." Rose smiled and tossed the rag onto the table, exchanging it for a simple metal goblet from which she took a long draught before wiping its crimson liquid with the back of her hand. "I know that you probably don't feel a whole lot like talking right now, but I have found that it is always best to remind my pupils of how bad it can be if they refuse to participate in the discussion."

Yvette lifted her head and tried to speak, but all that came out was a sobbing moan of pain. Her brain refused to form coherent sentences. Rose's smile broadened, and she stepped forward to place her goblet a few inches in front of Yvette's face so that she could smell the tantalizingly fresh blood within it, just out of her reach. This didn't stop Yvette from trying as she strained against her bonds, stretching desperately to taste the rusty tang of the sanguine wine.

"If I give you a small sip, will you be willing to have a nice conversation with me?" Rose's voice dripped with sweetness. Yvette didn't care and nodded her head vigorously. The older sister returned the gesture and pressed the goblet to Yvette's lips, who sighed as she slurped the blood down greedily. Instantly the shallow wounds on her arms and legs began to seal themselves, and the deeper wounds on her shoulders began to knit back together. The pain died away to a dull ache and was on the verge of disappearing when Rose tugged the goblet away from her lips.

"Not too much! I wouldn't want you to be too full for our discussion!" Rose stepped back and placed the metal vessel on the table beside the knife that she had used to butcher Yvette's still healing skin. The daze of pain was subsiding to a manageable level, but in its absence, the dreaded anticipation of more pain crashed down on Yvette's chest. Rose moved close and caressed the side of her face, making shushing noises as she did so; Yvette hadn't realized that she was crying softly. She tried to flinch away from Rose's touch, but the older sister reached out with her other hand and held Yvette's head in place by squeezing her at the base of her neck.

"We haven't received word from your friends yet. Did you send some sort of code to them? Did you warn them?" Rose leaned in closer so that their faces were inches apart, Yvette could smell her perfume and felt her cold breath on her face. She wished that she was brave enough to glare at her torturer, but the best she could manage was a stony mask before she shook her head.

"Then why aren't they rising to the bait?" Rose snarled, moving to stand directly over Yvette so that she forced the younger vampire to stare straight upward with wide, glazed eyes dimmed with pain and befuddled with fear. Rose gave a frustrated sigh and stepped back.

A loud knock came at the door. Rose stepped quickly back from Yvette, and called out for the knocker to come in. The door practically swung open and a younger acolyte stood there, breathless.

"Sister Rose!" Yvette flinched at the voice that accompanied the sound of the door slamming into the wall. "They are here! The forest is attacking! The Mother Abbess sent me to tell you that she needs you by her!" Rose sighed and arched her shoulders and knuckled the small of her back.

"Abbess Laurine is often times melodramatic. The beasts must first fight their way through the village before they reach us."

"But the village is on fire!" The young acolyte squeaked. Yvette's pain-addled mind noted that the messenger's face would likely be flushed if she weren't already undead. She shook her head to try and clear it, realizing that something important was happening, but she couldn't seem to focus on it.

"What?!" Rose snarled. "Are you certain, child?" The acolyte made a strange squeaking noise and nodded vigorously. Rose pursed her lips for a few moments, unreadable thoughts that only she could see passing through her vision. Yvette's eyes refused to focus on anything, and the world was a shifting array of blurring images. Finally, Rose gave a mirthless chuckle and strode toward the door.

"It seems your friends are more troublesome than we first thought. Don't worry, little duckling, I'll be back to deal with you shortly!"

With that, Rose swept out of the room and slammed the door behind her. There was an audible rattling followed by a click as she locked the door behind her.

Yvette stared at the closed door, her eyes still blurry and unfocused. Her brain screamed at her that there was something important happening and that she needed to think. But the only thing that she could focus on was the memory of pain the past several days had contained. Everything was a blur of hurt, her arms bore the scars that not even the sporadic vampiric feedings could heal completely due to their frequency and depth. Her stomach clenched at the thought of a renewed session with Rose when she returned. Some part of her even welcomed the prospect of death that the arrival of the forces of nature would herald for Yvette as she had likely outlived her usefulness.

This thought caused a jolt of fear to pass through her chest, and with it came a moment of clarity. She hadn't been a vampire for long, but she also did not know what happened to her when she died. Before, when she had been a sister of Basilea, she knew that if she had lived up to her covenants, she would be welcomed into the golden meadows of Kolosu with the Shining Ones, and that all her pain from this life would be forgotten. Now, she did not know what awaited her when the darkness took her. She knew as an abomination that the Shining Ones would be repulsed by her presence, and that none of the Elohi would be swooping down to carry her off to her glorious reward.

Perhaps there was nothing there waiting for her. This thought caused her to shudder. She didn't want to die. The shadows all around her seemed to press down, making it difficult to breathe. She strained against her bonds in a sudden fit of panicked rage. The leather straps screeched in protest but held firm. Yvette found her hand slipping on her blood as it slicked the underside of the straps, making it impossible to find purchase to pull against them. It took her crazed mind a few moments to process this information as she continued to struggle. She had been in this chair dozens of times before, and she had thought that the strap had begun to loosen with her efforts of straining against it, but all that had won her was a mere inch or so gap on her left wrist that was still too small to pull her hand through. It was more than her right hand, which was paralyzed under the crushing pressure of its strap. But freedom seemed an impossibility all the same.

She tried again anyways, her panicked breathing wouldn't allow her to quit. At first it seemed impossible, as her hand was just too big to fit through the loop, but she continued to twist, and the leather began to tug at her skin painfully. She pulled harder and gave a small scream as the skin of her hand began to sluff away under the pressure of the buckle. This exposed raw flesh underneath and caused fresh blood to pool on the armrest where the strap was attached.

Yvette groaned and relinquished her efforts for a moment, the pain of her exertions washing through her body. But this was a different kind of pain, not one that bore the sickly edge of poison that Rose's torture had used. No, this was a sharp pain, and it had the curious effect of clearing the fog from her mind. She looked down at her bloodied left hand which she had been trying to free. The strap rested just below the joint of her thumb where she knew that it would not pass over no matter how much she strained, unless she could collapse her fist just a little bit more.

She suppressed a groan as a horrible thought came to her. The strap she had been working on was too tight to fit her hand through *as it was*. But if she was able to make her hand shift to be a bit narrower... It was a desperate plan, and one that she wasn't sure she could endure, much less follow through. She eyed the metal goblet which Rose had left. Yvette hoped that there was some blood left in it that might repair her hand after she was free.

Yvette took some deep breaths to calm her nerves, then slowly she began to press the outside of her thumb into the blood soaked wood of the chair's armrest. She pushed harder and harder until she felt the joint beginning to give way. A sickening cracking sound sent a stream of fire up her arm, and Yvette cried out in agony as her hand folded unnaturally with its collapsed joint.

Yvette sucked in great gulps of air as her vision blurred and her body tried to desperately deal with the pain in her hand. Gradually, her vision began to clear, and she attempted to tug at her hand. With its painful new position, it slid through the strap with little effort.

With one hand freed, Yvette pawed at the buckles holding her right hand captive. Gripping the strap with only her fingers while her thumb dangled uselessly to one side at a painful angle, she fumbled to loosen the brass that held it in place. She stopped several times for fear of blacking out from the pain. The cold thought of Rose's imminent return forced her to press on. Finally, after several attempts, the buckle's tongue slid free and Yvette's good hand pulled out of its restraint.

She bent quickly and undid the straps at her feet and stepped clear. She stumbled over to the table on weary legs and reached for the goblet. Her hands gripped clumsily for the stem of the glass, and in her haste, it tipped onto its side, spilling much of its contents across the table before she hastily grabbed it and pulled it to her chest. The remaining ruby liquid splashed over one edge and trickled down over her hand. There was little more than a few mouthfuls left, and she hoped it would be enough.

Breathing heavily, Yvette tipped the glass back and poured the blood into her mouth. As soon as it touched the back of her throat, she felt her body beginning to grow warm. Her hand crackled and snapped like a pile of dead leaves, and she felt the bones shifting position underneath her skin, repairing her broken thumb and wrist. She marvelled that this process was not painful as had been the breaking of her joint, but she was thankful for such small mercies.

She drained the goblet, feeling her strength restored with each thirsty gulp. Casting the vessel aside, she looked around hungrily for more. She looked down at the spilled pool of crimson on the table and fell to licking it up like an animal. Her pain gave way and justified her embarrassing position as she licked hungrily at the wooden surface. She lifted her head back, a bead of red trickling down her neck from her open mouth, and she sighed. The pain was subsiding, although she still felt the stinging after effects of the poison.

She cast her gaze down to the table once more and saw the small paring knife which had been the source of so much pain for her. She picked it up delicately. The blade was nothing special. A simple piece of metal with two pieces of wood riveted together to form the handle. In all, the blade was only a few inches long, but Yvette knew its edge was razor sharp, and she could smell the poison lingering along its length. A cold sensation began to spread out from her stomach as she stared at the simple knife.

There came a rattling noise from the doorway, and Yvette turned in terror as she heard a key being inserted into the lock. She sprinted over to hide beside the door just as it eased open, the person opening it being cautious not to let the door open too wide. Yvette could smell Rose's perfume, and her throat constricted at its scent. Rose stopped at the threshold and Yvette could almost feel her eyes roaming around the room.

Step forward! Yvette willed the older sister to step further through the door. Yvette knew that she would have only one chance at killing her, and if that failed, then she shuddered at the thought of what Rose would do to her.

"Oh, my lame little duckling..." Rose sighed. Then the door hurtled back to slam against Yvette, crushing her against the wall. Involuntarily, she cried out and crumpled to the floor, the knife tumbling from her hands. Slowly, Rose stepped around the door and closed it behind her.

"Such a waste!" Rose clicked her tongue disapprovingly as she knelt before the dazed Yvette. Rose reached out and picked up her paring knife from off the floor, her eyes flashing dangerously as she looked over Yvette's slumped form on the ground. "You're so resourceful! We could have used someone like you helping us! Instead you had to latch on to a memory of a dead mother who you will never see again and wouldn't love you in your present state in any case!"

Rose leaned forward and stabbed down viciously with the knife, burying its full length into Yvette's thigh. The young sister gasped as the familiar sensation of agony washed over her, the poison working quickly to blur her senses and awaken her faculties to every subtle twist of the corrupted steel now embedded in her leg.

"There is no fighting this, child." Rose sighed, gripping the knife handle. Yvette tried to stifle a scream so that it came out as a muffled groan instead. "If I thought there was any chance for your redemption, I would do everything in my power to save you. But this has just proven that you are unfit for our coven." Rose lifted her free hand and caressed the side of Yvette's face once more.

"Such a shame," she repeated and then lowered her hand to Yvette's throat and began to squeeze. Yvette struggled, her hands clawing at Rose's. Yvette knew she could survive without breathing, she was undead after all, but her body was conditioned to breath and the lack thereof caused panic to ring in her head. But beyond that, the pain she felt was not due to lack of air. Instead, she felt Rose's claws digging into the side of her neck and the blood they drew trickled down her throat. Yvette felt the sharp nails digging deeper and deeper into her flesh, every moment drawing closer to her spine and her jugular.

"Goodnight, sweet little duckling," Rose whispered. Something broke within Yvette. The fear of death once again shook her, and the inability to draw breath magnified the sensation. The edges of her vision were turning red as the pain amplified in her leg and her neck. She looked into her tormentor's eyes as they stared down at her, madness was there, but so was regret and anger. Something tugged at Yvette's awareness and she focused on it desperately, hoping for salvation.

Gathering all her remaining strength, Yvette kicked outward with both feet. The knife wound in her leg screamed out in protest, but she had endured far worse and so ignored it. The kick landed squarely in Rose's chest and threw her back, not very far, but enough that she released her hold on Yvette's neck in order to catch herself. Capitalizing on this moment, Yvette lunged forward and ripped the knife from her thigh. She brought it up quickly and caught Rose a glancing blow to her cheek which left an angry red line that spread from jaw to her nose.

Rose screamed and fell backward, clutching her face. Yvette didn't stop. She reversed the grip on the knife and stepped forward, stabbing repeatedly at her attacker. Rose raised her arms to ward off the blows, but each of Yvette's attacks cut flesh there, and soon the older vampire began to wail in pain even though Yvette's attacks had slowed. The poison was doing its work for her.

"It really is quite painful, isn't it?" Yvette growled, forcing herself to stand above the cowering form of her abuser, even though one of her legs refused to take her full weight.

"Please!" Rose screamed. "Make it stop!"

Yvette waited for several long moments that were filled with the screaming sobs from Rose, who gripped her wounds and rocked back and forth. After some time, she leaned down and put her face within inches of Rose's so that her eyes filled her vision.

"No," Yvette said. "Not until I am through with you."

* * * * *

Ashal stared upward as she ran up the switchback path that lead up the side of the plateau where the abbey lay. This was better than looking down to see the village in flames while Thistle's elementals scoured the dried up buildings.

226

Ashal's memory flitted to the little girl and her father who had involuntarily sheltered her during their first ill-fated foray into the cursed village and wondered if they were even now coughing on the fumes of the smoke down below them. She quickly pushed such thoughts away; she couldn't afford to grow sentimental this late in the attack. Instead, she fixed her sights on the abbey gate which she was surprised to see was still standing open, just as Yvette had said it would be.

Something gnawed at the inside of Ashal's stomach. She kept glancing around at the pathway, searching for traps. This path was designed to be a nightmare for attackers. Its zigzagging path made a perfect setup for ambushes and created a lot of natural bottlenecks which would make it difficult for attackers to employ their superior weight of numbers against smaller blocks of defenders. Yet, apart from the withered husks of the villagers down below, there had been practically no resistance leading up to the abbey. Ashal found herself almost wishing for a counterattack, or a charge of Basilean vampires to come surging out of the open gates. But nothing was there, and the seeming arrogance of Laurine and her ilk was unsettling to Ashal.

They rounded the final bend in the path and came to a halt before the large, looming gate before them. The air suddenly became quite still as the only real sounds besides the heavy breathing of the soldiers was that of the burning village down below, nothing else disturbed the chill air. The gate stood open with its portcullis raised, as if inviting them in. A small panic began to settle into the back of Ashal's mind. She was among the first of the troops that had made the climb, and the soldiers around her paused as well, each one staring at the open gate as if trying to work out the puzzle.

"The way is open!" Ashal heard Thistle cry out, his voice ragged with urgency. Ashal shivered as once again her stomach twisted. There came the thundering sound of something large stomping its way up the path behind her and Ashal twisted to see the lumbering form of Bitter Bark just as he stepped over the line of soldiers of which she was a part. The living tree stepped out in front of the assembly of warriors, his gaze sweeping over the battlements. The wind shifted, and with it came the smell of smoke from the village, which was now properly in flames; there would be no recovery of any of the buildings. Ashal felt herself wondering if there would be any survivors and where they would go.

"Bitter Bark! Please! We have our opening! Yvette has kept her word!" Thistle's voice tore through the still air. Bitter Bark turned back to look at his troops, his eyes focusing on the druid.

"An ill wind blows here. Something is wrong," the treeherder's voice rumbled.

"We can't go back!" Thistle replied. "Those fires will rage for hours yet! The way is blocked. Would you have us wait here, exposed to whatever attack Laurine would throw at us?" Bitter Bark shook his head and waved a hand.

"I see your point, Thistle. But something does not sit well with me here. Why have they not attacked us yet? This is obviously a trap. An attack awaits us on the other side of that gate."

"If we do nothing, we are exposed to attack in any case! And we will fare better in there than we will strung out along the pathway leading up here!" Thistle growled.

"May the Lady watch over us," Bitter Bark responded. Ashal could sense the reluctance in his voice, and she found herself agreeing with him. But Thistle was right, they were more exposed where they were than inside the abbey walls, even if it was an ambush. At least that's what she hoped was true. Bitter Bark turned back to the gates and raised his arm into the air.

"Advance!" The deep voice boomed out, dropping his arm in a chopping motion. The wall of warriors behind him surged ahead. The charge slowed somewhat as the warriors had to squeeze through the gateway to the large courtyard on the other side. Ashal quickly pushed her way through and marvelled at the architecture of the buildings which made up the abbey compound. In particular, the large building at the center of the others which was marked with a large bronze statue of what looked like an angel at its pinnacle.

There were no enemy soldiers waiting for them in the courtyard. In fact it was completely empty. Ashal fixed her gaze on the large building with the bronze statue, thinking it to be the most likely place where Laurine would hide. She ran toward it, and just as she was about to reach for one of the handles, the great wooden doors burst open and a group of Basileans clad in silver plate and wielding large swords rushed out. Ashal dodged two quick sword thrusts and danced backward. Two naiads who had kept pace with her in her charge toward the building were quickly cut down by the vicious attacks of the shining paladins.

The Basileans did not pursue as Ashal retreated backward toward the line of warriors hurrying to catch up with her from the gate. Instead, they formed a defensive line with their swords held at the ready. Behind them, a figure emerged and Ashal's breath escaped her in a hiss as she recognized the smooth features of her enemy. Laurine walked out behind her guard and raised her hands to the heavens. Ashal's vision did not stray from Laurine's face as a strange, purple mist seemed to coalesce around her palms before tumbling softly to the ground. A slight tremor shook the earth as the mist made contact with the dark, freshly disturbed dirt beneath their feet. The panic returned to Ashal, and she grabbed a nearby naiad who held one of their strange harpoon guns.

"Bring her down!" Ashal screamed, pointing at Laurine. The naiad raised her weapon and fired a bolt at the chanting abbess. One of the paladin guards standing beside the abbess leapt in front of the harpoon and it pierced her chest. The armor clad woman tumbled to the ground. The rest of the paladins closed ranks around Laurine so that she was lost from sight behind them.

"Prepare to charge!" Ashal bellowed and leveled her spear at the gathered group of Laurine's defenders. As she did so, she heard a large crash from behind her and turned to see that the portcullis had fallen, cutting off the warriors who had poured into the courtyard from those that still sat on the path outside. Ashal groaned but turned back to her goal at hand.

As she braced herself for the sprint toward Laurine, there came a grating sound from below her feet. She looked down to see a skeletal hand protruding from the dirt, its bony digits wrapped around her foot. She grunted and stabbed downward, severing the hand with her spear. As soon as she did so, however, more hands sprouted from the earth, followed by the macabre grin of hundreds of skulls as they pulled themselves from the ground.

Chaos ensued. The warriors tried to kill the newly sprung undead troops before they could rise, but there were far too many of them. Soon, there came a rain of arrows falling on the combined warriors. Ashal looked to the battlements and saw more skeletons, these ones with bows loosing arrows indiscriminately into the combined mass of bodies, both living and dead. Several tried to target Bitter Bark, who stood in the middle of the courtyard bellowing orders.

Knots of armored skeletons began to form among the living soldiers. Ashal spun about to look at Laurine and found herself staring into the empty sockets of an undead spearman's skull. She reacted quickly and thrust her own spear forward, piercing its chest and severing its spine from the rest of its body. The undead thing crumpled to the ground, but behind it stood two more to take its place. She warded off their attacks and pushed them away with the haft of her spear where the naiads to either side of her quickly finished them with their simpler weapons of oaken clubs and long knives.

All around Ashal, the sounds of battle washed over her as terrified screams and muted collisions of blade on bone punctuated the air. The undead were uncomfortably quiet in the way they fought; the sounds of the dead and dying came only from the living. The clatter of bones and the ringing of steel cut through the evening air. In the distance, the sun was beginning its full descent. Soon the abbey would be cloaked in darkness and the battle had only just begun in earnest.

Ashal glanced at the portcullis and thought she saw signs of battle coming from the other side. No relief would be coming from the rest of their army. They had fallen fully into Laurine's trap, even knowing it was there! Ashal cursed and pushed herself back to the front line where they were still fighting to make their way toward the large building; Laurine and her bodyguard stood there, as if waiting for something else.

The rumbling had ceased, but now there were undead soldiers scattered throughout the courtyard, easily equalling the forces of nature, warrior for warrior. The real battle for the abbey was finally underway.

Twenty-Three

THE INNER SANCTUM

The battle raged like the seething tide caught in a maelstrom. There were no clear battle lines here, no rules of engagement or commanding officers to determine the course of actions. This was the forces of nature struggling against an impossible foe whose very existence was an act of defiance to the natural world. Raw, seething fury clashed against unyielding indifference as beast fought corpse in a series of clumped brawls that had developed from the soldiers of the abbey springing up from under the feet of the denizens of the forest. This was no grand battle of which songs were sung and tales were told, this was a relentless struggle for survival. There was nothing glorious about this wanton violence.

Ashal found herself on the edge of this sprawling pit of bloody conflict with skeletons behind her and a band of armored vampires in front. Laurine stood before the grand building that made up the center of the abbey's compound, a smile on her lips as the purple mists fell from her hands, summoning forth her warriors from the very earth. Ashal stared at her enemy, a furious heat stinging at the corners of her eyes and threatening to spew forth from her mouth.

She gritted her teeth and charged toward Laurine's bodyguard of vampires clad in Basilean armor, not caring that this was likely suicide, or that even if she made it through to Laurine that she would likely be blasted by her fell magic in any case. She ran because she was tired of waiting. She ran, and the years that she had spent in exile waiting for this moment charged with her. The weight of her mother's death and Magdolon's disappointment urged her onward. Gravel's dead eyes would not let her slow her pace.

She collided with the first vampire, Ashal's shoulder hitting her square in the center of her chest and throwing her off balance. Quicker than a thought, Ashal's spear stabbed forward, catching the vampire just above her gorget, spearing up through her lower jaw and into her skull. The former Basilean paladin was dead before she hit the ground. Ashal pulled her spear free and repeated the attack. This time, the vampire ducked away from her charge, and she felt a sharp sensation as her attacker's sword caught a glancing blow across the back of her arm.

"Follow the Neritican! The newcomer!" Ashal dimly heard Bitter Bark's voice rumbling above the clash of battle behind her. "If we kill the necromancer, her army will fall!" Ashal didn't hear anything else as she was quickly thrown to the ground by a gauntleted fist that connected with the side of her neck.

She rolled in the dirt, gasping for air until a heavy boot landed on her sternum painfully, causing her ribs to creak beneath its weight. She stared up into the furious eyes of another vampire, her gleaming sword held high above her head. Ashal fumbled with her spear, trying to stab upward and dislodge her attacker, but it was no use. The vampire batted the spear away and took aim with her blade once more before an obsidian axe suddenly collided with her chest. Ashal found herself gasping for air as the pressure released and the foe fell to the ground beside her. Dead eyes stared out from the shadow of the vampire's helm. A large salamander stepped on the body to dislodge his axe and nodded down at Ashal who blinked her thanks as she forced herself to stand.

The maelstrom of battle swirled around her on all sides. Although Laurine's guards were killing far more than they were losing, they were savagely outnumbered, and the creatures of the wood pressed their advantage to deadly effect. Ashal looked through the mass of bodies pushing against each other and spied Laurine standing on the other side. Her smile still had not faltered despite her precarious position. She lifted a hand, and a green spout of lightning flared up from her fingers and struck the ground with a deafening crack of thunder within feet of where Ashal stood. The concussive blast forced Ashal to her knees, along with all the rest of the fighters around her. When she looked to where the blast had struck, she saw three dead naiads, their bodies blackened by the heat of the lightning bolt.

Ashal's ears were ringing, and everyone in the immediate vicinity was struggling to find their feet. Some looked around with terror on their faces as their eyes refused to focus. Some of the vampires, with their chilled blood and inhuman reflexes, quickly took advantage of this lull in the fighting and fell upon their attackers. Ashal stumbled forward to try and challenge them, but her clumsy steps refused to carry her, and she found herself leaning on her spear as the ringing in her ears finally began to fade.

The vampires cut down several of the naiad warriors who had been fighting around where the lightning had struck. This proved to be too much for the rest, most of whom were more proficient with their harpoon guns than any kind of hand to hand fighting. The naiads tried to turn and flee from the vicious onslaught, only to run into the backs of a regiment of salamanders who were struggling to hold back the line of skeletons from assaulting the rear. The naiads panicked and scattered. Some tried to push their way through the salamanders and met their ends on the rusted tips of the skeletons' blades. Others turned and tried to flee around the reptilian soldiers, and while some of these successfully made it to the walls, most were cut down in the attempt.

The vampires yelled their triumph and surged forward into the back of the salamander regiment, cutting down many of them before they were even aware they were under attack. The salamander line shuddered as it took casualties from both sides, and Ashal was certain that they would break just as the naiads had, but miraculously they held strong. Perhaps it was the realization that they had nowhere to flee that kept them in the fight, maybe it was pure stubbornness. Ashal didn't care and quickly ran up on the already heavily wounded group of vampires. The salamanders decided that these new attackers were a bigger threat than the skeletons behind them and also turned to face the new foe.

With their attention focused on the salamanders before them, Ashal was able to dispatch two vampires in short succession, hitting them unawares. The reptilian warriors cut down another three with their heavy axes. Seeing this combined ferocity, the already diminished group of vampires scattered, the remnants of their unit disappearing into the chaos of the battle. Ashal lifted her spear to her allies in salute, but they were already turned back to their former foe. Ashal watched in horror as skeletal hands reached out and pulled the salamanders into a sea of bone that ripped and tore at their scaled hides. Ashal tried to block out their screams and turned to look back at Laurine.

The necromancer now stood exposed with nothing between her and Ashal, yet still her smile had not slipped. Laurine locked eyes with Ashal, then her head turned to the side to glance over her shoulder. Ashal turned to follow her gaze and groaned when she saw two groups of armored horsemen galloping out from between the large building and one of the ancillary ones on the edge of the battle. They were aimed to crash into the flank of a group of centaurs who had broken free of the battle and were rounding about to try and hit a knot of skeletons in the rear. The centaurs were completely oblivious of the peril they were in and Ashal watched the vampiric knights slam into their far flank. The first centaur died without a sound, and the Basilean vampires quickly made short work of the rest of the unit, killing them all in a mercilessly efficient and bloody manner.

Ashal closed her eyes and shook her head. She couldn't do anything about that now. She opened her eyes and looked back at Laurine, fixing her as the priority in her mind. Laurine's smile grew wider in triumph, and she raised a hand to point it at Ashal, who crouched defensively waiting for the magical blast. It never came, however, as Laurine suddenly doubled over clutching her stomach. Ashal's eyes narrowed in confusion, was this some kind of ruse? She didn't dare hesitate, however, and sprinted forward.

The abbess pulled her hand away from her stomach and Ashal was shocked to see it covered in blood. *The wound I gave her!* Ashal realized suddenly. She forced her legs to move faster to try and close the gap between them. Laurine lifted her hand and a spout of fire shot out of her palm, forcing Ashal to jump to the side in order to avoid it. Laurine rose to her feet and ran back to the

233

doors to the great building, casting another blast behind her as she did so before ducking inside. Ashal cursed and ran after her.

The doors opened up into a darkened hallway that turned pitch black as the door closed behind her. Ashal stood for a few moments to let her eyes adjust to the gloom. The sounds of battle were muffled by the heavy door as it thudded back into place and sealed off the world outside. The darkness was almost absolute, the only light coming from up ahead. Ashal realized that there was only one way to go and so moved toward the faint light that was emanating from the other side of an archway. As she drew closer, she saw that the light was coming from two burning braziers that were insufficient to dispel the gloom of what appeared to be a massive hall that likely stretched all the way up to the bronze statue overhead and took a large majority of the width of the building as well.

There were wooden pews which stretched away on either side of the aisle until they became fuzzy shapes in the gloom. Situated in between the two braziers was a large dais with stairs that lead up to a massive wooden throne. Laurine sat there, her head resting against its back and her eyes closed. A line of dark liquid ran from the corner of her mouth, and she held so still, that for a moment, Ashal wondered if her chance for vengeance had been stolen from her. Then the abbess's eyes snapped open and she leaned forward to stare at Ashal from across the massive hall.

"I must remember my limits." Laurine's weak voice voice sounded cold and hollow, amplified by the echoes it created. "I think the Shining Ones may have sent you to remind me of them." She sighed and fell into a coughing fit.

"I would have thought you had abandoned your faith long ago. About the time you killed my mother." Ashal moved forward cautiously, her eyes darting between the various shadows. Laurine finally controlled her coughing and sat back, wiping her hand across her mouth which only served to smear the blood across her cheek.

"I have paid for my sins a thousand times over, child. Your mother's death weighs no more heavily upon me than the hundreds of others whom I have been forced to deal with. I would do it all again, too, if it meant salvation for my people and an end to the evil in this world."

"End of the evil in this world?" Ashal gave a dry laugh. "You are part of that evil! It is all around you, and you use it to meet your own selfish ambitions!"

"No, child, it is you who are mistaken. This village was safe, its inhabitants secure against any and all who would dare bring them harm. Until *you* came here. If anyone is to blame for being the cause of all this suffering, it is you. After all, I did not start the fires which even now tear through the homes of those I serve, suffocating them with smoke and crisping their flesh with flame."

"Your people lived in constant fear! You turned all those who had committed even the most basic of crimes into the walking dead! How is that safety?"

"If my people feared me, it was their choice to do so. But how is your solution better? Is death better than the life I gave them?" Laurine glared down from her throne. By now, Ashal had reached the end of the pews and only a handful of feet separated her from the foot of the dais. Laurine's words hit her like a blow to the stomach. The necromancer tilted her head and stared at the naiad.

"How are your actions any better than those that you have accused me of doing?" Laurine asked, pushing herself unsteadily to her feet as she did so. Ashal shook her head and forced herself to look up at her.

"I have come to end a darkness that I know will only cause further harm. I have seen what you have done, I have been a victim of your machinations, and now I will end it."

Laurine chuckled menacingly.

"Is that what separates us? Because you have suffered by my actions, that is what makes me evil? Very noble of you." Laurine raised a hand and purple mist began to coalesce around it. "Let me ask you this, child, how many bodies lay on *your* noble path to vengeance?" As she spoke, white wisps of smoke began to circle through the air around Ashal's head, and she heard whispers within her mind.

Why would you do this? The voices cried out in a familiar tone. Ashal now saw the stone pillars which surrounded her, holding up the high roof of the great hall. A magical wind began to blow through them, whistling in and out of the pews behind her and screeching against the stone that surrounded her. A quiet terror settled into the pit of her stomach and she glanced around, trying to find where the voices were coming from. The pressure of the room settled around her shoulders with a familiar weight.

"How many are outside even now, dying for your chance at revenge?" Laurine's voice held the same, ethereal quality of the voices within Ashal's head. The white wisps began to grow in number, forming a wall of white between Ashal and Laurine. Some of the wisps began to form into shapes. Mouths and eyes began to appear, the lips of which moved in time with the accusations that grew within Ashal's mind.

Our blood is less precious than your mother's? One voice seemed to say in a little girl's voice, and Ashal swore it was the same as the little girl who'd offered them shelter. What was her name? *Sasha!* A voice called out to her in her mind. An image flashed in Ashal's thoughts of the little girl curled up in a terrified ball in her father's arms as the fires of the elementals devoured their home around them, the smoke choking the air from their throats.

How much of your friends' blood have you washed your hands in? Another voice called. This one sounded vaguely of Gravel's, and Ashal could see his dead, pale face before her now, his mouth dribbling blood and his milky eyes that seemed to stare straight though her.

"No!" Ashal cried out. "I'm sorry!" She stepped backward, away from the wall of wispy faces that were now forming out of the fog. She turned to look away and found herself staring into the eyes of Magdolon.

I am so disappointed in you. Another voice spoke, but it wasn't Magdolon's, although his face was angry and fit the tone of the words. Something stirred within Ashal, even though her heart felt like it was being ripped from her chest. She cried out, her despair denying her the dignity of silent suffering. The visage of Magdolon stepped forward and pulled its spear from its back.

You have fallen from grace, and you must pay for your transgressions. Magdolon raised his spear, aiming for her throat. *The only suitable punishment is death.* Ashal stared up into his face as a whirlwind of whispers echoed through her mind. Her heart began to beat faster in anticipation of Magdolon's strike, and she dropped her spear from her tired hand, falling to her knees in order to welcome the oblivion and the release it brought.

Somewhere in the midst of all this noise came a single note. It rumbled like the distant thunder of a summer storm, the kind that brought warm rain that wrapped the world in a blanket of comfort. It stood out against the backdrop of wailing misery like a diamond set against black velvet, shimmering and bright. Ashal reached for it within her mind, stretching to cling to one last bit of warmth in her final moments. The bass rumble enveloped her, and for a moment, she found herself standing on a beach bathed in moonlight, standing beside Magdolon. She recognized the scene from her memory. This was the night before they had left on their journey here. Magdolon was speaking, and Ashal clung to his words.

"Your path has been difficult, *Lueshwy'n,* but you have strengths that many do not. These strengths will carry you in ways that no other Child of the Deep could manage. Yours is not the way of the Trident and the Conche. You have darker roads to walk, and more difficult." Magdolon's voice rumbled with the pleasant sound of thunder which had called to Ashal in her mind. He turned to look at her, and Ashal peered into his eyes. Stone itself would crack under that gaze, and yet it held such warmth as it beheld her. Ashal felt her throat tighten as she recognized the pride which Magdolon's look conveyed as it stared down at her. He spoke again, and Ashal felt something from deep inside her call out in desperation at his words.

"Beware the riptide of your emotions." He spoke softly and leaned in close, placing his forehead against hers. "If you are not careful, they will pull you out to sea and leave you to drown. Just like the riptide of these waters pulled you into the blue despite you being a stronger swimmer than any human or dwarf who might also have swam here. So might your desires for revenge draw you out into a place where you will be destroyed."

Yes, I know! Help me! She tried to call out to him, but the boundaries of memory would not let them leave her mouth. Instead, she listened to Magdolon's words.

"Your anger is a tool, and you must use it. Your desire for vengeance must be equal to your desire for justice. You are not simply getting revenge for yourself. You are also avenging all the widows, the orphans, and the dead that Laurine and the others who have wronged you have left in their passing. You must be strong. You must control your anger, your desire. Do not let this quest change you into something less than you are."

The emotions within her stirred once more. *I'm so sorry that I have disappointed you...* She whispered in the darkened corners of her mind. Then, something happened. The memory shifted, and Ashal felt her pulse quicken as the memory of Magdolon lifted her chin with his hand so that he was staring directly into her eyes, as if he was looking past what the memory held and into Ashal's very being.

"Is that what you think you have done?" His voice rumbled, and Ashal gasped. Magdolon smiled a sad smile and continued speaking. "The riptide has taken you very far away from yourself, has it not, *Luesh'wyn*? Remember what has brought you to this place. It is not just for you that you have come to this point. This is what I have been telling you all along. You are here to end the suffering of all those not only who Laurine *has* hurt, but also those whom she *will* hurt."

But what about all the wrong that I have done? What of Gravel, and the villagers down below? Those who are dying even now? How am I any different than Laurine? I sacrifice others for my own desires. How can I claim to serve justice? Even as she cried out in her mind, she felt a growing warmth that seemed to spread inside of her. Magdolon's eyes sparkled as he spoke, and a smile played across his face.

"I cannot answer that for you, for it would only make cheap the response. Your mistakes are many. You have made many poor choices on this path. But your death will not erase those mistakes, and you cannot change your path if you are dead. Do not let your memories be the end of your life, let them fill your life instead. Use them, do not be controlled by them."

Magdolon smiled one more time, and Ashal wanted to reach out and crush him in a tight embrace as the memory, or whatever it was, began to fade away. But then it was gone and Ashal found herself staring at the phantom version of her mentor, poised to strike. The terror in her stomach was gone, the ghostly whispers subdued to the back of her mind. Ashal took a deep breath and stared into the face of her would-be killer.

"I am ready."

The phantom's spear rushed toward her face. At the last possible second, Ashal leaned her head to the side and the spear passed within inches of her cheek. In the same motion, she bent and picked up her own spear, ramming it up and through the figure's chest as it over-extended itself into its thrust. Ashal found herself clucking disapprovingly, noting that the real Magdolon would never have exposed himself in such a way.

The creature evaporated in a spray of mist, and the voices in her mind rose up, wailing. Ashal ignored them and turned to where she knew Laurine must be. She ran at the wall of wisps. The faces and mouths there screamed at her in protest, but she refused to listen and passed through them to land on the bottom step of the dais.

Laurine stared downward in shock and anger. She screamed and raised her hand to release a bolt of fire. Ashal dodged to the side and began running up the steps. Laurine loosed another blast of heat, but Ashal again dodged neatly to the side and the fire passed by harmlessly. Ashal used her momentum to launch herself up the last few steps and focused on Laurine's eyes as they widened in surprise.

The tip of Ashal's spear pierced the base of Laurine's ribs and moved up though her heart to burst out the top of her back in a spray of blood. The impetus of Ashal's charge carried them backward until Laurine toppled onto her throne with a shocked expression on her face.

"I am the daughter of Ai-ellain, High Lord of the Deep. I take vengeance for her and all the other orphans and victims you have created in the wake of your evil crusade! Go now to whatever abyss will take you." Ashal watched as Laurine's eyes clouded over and lost focus before her head lolled to one side.

Silence enveloped the great hall, and Ashal felt a great weariness grip her limbs. She sank down to sit on the highest step of the dais. She realized that the sounds of battle had grown quiet. She wondered if the fighting had ceased, and if it had, which side was the victor. She leaned her head back and stared up into the darkness above her.

"I'm sorry, Gravel," she said, realizing that it was the first time she had openly spoken of his death out loud. "I am so sorry for what I did, and what it cost you. I am sorry for all the pain that my actions have caused for everyone by me. I swear today that I will make it all right, as best I can, starting with this." She reached over and patted her spear which still lay embedded in Laurine's chest. Then she closed her eyes and pictured Magdolon's face as it had appeared in her memories.

I promise that I will keep swimming against the riptide.

A sudden crash and the sound of feet running across the stone floor brought Ashal back to herself, and she stared out into the gloom where she could just make out the entrance to the great hall. The door was open, but the light outside had fallen to the star-lit night and did little to illuminate anything.

"It is true! The abbess is dead!" A woman's voice carried through the dark, and four vampires clad in Basilean armor covered in various colors of blood and sap stepped forward into the flickering light of the braziers. They stood at the foot of the dais and stared up at Ashal, who still sat holding the end of her spear that had impaled Laurine. One of them turned to another and pointed off into the dark to the side of the throne.

"You! Go and fetch Sister Rose! She will need to know! We will take care of this one." The appointed one ran off into the dark, her footsteps echoing in the dismal light. The speaker turned her attention back to Ashal, and all three of the former paladins spread out at the base of the dais and began walking up toward Ashal.

"It takes three of your warriors to kill me?" Ashal said, still feeling tired as she willed her leaden limbs to pull her weapon free from the rapidly cooling corpse behind her, but the spear was stuck solidly in place. She sighed and pulled her knife from her belt instead, falling into a defensive stance as she did so. The vampires advanced slowly, their swords held ready. Soon the vampires would be in range, and then it would all be over in any case.

Another step closer. Ashal drew a deep breath and prepared to lunge.

"Hold sisters!" A familiar voice said from the shadows. "This one belongs to me."

Twenty-Four

THE EBBING OF THE TIDE

Yvette seemed to materialize out of the darkness. She was dressed in the ragged remnants of her sisterhood habit that were stained deep red at the cuffs and along her shoulders. Her dark hair was matted to her scalp in places, and in one hand she carried what looked like an old burlap sack that was also stained a deep crimson. She stopped at the foot of the dais and looked up at the three vampire sisters that stood before Ashal.

"Yvette! What are you doing here? I thought you were locked away as Rose's plaything!" The middle vampire spoke, not tearing her gaze away from Ashal.

"Oh yes! Indeed I was," Yvette replied. "But I guess you could say I have done my penance and earned my freedom." The young sister laughed, a sound that rankled Ashal's nerves as she stared at the awkward exchange.

"I can't even begin to understand what that means. But you have no claim to this naiad. She has slain the Mother Abbess, and I am going to kill her for that."

"That is where you are mistaken, Sherinne." Yvette smiled and pulled the sack away from what she was holding. Ashal gasped at the gruesome sight of a woman's head, her face contorted into a frozen mask of agony with her mouth wide open and her eyes rolled into the back of her skull. One of the armored vampires on the dais, the one Yvette had named Sherinne, turned to look after seeing Ashal's reaction and also took a sharp breath.

"What have you done?!" Sherinne whispered. Yvette smiled and threw the decapitated head up to land at Ashal's feet and in clear view of the other two vampires.

"I've followed our laws for succession. I've killed the matron of our coven. That makes me the new matriarch. And my first order is for you to stand down." The armored sisters did not move for several seconds, which caused Yvette to frown.

"I said stand down! That means you should come down from there and listen to my other directives!" Her voice boomed, echoing in the darkness.

The loud sound caused everyone to flinch, including Ashal who remained in a defensive crouch with her knife in hand. The other three took several cautious steps backward until they reached the bottom step before lowering their swords.

"What is your will then, Matriarch?" Sherinne spat, her voice dripping with contempt. Yvette stared at her for a moment, a sweet smile on her lips as she walked closer. Sherinne was a good head and shoulders taller than the diminutive Yvette, but even so, Sherinne took a step backward after a tense moment of staring had passed. Then, in a blur of motion that Ashal could barely follow, Yvette's arm shot out and a small, red line cut itself across Sherinne's cheek. The taller vampire staggered back, clutching her cheek.

"You little," she began before suddenly breaking off into a scream that caused the air to vibrate. Sherinne fell to her knees, clutching her face where Yvette had cut her. Her mad shrieks continued almost unbroken for several agonizing moments. Yvette lifted her head with a finger and made shushing noises. Then, almost contemptuously, Yvette backhanded her, cutting off the screams in an abrupt moment of violence as Sherinne crumpled to the floor.

"My first wish is for you two to run outside and call a stop to the fighting. Wave a white flag or something. I wish to speak to the commander of the enemy's forces." Yvette looked back and forth between the two remaining sisters meaningfully. They hesitated only a moment, their eyes darting from Yvette to Sherinne's body on the floor, before turning and sprinting into the dark, headed for the door to the courtyard. After they left, Yvette turned to face Ashal, who still had not moved from her position at the foot of Laurine's throne.

"A very ingenious poison that Rose concocted to torture me... Well, perhaps not me specifically, but those of my kind. Really strong first bite that'll turn the world into a red haze of pain, but the worst part is after that initial burst of pain and the suffering that comes as it slowly burns you up from the inside. Good thing the antidote is simple, though." Yvette looked down at the crumpled form Sherinne on the ground. "I'll let her suffer a bit longer once she wakes up before giving it to her, I think, to make an example of her."

Ashal still hadn't moved, and Yvette looked up at her and sighed. "You can come down from there, now. I'm not going to hurt you. In fact, I must thank you for saving my life. At least I assume that it was you that got Bitter Bark to lead the attack and also, based on what evidence I see before me, the one that killed Laurine?" Ashal relaxed only slightly, allowing herself to rise up from her crouch into a standing position.

"Yes. I was the one to end her," she said simply. Yvette nodded her head and shrugged.

"Thank you, then. Too bad it was too late." This caught Ashal off guard.

"What do you mean too late? Too late for what?"

"Hmm? Ah! Rose and Laurine both knew you were planning to attack and already sent for Basilean aid. Thankfully you arrived before they did, but I imagine that they are likely only a few days march from here, perhaps less. They are coming with strict orders to burn the forest down and end the threat to the Abbey of Danos."

"How do you know this?"

"Well, Rose liked to gloat, and she would pull me out of my pain-filled, poison induced agony long enough to show me the letters. She couldn't conceive that I might survive her 'sessions' with me, so she wanted to crush me entirely, both my spirit and my body, by letting me see just how utterly I had failed. At least that's what she said, or what I think she said. I was really in and out of that conversation to be honest. But I do know that the Basileans are coming."

"But they will see that you are undead. Won't they turn on you?" Ashal felt as though the ground was shaking beneath her feet. Yvette flashed her a winning smile.

"How will they know? You have burned all the evidence of Laurine's… indiscretions. All that's left are a bunch of scared sisters who somehow managed to survive the forest's attack by huddling in the cellars, waiting for their brave rescuers to save them. As for their sense of evil… well, we can blame that on the heinous actions of you forest dwellers and the wanton violence you visited upon us. Besides, there are other ways of dulling their senses…"

"Can't you stop them from burning the forest?" Ashal shivered as if the room had suddenly dropped in temperature.

"I might, who knows?" Yvette shrugged. She pointed at Laurine's corpse. "Take your spear, I remember how much that means to you." Ashal hesitated but proceeded to pull the weapon free as she was bidden. After dislodging her spear rather unceremoniously, she walked slowly down the dais.

"Thistle and I used to plan what we would do when something like this happened. How we would escape and go and explore the world together. That was before Laurine had arrived, of course, and before I was… well, you know." Yvette rubbed the side of her neck meaningfully.

"After that, things began to change. Thistle had always said that I could have a home in the forest, that he would make a place for me and my mother, but Mother never would leave her devotions, and I wouldn't leave mother. After she… passed… I tried to follow Thistle into the forest, which is where I met Magdolon and he persuaded me to stay. Once I was given the Gift of Oskan, as the sisters here call it, I found that I was no longer welcome in the forest. Thistle said Bitter Bark would kill me if I set foot in his precious woods, if any of my sisters did. Honestly, he was one of the major reasons we couldn't leave the abbey."

A creeping realization stole through Ashal as she approached Yvette. Her hands twisted around the haft of her spear.

"Bitter Bark was keeping you here?" Yvette nodded in response.

"Of course, Laurine and Rose were content to live here and slowly build up an army from the villagers and occasional traveling pilgrims or whatnot. They loved the long game of steady growth. Low risk and all that. I myself play a different game. What is life without a little risk?"

"Did you plan all of this?" Ashal asked, the sinking sensation in her stomach already confirming what she dreaded.

"All of this? No! Well… Some of it, yes. My original plan did not involve me getting caught and tortured, but it was always a risk that I had to take. Thistle was such a willing accomplice, he really is so sweet. He just wanted his sister back. He did everything I asked of him, and Laurine and Rose were so scared of losing their little empire they built here that they reacted to the threat of an invasion exactly as I hoped they would. Now they are both dead and the last phase of our plan can begin."

"But you've lost everything!" Ashal sputtered.

"You mean the army of desiccated corpses and withered skeletons that you cut down, weakening your own forces in the process? What good were they to me here?" Yvette sighed contentedly and ran her fingers over the armrest of a bench pew. "We lost some of our coven tonight, but it was an acceptable amount, and we will be able to rebuild once we reach a real civilization center."

"But the Basileans will know what you are!"

"Ah, yes, our Hegemon's loyal followers. The ones who have been sending envoys and such to visit us for the past several years? The ones who would never comprehend that those who wore their holy symbols and sang their sanctimonious hymns could ever be something other than what they profess to be? The Hegemony has many weaknesses, not least among them is their hubris which won't allow them to doubt those that wear the sacred cloth. Of course it is possible that we overstretch our reach and make a mistake. Perhaps we'll draw too much attention, or the wrong kind, and someone will piece things together and report us before we can silence them. But as I said, I enjoy a game with risk."

"Why are you telling me all of this?" This caused Yvette to giggle like the young woman her face suggested her to be.

"You know, it's ironic, but I have to gloat to someone, and who better than you, because…" Yvette quickly crossed the distance between her and Ashal so that her face was inches from her ear, and before Ashal could react she whispered, "there is no one who will believe you that could stop me." She took a few steps back and smiled.

"I suppose some part of Rose's teachings made an impact on me, because it *is* fun to tease like this!" She took a deep sigh. Ashal gripped her spear. Yvette harrumphed and shook her head.

"Oh, calm yourself. We're not going to fight right now. I don't want to, and even if we did and you won, it still wouldn't change anything." She stood and walked toward the door leading to the courtyard, motioning for Ashal to follow.

"Let's go, they are likely waiting for us out there." With that, she disappeared into the gloom. Ashal hesitated for a moment, still clutching her spear to her chest, then she too walked into the dark.

The door was already open, and when they reached it, Ashal could see ribbons of orange light along the horizon and could smell the telltale signs of smoke in the air. As they stepped outside, they saw that the armies had divided the courtyard in two. Bitter Bark and his forces stood on the far side where the remnants of their army had finally broken through the portcullis and stood beside their comrades. The vampiric sisterhood claimed the other half of the courtyard. Their numbers were fewer than their foe, but the bodies that littered the ground were made up of far more woodlanders than those that wore the Basilean colors.

The crowd of sisters parted as Yvette approached, forming a pathway through their numbers. Several of them eyed Ashal as she walked past, following Yvette. She tried to suppress a shudder as she imagined a rabbit walking down a row of wolves. They reached the space between the two armies and Ashal could see Bitter Bark and Thistle approaching from the other side.

"I deliver unto you your savior," Yvette said as they came together. "Though it is mainly because I owe her as much and I hate being indebted to anyone."

"This doesn't change anything, abomination," Bitter Bark rumbled. "We do not parlay with your kind."

"And yet, you stopped the fighting... Interesting." Yvette tilted her head and squinted.

"We have fought each other to a standstill," Thistle ventured haltingly. "Yvette! I was surprised to see you here, and now. I thought we might have to rescue you."

"That was unnecessary. Ashal saved you, and I saved myself." Yvette placed her hands on her hips and stared at the rest of them.

"What is the meaning of this? Where are your masters?" Bitter Bark's voice cut across them.

"I am the master, now, or matriarch, if you will." The young vampire smirked. The treeman made a sound like waves crashing against the rocks, and Ashal realized that it was laughter after he spoke.

"So you are leaderless, then? What happened?"

"Your little naiad here killed Laurine, I took care of Rose. Now, I plan on taking care of you." This caused Bitter Bark to grow serious and he stared down at her.

"I don't know what you plan, little thing, but you are outnumbered and have lost your strong leadership. It makes no difference in any case. But if you surrender, I will grant you all quick deaths."

"What is the meaning of all this?" Thistle stepped forward and looked up at Bitter Bark. "Laurine and Rose are both dead! The abbey is in ruins and the village has been cleansed! There is no more need for bloodshed!" Yvette gave a dry laugh behind him.

"Did you really think he would ever leave us in peace?" Thistle said nothing, but his shoulders drooped and his gaze went to the ground. Yvette stepped up and placed a hand on the druid's shoulder. "You really believed that there was a way for us to return to what we were, didn't you?" Her voice took on a strange tone as she spoke, husky and very forlorn. That moment hung in the air for a long moment, the only sound that of the crackling fires below.

"Thistle. Get behind me." Bitter Bark said, and the moment shattered. Thistle looked up at him, then back at his sister who still stood with her hand on her shoulder. She nodded at him.

"It's best if you go, Thistle. There is no place for you with me any longer. My people will not accept you." She made to pull her hand away, but the druid reached up and caught it.

"No! Don't leave me again!" His voice was strained. Ashal felt a pang of regret and pity for the druid. She had always known loneliness, but she had always had Magdolon, too, so it was not the same kind of forsaken isolation that was written so plainly across Thistle's face now. The forest was not a kind or nurturing place, it was a delicate balance. That kind of balance had no time for innocence or pity. It was no place for a child born of humans.

Thistle stood staring at the last remnant of human touch he had ever known, but she was cold and dead. A cruel mimicry of what he had lost. His eyes shimmered in the dim light of evening, and Ashal watched as they flowed over and tumbled freely down his cheeks. For a moment, Yvette paused, her hand rising to his cheek. She stopped before touching, her hand poised to wipe away the tears. Then she stepped back and pulled her other hand from his. She gave a sad shake of her head.

"Go back to your forest, druid, it is the last home that you have, and soon even that will be taken away from you." Her gaze flicked back to Bitter Bark. "And you, ancient guardian, your time here is coming to an end. The Hegemony is sending its best for you. An army is coming to burn your beloved woods to ash. Even if you kill every one of us here, which I doubt your strength in that, it will not change that you have attacked an abbey of Basilea, and now they are coming for you!"

Ashal felt the air change suddenly around them. Bitter Bark's face was contorted into a mask of rage. He took a step forward and the force of it shook the very ground. Ashal pulled her spear free.

"What?" Bitter Bark's voice was low, but it cut through the dark like a knife.

"Yes, Laurine sent for aid shortly after I returned from the forest and was coerced into revealing that you were preparing an attack. We received a response that they were coming and that they should be here any day now."

Yvette's face split into a sneering grin. Thistle seemed to shake himself at this and turned back to face her.

"But you had no idea when or even if we were going to attack at that time! We've been trying for years to get him to attack and he never did. What was different this time?" Yvette turned and nodded at Ashal.

"She was."

"But how..." Thistle began, but he was interrupted by a monstrous howl from Bitter Bark.

"You filthy corpse!" His voice bellowed across the courtyard, and he swung his fist at Yvette. His blow never connected, however, as a column of fire erupted in the middle of his chest. The flames spread out from there and he began to scream in pain. The sound was inhuman and feral, it sounded of the keening cries of a thousand dying wolves and the crumbling of an avalanche crashing through the mountains. Before the mighty willow giant stood Thistle, his hands outstretched and orange heat radiating from his palms.

Ashal watched in horror as the striped bark of the tree herder blackened and flaked into ash as the air turned to pure, blistering fire around him. Bitter Bark crumbled, his scream still screeching through the night, before toppling onto his side, fingers of orange fire still licking hungrily at his wooden cadaver. Thistle stood over his work and stared at his hands in horror. Behind him, Yvette was laughing hysterically.

"Well done, Thistle, now you really have ruined everything, haven't you?" she exclaimed in between bouts of dark merriment. "Now you have no home to call your own!"

"Thistle!" Ashal whispered. "What have you done?!"

"He was going to kill her!" The druid didn't look away from his hands as he spoke. "I had to stop him!"

"And now you've destroyed the last being in this world who could have possibly held any sentimental attachment for you," Yvette said, her laughter subsiding. Ashal heard a terrible sound rising up from behind her and she realized it was coming from the woodland creatures. A great, howling cry had gone up among them, unified in its grief as hundreds of voices were bound together. The boiling mass of fur and scales beat at their chests and cried out their sudden grief into the sky.

"It seems as though we have a fight on our hands after all." Yvette sighed and turned to walk away. "Go on then, druid, go home to your forest and face their justice. It will be more merciful than if you follow me, I promise you." She didn't spare a backward glance as she stalked back toward the Basilean vampires arrayed in ranks and awaiting their orders.

Thistle sank to his knees, a blank stare on his face as the keening of the forest dwellers grew louder and louder.

Twenty-Five
ON WINGS OF FIRE

Everything seemed to grow quiet for a few precious moments. The night sky above them was choked by the fires and the smoke so that only the brightest stars shone through. The cries of the foresters fell on numb ears as Ashal sat staring at the slumped figure of Thistle while he stared after the retreating figure of his half-sister. Bitter Bark's corpse still crackled as the fire continued to eat away at his limbs, leaving only red embers and ash in their wake.

"Ashal!" A voice called out, snapping Ashal out of her stunned moment of vertigo. "What is this thing that is happening?" She turned to see a massive scaled water serpent speeding toward her. It slithered to the side, and Shesh'ra leapt down from behind its massive, finned head to land beside her.

"I..." Ashal hesitated, how could she answer that question? Shesh'ra's face was twisted with grief and rage and she didn't wait for Ashal to respond, instead moving past her to kneel beside Bitter Bark's smoldering body.

"I'm so sorry." Ashal felt herself cringe at her words, they seemed so pitiful even to her. Shesh'ra did not respond for several moments. Then, suddenly she rose and walked over to the druid. Grabbing Thistle by his long hair, she pulled his head back and slammed her fist into his nose. Blood fountained out of his face and he tumbled to the ground, not resisting as Shesh'ra knelt down and began to pummel him repeatedly across his mouth. Ashal ran forward and threw herself around Shesh'ra, pulling her off the nearly senseless Thistle.

"Do not for to stop me, child!" Shesh'ra howled. "This one is to die by my hand!"

"Maybe so," Ashal panted. "But not like this! Not when he is defenseless and broken! You are better than that!" Shesh'ra pushed away from Ashal and stepped back.

"What is it that I should be for doing then?" Ashal was shocked to see tears falling from her eyes, the sight was somewhat terrifying to her.

"Take him back to the forest. Let him face the justice of all the woodland folk. It is their right to justice, too." Shesh'ra closed her eyes and leaned back, her fists shaking at her side.

"Fine! Yes, go." She said at length, waving her hands at Ashal. She turned to her mount and climbed quickly back to her saddle at its head.

"What are you doing?" Ashal asked as she pulled Thistle to his feet, he groaned as he came up.

"I will not be for leaving Bitter Bark's body to the abominations. Mine will stay here so to keep them away, and for to give you the time to flee. Take those who will go. Take them to the trees. We will come when our anger finishes grieving this night." Ashal watched as Shesh'ra raised her weapon to the sky and several figures broke off from the main body of the remaining army. Ashal realized that they were more giant serpents, their riders urging their mounts to greater feats of speed. She soon saw several other, smaller figures running out ahead of them and recognized the figures of centaurs galloping in front of the sea serpents.

As these charging figures reached them, Shesh'ra spurred her serpent to begin moving as well, screaming forth a battle cry as she did. Together the surging tide of angry woodlanders bellowed their defiance as they ran toward the gathered body of vampiric Basileans on the other side of the courtyard. Ashal watched in awe as they collided with the front lines of what was left of Laurine's court, but knew she could not stay and witness the entire fight. Turning, she ran back to the rest of the army which had held position, their mournful cries having fallen to silent, dreadful sobs of anger and grief.

"We must go!" Ashal yelled as she drew near. "Shesh'ra wants us to retreat. We have accomplished all that we can tonight. More bloodshed will not solve the problems that are coming! We must sound the retreat!" Some of the forest dwellers shuffled on their feet. A few looked angrily at Ashal and then at Thistle who leaned on her shoulders for support.

"Did you not hear me?! We must fall back! I know you want revenge! I know you want justice! But those things must wait! There are bigger things that are coming. You will have your justice, but now you must survive in order to see it realized. We must fall back to the forest!" Her voice was almost swallowed by the sounds of battle behind her, but finally a lone naiad stepped forward with a conch shell in her hand like those that Ashal had seen along the coast. The lone naiad stared at her with eyes of steel and did not take them away as she blew into the shell a single, long, mournful note that cut above the din of fighting and the uncontrolled fires of the village below them.

"We will not go without Bitter Bark," a voice cried out of the gathered troops. Without waiting for Ashal's response, several salamanders and a few of the living trees broke rank to hurry toward the treeherder's smoldering corpse. With a little effort, they picked up the remaining pieces of his body and then fell back to the rest of the army. The naiad with the shell blew another long note, and as one, the army turned and began to move toward the gate.

Ashal looked behind her at the battle being waged with the remnants of the abbey. It was hard to tell, but it seemed as though Shesh'ra was holding her own, for now, although the vampire sisters didn't look as though their heart was in the fight, either. The last Ashal saw before ducking through the gate was that of Shesh'ra leaping from her serpent as it fell to the ground with several weeping wounds in its sides. The vampires were closing in around them, but she also saw several of the sisters retreating into the Great Hall. Then they were lost from view as she passed under the ruined portcullis.

The army descended into the flames of the burning village. The fires were still so fierce that at first only the hot-blooded salamanders could make their way through the blistering streets, putting out fires as best as they were able to allow others to pass. Gradually, the rest of the forces began to push through the heat. Ashal was one of the last to enter the town.

She felt the heat on her skin, her scales shimmering in the orange light of the destruction all around her. Everywhere she could see there were collapsed buildings and the smell of ash and burning meat from the various bodies that were wrapped in their cloaks, burning up in their universal funeral pyre. Ashal tried not to think of the poor villagers who had not been turned and their fates, but it was hard to ignore how unlikely it was that there would be any survivors.

They found themselves in the market square where Ashal had first tried to kill Laurine. Fire ringed the open cobblestones, and all that remained of the pathetic vendor booths that had occupied the space was smoldering ashes which the soldiers kicked up into the hot wind. Ashal coughed and covered her mouth to deal with the smell and the smoke that was growing thicker the further they retreated.

The army cut across the square and started filing down one of the larger streets, starting with the salamanders who would try and clear a path for the naiads and forest shamblers that came after. They were almost all through when the large building beside the street collapsed with a lumbering groan as its timbers gave way to the flames. The wreckage spilled down to land on a group of naiad soldiers right in front of Ashal and Thistle who were among the last of the struggling column.

Ashal cursed and lowered Thistle to the ground where the druid sat staring into space. She ran over to the flaming piles of rubble and tried to pry up some of the more intact beams that lay across the strewn bodies of the naiads underneath. She cried in pain as the white-hot coals burned the flesh of her palms when she went to grab a long shaft of wood. She did not release it however and instead heaved, throwing the wood slightly to the side, but it was not enough. Several other naiads who were with her came forward to try and help, but they were even less successful than her in moving the debris.

Ashal clenched her jaw in pain and stumbled back to where Thistle sat. She grabbed his shoulders and shook him. His eyes shifted and focused on her, but he didn't move otherwise.

"Can't you do something?" she yelled. Thistle blinked and then looked past her.

"Why?" His voice was barely above a whisper. Ashal stared at him for several seconds, then slapped him across his face, the sting of her freshly blistered fingers causing her eyes to water. Thistle's head snapped to the side under the blow and he raised a hand to his lip which was spouting fresh blood from a split where his tooth had cut him.

"Maybe you can find some redemption for that wretched soul of yours," she growled. "Can you do anything or not?" Thistle looked up at her with a dazed expression.

"What would you have me do?" He asked, his voice flat as his eyes that didn't look like they were focused on anything.

"Fire magic is your specialty, right? Can't you cause the fires to lessen there, or pull the heat out?" Thistle gave a laugh at this.

"That's not really how it works. I cause fire, I don't control it once it's left my hands." He gave a humorless chuckle and rose to his feet. Ashal glared at him.

"Is there anything you can do? There are people dying underneath that!" She pointed at the wreckage. Thistle leaned back and closed his eyes for a moment, then opened them and stared at the smoking pile of debris.

"There is one thing I could try," he said and held his hands together at his side. He then reached up, separating them and pointing each of his fingers toward the sky. Ashal felt the air shift, then Thistle brought his hands down and pointed them at the fire. She felt a sudden strong gust of wind that pushed down from the heavens and howled through Thistle's outstretched hands. Ashal's ears popped as the wind began to whip across the smoldering pile of the ruined building.

At first the fire sprang up, hungrily grasping at the fresh air. But as the wind strengthened itself, and the longer Thistle's arms stayed outstretched, eventually the flames began to die down, suffocated by its intensity. Ashal's ears rang from the wind, and when it abruptly stopped, she felt lightheaded as the pressure in her temples alleviated.

"There." Thistle grunted, waving his hands toward the ashen pile of burnt wood and brick. "Save who you can."

Ashal and several other soldiers ran forward and began to pull bits of rubble that were still warm, searching for survivors. It was a disheartening endeavor as they pulled out several bodies as they searched, but no survivors. Then came several shouts and Ashal hurried over to find the body of a young naiad lying on the ground between two rescuers. Her face was a mass of burns and dried blood that at first Ashal did not recognize her, but as she stared closer, she felt a troubling sense of familiarity.

"Onwei!" The name fell from her mouth almost without realizing it. It was the naiad who had welcomed her before the battle! She almost thought that she was dead, but her chest rose and fell with a frightening irregularity. One of the bigger naiads stooped and picked her up in her arms, cradling her like a little child. Onwei screamed at the sudden movement and then grew very still. For a moment, Ashal feared the worst, but she wasn't allowed to dwell on her thoughts as the group quickly began to move again. The fires in the village were beginning to die down, but the weakened buildings were collapsing around them. The threat now lay in escaping the village before they became buried beneath its ruin.

Corridors of smoke and ash clouded Ashal's vision. The labyrinth of embers stretched out for an eternity before her, blinding her from seeing anything more than a few feet away as she ran blindly behind the figure in front of her. She gripped Thistle's arm and pulled him along, the druid offered no resistance. Together they stumbled through the ashen night as motes of white drifted down like hellish snow. Several times, Ashal ran into the back of the naiad in front of her as they found themselves stumbling into a dead end and had to double back due to another collapsed building, or a fresh resurgence from the fires billowing up to block their way.

After what seemed an eternity, though, they stumbled out of the smoky dark and into the clear air of the night. Staggering, they found their way through the outer gates and stumbled toward the welcoming shadow of the woods. As Ashal entered under the eaves of the forest, she glanced back and gasped at the sight of the mountainside completely alight in flames. Great pillars of black smoke curled up toward the moonlit sky. The fires had spread to the abbey proper now, and the various buildings there were just beginning their slow descent into a fiery oblivion.

Ashal felt a strange pang in her chest, a flash of remorse, and a wave of uncomfortable familiarity with the scene. She closed her eyes and pushed Thistle deeper into the woods as she remembered how fire had fulfilled her last endeavor on her road to vengeance. Meanwhile, the edge of the Abzkhala Mountains began to burn.

Tales of Mantica

Twenty-Six

THE FOREST'S LAMENT

The smell of smoke still lingered in the air, and that was what woke Ashal from her deep sleep. Her eyes flashed open as the smell registered with her senses, and for a moment she thought she was back in the village with the acrid air burning in her lungs. It took her several moments to realize that the red light was the sun piercing through the lingering haze, and that she was lying at the edge of the sacred grove where Bitter Bark had delivered his rallying speech to his children.

She sat up and rubbed her eyes, they felt gummy and her lids stuck together whenever she tried to blink. The back of her throat was raw, as if she had spent the evening screaming; and despite having slept for several hours, her limbs were heavy and it took her several attempts before she could push herself to her feet. She felt the callouses on her hands, already healed by some of Thistle's more rudimentary magic the previous night before the other naiads had come to take him away. Ashal had been too tired to protest when he'd insisted on trying to heal the burns there and had honestly been relieved when the throbbing had subsided under his magics.

"You should be for the resting, still," a cracked but familiar voice caused her to turn abruptly toward its source. Shesh'ra sat with her back toward an ancient oak tree. Her right shoulder and much of that side of her body was covered in a strange moss, and her eyes were clouded with pain.

"Shesh'ra! You're alive!" The older naiad coughed rather violently, cringing after each convulsion.

"This thing is true," she sighed. "But the abominations were not lacking in their desire for my end." Ashal walked over to her and saw that the moss was covering what looked like blistered skin underneath. Several long gashes had been carved into the side of Shesh'ra's face, as well. Ashal's eyes fell as she looked at the extent of her wounds. The centurion made a sound that appeared to be coughing, but Ashal realized that it was meant to be a laugh.

"Do not be troubled, spawnling, my end is still a far time ahead of me. Although I do not know that I will hoist a spear before then." Ashal bristled at being called a spawnling, but quickly brushed it aside as she listened to Shesh'ra's diagnosis.

"Couldn't they put you in the spring to try and heal you? Like they did for Magdolon and myself?" Ashal asked, Shesh'ra shook her head.

"My wounds are not those of the worst we have. My pain will ebb with the coming and going of the time. The waterweed does help with the burns. This is where my strength was able to carry me to, so this is where I will be sitting until it returns and carries me further."

She looked up at Ashal, a frown coming over her face. "Poor Onwei is of the worst. Her face is to be a mass of reminders from this terrible night. That is if she is to live."

"Will she?" Ashal asked. Shesh'ra shook her head.

"This is a thing that only the Lady shall say." She groaned and leaned her head back against the trunk of the tree.

"I should let you rest," Ashal began, but Shesh'ra cut her off.

"You will be silent, and you will listen." Her voice was not gruff, and the rebuke held a pleading edge that caused Ashal to pause. She nodded and the older naiad continued. She pulled a cloth bundle from where it had lain beside the tree; Ashal hadn't even noticed it. Shesh'ra handed it to her, and when she touched it, a shiver ran down her spine.

She pulled the cloth away and gasped as the largest emerald she had ever seen fell into her hand. It was rough and uncut for the most part, but it was easily the size of her fist. One side was smooth and translucent, its polished surface reflecting the orange light of the smoke filled morning like a mirror.

"I can't accept this," Ashal stammered, still staring at the raw gem. "After all the pain and suffering I have caused, not just to you but to the whole forest…" Again Shesh'ra cut her off.

"You can and you will take this thing. It is not my gift for you to refuse. This comes from the Lady." This caused Ashal to cock her head to the side and raise an eyebrow.

"Do not be for giving me this face, spawnling," Shesh'ra snapped. "Before the battle was met, Bitter Bark did name me as protector if he were to meet his end. The Green Lady, she is part of all trees, all rivers, all oceans. She knew of Bitter Bark's death and did reach out to speak with the new protector of the forest, not that it is of a matter for soon the forest will be for ash and there will be no needing for a protector if the forest is but dust. However, I did see the Emerald Mother in a vision of sleep in the midnight hour." Her eyes grew sharp at this, and when she spoke, she seemed to lose her accent.

"She told me that it was time you went home."

"But that's impossible!" Ashal exclaimed. Shesh'ra shook her head.

"Not with the rock that is in your hand." She pointed to the emerald. "This stone, it holds the sigil of the forest. It will be that which gives you pardon.

There may be some that will be wanting to question what it is. But there be none what will sneer at the sigil. Look there, in this part which appears as glass, you will see it." She motioned for Ashal to hold the emerald up to her eye and look at the sun through the polished side of the glass. Ashal was confused at first, but as she looked, several shadows began to move within the green gem. She gasped as swirls began to appear.

These swirls clumped together until the formed the symbol of an ancient tree with roots that stretched down and away, out of Ashal's view. The longer she stared, the more real the image seemed to become, to the point that Ashal began to have trouble distinguishing the individual swirls and lines and felt like she was looking at roughened bark with gigantic branches and hordes of leaves clinging to its limbs.

"You see?!" Shesh'ra gave another coughing chuckle. "There is none who will dispute this thing when they see. But you must keep it close. Do not be for giving it to the first naiad you see. Make sure it is shown in a place with many eyes, so that enough will believe you and not try to cover the truth."

"She could've made it a little easier to hide, then," Ashal grumbled as she pulled her gaze away from the gem.

"We do not seek to spit on the gifts of the Emerald Mother," Shesh'ra chided, growing serious. "You have a path that is full of many dangers to pass through. Your home will not be a welcoming one, I think."

"I don't understand why a goddess would waste her time to even consider someone like me. It all seems so… unreal."

"Yet the proof you hold that is in your hand. I did not make this thing, I do not know how I could. It was here when I did wake from my vision." Shesh'ra motioned to the ground beside her.

"I'm not sure that I am ready to return home." Ashal rolled her eyes. "I have lived above the waves for longer than I ever did below them."

"What was this whole thing that you have done here for?" Shesh'ra motioned with her uninjured hand, pointing to the sky above that still held traces of smoke and then to her burned side. "Is this not all part of the revenge for which you seek for a home you do not know you want?"

"You're right! I am sorry!" Ashal protested. "But now that it is behind me, I'm not sure how I should move on. My life has been obsessed with finding justice for my mother, and now that that is through… I just don't know. I'm scared to go back to a world that I barely remember."

"Fear is a poor excuse to not act." This caught Ashal off guard and she stood a moment with her mouth open, unsure of how to respond.

"Close your mouth," Shesh'ra coughed. "You begin to look like a bottom feeder fish like this." Ashal obeyed, but her brow furrowed at the older naiad who shrugged, her eyes already glazing over as another wave of pain overtook her.

"Go or do not," Shesh'ra said at length. "The Mother's blessing is given to you. The way is already there for you to use or no. It is the choice that must be made by none but you. Go home, or leave and do nothing, and be nothing. Let this act that you have done already be the legacy that you will leave. None will stop you. None shall force you, though there will be many who might try." She broke off into a fit of coughing and doubled over. Ashal knelt beside her, holding her arms out in case she needed support. Shesh'ra pushed her away and sat up with a deep, strained sigh.

"I will have to think on it. I'm not sure what path I will take," Ashal said after several long moments of watching Shesh'ra's face twist with pain. The older naiad sighed and shook her head.

"Do not be for waiting for a lengthy time to decide, spawnling," she said at length, opening her eyes to level a hard gaze at Ashal. "There are many drowned secrets in your home that you must drag to the surface. If you are to wait too long, then they will take root and then the truth will fail you in being enough to be for setting you free."

After this, she closed her eyes and leaned her head back against the tree. Ashal sat for a few moments longer, then decided that she had fallen asleep and rose to walk away. She lifted the emerald in her hand to look at it once more. The sunlight glistened off of its flat surfaces and cast a green light out of its facets.

"There was one thing more that I was to tell you." Ashal gasped and whirled around at Shesh'ra's voice crackling through her thoughts. The older naiad smiled at her discomfort before continuing. "The traitor did wish to give you his thoughts. He is to be held in a small cave beside the one that you and your defender did stay in before. Go there. You will not be having a hard time in finding it." Again, Shesh'ra closed her eyes. Before Ashal could respond, she was fast asleep.

Ashal pursed her lips and frowned. What could Thistle want to say to her? She sat for a moment pondering this question, then set off walking toward the cave where she had spent those days in what seemed so long ago. It was difficult to believe that it had only been a few days since she had last seen Magdolon, and her throat constricted as she thought of their parting. She pushed those thoughts aside and kept walking.

Shesh'ra was right, it wasn't hard to find Thistle. But he wasn't inside of a cave, he was leaning beside a tree with his hands bound in front of him. His eyes snapped open as she approached and he stared at her, a moribund smile creeping across his face.

"Don't worry, my guards are around here, watching me. They know I have nowhere to run to. This forest is as secure a prison as any you'll find in the world. The trees themselves are angry with me, and if I tried to flee, I'd likely be dead before nightfall and tangled in some brambly patch of living thistle with a vine wrapped around my throat." As he spoke, a musty wind rose up behind

Ashal, filled with the smell of loam and wet earth. The trees began to rustle, and Ashal could almost feel the agitation in the air, it buzzed through her teeth and caused her bones to ache. Thistle took a deep breath and leaned back, as if taking in the pleasant forest air.

"Ah!" He sighed. "Can you hear it? The trees are mourning their departed shepherd. Their song is so melancholy and filled with that bittersweet sadness that only grief can purchase." He shook his head.

"I don't hear anything," Ashal said, rubbing the side of her head.

"Yes you do, you're just not hearing it properly," Thistle replied. "You are a denizen of the Green Lady, as such you are *blessed* to be able to hear the cries of the trees. I can see it in your face. The way you keep touching your temples." He spoke with a sneer in his voice. Ashal glared at him, but he just smiled.

"Listen carefully," he instructed. "Clear your head of thoughts and let what comes to mind take on its own voice. You'll see what I mean."

"What does this have to do with anything? What do you want, Thistle?" Ashal snapped.

"Consider it a dying man's wish." Thistle gave that same, sad smile. "I think it might help you in the future, and I feel that I owe you this much at least." Ashal sighed impatiently but did as she was asked. She continued staring at him but tried to push out all other thoughts. Almost instantly, the buzzing in her bones shifted and flowed up into her head, the pressure on her body seemed to relieve and words began to form in her mind. It *was* a song, just like Thistle had said. A low thrumming noise like the beat of a large drum acting as the rhythm with the rustle of the leaves being the melody.

"You see?" Thistle chuckled. "When the trees want to make themselves heard, they can be quite persistent. It's best to let them have their say." Ashal made to answer him, but the words became more defined in her mind and she was driven to distraction as the dirge-like canto forced itself upon her, the words flowing unbidden into her mind.

Listen to me and hear what I say
For I will tell you the best of dreams
I had while upon the midnight hour
The visions of life and emerald things.

I saw myself upon a hill
The sun afar was sinking low
And in my gaze I thought I saw
A tree whose limbs began to grow.

> *Then through its leaves a golden hue*
> *The blessings of our Mother Green*
> *Did whisper these soft words to me*
> *'A forest there will soon be seen'.*
>
> *And so it was as She proclaimed*
> *The verdant canopy laid bare*
> *And lasted for a thousand years*
> *The Bitter Bark for it to care.*
>
> *A song for the Fallen Willow*
> *The crimson fires have laid him low*
> *The wind his ashes now will blow*
> *To us his children here below.*
>
> *The flames now come for us as well*
> *And we shall meet our burning harm*
> *The pyres of our end are near*
> *Where we will fly to Mother's arms.*

"It's beautiful!" Ashal gasped, a hollow ache forming in her chest.

"A bit rushed, I'll admit," Thistle agreed, "but a genuinely touching effort overall."

"What do they mean the flames now come for them?"

"What do you think?" Thistle eyed her skeptically. Ashal raised an eyebrow.

"I have no idea, which is why I asked."

Thistle sighed and shook his head.

"The Basileans are coming, and they have reports that the forest rose up and ransacked one of their abbeys. What do you think their reaction will be? What do you think will happen to the trees that make up this forest?"

"But surely there is something that they can do? Can't they fight? Or leave?" Ashal's eyes widened in shock.

"A tree is not like a person, or an animal. A tree cannot move, with the exception of the shamblers, which are not regular or proper trees but more like spirits of trees. It cannot pull its roots up and crawl away from danger. To do so would be to die for them. They cannot retreat before the horde of torches that is drawing nearer and nearer to them with each moment. They were created to give, they are the ultimate gift, and their existence is one of sacrifice. They exist to give shelter to the creatures of the wood, to give food to those in need, to give us the very air we breathe! They do not fear for their own safety, and they will do nothing to stop what is coming."

260

"But they are crying out even now!" Ashal cried, her eyes beginning to burn. "Can't the Basileans hear them, too?" This caused Thistle to laugh heartily.

"Mankind has long since stopped hearing the trees, since before time really began. Even many elves won't be bothered with it these days, except perhaps the Sylvan Kin. Very rarely do they try to talk to either humans or dwarfs. Especially not those wearing the robes of the Hegemony. They'd much rather cut an oak down rather than listen to it. They'd prefer to have logs for their fire more than understanding from their fuel."

"Why would you teach me this, then, if there is nothing I can do with it?!"

"Because I don't think that this is the last time that you will hear the forest speak to you. You should know how to listen when that time comes."

"Is that why you brought me here? To torture me with sorrowful songs and remind me of the pain that I have caused?" Ashal stabbed a finger toward him, but Thistle didn't respond; instead he slowly sank down to sit on the long grass at the base of the tree which he stood against.

"Not at all," he said quietly. "Your choices helped propel us to this point, you have your share of the blame, but it is not the only portion that should be doled out." He held up his hands at this. "I have my own conscience to appease in this mess as well."

"Then what?!" Ashal glared at him. He lowered his hands.

"I asked you to come so that I might thank you."

"What?" Ashal paused, her brow furrowing.

"Last night, when you slapped me... when you pushed me to help those trapped in the collapsed building. You gave me something there." His voice was low, it echoed the funeral march of the song still repeating in the back of Ashal's mind.

"What did I give you?" she hissed.

"A choice." He smiled and looked away from her.

"I didn't do any of that." Ashal shook her head. "We needed something from you. I demanded it, and you gave it."

"You couldn't have forced me to do what I did," Thistle responded. "All you *could* do was provide me with the opportunity to choose, and I'm glad that you did." A silence spread out between them. Ashal could not find words that fit what he had said, so she chose another, more cruel topic to discuss.

"What will happen to you now?"

Thistle sighed and stared at the ground.

"I am to share the fate of the trees. When all the other creatures of the forest flee from the Basilean torches, I will be trussed to this tree and left to burn with the others of Bitter Bark's children." He laughed. "It is both a fitting and ironic end, I think. Fitting in that it is justice in its most basic sense, and ironic in that the very thing I am thanking you for is what makes this death so much more terrifying to face."

261

"Do not blame me for your fate," Ashal said.

"You misunderstand me. I do not blame you, even if it would be an easier end for me if I did. But I choose the harder way." He stood up slowly and brushed the grass off his legs. "And I thank you for giving me that choice as well."

"This has been a very confusing conversation. I'm not sure how I feel about my actions being a comfort to you after what you have done, but it seems you are at peace with the consequences of those actions." Ashal turned to walk away. "Good speed into whatever awaits you on the other side of those flames, Thistle."

"One last thing, before you go." Ashal turned back to face him and he held out his hand, a small, brass token gripped in his fingers. "I wanted to give this to you, a token to remind you of the choices that we made here."

"Your choices are your own," Ashal replied without moving to take the token.

"In that you are correct, but we all made decisions that lead us to this point. Take this to help you remember that, so that you don't lose your own humanity in your journey ahead." This caused Ashal to shake her head.

"*My* humanity? Do I look like I belong to your race? Why should I want to be reminded of the frailty of humanity?"

"Take it as a reminder of your choices, then." Thistle sighed. "Before Yvette changed into what she is now, she used to tell me stories of the great heroes of humanity from her lessons. We humans can be weak, but we aspire to greater things, and our stories reflect that. You have accomplished some great things here. Some very difficult things. But I think that the future holds many more trials for you. Let this help remind you of the choices that you have." Thistle then smiled, not a half smile filled with melancholy, but rather one that caused his eyes to shine.

Ashal hesitated, then moved forward and held out her hand to take the token.

"I am not the one whom you will save," she said as she took it from him. Thistle's smile faded and he nodded.

"Then take this as a momento mori. Remember that one day this will all end, and on that day, I hope you will have become what you wish to be." Ashal looked down at the token, it was a wax stamp which showed the image of a man surrounded by a single flame.

"It was my seal that I would use when communicating with Yvette," Thistle said, once again sliding down to sit beside the tree. "It was how she would know my communications were authentic. Another irony I suppose."

Ashal stared at the seal for a moment longer then turned and walked away without a glance backward, her steps leaving Thistle to fall behind her until he finally disappeared from view. As she walked, a sudden impulse seized her and she turned toward the cave with the healing spring.

It didn't take her long to arrive, and when she did, she was surprised to see a crowd of naiads, centaurs, and salamanders hovering around the entrance. Ashal walked cautiously up to the closest naiad, a young female whose scales were the dark brown and gold of a sea bass. Her large, golden eyes stared up at her when Ashal touched her shoulder.

"Excuse me," Ashal said quietly, glancing around nervously. "I'm looking for a young naiad they said was brought here, do you know who I should talk to about finding her?"

"What is she called by?" The naiad responded in the same thick accent as Shesh'ra.

"She said her name was Onwei." Ashal replied, and a sick sensation clenched at her stomach as she watched the other naiad's face fall.

"You knew of Onwei?"

"Yes, she's really the only other person I know here in the forest besides Shesh'ra," Ashal said, noting the way she had said 'knew' as if in the past. "She welcomed me just before the battle, honestly it was a brief introduction. But I was there when they pulled her from the wreckage of the house and just wanted to see how she was doing." Abruptly, the naiad threw her arms around Ashal and pulled her close.

"I thought it would be you," she said in a choked whisper. "They were of the knowledge that it was a naiad that we were unknown to that did for saving Onwei." Ashal stood awkwardly, her hands hovering by her sides as the girl embraced her.

"Umm, yes, I was part of the rescue effort. Although I didn't know what happened to her after she was pulled free. Is she okay?" Ashal pushed the girl back whose eyes were glassy from weeping.

"Onwei did return to the Depths before the sun rose this day." The naiad struggled to get the words out, but Ashal felt their impact in her chest.

"Are you sure?" She felt the words leave her mouth, but she recognized how hollow they sounded even as she said them.

"I was beside her when she did leave." She sobbed, the tears flowed freely now. "She was to be my mate here, and there was much hope in me that she would swim the current back to me. But now she is lost."

"Oh." Ashal's head felt like it was stuffed with cotton. "I'm so sorry for your loss."

"Thank you for the effort which you gave in returning her to the woods." Onwei's mate sniffed. "I am sorry, but I know not what you are even called."

"My name is Ashal."

"I am called Turessa." She gave a sad smile and pulled away from Ashal. "Will you be for staying with us here?" She motioned to a spot beside her, a pleading in her eyes. Ashal's heart quickened and her feet shuffled back a few paces at the thought of sitting down there.

"No," she stammered. "I have other things I need to see to, and I really must be going. Again, I am so sorry." Ashal didn't wait for a response, but simply turned and walked away as fast as she could without running.

She found her way back to where Shesh'ra was still sleeping against the side of her oak tree. Her slumped form shuffled slightly when Ashal approached but otherwise remained still. She moved quietly over to her pile of things and quickly gathered them up and tied them into a bundle with some strands of willow branches that lay scattered about the clearing.

"I do beg excuse for my intrusion." A voice startled Ashal, and she turned toward it. Another naiad was standing there, in her arms were several strange objects that were out of place this deep in the forest. There were a few pairs of boots, some wrinkled cloth that was singed badly on one side, and various other knickknacks that looked like some kind of ill-advised raiding plunder from the village. Ashal's breath caught in her throat as she recognized one of the items in the naiad's arms. She ran forward and grabbed a small sackcloth doll out of the mangled assortment, causing the naiad to curse as the rest of her armful went tumbling into the dirt.

"Where did you get this?" Ashal's voice was frantic as she eyed the one-eyed child's toy.

"These remains are for what the refugees did leave in their flight from this forest."

"What do you mean refugees?"

"It was among the last of Bitter Bark's commands that we were to take as many of the humans of the village away from the flames before they did perish and stop them from dying by fire. Then to release them if the human warriors were to be leaving that would come for to investigate the abbey. Shesh'ra did order them gone this morning before she was tended to for her own wounds. She did say that there was to being no purpose in staying if Basilea already was to being aware of our attack and who it was that did it."

"Were you to be thinking that we were of the savage?" Shesh'ra's cracked voice cut through Ashal's thoughts as she stared at the doll. Ashal turned to face the wounded centurion.

"I don't know what to think anymore, quite honestly."

"Here be the items that the humans did leave upon their flight, as you did command." The other naiad gathered up the rest of the fallen items and deposited them beside Shesh'ra, who nodded her thanks.

"I will be seeing to them later, when the pain does not fill me with desires for sleep." She waved a hand and the other naiad turned and departed into the shadow of the wood.

"Bitter Bark saved the villagers?" Ashal asked.

"Not all." Shesh'ra shook her head and grimaced. "But some. He did always have a place in his heart for the human pups. It was why he did take to Thistle so kindly." Ashal opened her mouth to speak again, but Shesh'ra interrupted her.

"You do the talk too much, and my head and body do ache. If it is to be acceptable to you, I would rest at this time. If you are to stay until I wake, we may speak of this thing more then." Without waiting for a response, Shesh'ra lowered her head and closed her eyes. It wasn't long before her breathing evened into the relaxed pace of sleep.

The forest seemed to press in on Ashal in the sudden silence that followed, and she felt the urge to rush over to collect her belongings that lay nearby. She pulled out the emerald that Shesh'ra had given her and considered throwing it away into the undergrowth. But she hesitated with her arm cocked, ready to throw. She slowly lowered the gem and stared at it for a long time, focusing on the image of the tree that began to form whenever she allowed her gaze to linger for too long. She glanced again at the sackcloth doll still in her other hand, and then back to the emerald. Finally, she dropped both into her makeshift satchel of belongings.

Hoisting the bag onto her shoulders, she then bent to pick up her spear and strap it to her back in a way that she could easily pull it free. She felt a surge of regret as her eyes fell over the imagery of the stingray worked into the base of the speartip, and she almost could hear Magdolon's voice in the back of her mind, warning her of letting her emotions control her.

She paused and looked out at the clearing that was so important to the creatures who lived here. Soon it would all be consumed by the wanton destruction of the Hegemony. She wondered, briefly, what would have happened if she hadn't arrived here. If she would have simply gone on living with Magdolon in exile, how would things have turned out differently? Would Gravel still be alive? Would Onwei? Would the forest still be poised for the flame? Where did the responsibility for the events now in motion end with her?

The comforting weight of the spear on her back helped still the dissenting voices in her mind, and she found herself falling into one of Magdolon's breathing exercises that he had created for fighting on land. Deep inhalations and slow exhalations. The buzzing in her mind began to fade. The thrumming lament of the forest could still be heard in the back of her mind, but now Ashal began to see that the trees were not directing their anger at her. This dirge was not to punish her, indeed it was a bit presumptuous of her to think that it ever had been. She realized that she was holding Thistle's token that he'd given her and looked down at its symbol once more.

The figure of the burning man stared up at her. She felt some sympathy beginning to fester for the doomed man. The fires that consumed him were not his own making, yet still he suffered from them. So many thoughts whirled in her head as she stared at the seal. So many emotions attached to each errant memory. For now, all she knew was that she couldn't stay here. Not because she was being forced away, nor because of the pain that she'd caused, but because this wasn't where she belonged. This was not her home.

She sighed and stowed Thistle's momento in her pouch. She thought about leaving a note for Shesh'ra explaining her sudden decision, but she realized that it wouldn't matter. Besides, she had a sneaking suspicion that the older naiad already knew what she'd decided in any case and understood her reasoning for it.

Her mind cleared as she fixed her eyes on the north. Reaching back, she touched the worked metal of the stingray once more. Then she began to walk, and the forest seemed to part the way before her.

Ashal was going home.

THE END

Look for more books from Winged Hussar Publishing, LLC – E-books, paperbacks and Limited-Edition hardcovers. The best in history, science fiction and fantasy at:

https://www. wingedhussarpublishing.com

or follow us on Facebook at:

Winged Hussar Publishing LLC

Or on twitter at:

WingHusPubLLC

For information and upcoming publications

Look for information on
Kings of War and Mantic Games at:
manticgames.com